OUTSIDE LOOKING IN

Novels

Water Music (1982)
Budding Prospects (1984)
World's End (1987)
East Is East (1990)
The Road to Wellville (1993)
The Tortilla Curtain (1995)
Riven Rock (1998)
A Friend of the Earth (2000)
Drop City (2003)
The Inner Circle (2004)
Talk Talk (2006)
The Women (2009)
When the Killing's Done (2011)
San Miguel (2012)
The Harder They Come (2015)
The Terranauts (2016)

Short Stories

Descent of Man (1979)
Greasy Lake & Other Stories (1985)
If the River Was Whiskey (1989)
Without a Hero (1994)
T.C. Boyle Stories (1998)
After the Plague (2001)
Tooth and Claw (2005)
The Human Fly (2005)
Wild Child & Other Stories (2010)
T.C. Boyle Stories II (2013)
The Relive Box (2017)

Anthologies

DoubleTakes (2004), coedited with K. Kvashay-Boyle

OUTSIDE LOOKING IN

T.C. BOYLE

BLOOMSBURY CIRCUS
LONDON · OXFORD · NEW YORK · NEW DELHI · SYDNEY

BLOOMSBURY CIRCUS
Bloomsbury Publishing Plc
50 Bedford Square, London, WC1B 3DP, UK

BLOOMSBURY, BLOOMSBURY CIRCUS and the Bloomsbury Circus logo
are trademarks of Bloomsbury Publishing Plc

First published in Great Britain 2019

A catalogue record for this book is available from the British Library

ISBN: HB: 978-1-5266-0468-2; TPB: 978-1-5266-1036-2;
eBook: 978-1-5266-0466-8

2 4 6 8 10 9 7 5 3 1

Text design by Michelle Crowe
Printed and bound in Great Britain by CPI Group (UK) Ltd, Croydon CR0 4YY

MIX
Paper from
responsible sources
FSC® C020471

To find out more about our authors and books visit www.bloomsbury.com
and sign up for our newsletters

Ariane Fasquelle,
in memory

Turn off your mind, relax and float downstream
It is not dying, it is not dying

—John Lennon–Paul McCartney, "Tomorrow Never Knows"

Whither is fled the visionary gleam?
Where is it now, the glory and the dream?

—William Wordsworth, "Ode: Intimations of Immortality
from Recollections of Early Childhood"

OUTSIDE LOOKING IN

Prelude

Basel, 1943

Was it poison? Was it out of bounds? An unacceptable risk? She couldn't have said, but she was in a state all day, though she kept telling herself she was being foolish—if anybody in the entire building knew what he was doing, it was her boss. Since she'd come to work for him just over a year ago, she'd never seen him falter—he was precise, cautious, solid, and he didn't take chances with his own safety or his assistants' either. Which you couldn't say for all the chemists who worked here. Some of them— she'd heard the gossip—got sloppy as the day wore on, not bothering with their safety goggles, crossing the floor with pipettes of nitric acid or sodium hydroxide as if they were on their way home with a bag of groceries, even in one case (though this was only rumor), drinking on the job. And who was left to clean up the mess, to accept blame and cover for them if need be—to lie right to the face of the supervisor? Their lab assistants, of course. Who else?

Herr Hofmann wasn't like that. He followed safety procedures to the letter, always, whether it was eight in the morning or five in the afternoon, whether they were preparing the chemicals for the first process of the day or the last. She admired his efficiency, his attention to detail, his professionalism, but there was so much more to him than that. For one thing, he'd had no qualms about taking on a female assistant, the only one in the whole company, and for another he was no cold fish, but a man with red blood in his veins. He was unfailingly pleasant, even on the off days, always with a sympathetic look or a smile for her, and under his lab coat you could see the effects of his bodybuilding and the hours he spent training with the boxing club. His hair might have been thinning and he wore spectacles in the lab, but he swept his hair back like Adolphe Menjou so you hardly noticed, and the spectacles only made him look distinguished. Maybe she was in love with him, maybe that was it, which of course she would never have admitted to anyone on this earth, not even her best friend, Dorothea Meier, and certainly not her mother, who if she had even an inkling that her daughter had a romantic fixation on an older man—*a married man, no less, with children*—would have marched right up the steps of the building and dragged her home by the scruff of her neck.

It was April. The day was bright beyond the windows, spring in the air, the whole world singing, and she was in a state. So what if there was a long and honored tradition of scientists experimenting on themselves—August Bier opening a hole in his own spine to discover if injecting cocaine directly into the cerebrospinal fluid would prove an effective anesthetic; Werner Forssmann running a catheter from an incision in his forearm up a vein to his heart to see if it could be done; Jesse Lazear purposely allowing an infected mosquito to bite him in order to prove the insect was the vector of yellow fever— there were as many failures as there were successes. Lazear had his proof, but died seventeen days later, so what good did it do him?

Or his wife, if he had one? But that wasn't going to happen to her boss, she told herself—nothing was going to happen to him. He was taking so small a dose of the compound, a mere 250 micrograms, it couldn't possibly have any adverse effect, and if it did, she would be there at his side to see him through it.

She'd come to work that morning in high spirits, never suspecting what he had in mind or that this day would be any different from any other. Because the weather was so fine she'd bicycled to work rather than take the tram, and the fresh air and sunshine had made her feel as if she didn't have a care in the world. "Good morning to you, Fräulein Ramstein," Herr H. had called out cheerily when she came through the door after hanging her jacket in the closet and slipping into her lab coat. He was at his desk, peering up from his notebook, grinning at her. "Did you see the way the daffodils are pushing up everywhere? I thought somebody'd smeared the whole landscape with butter while we were asleep."

"Yes," she murmured, "yes, it's all so beautiful—summer will be here before we know it," and if it was a banal exchange, so much the better, because everything was ordinary, business as usual, and nothing was going to happen to her or her boss, not now, not ever.

But then, grinning still, he gave her a long look and said, "Didn't you find it unusual when I went home early Friday afternoon?"

She had, but she hadn't said anything then and didn't say anything now either—she just stood there at the doorway, waiting.

"Of course, you know it's not like me—I don't think I've missed more than maybe two days in all the"—he paused, counting up the years—"fourteen years I've been at the company, but I felt so strange, or disoriented, I guess, I was sure I had a touch of the flu or a fever or something." He paused, held her with his eyes. "But it wasn't that, it wasn't that at all. You know what it was?"

She didn't have a clue, but it was then, at that precise moment, that the anxiety began ticking away inside her like one of the time bombs the partisans were using against the occupiers in Vichy and the Netherlands.

"The chemical, the *synthesis*. You know how careful I am, how rigorous—especially with toxic compounds—but nobody can be perfect a hundred percent of the time and I realized the next morning I must have got a trace of the solution somewhere on my skin during recrystallization, on my wrist or forearm, I suppose—or even my fingertips when I pulled the gloves off. A trace. That's all. And I tell you, I've never experienced anything like it. It was as if I were intoxicated—drunk suddenly, right here in the laboratory, in the middle of the day. But more than that, and stranger, when I got home all sorts of fantastic shapes and images kept spinning in front of my eyes, even with my eyelids closed."

She said the first thing that came into her head: "You were poisoned."

"Yes," he said, rising from the chair and crossing the room till he was standing right there before her, peering into her eyes as if looking for something he'd misplaced. "But how? And what does it mean?"

She couldn't think. He was too close to her, so close she could smell the lozenge on his breath. "I don't know," she said. "That you're lucky?"

He laughed aloud. "*Lucky*, that's exactly it. We've got something here, I feel it, I really do."

"No," she said, taking a step back, all the precautions, all the rules, everything she'd learned in her apprenticeship and her time here as a full-fledged employee, all the horror stories about inadvertent poisonings, splashes and caustic burns flapping through her brain like flocks of black-winged birds—*Never pour water into acid, All volatile materials to be handled in a hood with the exhaust fan on, Always cover up and always wear gloves*. "What I mean is you're lucky it wasn't worse. Lucky"—she paused and felt something float up in her, some amalgam of fear and loss and love—"lucky you're alive."

The chemical was one of the ergot compounds Herr H. first synthesized in 1938, when she was just sixteen and working as an au pair in Neuchâtel and he an ambitious young chemist hoping to synthesize an analog to Coramine, a cardiovascular stimulant produced by Ciba, one of the company's biggest rivals. The structure of Coramine—nicotinic acid diethylamide—was strikingly similar to that of lysergic acid, the basic constituent of the ergot alkaloids his mentor, Arthur Stoll, had isolated eighteen years earlier, and so Herr Hofmann reasoned that it would have similar properties and uses. He spent three years on his investigations, which yielded one useful product—ergobasine, marketed by the company for obstetrical use, as it promoted dilation of the uterus and stanched bleeding after birth—and a series of lysergic acid derivatives that unfortunately didn't show much promise, including the twenty-fifth iteration, lysergic acid diethylamide. The pharmacological unit found it 30 percent less effective than ergobasine, though it did seem to have a mild stimulatory effect in animal trials, producing a degree of restlessness in rats, rabbits and dogs. But Sandoz was not in the business of marketing stimulants for the lower animals, and the compound was shelved, along with its twenty-four predecessors.

The thing was—and he'd tried to explain this to her the previous week—he just couldn't get it out of his mind. He was paid to experiment, to be creative, to unlock the chemical secrets of natural substances (like ergot, a parasitic fungus of grains that had been used in preparation by midwives from time immemorial) in order to produce new medicines for the company so that the company could market them and make a profit for its investors, and, by extension, its employees. That was his job, his fulfillment, his pleasure in the work—the natural world presented a mystery and it was the object of science to chip away at that mystery and see what lay beneath it. He had a hunch about this synthesis, that was what he'd told her ("*Ich habe ein Vorgefühl*"), this one above all the others, and though it was unusual to continue experimenting on a drug once Pharmacology had passed judgment on it, he couldn't help feeling there was something here they were all missing. And so, on Friday she'd assisted him in preparing a new synthesis for further trials. And on Friday he'd inadvertently poisoned himself and had to go home early. Now it was Monday, the first day of the workweek, and he was proposing to poison himself all over again, intentionally this time.

He was right there, as close as he'd ever been to her, and her heart was pounding in her chest. Strangely, his eyes didn't seem to blink— he was fixated, not on her but on something beyond her, through her, an *idea*—and for the longest moment he didn't say a thing. When he told her what he was proposing, she let out a little cry—she couldn't help herself; she was that shocked. "But wouldn't it be better to test it on animals first—in the event, I mean, in case there are adverse effects, or you, you—?"

She had to look away from him. It wasn't her place to question him—he'd gone to university, he was an educated man, he was her boss, and she was a girl still, just twenty-one. She hadn't even gone to high school. None of the girls she knew had—in her place and time women were expected to marry and raise a family. Period. Oh, maybe they'd work for a year or two as au pairs or apprentices in a shop, as typists or assistants in a chemistry lab, but marriage was their prospect and their destiny and that made a high school education strictly de trop.

"Ha!" he said, spinning away from her like a dancer, as excited as she'd ever seen him. "We've already been down that road, as I told you—all that would happen is that the stiffs over in Pharmacology would dose a couple of dogs and the dogs' pupils would dilate and their body temperature rise and they'd pace back and forth in their cages, but dogs can't talk, dogs can't tell us about the kind of psycho-active properties this compound might have, *does* have, I'm sure of it."

"You're no guinea pig," she said, because she wouldn't give it up. Ergot was dangerous. She'd looked it up in the library because she wanted to be informed, wanted to *learn,* and what she learned frightened her all the more. It poisoned whole villages in the olden days when people consumed it in their bread, the fungus ground up into flour along with the grain it infested, and no one suspecting the truth of the matter. It caused convulsions, diarrhea, paresthesia, and worse, mania, psychosis, dry gangrene that made your nose, ears, fingers and toes shrivel and drop off.

"But I am," he insisted. "I am. And you're going to be my witness."

The noon hour came and went. She didn't go home for lunch, but instead sat outside in the sun and nibbled at the sandwich her mother had made her that morning. Everything around her was buzzing with activity, people from the shops and offices picnicking on park benches or spreading blankets on strips of grass, bees at the flowers, birds in the trees, pigeons rising up and fluttering down again like windborne leaves. She wasn't hungry but she forced herself to eat, trying not to think about what lay ahead—which was nothing really, she kept telling herself, because ergot was only toxic in much higher and repeated doses, so that the photo she'd seen of the gnarled decaying feet of a peasant afflicted with ergotism was the end result of continued ingestion—bread, daily bread. She took a bite of her sandwich, then turned it over in her hand and examined it, the neat semicircle her teeth had made, crumbs, the pink of the ham, the yellow of the cheese. The sun warmed her face. Her mind drifted. She chewed. Swallowed. Watched a cloud in the shape of a scythe slice across the face of the sun and melt away.

Herr Hofmann, always mindful of the company's time, put off the experiment till late in the day. She kept herself busy cleaning the lab equipment, washing and drying beakers, funnels, stirring rods, wiping down the counters she'd already wiped down twice, but all the while she was keeping an eye on him where he sat at his desk making notations in his laboratory journal. The afternoon wore on. She was in the midst of rechecking the inventory for lack of anything better to do, when all at once he pushed back his chair, stood up and swung round on her. "Well," he said, "are you ready, Fräulein?"

It was four-twenty in the afternoon—he made a note of it for the record and so did she—when he diluted 0.5 cc of $\frac{1}{2}$ promil aqueous solution of diethylamide tartrate with 10 cc of water, gave her a "here-goes" grin, raised the glass as if he were toasting her and drank it down in a single swallow. "Utterly tasteless," he pronounced, looking past her to the window and the glaze of sunlight on the panes. "If I didn't know better I'd think I was just taking a sip of water." Again he flashed the grin. "For the purpose of moistening the throat. Always advisable to keep the throat moist, right?"

Her response was so muted she could barely hear herself. "Yes, I think so," she murmured, but she was watching him closely, feasting on the sight of him actually, this shining man, this genius, and why couldn't he have chosen somebody else for the trial, somebody who didn't have so much to lose? He could have called for volunteers, paid someone—Axel Yoder, the halfwit who pushed a mop up and down the hallways all day long as if it were attached to him. Or the squint-eyed woman in the butcher's shop down the street. He could have paid her, couldn't he? What would she know? Or a monkey—what was wrong with trying it on a monkey?

Twenty minutes later, nothing had happened. They'd both gone back to their work, the sun held steady, a telephone rang somewhere down the hallway. She could barely breathe. She was aching to ask him if he was feeling anything yet—any effects, anything whatever—but she felt shy suddenly, as if it would be an imposition, as if somehow the experiment would be in jeopardy if she were the first to speak. The toxin was in *him,* this was *his* body, *his* trial, and what could be more private than that? She thought of Werner Forssmann then and how he'd had to physically restrain his nurse so she wouldn't interfere with him when he worked that catheter all the way up his antecubital vein to his heart, and then she was wishing she'd taken the compound with him. Or instead of him.

Every minute fell like a sledgehammer. She wanted to get up, wanted to go to him, if only to press a hand to his shoulder to assure him she was there still, but she fought the impulse and fought it again. And then, just as the church bells tolled the hour, he suddenly shifted around in his chair, glanced over his shoulder at her and began to laugh. Laugh! And not just a titter or a cackle, but a booming full-chested roar of a laugh that just kept coming and coming till he had tears in his eyes and she was on her feet and flying to him, crying out, "What? What is it?" And absurdly, "Are you feeling it?"

He tried to get up, then sat heavily. The laughter caught in his throat. "I feel, I feel"—he was struggling to get the words out— "light . . . headed . . . dizzy, maybe. And"—here he laughed again, sharply, more a bark than a laugh—"gay, gay, Fräulein, and why would I feel gay?"

She was standing over him now, barely able to breathe herself, and she did the only thing she could think to do: she touched him, ever so lightly, on the forearm. He rotated his head to stare up at her, his question still hanging in the air, and she saw that his pupils were dilated like the pupils of the dogs in the laboratory trials he'd told her about, so wide open they drove all the color out of his eyes. Normally, his eyes were the color of caramel; now they were black, shining and black, and she made a mental note of that so she could write it down later, and why did she have such an ache in the pit of her stomach and why was she thinking of *Dr. Jekyll and Mr. Hyde?*

"I must . . ." he began, then laughed again, waving an arm in front of his face as if he were conducting an orchestra only he could hear, "must . . . record . . ." In the next moment he took up his pen and very slowly and meticulously wrote a single line in his notebook: *17:00: Beginning dizziness, feeling of anxiety, visual distortions, symptoms of ataxia, desire to laugh.*

She'd drawn her hand back when he'd begun waving his arm, and she wasn't so much thinking that this was the first time they'd ever actually touched, aside from brushing past each other in the performance of their daily routines, but of what he'd written in the notebook. *Ataxia, anxiety.* Would he need an emetic? A tranquillizer? Should she call a doctor?

As if reading her thoughts, he turned his face to her again—black eyed, his features slack and distorted—and murmured, "It's all right, Susi, I'm fine, everything's fine, it's just that—well, let's see, let's give it a . . . bit more time." He glanced at the clock, let out another laugh. "It's only five. We wouldn't want to . . . to cheat . . . the, the company out of our last hour's work of the day, would . . . we?"

Everything stopped right there, right in that instant: he'd called her *Susi.* Never before, never once, had he let slip the formal bonds of their relationship, under which, rigorously, unfailingly, she was Fräulein Ramstein and he Herr Hofmann. As upset as she was, as frightened, she was rocked by it: he'd called her by her first name, almost as if they were on an equal footing—almost as if they were friends, very close friends, male and female, as if she really was more to him than a starched lab coat and a pair of willing hands. She didn't know what to say. *Cheat the company?* No, was the proper response, but then he clearly wasn't in his right mind and to expect him to continue work—or her to—was absurd.

He abruptly turned back round in his chair, the four legs grating on the floor so that the sudden noise startled her, and he began paging through his notes as if he were riffling a deck of cards. The pages hissed under the pressure of his fingertips, a noise that struck her as frivolous, and beyond that, wrong: this was the official record, not a plaything. He released the pages, took them up, riffled them again. Then again. "Please, Susi, dear Susi, give me, give *us,*" he said, and here came the laugh, "give us a few minutes . . . and we'll . . . we'll see, because when you examine it, really examine it, time has no meaning, whether it's company time or free time or the, the . . . time . . . they clock at the Greenwich Observatory. *Nicht wahr?"*

She was still floating on that *Susi, dear Susi,* when things became complicated (or more complicated, that is, considering that her boss was self-poisoned and acting as if he were a slurring drunkard in the back room of a whiskey bar). Suddenly he jumped up from the desk as if he'd been stung, as if the desk itself had come to life and attacked him, and when he swung round on her she saw that all the color had drained from his face. He wasn't laughing now. Now he looked ill, seriously ill, the knowledge of what he'd done to himself rising up to infest the swollen black pupils of his eyes. He looked to the ceiling, looked to the walls. "The light," he said. "The light."

"You want me to turn off the light?" She crossed the room to the switch on the wall and shut down the overhead lighting, though the lab was still flooded with sunlight so that you could hardly tell the difference.

"That's not it," he insisted. "That's not it, that's not . . . it at all." He was standing in the middle of the room, swaying on his feet. "Home," he said abruptly, his fingers fumbling at the buttons of his lab coat. "Take me home. I need to . . . Help me, Susi, *help me."*

If she was frightened—and she was—she didn't have time to dwell on it. She'd never been to his house, but she knew he lived in Bottmingen, out in the suburbs, some ten kilometers away, and the immediate problem, a problem that could have life and death consequences for all she knew, was to get him home where he could be properly cared for. She helped him out of his lab coat, her own fingers trembling, and then she was handing him his jacket, which he merely stared at as if he'd never seen it before, and she helped him with that too. And his cap—he couldn't very well bicycle all the way home without his cap. It took him a moment, turning the cap over in his hands as if trying to reference it, and then he reached up and pulled it down firmly over the crown of his head.

She made a quick survey of the lab to be sure everything was in order and led him out the door. Never once did she think of going to his colleagues for help—just the opposite: she went out of her way to avoid them. She looked in both directions up and down the hall and then hurried him to the back stairway, where there was no one to see him but Axel Yoder, eternally plying his mop. She did this reflexively, to protect him. He was more than merely respectable—he was a cornerstone of the research department at Sandoz—and it would be devastating if anyone were to see him in this condition because they would assume the worst, that he was drunk, drunk on the job. That would never do.

Her next worry was how to get him home. He bicycled to work every day, rain or shine, winter and summer, but was he in any condition to bicycle now? She would have called a car, but it was wartime and there were no cars available, except maybe for the mayor or the president of one of the big chemical companies, so she really had no choice in the matter. "I'm taking you home," she said to him firmly, reassuringly, no arguments, and suddenly their roles were reversed— she wasn't addressing her boss and superior but a child, like Liliane and her sister Juliette, the little girls she'd instructed and chastised and watched over day and night when she worked as an au pair. "You think you can bicycle?"

They were standing out on the sidewalk now, the mild evening sifting down around them, sunlight draping banners across the street all the way to the end of the block and the air charged with the scent of flowers and the cooking smells from the cafés. It was a beautiful evening, the sort of evening she would have reveled in under other circumstances, but all that mattered to her now was that it wasn't raining and wasn't going to. There were pigeons at their feet, ubiquitous pigeons, parting and regrouping as she wheeled both bicycles up and held his out to him by the handlebars. He hadn't uttered a sound since they'd left the building, just let himself be led by her like a schoolboy, but now he began giggling uncontrollably, and a couple, passing close by, arm in arm, gave him a look.

"Can I bicycle?" he repeated in an odd tone, taking hold of the handlebars and swinging one leg over the crossbar, his movements syrupy and slow, which lulled her for just the instant it took for him to push off and begin pedaling furiously up the street. "Just you watch!" he cried, glancing back at her with a triumphant look, and in his distraction he very nearly ran down an old man with a stiff leg limping across the street. But panic and more panic: before she could even mount her own bike he was already at the end of the block, slashing left at the corner directly in front of a tram that somehow managed to miss dragging him under its wheels, and the chase was on.

There were people everywhere, on bicycles, in carts, on foot, men carrying satchels home from work, women with groceries, children darting out after hoops or balls till the street was like an obstacle course—and dogs too, dogs popping up to chase along, disappear and pop up all over again. The tram. An automobile. A wagon laden with beer kegs. Herr H. was wearing the loden jacket she'd helped him on with not five minutes before and she struggled to keep sight of it, weaving in and out of the traffic. She was pedaling with every-thing she had but she didn't seem to be gaining on him, and were they racing now, was that it? But wait, there he went, darting down a side street and into a scrum of bicyclists who were all but dressed identically to him, so that for one frantic minute she lost sight of him and wound up homing in on someone else altogether until she saw her mistake, her legs churning, her heart thumping in her chest, and where was Herr H.? Where *was* he? She pedaled on, frantically scan-ning the road ahead, until a figure separated itself from the scrum—loden jacket, pale cap, the hard-muscled V of his back—and she shot after him.

It wasn't until they were on Bottmingenstrasse, with its long vistas and thinning crowds, that she finally caught up with him. He hadn't slackened his pace, not for a minute, and it was only fear and adrenaline that kept her going, because what if he had an accident, what if he ran off the road into a ditch and broke a leg—or worse? She was responsible. She was the one he'd cried out to for help and no one else. Of all the people extant—his colleagues, his intimates, his *wife*—she was the only one on this earth who knew he wasn't in his right mind, that he was poisoned and in danger, mortal danger. As she drew even with him, fighting for breath, she called out, "Herr Hofmann, slow down, will you, please?"

The wheels whirred. The breeze fanned her sweat. He didn't turn his head—just kept pumping and pumping as if she weren't even there. "Herr Hofmann!" And then, her lungs burning and her legs like rubber, she lost all control and began shouting at him—or no, shrieking, actually shrieking. "Stop it, will you? Albert! *Albert!*"

That was when he turned his head. "Fräulein?" he gasped, slowing now and giving her a puzzled look. "What on earth are you doing here?"

She was curious about his house—and his wife, Anita, a pretty, dark-haired woman of thirty or so she'd met only once in passing—but of course lab assistants didn't get invited to Sunday dinner or to socialize or sit around dipping croutons into the fondue in the bosom of the family, and in any case, Bottmingen wasn't exactly in the heart of town. The odd thing was that she hardly noticed the place when they finally arrived—it was a house and he lived there and that was all that mattered. She was sweating, exhausted, her heart about to burst through her chest, but she followed his lead, making a sharp right turn and pedaling up the gravel drive to the front of the house, where he just dropped his bicycle on the lawn and bolted inside, leaving the door wide open behind him, the keys dangling in the lock. Even as she propped her own bike against the tree in the front yard, wondering if she should follow him in and explain the situation to his wife as best she could, she heard him shouting within. "Anita! Anita, where are you?" There was a clatter, as of something metallic crashing to the floor, then a silence. A beat. Two beats. And then a long drawn-out moan of despair: "Anita!"

Tentatively, she made her way up the steps and into the front hall. The sun was out still but it was shadowy inside, none of the lamps lit and the light from the yard held trembling in the windows. "Herr Hofmann?" she called, afraid to enter uninvited.

His voice cracked as he cried out his wife's name one more time, and then it dropped almost to a whisper: "I'm here," he said. "In here."

She found him in the sitting room—sofa, chairs, end table, lamps, everything in perfect order—staring wildly about him. "She's . . . she's gone," he said, and all the breath went out of him.

"Gone? What do you mean?" It was nearly six in the evening—any wife, let alone the wife of such a man, would have been at home, cooking the meal, looking after the children, there to greet her husband at the end of a long day.

"Gone," he repeated. He pressed his hands to his temples, as if the internal pressure were too much to bear. "And I'm left here dying, I tell you, *dying*. I'm poisoned, can't you see—?"

That froze her inside—could it be true? Was it fatal? Had he miscalculated the dose? None of the dogs had died, had they? But then who knew what effect an experimental drug might have, a new drug, one nobody had ever tested before on a human subject?

"No, no, you're not dying, not at all," she said, fighting to keep her voice under control. "You'll be fine, you will—you just need to, to sit a minute," and she helped him to the armchair, where he dropped down like a stone. In the next moment she was making a frantic circuit of the house, shouting herself now—"Frau Hofmann! Frau Hofmann! Are you home?"—but there was no answer. The wife did seem to be gone, and the children too. She couldn't help feeling a flare of anger—if she were the wife of a man like Herr Hofmann, like *Albert,* she would be there for him every minute of every day and night.

Sixty seconds later she was back in the sitting room, repeating what he already knew: "She's not here."

He said one thing only: "I can't stop it."

"Milk," she said, "what about milk—to absorb the poison? Do you have any milk?"

He didn't answer, so she went to the kitchen herself, feeling like an alien in this house where he lived, where he spent his nights, where he climbed into bed with his wife who wasn't even here when he needed her most . . . She flung open the door of the icebox, but there was no milk. A bottle of beer, yes, cheese, a plate of sliced beef, *rösti* and haricots verts laid on the shelf as if set aside for his dinner, but no milk.

When she came back to him, very nearly in tears now, to say that there was no milk in the house and what did he want her to do—the doctor, should she call the doctor?—he flinched as if he didn't recognize her, as if she'd come to do him harm rather than rescue him. His face was in shadow. He held a hand over his eyes. "The doctor," she repeated. "Should I call the doctor?"

Suddenly he lurched up in the chair, his face flushed and his eyes snapping at her. "What the hell do you think? God help me, yes— call the doctor! And, and . . . the neighbor, Frau Rüdiger, go next door and ask her for milk, as much as she can spare . . ."

She was in motion again and glad of it, glad to be doing something, anything, bolting out the still-open door and across the yard to the neighbor's house, where she pounded on the door until it was answered by a bewildered-looking woman with fleshy pouches for cheeks and drawn-down little specks of blue for eyes. "Help us, please, it's an emergency, we need milk and we don't have any," she said in a breathless rush, "and the doctor, call the doctor, *please*—"

"The doctor?" the woman repeated. "But who are you?"

The explanation took all of ten seconds and then the woman had the milk in her hand, two full liter bottles, and they were hurrying across the yard to the open door of the Hofmanns' house and the woman was saying, "Poisoned? How?" But then the woman stole a glance at her—the sweat at her temples, her hair come undone, the frantic look in her eyes—and said no more.

The doctor, who was local to Bottmingen, was there within half an hour, wheeling up the drive on his own bicycle, his bag strapped on behind. When he came into the sitting room, Herr H. was stretched out on the sofa, a comforter pulled up to his throat and both bottles of milk standing empty on the end table at his side. Herr H., who'd been forcing his eyelids shut with the pressure of his fingertips, dropped his hands and flashed open his eyes as the doctor entered the room, and he looked more startled than relieved. After his outburst he'd sunk back into lethargy, muttering to himself, moaning, exclaiming, the whole time acting as if she weren't there in the room with him, as if he couldn't see her or trust the evidence of his senses. Now he tried to say something—a name, the name of the doctor, or no, the drug, the poison—but it was garbled and confused and though it really wasn't her place she couldn't help speaking up. "It was an experiment," she said, feeling ridiculous, feeling guilty, as if she were the one responsible or at the very least a coconspirator.

The doctor was an old man, dressed in a shapeless blue suit and a collar that didn't seem to fit him. His hair was white, his face red, and he lifted his eyebrows in puzzlement, as if he didn't know whether to question her or the patient or even to step back a moment and make introductions, because who *was* she established here in his patient's sitting room and where was the patient's wife?

"It was a new compound we—Herr Hofmann, that is—synthesized in the lab, lysergic acid diethylamide, and Herr Hofmann had a hunch, and he . . ." She had to break off—she was afraid she was going to start sobbing. "He, he—it was the minutest dose, just two hundred fifty micrograms . . ."

"When was this?" The doctor gave her a sharp look, his voice harsh and accusatory. "And who are you, exactly, Fräulein?"

Very slowly, in bits and pieces, the explanation came out, and Frau Rüdiger was there to back her up on the details of what had occurred since she'd brought Herr H. home, how they'd given him milk, how he'd cried out that a devil had taken possession of his soul, how he'd had trouble standing, how Frau Hofmann, today of all days, was absent, having gone to Lucerne with the children to visit her parents, and how Frau Rüdiger had telephoned her so that she was rushing home even now. All the while, Herr Hofmann just lay there on the sofa, staring at nothing.

"All right, then," the doctor said, turning to him. "How are you feeling, Albert? Can you speak?"

Herr Hofmann—black eyes, fingertips alive at his temples—only nodded.

"This young woman—your assistant, is that right? This young woman claims that you've ingested a very small dose of this substance, two hundred fifty micrograms, yes? Nod if that's true."

Herr Hofmann nodded, and then he was trying to say something. The doctor leaned in, cupping a hand to one ear. "Yes," Herr H. said, his voice so soft it was barely audible. "Yes—*micrograms.*"

The doctor didn't reply, just pursed his lips and reached behind him for his black bag. He took the patient's temperature, which was slightly elevated, applied his stethoscope and finally pressed a finger to Herr H.'s wrist to count his pulse. A long moment crept by, Frau Rüdiger looking as startled as if she'd stumbled upon some satanic rite in the sitting room of her next-door neighbor who'd always seemed so unassuming and substantial but was now revealed as a deviate, while the doctor's eyebrows rode up and down like pale markers in the gathering gloom as the evening deepened and Susi took it upon herself to go around the room and switch on the lamps as if this were her own house and her own privilege.

"Everything appears normal, Albert," the doctor said finally, turning aside to replace his instruments in his bag. "You'll be fine—just let it pass. And it was wise"—he looked back to the patient now—"to consume the milk, which I'm sure is acting as an antidote to whatever you've managed to poison yourself with . . . what did you say it was?"

And Herr H., pushing himself up to a sitting position now, smiled for the first time since they'd left the lab. The color was seeping back into his face, as if the crisis had passed—or was passing. He was silent a moment, his eyes sweeping over the room until finally coming to rest on the doctor's. "Lysergic acid diethylamide," he said. "Synthesis"—a brief stumble over the syllables—"synthesis number twenty-five."

The doctor left, weaving off into the declining sun on his bicycle, but not before taking her aside and admonishing her to keep a close watch on the patient and call him right away if he should take a turn for the worse. "You never can tell with cases of poisoning," he said, looking her full in the face, "especially if there's no known antidote. And how could there be since the agent itself is all but unknown, isn't that right?"

She could only nod.

He looked at her sharply and she thought he was about to deliver a lecture on the dangers of ingesting foreign substances, but finally, his voice shot through with scorn, all he said was, "Don't you people have animals for this sort of thing?"

Frau Rüdiger, wringing her hands in the doorway—and she had a story to tell, oh yes indeed—said she hoped everything was going to be fine but that she had her own family to attend to, *if that was quite all right*. Snatching a quick look at Herr H., where he lay stretched out on the couch, staring at the ceiling and moving his lips as if conversing with someone who wasn't there, she said she'd look in later when Frau Hofmann returned, and added, oddly, "Do you understand?"

Frankly, Susi didn't understand, but no matter the awkwardness of the situation—alone now in the house with her boss—she was determined to see it out. She thought of her mother then. Her mother would be worried and she really should telephone her, but then she couldn't get past the further awkwardness of asking permission—and whom was she going to ask? The wife wasn't home yet—the wife was on the train from Lucerne, half-mad with worry, no doubt—and Herr Hofmann was in no condition to respond. In fact, for the next hour he just lay there on the sofa without moving except to blink open his eyes now and again and exclaim, "The light! The light!"

She was sitting in the chair across from him, trying to read a book she'd slipped from the shelf—Hesse's *Narziss und Goldmund*, which she found heavy going, especially with the way her mind was wandering—when she heard a quick tattoo of footsteps on the porch and the click of a key in the lock. In the next moment Frau Hofmann burst into the room, her face burnished and eyes wild, shrugging out of her coat and dropping her purse to the floor in a single motion, and then she was on her knees in front of the sofa, clutching her husband to her and repeating his name over and over as if in prayer.

Susi didn't know what to do. She started to get up, then thought better of it. She wanted to explain, officially, to give Frau Hofmann an account of all that had happened, what the doctor had said, Frau Rüdiger, the milk, the bicycle ride, everything, but it was as if she'd been bound in place like Werner Forssmann's nurse. Everything was so odd. She was here in this house she'd pictured endlessly in her imagination, here among all the things it contained, the family pictures, the ancestral china, the carpet he walked on in his slippered feet, but this wasn't where she belonged and it was dark beyond the windows, and her boss, the most proper man in the world, the man she esteemed more than any other, was responding to his wife's embrace with mounting passion, his arms clutched to her shoulders and his mouth pressed tight to hers in a deep erotic kiss . . .

"Albert, Albert," the wife murmured, coming up for air, "what have you done to yourself? What were you thinking?"

He didn't say a word, just tightened his grip on her and tried to kiss her again, but she pulled away and for the first time seemed aware that they weren't alone in the room, throwing a quizzical glance in Susi's direction before turning back to him—to his kiss. "You gave us such a fright," she whispered, and then she was repeating his name again, over and over, as if to take possession of it.

"The children—?" he began, but couldn't finish the question.

"I left them with Mother because I didn't know . . . I thought— Oh, Albert, I was frantic, *frantic*. Don't you ever do anything like this again, hear me?"

For answer, he pulled her back down to him.

The room went deep then, enclosed, narrowing, a submarine plunging into the depths where only the two of them could go, and Susi, without a word, laid the book aside, pushed herself up from the chair and tiptoed out of the room.

She found her bike propped against the tree where she'd left it. It was chilly out now, but the crickets sang their night song and the frogs, awakened after a long winter's sleep, joined in. She was out in the country, on her own, and it must have been past ten at night. Her mother would be furious. She swung a leg over the crossbar of her bike, pushed off and began pedaling down the dark driveway to the darker road, and there was no moon in the sky to guide her, only the pale distant luminescence of the stars God had put in the heavens to mark His boundaries.

She was late for work the next morning. Her mother had awakened her at the usual hour but she'd fallen back asleep, never more exhausted in her life. She'd got home very late and her mother had greeted her at the door with a stony face, but she explained herself patiently till gradually her mother seemed to relent and heated a pan of barley soup over the stove for her, all the while complaining *You couldn't have telephoned even?* and she reiterating how desperate the situation had been—and she didn't have to exaggerate, that was for certain. When finally she did get to bed, she couldn't sleep, her mind replaying the day's events in a continuous loop, coming around again and again to the way he'd cried out her name—*Help me, Susi, help me!*—and then the image of him holding fast to his wife, of their lips, their tongues, the way he moved against her and she against him as if there were no constraints, as if she herself wasn't sitting right there in the corner of the room. And she wasn't in that room as an interloper either, she was there as a Good Samaritan, a friend, a savior—and what did that get her? A lonely ride home in the dark and not a word of thanks.

The first thing she saw on opening the closet—his jacket, hanging on its hook like the most ordinary thing in the world—flooded her with relief. He was there. He was all right. He hadn't died in the night or lost his mind or succumbed to delirium. She fought down the flickering memory of his vacant eyes, his reddened face, his mussed hair that stood straight up on his head like the hackles of an animal and the way he'd shouted at her when she asked, in all innocence, if she should call the doctor, then she hung her scarf and jacket on the hook beside his, slipped on her lab coat and stepped into the laboratory.

At the moment she caught sight of him in the far corner (not at his desk but at the window, his back to her), she was struck by the aroma of fresh coffee, a rarity in these days of rationing and hardship, and something else too, a lighter fragrance, a whiff of nature in this place where the natural invariably gave way to process, synthesis, titration and extraction. That was when she saw the flowers, the daffodils, a whole bouquet of them, arranged in a beaker on her desk. She was struck dumb. No one ever gave her presents, except for her parents and her brothers, and only then on her birthday and at Christmas, and before she could even think to call out a *Guten Morgen* to him she was pressing her face to the soft cool petals and breathing in the scent of the outdoors.

"Oh, I see you've found the flowers, Fräulein." He'd turned round now, grinning at her, his hair swept back, the spectacles pinching his nose, his lab coat spotless and his tie perfectly aligned, everything right again, everything the way it should be. "I wanted to do something more for you, to thank you, that is, for yesterday . . . roses, I thought of roses, but the shops weren't open yet and, well, I picked these for you along Bottmingenstrasse on my way in this morning. I hope you like them."

Her first emotion was guilt over the resentment she'd fallen prey to on her way in on the tram, but now, as if a switch had been thrown, she felt nothing but warmth for him—he was his old self, and his old self was gentle and giving, and he did care for her, he *did*. And then, as he crossed the lab to her to take both her hands in his own, she gave way to relief and a kind of amazement at how well he looked, fresher than ever, in fact—if she hadn't known better she would have thought he'd just returned from a week at a spa, at Montreux or Baden-Baden, his whole body aglow as if he'd been rebuilt, cell by cell, overnight.

"I do," she said. "I love them. But you didn't have to—"

He held up a hand to silence her. "Let's have a cup of coffee—you do enjoy coffee, don't you, Fräulein?—and sit down a minute to discuss what's happened here. I have so much to tell you."

So they sat—at his desk, on company time—and sipped their coffee, with sugar and cream, no less, and he told her everything, from the minute the drug had come on to its gradual dissipation late in the night. "I experienced things, Fräulein, I'd never thought possible— saw things, saw whether my eyes were open or shut, a whole kaleidoscope of swirling images and colors, and that was only the beginning.

It was the most"—he hesitated, then laughed—"eye-opening experience I've ever had. Susi, I saw the world as it truly is," he said, his voice so rich and resonant he might have been singing, "—the immaterial world, the spiritual world, Kant's *Ding an sich* in every object."

She didn't know what to say. She barely knew who Kant was.

"Table legs. The antimacassar on the chair. The end table, the telephone, my shoes! Everything has a life of its own totally independent of us and I never knew it, never even imagined it, because I've had my head down my entire life, my nose in books, in beakers, peering through microscopes at a busy universe no one before van Leeuwenhoek had even guessed at! Do you see? Do you see what I'm saying?"

He was his normal self, that was what she'd been thinking a moment ago, but now she wasn't so certain—could he still be under the influence of the drug? Was he delirious? What was he talking about? She raised the cup to her lips, blew briefly across the surface to cool it, and looked into his eyes. "Yes," she said, "I think so. It does have psychoactive properties, just as you predicted, is that what you're saying?"

His eyes were strange—not dilated now, not black, and back to their normal color—but infused with something like, like . . . mania. Or no, enthusiasm, extreme enthusiasm for this new product and what its possibilities were for the company, for the world, because it was his creation, his alone, and he couldn't contain the excitement of it. "I won't say it was all bliss and I don't know what I said or did"—a long look for her now, deep into her eyes, so deep she had to turn away—"and forgive me for any . . . indiscretions, but if I saw the devil, if I thought I was losing my mind when in fact I was only prying loose the grip of my ego, I saw God too, shining until His face engulfed the sun and a second sun and all the suns beyond it and I was left with a peace I've never felt in all my days—or even dreamed of."

He straightened up in the chair, threw back his head and drained his cup. "This is a revolution, Susi, and make no mistake about it. We have something here more powerful than any bomb, any reagent, any synthesis anyone has ever come across—I'm sure of it, as sure as I've ever been about anything, but of course we need more experimentation, more human subjects, and my experience alone is woefully insufficient, I know that . . . but I feel it in my bones, in my heart, my brain, in the neurons, Susi, the *neurons*."

O f course, no one would believe him, at least not at first. Three days after his self-experiment, she typed up his report on the experience and at his direction sent copies to Professor Stoll, his immediate superior at Sandoz, and to Professor Rothlin, director of the Pharmacological Department. It didn't take long to get a reaction— within the hour Professor Rothlin was tapping at the door. At the moment, Herr Hofmann was in the middle of producing another iteration of the chemical for further trials—he'd been doing almost nothing but for the past three days—and he called impatiently over his shoulder to her to *please* see who that was and what they wanted, and if he was impatient, edgy, really, she excused it because the synthesis was so complex and tedious and the resulting product so unstable even light would rapidly degrade it, and of course, all this meant so much to him. This was his discovery, his child, and he would settle for nothing less than the purest synthesis it was humanly possible to produce.

"Yes," she said, "of course," and went to the door expecting one of the other young chemists or perhaps a secretary from the main office with some form or other, so it took her a moment to collect herself when she saw who it was standing there before her.

The director barely gave her a glance, just strode into the room, huffing and puffing and waving the report in one hand. "Albert, Albert, what in God's name *is* this?"

Fortunately, Herr H. was in the second stage of the process, which involved cooling the isomerized synthesis prior to mixing it with an acid and a base and evaporating it to produce the active substance, so he was able to step away from the hood, strip off his gloves and nonchalantly shake the director's hand. "What do you mean?" he said, breaking into a grin. "My report?"

"Exactly, yes. Because obviously you've made some error in calculating the dosage—"

"Not at all—and my lab assistant, Fräulein Ramstein, who was at my side throughout the entire process, can back me up here, isn't that right, Fräulein?"

And here was a role she knew how to inhabit: modest, pretty, bowing her head in accord as the sun sent a slant of light through the window to illuminate her where she stood, and it was almost as if they were in a scene from a film, the heroine stepping forward to exonerate the hero when he most needed it. "Oh, yes," she said, "we were very precise about that. Two hundred fifty micrograms."

"Ridiculous," the director said, and he'd begun to pace up and down the room now, a delicate-looking man of her father's age, wearing whiskers. "Do you really expect me to believe that the merest trace of this substance—two hundred fifty millionths of a gram—can have any effect whatever? Especially for a man of your size—what do you weigh, Albert? Seventy kilograms?"

"Seventy-two."

"There, you see? A man of seventy-two kilos affected by a barely measurable dose?" He'd reached the windows and come back again, twice, and now he swiveled round on his feet and pointed a finger at Herr Hofmann—and at her, her too, because she was indivisible from this. "There's something very wrong here. Either that or you've discovered the alchemist's elixir."

Herr Hofmann tried to interject, but the director waved him off. "No, no, Albert, I'm sorry, but this is just too fantastic to be credible. I'm going to need to see all your laboratory notes, everything you've done with these lysergic acid amides, and I want to be personally involved in any further trials—animal or human—so that I can judge for myself." He paused, the hint of a smile hovering over his lips. "You're a solid man, Albert, one of the best we have, and I know as well as anyone here that you're not given to miscalculation, exaggeration—or what, fantasy?" The director let out a little laugh. "You're not a fantasist now, Albert, are you?"

Whether he was or not—and, of course, the director was just having a little joke—the compound Herr H. had discovered was simply too intriguing to resist, and within the week the director himself, and Professor Stoll too, had come to him for a trial dose, and so they became the second and third human guinea pigs to experiment with the drug. They remained incredulous regarding the dosage right up to the moment of ingestion, but Herr Hofmann, insisting that the quantity he himself had taken was an overdose, gave his colleagues less than a third of that, 60 micrograms only, and yet both reported the most astonishing effects, seeing lights, colors, experiencing synesthesia and visual distortions, though neither suffered the terrifying visions Herr H. had summoned, nor the glorious ones either. Which Herr H. attributed to the reduced dosage. Still, the effects were beyond what anyone could have expected, and both men encouraged him to continue trials, which he did succeed in doing on separate occasions with two other volunteers from the Chemistry Department.

All this was very gratifying. She began to feel an attachment to the work she'd never experienced before because she'd been there from the very beginning, at his side, his helpmeet, and in a sense the compound was as much her child as his. Work, which had seemed so dull and repetitive, was suddenly absorbing, radiant even, so much so that she began to think she'd like to go back to school and become a chemist herself. Of course, she kept all this hidden from her mother, because her mother wouldn't have approved and because LSD-25, as they were calling it in shorthand, was the secret sweet chemical bond between her and Herr H., and she valued that more than anything in the world.

Spring gave way to summer, the days collecting beyond the windows like so many invitations to another realm, each one softer and lovelier than the one before, and she and Herr H. worked at synthesizing, purifying and crystallizing the product until it was as close to perfection as they could make it, and sometimes, when the mood was right, they took their lunch hour together on the patch of lawn out back of the building. It was during the second week of June—June the twelfth, actually, and she would never forget the date—that she approached him about something she'd been revolving in her mind for the longest time.

They were sitting side by side in the grass on the blanket he'd spread, casually chewing their sandwiches, books open before them, as relaxed with each other as—well, she didn't want to push the simile because he was married and always would be married and she'd never be married to him, but it wasn't like brother- and sisterhood either, and no one, least of all her mother, could ever know what she was feeling. At any rate, she took the last bite of her sandwich, chewed, swallowed, and screwed up her courage, sure he would deny her, say no, claim that she was a girl still and not a woman—not a woman at all, but a girl under her mother's aegis—and the words were out before she could stop herself. "I want to be a guinea pig," she said.

He turned his head and gave her a long look, as if he'd never seen her before—or no, as if he were seeing her suddenly in a whole new light. It took him a moment, his eyes fixed on hers, working things out in his mind, and then, his voice soft, he said, "What will your mother say?"

"I don't care what she says." She was conscious in the moment of a multiplicity of things, the way the light caught his eyes when he wasn't wearing his glasses, the breeze, the smell of chemicals from the company's smokestacks, two toddlers with their mother, a dog running free at the edge of the grass, clouds, shade, the world as it is.

"You mean you won't tell her?"

"No, I'll keep it a secret." She hesitated. "Between you and me."

He let out a laugh. "Right, and Professor Stoll, Professor Rothlin, all our colleagues, all their assistants, the janitorial staff, and, and—"

"I don't care," she said. "I want to be part of this."

He shrugged. He was leaning back, bracing himself on both elbows so that you could see the muscles of his chest stand out against the fabric of his shirt. "Today?" he said. "Would you like to try it today—just a moderate dose, nothing like what I ingested, but more than Stoll and Rothlin and the others, say one hundred micrograms? Just to be sure you're going to fully experience the effects?"

In answer, she just smiled.

I t felt almost illicit, just the two of them there in the lab at four in the afternoon, he measuring out the dose and mixing it with water, just as he'd done two months earlier on the day she'd chased him down Bottmingenstrasse on her bicycle and gone into his house and seen him transformed. "Are you ready, Fräulein?" he asked, just as he'd asked on that chaotic day, the same words exactly, only now he was holding out the glass to her and he would be the observer and she the subject. Was she frightened? A little, she supposed. She couldn't quite suppress the image of him as he lay there helpless on the sofa and how he'd cried out and how frightened she'd been, but she had confidence in him—he'd taken an enormous dose, an overdose, that was all . . . and if old men like Stoll and Rothlin could go ahead and take the drug, well, she could too.

She drank, conscious of his eyes on her. The lab was quiet. The sun, which had shone so brightly at lunch, had disappeared behind the clouds and the room darkened a shade. She gave him a smile and handed back the glass. "No taste at all," she told him, and they were both smiling now.

"Good," he said, "good. And please remember to record all your impressions and keep as accurate a time line as you can. You shouldn't

feel anything for perhaps forty minutes to an hour or even longer,
depending—"

"Depending on what?" Her smile vanished, just like the sun. It
came to her—again, but thunderously now—that she'd just poisoned
herself.

"Each person's chemistry is different," he said, studying her closely.
They were standing there casually at the counter, as if they'd met at
the bar of a hotel or a ski chalet in the Alps and weren't in the office
at all. "So, and you must know this from our animal trials, each individual's reaction time—and the reaction itself—is going to be different. Especially with women. Women are different from men, I don't
have to tell you that, different in every way, and there's no saying how
you'll process this . . ." He trailed off, and she wondered what she
must have looked like just then, her limbs rigid, her face clenched, a
shrill pharmaceutical alarm ringing through her body. "Which won't
be a problem, Fräulein, not at all, so please don't worry. The dose," he
said, "the dose is so very small, *ja*?"

She tried to smile, but her heart was in her throat: What had she
done?

"Just think," he was saying, and he had his hand at her elbow, leading her back to her desk, "you have a distinction now, you among all
the other women in the world—you're the first, Susi, the very first."

He was right. He was always right. Her reaction was mild, to say
the least. Within the hour she began to see colors in everything,
an intensity of color she'd never dreamed was there, and things
began to shimmer as if in a reflection off a wind-rippled pond, but
it was pleasant, all pleasant, and more than that, beautiful beyond
compare. At six, she insisted she was all right—and maybe she felt a
little giggly, like a girl in a horde of girls at a school party, but that
was all right too. "Are you sure, Fräulein?" he kept asking her when
she told him she was perfectly capable of getting home under her

own power and she kept saying, "Yes, yes, yes," and giggling, and in the end—she was going to show him what she was made of— she wouldn't even let him take her to the tram stop but managed everything on her own, even if the ticket taker's face devolved into a clown's mask and the woman behind her had a voice that came to her in the brightest colors, bright green, vernal green, banana yellow, a voice like a glade in the deepest jungle in a country far from her own. Then she was home and she was sitting down to the evening meal with her parents and her brothers and no one questioned her and no one knew that anything had changed at all. She didn't see heaven, she didn't see hell, there were no demons, there was no God, just . . . color, vivid jolting gorgeous color that took her up the stairs and into the enclosed nest of the bed in her room, where the ceiling came to life and all the stars burned right through the roof.

She took the drug twice more in the course of the next year and dutifully recorded her reactions, which were more or less the same each time and more or less pleasant—more pleasant than less, actually. Toward the end of that year she was in the grocer's one evening when she ran into a boy from the neighborhood who'd been away in the army and just come home the day before. She hardly recognized him because he wasn't a boy any longer but a man, and if he bore a resemblance to Herr Hofmann, if he was trim and neat in his uniform and wore wire-framed spectacles, all the better. Three months later he asked her to marry him and she gave her notice at Sandoz and never went back there again.

PART I

Cambridge, 1962

1.

He didn't believe in God, because God didn't make any sense to him, and what he was hearing from some of the people in the Psych Department made even less, if that was possible. Rational people, grad students every bit as serious and committed as he was, suddenly seemed incapable of talking about anything but the oneness of being and the face of the Divine, as if they were mystics instead of scientists. He hadn't come to grad school for God or mysticism or mind expansion or whatever they were calling it, but for a degree that would lead to a job that would pay his bills and get him a house and a car that actually started up when you inserted the key and put your foot down on the gas pedal. Unlike the piece-of-crap Fairlane he was sitting in at that very moment, which he'd coaxed to life with a judicious blast of ether down the throat of the carburetor and had to be goosed every five seconds to keep from dying, and that had nothing to do with any deities except maybe the ones sitting in the board rooms in Detroit. Of course, the car was eight years old, with tires worn as smooth as the sheets of Corrasable Bond he typed up his class notes on and rusted-out rocker panels and springs so worn you hit bottom every time you went over a bump, which was just another kind of humiliation, and where *was* she? Jesus. To be late—late for anything—was totally unacceptable, not to mention rude and unprofessional and about twenty other adjectives he could summon, but tonight of all nights?

It was cold, somewhere down around zero, but he was sweating because he always sweated when he was nervous—or worked up, as his father liked to put it—and he was nervous now. And late. He jerked his head around to stare up at the window that cut a glowing rectangle out of the void above him, no curtains, no blinds, everything open for everybody to see—and no Joanie and no babysitter either. The car sputtered, caught again, and he brought his hand down on the horn and hammered it, twice, till Joanie appeared in the window with her pale pinched face and gave him an irritated flap of her hand that could have meant anything from *Go crawl off and die* to *I just broke my wrist,* and then she was gone and he immediately hit the horn again and kept hitting it until a new face thrust itself through the blinds of the apartment next door—Mrs. Malloy's, with her jaws clenched and her hair flattened to one side of her head—and he eased up.

What he felt like doing was just driving off and leaving her there, but that wouldn't work, of course, and he'd never do it anyway, because then there'd be a whole long soap opera of tears and recrimination to get through when he came back. Plus, Tim had insisted he bring her ("This isn't just for you, you know"), and the last thing he wanted was to disappoint Tim. Or countermand him, or whatever you wanted to call it. On top of it all, he was feeling increasingly ambivalent about the whole thing—scared, that is—and he needed her. Now more than ever. And where *was* she?

He was turned sideways, feeling around on the floor for something to pin down the accelerator so he could go up there and drag her out of the house if that was what it was going to take, when a shadow drifted up the dark tube of the shoveled walk and suddenly cohered into the shape and form of the babysitter, Mrs. Pierzynski, and he

caught his breath. He watched her come lumbering past the car without even realizing he was there—knock-kneed, rubber boots, scarf,
mittens, knit hat—and then stamp up the steps, the door opening
and closing in a quick flash of light and the figure of Joanie replacing hers on the landing. In the next moment there was a rush of cold
air and Joanie was sliding into the seat beside him, smelling of the
perfume her mother had given her for Christmas.

"Jesus," was all he said, and then he put the car in gear and lurched
out onto the icy street, feeling the wheels slide out from under him
for one terrifying moment before finally taking hold where the plow
had scraped the pavement.

"What?" she said. "Don't blame me—you're the one who insists
on treating him like a child. Fitz, Corey's thirteen years old, *thirteen*.
He doesn't need a babysitter—it's just a waste of money we don't
have."

"You're the one who infantilized him."

His wife's face, elaborately made up, false eyelashes, lipstick so red
it looked black in the dim glow of the dash lights, hung there beside
him as if it were floating free, one more satellite in orbit. "How would
you know? You're always at the library."

"You baby talk him."

"It's not baby talk—it's a code, we have a code between us, okay?
Mother and son? Our own special vocabulary." He heard her purse
snap open, the rattle of the cellophane on a fresh pack of Marlboros.
They were silent a moment, then she said, "Don't blame me. It's ridiculous, is what it is—you tell me he can't be home alone for a
couple of hours on a Saturday night?"

The heater was up full, roaring against the windshield. Sweating,
he turned it down, and when he tried to shrug out of his overcoat
she was busy lighting her cigarette and didn't even make a pretense
of trying to help him. "Keep your hands on the wheel, will you?" she
snapped in an irritable little buzz of a voice that brought his anger
right back up again. He was going to say, *It's not just a couple of hours,*

but the thought came like a punch in the stomach, and her whole attitude—and the fact that they were late—made him go on the attack instead. "Screw you," he said. "Really, screw you."

The upshot was that when they finally came up the front steps of Tim's house (after the added tension of driving around the same block three times, squinting at numbers on dimly lit mailboxes), they were angry, pissed off, stewing, in exactly the wrong mood for the session he'd let himself get talked into, which he, in turn, had talked her into. And if that wasn't enough she'd insisted on bringing along a bottle of Bordeaux they couldn't afford, as if this were a suburban dinner party with the local minister and the superintendent of schools and the guy who owned the car dealership. He felt ridiculous, the vise tightening one more twist in the fraught moment he found himself standing there in a sudden blast of wind, cradling the wine and pushing the doorbell nobody was answering.

"You always bring wine," Joanie said, her voice flat and instructional. She'd spent half an hour on her hair and makeup and she was wearing her best dress, her best coat and a pair of black pumps that were new last fall. "It's expected. It's civilized. And you hand it to the wife, not him—"

"Hand it to whose wife?"

"Your prof's—*Tim.*"

"His wife's dead."

"What are you talking about—I thought you said he had kids?"

"You don't need a wife to have kids, not once they're born. She killed herself is what I hear, I don't know, before he even came here . . . Out west. In California."

The wind was bitter, riding a dank undercurrent of moisture off the sea, and he shivered in his blazer, cursing himself for leaving his overcoat in the car. He pressed the buzzer again. From inside came

a low murmur of voices rising and falling in conversation, a snatch
of laughter, the low-end repetitive thump of the bass line of a jazz
record, and that was a surprise—he didn't know Tim was a jazz
buff; he would have figured him for Bach, Handel, Mozart, maybe
Shostakovich if he really got adventurous.

"Still," Joanie said, because she always had to get the last word in,
"you don't come empty-handed to somebody's house."

That was when the door swung open on a tiny moon-faced girl
who looked to be Corey's age but for the breasts that swelled the fabric of her white turtleneck. "Hi," she said, smiling dutifully at them,
"come on in. I'm Suzie, by the way, the *daughter*," and then, before
he could hand her the wine or even calculate if it was appropriate to
present it to a child, she'd turned and padded away on her bare feet
and he and Joanie were left standing there in the entryway.

The house was warm, the voices louder now, the jazz defining
itself as John Coltrane's latest LP, which he himself didn't have the
money for though he was dying to have it and could see the cover
in his mind's eye, all blue, the saxophonist's head looming over the
neck of the instrument as he lost himself in a passion that was as
evident on his face as a sexual climax. It was a profound, aching
kind of music, and he'd fallen under its spell at the record shop one
day, listening to it over and over when he should have been elsewhere,
should have been studying. He looked at Joanie. She looked at him.
He shrugged. "I guess we just go in?"

In truth, she was the one with the confidence in this relationship,
not that he felt in any way inadequate, just that sometimes in social
situations he tended to try too hard and that left him off balance, at
least until she took charge. Which she did now, leading him by the
hand through the foyer and into the living room, where there was a
fire going and twenty people standing around with drinks in their
hands as if they were at a cocktail party. If he hung back—just briefly,
just for an instant—it was because this wasn't what he'd expected at

all. What *had* he expected? Something more intimate, more clinical, monkish even. This was supposed to be his initiation into the inner circle, not just another cocktail party.

It was no small thing either—the inner circle was the only circle as far as Tim was concerned and if you weren't part of it he didn't have much use for you. The Psychology Department (and its offshoot, the Center for Research in Personality) might have relegated Tim to a converted closet on the second floor as befitting his beggar's status as visiting lecturer, but no matter the size or location of his office, he was the shining star everybody wanted to study with. Half the students in the grad program were already on board, gravitating to him and Professor Alpert (Dick) because they were the young guns, the ones with the fresh approach, espousing a whole new methodology that was transactional rather than authoritative and hierarchical. Tim described it as a partnership with the patient, as if you were sitting across the kitchen table from him having a beer instead of laying him out on a couch and probing him like an Inquisitor. His first book, *Interpersonal Diagnosis of Personality,* had appeared five years earlier and it came down like a hammer on behaviorism and the traditional model of Freudian analysis. People were still buzzing about it. Tim was hot, red-hot, and Harvard was lucky to have gotten him.

The story had it that he was in Mexico writing his second book when by chance he stumbled across a new tool he couldn't stop talking about, a tool he insisted would revolutionize psychotherapy. It wasn't a theory or a method, but a drug—psilocybin—which had been synthesized by a chemist at Sandoz Laboratories from the so-called magic mushrooms of Mesoamerican culture, and it had powerful psychoactive properties that could dissolve a patient's defenses in a single session. Along with an earlier synthesis, lysergic acid diethylamide, it was just then being used in clinical trials as a potent new means of disarming the control tower of the brain, as Tim put it, thereby freeing the subconscious and letting all the unfiltered sense impressions of the world come winging in. No one knew quite how it worked, but the attraction was magnetic. You didn't need psycho-therapy anymore, that was the implication. You didn't need books and study and lab rats—all you needed was this, a little pink pill, as if it were magic.

He himself had been on the outside of all that, new to the pro-gram in September and one of the last of Tim's advisees to resist tak-ing that particular flight, and three days ago Tim had put it to him bluntly: "Listen, Fitz—can I call you Fitz or do we have to keep up with these Doctor/Mister games? Fitz, you're going to have to decide if psychology is really for you, or even what century you're living in, whether you're going to be transactional and experiential or go the crusty old Freudian way—or what, play with Skinner's white rats till you become expert in the psychology of rodents? Or pigeons, maybe pigeons is the way to go, operant conditioning, peck, peck, peck."

They'd been alone in Tim's office and Tim had got up to shut the door for privacy. There was a window, a filing cabinet, and just enough room for a desk and two chairs. Tim let a beat go by, then leaned back in his chair. "You don't want to be a pecker, do you?"

Well, no, of course not, and he didn't want to be hidebound or the brunt of a joke either, but he was reluctant—and beyond that, un-easy. He came from a long and undistinguished line of Irish drunks and he'd worked hard to get into the program, to get into Harvard, and he didn't want to screw with that, didn't want to have to worry about alcohol or this new miracle drug or anything else that could compromise what mattered above all else: the degree, the job, the house, a better life for Joanie and Corey. This was called ambition, class mobility, the American Dream, and he had it in spades. But Tim was persuasive, messianic even, and everyone in the inner circle had taken the drug—was taking it, regularly—and now, feeling left out, feeling pressured, he felt himself giving way.

"There's nothing to be afraid of—you know that, right?"

"I'm not afraid."

"Then what's the hang-up? This is nothing less than a revolution we're talking about, Fitz. The first time I ate mushrooms, the real thing, obtained from a *curandera* in Mexico—you know what a *curandera* is?"

"A shaman?"

"Right, a shaman, and we're talking a thousand years of history here, and you know what? I learned more about the mind in six or seven hours than in fifteen years as a psychologist. God's truth. And what I'm telling you, Fitz, is that this is a tool we can't afford to ignore, not as psychologists, not as human beings. You decide." He tented the fingers of both hands in front of his face and peered through them. "Ball's in your court, my friend."

So here he was, and here was the ball, and he was stroking it back.

Or trying to. At the moment he was stalled on the fringes of the room, clutching Joanie's hand like a child on a school trip. People chattered, the fire snapped. He had an impulse to back away, tug Joanie out the door, down the steps and into the car and just forget the whole thing, and he'd actually taken a step backward when Joanie's grip tightened round his fingers and she hissed, "Fitz, what are you doing?" It was the moment of truth and it seemed to break the spell. Suddenly everything came into focus—he knew these people, or some of them, and this was where he belonged, this was what he'd come for. It was now or never.

The better part of the inner circle was gathered round the fireplace, as well as a couple of people he didn't recognize, including a blonde with an angelic face and a cheerleader's figure who turned out to be Tim's girlfriend (or, actually, his date for the night, since they'd just met the day before). The room itself, high ceilinged, wainscoted walls, period furniture, was casually elegant, presumably reflecting the taste of the owner, a prof on sabbatical who'd rented the place to Tim for the year, or at least that was what he'd heard. A prof in the History Department, he thought it was—or no, International Law.

The bass thumped, the saxophone soared, and before he could think he was pulling Joanie across the room to where Ken Sensabaugh was standing with his back to him, waving a cocktail glass at two girls Fitz had never seen before and one he had—Ken's wife, wasn't it?—and then he was tapping Ken on the shoulder and Ken was swinging round on him and breaking into a grin. "Fitz, my man, you finally made it!"

Ken was a head taller than anybody in the room, which made him stand out, which, he realized, was why he'd gone to him first. But that was all right, because Ken had been the first to befriend him when he entered the program, and though they weren't exactly close, or not yet, he radiated a kind of energy and high spirits that were hard to resist, almost as if he were Tim's doppelgänger. Careful not to spill his drink—a martini he held pinched by the stem between two fingers—Ken bent forward to take Joanie's hand and bring it to his lips, as if they were all in some Noel Coward play, crooning, "And this must be Joanie I've heard so much about, Joanie Loney, Joanie, Joanie, Joanie Loney."

"The one and only!" Joanie said, grinning back at him. "And you're Ken, right? One of Fitz's classmates?"

That was all it took. They were there, in the heart of it, and in the next moment someone took the wine off his hands and he and Joanie each had a martini thrust at them and Joanie was chatting up Ken's wife, Fanchon, who had a pair of pillowy lips, spoke with a French accent and wore her black hair in a bouffant with the bangs hanging sexily in her eyes, like the girl in *The 400 Blows*. Some of the other grad students drifted over to say hello—Rick Roberts, Charlie Millhouse, a wife, a girlfriend—and make him feel at home when he was feeling anything but, and where was Tim? Wasn't this supposed to be a *session*?

Charlie—short, square shouldered, with an outsized head and eyes set too close together, which just managed to draw your attention to them all the more—had his arm around a redheaded girl Fitz hadn't caught the name of because he was bad with names and introductions, too hung up on subliminal gestures and the pure animal presence of other people to focus his attention. Which was a failing, he knew it, and the reason he always felt uncomfortable at parties. Or part of the reason. His mother claimed he was reserved. Joanie called him shy. But the truth was it just took him a while to get a read on people. Or that was what he told himself.

Charlie had a cigarette in one hand, the one attached to the arm thrown over the girl's shoulder, and an empty glass in the other. "You like this music?" he asked, jerking his chin in the direction of the stereo while Coltrane floated his arpeggios just out of reach and the party buzzed around them.

The answer was yes, a definite yes, but he couldn't tell from Charlie's inflection whether he was looking for affirmation or negation, so he just nodded and shifted his eyes to the girl, whose name popped into his head at that moment—Patricia—and tossed the question back at her. "And what about you, Patricia, what do you think?"

"I don't know," she said, turning her head to draw Charlie's cigarette to her lips and take a quick puff, which she exhaled in a thin blue cloud. "It's all the same to me. And the name's Alice, by the way."

Charlie, still holding fast to her, leaned in, his cheek pressed to hers, to pull the cigarette to his own lips. "The reason I ask," he said, exhaling, "is because to me this is exactly what Tim should play during the session, but he always goes for mellower stuff, string quartets, Satie, Debussy, and if it's jazz it's going to be the MJQ, you watch."

"Sorry, *Alice*," Fitz murmured, though the moment had already passed. "I must have misheard," he added lamely, and was his glass empty already? He hadn't come here to get drunk, had he? And where was Joanie? All the way across the room with Ken and Fanchon and some people he didn't recognize, her head thrown back, laughing at something Ken had just said. The sight of her reminded him all over again of how strange this was—and of what was to come—and he felt his stomach clench. "But yeah, Charlie, I don't know what to expect—this'll be my first time—so I can't pretend to know what the music protocol is, but I agree about Coltrane. He's our modern master, even beyond Bird or Miles or anybody."

"Pure mathematics of the soul, that's what I say."

"Wait a minute," Alice said, shimmying out from under Charlie's arm. "You mean this is your first time? Really?"

Fitz nodded.

She let out a nervous laugh. "Mine too. Jesus, from what Charlie told me, I thought everybody here was part of the club—what about your wife? Her first time too?"

"Yes, both of us," he said, swallowing the words as if he were taking a breath instead of expelling it. Across the room, Joanie was still laughing, but it was a laugh with a ragged edge to it because she was anxious too, everybody was, and everybody was waiting for Tim, and where was he, what was taking him so long?

As it turned out, Tim had been upstairs, preparing things, and now he appeared among them like an avatar, and everybody—jazz, talk and gin notwithstanding—turned to glance at him as he bounced down the stairs, clean and athletic and wearing the big booster's grin that never seemed to leave his face. He came straight up to where Fitz was standing with Charlie and Alice, pumped his hand and said, "Welcome, Fitz, welcome . . . and where's—oh, this must be her, right, the pretty young woman in the black dress over there with Fanchon? Joanie, right? Hello, Joanie!" he called out, waving her over.

Joanie wasn't shy, that was for sure, and when Tim held out his hand she took it in hers and went up on her tiptoes to peck a kiss to his cheek and tell him in soft martini-inflected tones what an honor it was to finally meet him and even more to be invited for this—and here she faltered, just an instant, searching for the word—"this *occasion*." And then she laughed and Tim laughed too before turning to the room at large and clapping his hands together twice to get everyone's attention.

"All right, then," he said, raising his voice to be heard over the cascading trills and hard punctuative blats of Coltrane's tenor, "let's gather round for the main event. And don't forget the questionnaires, which is the whole point of this, you all know that," gesturing toward the sideboard where the drinks were arrayed. "Over there on the bar, one each, and I want your impressions now and then after. And please answer all the questions, even if they don't apply." He grinned, held it a moment. "I mean, even if you have to write *Doesn't apply*, okay? Are you with me? Everybody?"

Officially, this was a session, one of an ongoing series in the study Professors Leary and Alpert were conducting to assess the potential of the drug for clinical use, but it was apparent that it was more than that too. All you had to do was glance round the room at the way people held themselves to see that. This was a ritual, a ceremony, and Tim was at the center of it, going round dispensing pills into upturned palms while the conversation died and the sub-zero vibe of the MJQ replaced Coltrane on the stereo, just as Charlie had predicted, and where was Charlie? There, off in a corner with his girlfriend, the redhead—what was her name?—swallowing pills, fifteen of them, because that was the standard dose, thirty milligrams.

Tim came to him and Joanie last, lingering a moment to reassure them that he'd be there to guide them throughout the entire trip (as everybody was calling the experience now, as if it were a journey to some distant place, which, if you believed Tim, it was), just as he'd be there to guide everyone else so there'd be no worries and no hang-ups. "Just let it go," he said, handing him and Joanie each a glass of water and slipping a brown prescription bottle out of the inside pocket of his jacket. The bottle had a black screw-off cap, no different from any other prescription container, except for the Sandoz label affixed to the front of it.

"Could I see that?" he heard himself say, and Tim, grinning, handed it to him.

INDOCYBIN, it read, and beneath it, (PSILOCYBIN), 2 MG, 500 TABLETS.

Then the Sandoz emblem, a triangle with a single *S* emblazoned in the center of it, and beneath that, RESEARCH MATERIAL. CAUTION, NEW DRUG LIMITED BY FEDERAL LAW TO INVESTIGATIONAL USE ONLY, followed by the usual warning, FEDERAL LAW PROHIBITS DISPENSING WITHOUT PRESCRIPTION.

"Well," Tim said, looking first to Joanie, then to him, "satisfied?"

He wasn't, not really. It certainly looked official—the bottle, the description, the warnings—but who was prescribing it, Tim? Tim wasn't a medical doctor. (Walter Pahnke, another of Tim's grad advisees, was, but Walter was conspicuously absent on this particular evening, and whether his presence was needed or not, at least it would have been comforting.) Fitz nodded, then found himself grinning back. "Why am I thinking of Superman?"

Tim laughed. "Everybody says that. It's the big *S*, the triangle, the whole works, and I'm not promising you you're going to be able to see through walls or mold diamonds in your fist or fly around the world at supersonic speeds—'It's a bird! It's a plane! It's Fitz!'—but you never know, you just might."

Turning to Joanie, Tim said, "Ladies first," and she held out her hand while he shook the bottle over it and counted out not fifteen but ten pills. "Beginner's dose," he said with a wink, then turned to him. Dutifully, Fitz presented his cupped palm, felt the fleeting tap of the bottle's rim at the base of his thumb, heard Tim counting aloud, "Two, four, six, eight, ten," while the MJQ tinkled through the chord changes of "Lonely Woman" and conversation started up around him again as if after a long withheld breath.

Tim's face glowed in the light of the table lamp, an Irish face, quintessentially Irish, right down to the cool hooded eyes and the faint twist of the nose. He'd turned forty-one back in October but looked ten years younger—no older than Fitz himself—and he was fit and handsome, his hair trimmed in the universal crew cut and hardly a trace of gray in it. He favored tweeds, like the suit he had on now, and he even managed to make the hearing aid he wore look stylish, its cord descending into the same inner pocket from which he'd extracted the pill bottle. "All right?" he asked.

"All right," Fitz heard himself say, and then he was throwing back the pills two at a time and washing them down with measured sips from the glass, all the while telling himself there was nothing to worry about—it was research, that was all, only research.

"It's like going to the doctor," Joanie said, meaning it as a joke, a bit of levity to break the spell of the moment, but then she saw that Tim wasn't laughing and her face went sober. Still, she was right: it *was* like going to the doctor, the only difference being that they weren't sick and Fitz hoped he wouldn't be, his biggest worry at this point (beyond losing his mind, that is) being that he would embarrass himself in front of everybody. The fact was that these little pink pills that looked so innocuous they might have been Pepto-Bismol tablets were a laboratory synthesis of the mushrooms the Indians called flesh of the gods, *teonanácatl,* and they were said to produce intense visions, synesthesia, out-of-body experiences—along with nausea, and in extreme cases, paranoid delusions and even convulsions.

"A word of advice," Tim said. "Don't fight it. And don't think nothing's happening or you've got a placebo or anything like that because there's no control group tonight—we're just having an experience, okay? To initiate you. Both of you. And the drug takes a while to come on, maybe forty minutes, an hour? Just relax. And enjoy. You are about to have the single most significant revelation of your entire lives."

Joanie looked pale, as if she'd been drained of blood. She was nervous, though she tried to hide it, and he was nervous too. Joanie just nodded and a flicker of a smile jumped and died on her lips.

"Trust me," Tim said. "Really."

For the longest while, nothing happened. There was a small uptick of excitement after the pills had gone round, but then everybody settled into anticipatory mode and the party subsided till it wasn't a party at all, just small groups of people quietly conversing in the corners—the darker the corner, the better. Light was oppressive all of a sudden, and Tim, in his wisdom, had gone round shutting off all the lamps and replacing them strategically with candles. At some point the jazz gave way to one of Bach's masses, and he and Joanie, following suit with what the others were doing, settled down on the floor in a spill of pillows Tim and his daughter—Suzie, wasn't it?— scattered round the room. He watched Tim's daughter go from group to group, arranging things as if for a pajama party, and he wondered about that, about the propriety of an adolescent—a child— witnessing whatever was about to happen here, but then, once she was sure everyone was settled, she said good night in a soft fluting voice and drifted up the stairs to bed.

Time elongated. Nobody was standing anymore. The pitcher of martinis on the counter went untouched, as if everybody'd had their fill of that particular form of stimulus, and when he glanced up at it—he kept glancing up at it, he couldn't help himself—it seemed to glow like a crystal ball, as if the flame of the candle Tim had set beside it were in the liquid itself now, in the gin, transfusing it with light. "You see that?" he murmured, sitting there beside his wife in their dark, dark corner and reaching out a finger to point to it, where it was whirling now, not *on* the counter or *of* the counter, but in the space above it, ginfire, whirling.

"What?" she said and turned her face to him, her eyes gone huge as goggles.

"Ginfire. The martinis."

Bach's voices braided themselves, separated, braided again.

She laughed. "I'm not thirsty."

"No, no," he said, "that's not what I mean—I mean, look at the pitcher, don't you see it?"

"I see it," she said.

"You see what it's doing?"

"Yeah," she said, "oh, yeah," her voice soft and distracted, barely there at all. "And the puppet," she said, "you see the puppet?"

He didn't see the puppet, not that he didn't want to, but now all at once every ordinary object in the room came alive just as if it had a heart inside it pumping blood—highboy, bookcase, Persian rug, rocker, armchair, the nautical scene hanging over the mantelpiece—everything stirring, buzzing, fracturing the room with light, and he said, "I think it's coming on," and she said, "Yeah."

Time must have passed—time always passes, the globe spinning through its diurnal cycle, elliptical orbit, axial tilt, clocks ticking, Big Ben, horology, *Greenwich mean time*—but he had no more sense of it than if he were locked deep in a dreamless sleep. Except that this wasn't sleep but its opposite, a kind of hyper-alertness that set all his senses on fire till the MJQ replaced Bach and became his heartbeat all over again and every note had its own particular and individuated color shining through it and Joanie's face was something she'd borrowed from Miró, from Picasso, and he wanted to tell her about that but he was pre-verbal now or maybe post-verbal. If he was speaking, if he could have spoken—or even wanted to—he would have said *ineffable,* would have said *discontinuous,* would have said *wow.*

For the longest time that was no time at all he just stared at her as she changed faces and shapes and coalesced with everything else in the room and everything beyond it too. Someone, somewhere, laughed. The fire snapped like human fingertips, flames were themselves, shadows became light and light shadows. He laughed aloud, he couldn't help himself, laughed like Corey when he was four years old and they rode the Ferris wheel high into the sky together while the Fourth of July fireworks rent the night overhead, and then Tim was there, saying, *You all right, Fitz? Everything good?,* and he didn't know how even to begin to answer and just laughed again, which told the whole story in itself, beginning to end. Tim dissolved. The candles ex-

ploded and fell back into themselves, over and over. There was nothing he could do but sink back into the pillows, crushed by all that
sparking beauty, until he felt Joanie's hand exploring his inner thigh
like the warmest and best-adapted probe he could imagine, and then
her mouth was on his and his hands were doing their own examina-
tion of her breasts that were right there front and center despite the
dress, the slip, the rudely inconvenient conical lift-up bra that was
alternately made of lead and silk, and they couldn't do it here, could
they, on the pillows in a dark corner of his professor's house while
everybody else was seething around them in spirit if not the flesh?

No, no they couldn't, and Joanie grasped that before he did, rising silkily from the floor to the glassy accompaniment of Milt Jack-
son's vibraphone to tug his hand as she'd tugged it when they came
through the door just minutes or eons ago, so that he stood too, hard
as a rock and tent-poling the fabric of his trousers, till they were
flowing together in liquid grace up the dilating stairway to the first
unoccupied bedroom they could find.

I n the car on the way home—*You sure you're okay to drive?* Tim kept
asking, even following them out onto the frozen crust of the night
before being waved off—he'd felt everything receding like a wave
drawing back from a beach. The car was a coffin. Ice crunched under the wheels. He was moving, they were moving, and if he didn't
quite feel as if he was back in his body yet, his body knew what to
do, gas pedal, brake, two hands on the wheel, navigate, stay in your
lane, own the road. There were lights sparking at the margins of his
eyes as if he'd been knocked unconscious and come awake again, but
this was usual, explicable, nothing like the rhapsody of things that
had danced through his mind all night long even as he clung fast to
Joanie, his wife of thirteen years, his sweet sad beautiful fleshsack,
and fucked her and fucked her as if there were no other thing in
the universe but fucking. He thought about that, the streetlights the

only lights now, the tires crunching, and realized he'd uncovered a universal truth, *the* universal truth, because if mind was everything and thought uncontainable and God a construct, then fucking—sex, reproduction, the generational reissuing of the body that allowed the mind to be—was the foundation of all there was.

A match flared. The smoke of Joanie's cigarette rose up over the stale breath of the heater. He snatched a look at her, her profile, everything saturated in black but the glowing tip of the cigarette. "Well, that was really," he began, the sound of his own voice strange in his ears and the words so elongated they didn't seem to want to connect to one another in any rational way, "really, I don't know—what did you think? You like it?"

She didn't say anything. The night was a tunnel and they were right in the middle of it. After a moment she exhaled and brought the cigarette back to her lips. The tip of it brightened and a beat went by as the smoke circulated through her lungs and she exhaled again, then put a hand on his thigh to lean into him and pass him the cigarette, which tasted of wet tobacco and of her. "Uh-huh," she said.

"I didn't think it would be like that, I mean, I didn't know, I didn't—"

"Uh-huh," she said.

It wasn't till he turned into their street that he thought of Corey—saw him, saw his face the way it was when he was curled up asleep with all the animation gone out of his features and his hair splayed over the pillow and the one corner of the blanket he held gripped in his hand as if afraid somebody would take it away from him—and came back to himself. "Jesus, do you realize how late it is?"

Mrs. Pierzynski was waiting for them in the vestibule with her coat and hat on and a look of pure outrage on her face. "Do you know what time it is?" she demanded, and he did know because he'd looked at the clock on the dash when he thought of Corey and located himself in the instant. It was after twelve. Well after.

"I'm sorry," he said. "We were . . ." He was searching for an excuse, but there was nothing he could give her short of death and dis-memberment that would even begin to mollify her, and the truth of it, the essence of what they'd experienced—the *trip* they'd been on—would have been lost on this haggard red-faced pathetically ordinary woman who wouldn't have known transcendence if it swooped her up on angels' wings and sailed her high out over the glittering crest of the universe.

"That number you gave me? The emergency number? I must've rung that number ten times and nobody answered, so you tell me—"

Joanie was there now, Joanie the efficient, Joanie the politic, Joanie the peacemaker. "Forgive us, Mrs. Pierzynski, but we had an emergency—it was my husband, we had to take him to the emer-gency room because of something he ate, bad fish the doctor said, but thank God he's all right now, and I don't know what to say but forgive us, please, and here"—snapping open her purse and counting out bills, too many bills, into the woman's outthrust hand—"I hope this'll help."

A moment of constrained silence. The three of them there in the vestibule under the sick yellow overhead light. Outside, the grip of the night and the cold. "Some people," the woman said, her voice tight with anger, "have to be at work first thing Monday morning—*tomorrow* morning if you want to know, and I'm sorry for your trou-ble, but I mean, you couldn't even *call?*"

Then the door flung open on a fume of cold and the woman was gone and he looked at Joanie and gave a shrug, which was comical, so very comical, and they both broke down in giggles. He helped her out of her coat. She kicked off her shoes. And then he put an arm around her waist and led her off to bed.

2.

He had class all day Monday and didn't have a chance to see Tim till the following day, which shouldn't have been a problem, but somehow was. The need to see him, the *compulsion,* nagged at him from the moment he woke clear-eyed Sunday morning till he mounted the stairs to Tim's office at half-past seven on Tuesday night after a dinner of meat loaf, instant mashed potatoes and canned string beans at the kitchen table that made him feel bloated and out of sorts and anything but transcendent. Why he needed so badly to see Tim he couldn't have said, other than that he wanted to rehash the experience in the way people do when they've been profoundly moved by some event in their lives—and he had been moved. At least he thought he had. He'd seen things, visions, rippling visions shot through with color and movement, and they never stopped, even when he was deep inside Joanie, deeper than he'd ever thought it was possible to go.

They'd both filled out the questionnaire at Tim's while they were waiting for the drug to take effect (*How many people are present? How many are taking the drug? How many times have you taken this or similar drugs? How good do you feel about taking the drug today?*), but it was standard psychological survey stuff that couldn't even begin to prepare them for the intensity of what was to come. No, the key here was the report Tim required from all subjects of what was officially known as the Harvard Psilocybin Project. The idea was to individuate the experiences of as wide a sample as possible and then look for correspondences that would lead to the development of a method that could eventually be used in treatment. This was the rationale. This was why Sandoz was offering the drug gratis to qualified researchers around the country. This was why he'd taken his wife to Tim's house, why he'd written up his impressions in a narrative that ran to six single-spaced pages, and why it seemed so vital to get it to Tim as soon as he possibly could.

Coming down the hallway to Tim's office, he was surprised to hear voices. He knew Tim liked to keep evening hours, but up to this point he'd only been here during the day because, of course, he had obligations at night—dinner, a story for his son (they were reading *A Journey to the Center of the Earth* together), class preparation, bedtime—and he'd expected to find Tim alone, his feet on the desk, a book in his hand. And he wanted to find him alone, wanted to hand him his report (and Joanie's, in a sealed envelope) and sit there and talk it all through because he had a thousand things to say and he just couldn't keep a lid on them any longer. But Tim had a visitor—visitors—and he felt a sharp stab of disappointment even as he rounded the corner and saw Ken and Charlie there (and Ken's wife, who wasn't even a student), slouched against the doorframe of Tim's office. And Tim, beyond them, his feet propped up and the desk lamp casting an annulus of golden light round his face.

"Fitz," Ken called over one shoulder. "Hello, welcome—hey, come join the club."

Charlie turned round, looking surprised. "Hi, Fitz," he said, but his voice had no animation, as if he weren't really there, and that got the alarm bells ringing all right, even before Fanchon, her face shining and beautiful, gave him an electric smile and he heard himself fumbling over his words, "Hi, I was . . . I thought—Tim, is Tim in?"

"Who's that?" Tim called from inside the office. "Fitz?" He made as if to draw down his legs and rise from the desk, but then seemed to think better of it. "Come on in," he said, summoning his grin. "Good to see you. And wait, what's that in your hand?"

What was in his hand? The question didn't register because it was self-evident, wasn't it, besides which, as he came to the door, he saw there were two other people in the office with Tim, and that made him hesitant. One was the blonde from the other night, Tim's friend—girlfriend—and the other was the cadaverous Englishman Michael, who wasn't a professor and wasn't a student but who seemed to shadow Tim practically everywhere he went. Clumsily, he raised his hand with the two envelopes in it and murmured, "I brought the reports—from the, the session the other night? One for Joanie, my wife, that is, and one of my own, and I hope it's not too long, or, or—"

Tim waved the objection away. "Not to worry, Fitz—the way I see it, the more detailed, the better. But come on in—you want to talk? Have a seat."

There were two chairs in the room: Tim's, behind the desk, and the one reserved for students in front of it. The blonde was sitting in the student chair and the Englishman was perched atop the two-tier filing cabinet, his long thin legs dangling above a pair of scuffed desert boots. They all looked at one another for a beat, then Ken, behind him in the hallway, said, "Tim, you need a bigger office," and Tim, grinning wider, said, "Scotch. You drink scotch, Fitz?"

In the next moment everybody had a glass in hand and they were toasting to something—"The Project!"—and then Tim, the consummate host, was introducing him to the blonde, "In case you two didn't meet the other night, or did you?" Tim shrugged his shoulders, the grin widening to show off a set of teeth that couldn't have been whiter. "No matter. Brenda Maxxon, Fitzhugh Loney."

He took her hand awkwardly. The moment burst over him: she

was pretty in an incendiary way, with her hair teased out and a too-
tight cardigan that emphasized her full breasts. "A pleasure," she said,
sipping her drink.

"And you know Michael, don't you? No? Michael, Fitzhugh Loney.
Fitz, Michael Hollingshead."

Fanchon said something then and the group in the hall let out a
laugh.

"What's that?" Tim asked, tapping at his hearing aid. "Let's all
hear it, humor appreciated here, most appreciated, especially in this,
what—dungeon?"

"I just said, I wish we could be reading Fitz's report—and his
wife's. Aloud, I mean." She paused, pursed her lips. "I will bet it is,
what do you say, *steamy*, no?"

And Ken: "We couldn't help noticing you discovered one of the
side benefits of the research the other night—"

"The way you two were going at it," Fanchon said, her voice rising
high and birdlike till it twittered off the walls, "I thought maybe I
ought to step in and *formally* introduce you to each other because I
could have sworn you had just met or something—"

Everybody laughed now and if he reddened he couldn't help that.
It was just a moment and in that moment he saw that it was all in
good fun, a little ribbing, his initiation into the inner circle, and he
found himself laughing along with them, the scotch whiskey already
rising from his stomach to his brain.

Tim swung his legs off the desk then and leaned in to scan the
whole group, the pretty blonde, the Englishman with the high forehead and sunken cheeks, Ken, Fanchon, Charlie and himself. "Come
on, Fanchon," he said in a teasing lilt, "you know we're all profession-
als here."

The next night, despite the weather (mid-January, bleak as the bottom of a shoe, sleet turning to snow and back again), Fitz took

the family out for dinner. Or for pizza, actually. This was in fulfillment of a pledge he'd made to his son at the beginning of the
fall term—if Corey managed to get a B average or higher on his
report card he could pick any restaurant he wanted, as long as it was
a burger or pizza place and within a ten-mile radius. The payoff had
been more than a month in coming now and Corey, who'd done
better than just manage in his new school and wound up with A's
across the board tailed by a flurry of complimentary comments from
his teachers on his work habits and attitude, had been nagging him
about it since New Year's. Or not nagging—it wasn't in his nature to
nag—but offering up subtle and not-so-subtle reminders like, *They
let us out on the playground after lunch today and all we could smell was
pizza—from Scavone's, I think it was, which is only two blocks over?—
because they were like cleaning the ovens or something, I think. And you
know what I dreamed about last night? No, what? Pizza.*

So though he really didn't have the money or the time and the car
gave him the same aggravation as usual (addicted now, it seemed,
to ether, which cost a dollar twenty-five a can), they all drove across
town to Corey's favorite place—Carbone's—which, Corey claimed,
had the best crust in Boston, though to Fitz, who'd grown up on
New York pizza, it all tasted like cardboard with tomato paste and
shredded cheese dribbled over it.

The place was overheated and overlit, which normally would have
annoyed him but felt somehow comforting on a night like this
when you had to stomp the slush off your boots in the anteroom
and beat your hands together just to get a little circulation going.
And the smell—the scorched-oven aroma of bubbling pizza and hot
calzone—brought him right back to life after a long grim day of
sitting in class and the library and fielding questions from his too-
clever-by-half undergrads in Psych 101. He put a handful of change
on the table so Corey could wheel off to play one of the pinball machines lined up against the back wall, then went to the counter and
ordered a pitcher of beer with two glasses, a Coke for Corey and a

large mushroom pie with anchovies on one-third of it for Joanie, who had a taste for the super-salted, dried-out little strips of baitfish that neither he nor Corey managed to share.

He'd chosen a table by the window where they could look out on the frozen sidewalk and feel a sense of redemption. He poured out two beers. Joanie lit a cigarette. There was the ding-ding-ding of the pinball machines, the clank of the pizza oven opening and shutting, the drone of the jukebox, the red-and-yellow flash of the neon CARBONE'S sign that hung in the window just over their heads. "So what was it like?" Joanie asked, exhaling.

"What, last night?"

"You came home smelling like a brewery—or no, a distillery. Scotch or whiskey, one or the other."

"Scotch," he said, smiling. "You've got quite a nose—I mean, for a woman who was snoring when I got into bed. Maybe we can get you a job at one of the distilleries—quality control."

"Or a cop. I'd make a good cop, wouldn't I?"

He reached across the table and took her hand. "I don't know," he said, "I think I like you better as a sex object."

She was wearing a knit hat pulled down to her eyebrows. It had a little pompon on top and he liked that because it made her look so much younger than she was, girlish even, and it brought him back to another place and time altogether. She said, "Sounds good to me. When's the next research session?"

He shrugged, toyed with the glass Parmesan shaker in front of him. "I don't know, pretty much every Saturday night, I think."

"And we're invited?"

"I don't know—I guess. But I told you, I want to take things slow. It's a long semester and I've got a lot of weight on my shoulders right now, and I don't—I mean, experimenting once, just to see what it's like, that's fine, but nobody really knows what this sort of thing leads to. Even Tim."

She was giving him her randy look, a look she'd perfected when they were undergrads and didn't yet have the advent of a son to worry about, as if the act of coitus were free of consequences and human reproduction a kind of menu you chose from when you were established and ready and all your ducks set out in a row. "You mean out-of-body sex?"

"I mean, out of your mind and no coming back. We had a good trip, a *great* trip, right? But from what I gather, what I hear, it's not always like that. And last night—at Tim's office—it was so old-fashioned we could have gone back a hundred years, five hundred, scotch whiskey as lubricant and nothing beyond that. He's"—he paused, searching for the adjective—"welcoming, I guess, is the word. Very warm. He really went out of his way to make me feel part of the group—"

"Which took till what, one in the morning?"

"You jealous?"

Her voice seeped through the ding and buzz of Corey's pinball machine, soft and dubious and placatory all at once. "Not really. I'm glad for you. You've worked so hard and this was like the final barrier—now you're in—but is that really the way to conduct office hours? Isn't it, I don't know, unorthodox—to say the least?"

He'd stayed until the others had left, even the girlfriend and the Englishman (who kept glancing at his watch and finally at some point said, "Hey, Tim, I'm beat—see you back at the house, okay?" and Tim had said, "Take Brenda with you, will you?" and Brenda had puffed out her lips and Tim gave her a look and said, "Wait up for me, baby, I won't be long. Promise").

They sat in silence, both of them half-looped, or at least Fitz was, and listened to the footsteps recede down the hallway. The light on the desk held steady. Tim stretched, cracked his knuckles. He picked up his glass, set it down again, let out a sigh. "My guess is you're here to talk about your initiation the other night, your *experience*—am I right?"

"It was everything you said."

"No bumps in the road?"

"Not really. I mean, Joanie and I—"

Tim lifted a finger to his lips as if to hush him. "Yeah, I know," he said. "That's something, isn't it? Really, God is in the fucking, isn't that right? You've never had sex like that before? Pure magic, right?"

He nodded.

"How long you been married?"

"Thirteen years."

The figure floated there a moment and he couldn't tell from the look on Tim's face whether he felt that was just a blip in history or a life sentence, whether he was jealous or maybe regretful over the way his own marriage had ended or simply relieved to be free all over again to have women like Brenda in his life. He began to feel uneasy. Should he have fudged it? Should he have said six? Or what, twenty? Of course the former would have abridged Corey and the latter would have made him a child groom. *Not so long*—he could have said *Not so long*—but then the truth was he'd been married for more than a third of his life.

Tim leaned forward to take up the pack of cigarettes on his desk, extract two and pass one to Fitz, who put it between his lips, though he didn't really feel like a smoke and was trying to cut back, if only to save money. "You look starry-eyed, Fitz," Tim said, producing a lighter and leaning forward to touch the flame first to Fitz's cigarette and then his own.

For a moment, everything seemed to shift on him, the scotch inflaming his veins and fogging his head, and he looked down at his glass, which was empty, or all but empty, just the thinnest disk of amber liquid hugging the bottom of it. He didn't know quite what to make of what Tim had just said so he repeated the phrase, stupidly, and that was all right because this was a Socratic dialogue he was engaged in here and Tim—despite the hour and the circumstances— was still in his classroom, still teaching.

"I'm talking imprinting, Fitz. Just like Konrad Lorenz and his goslings. I told you this drug was a tool, did I not? The most powerful tool psychology has ever been able to lay its hands on, if people would only open their eyes to it." He tapped his cigarette over the empty bottle. "I'm the goose and you're the gosling, just like Lorenz when he took the mother away and hatched the chicks into a world in which it wasn't beaks and paddle feet and feathers that made a mother but white hair and a white beard and a belly full of what, Wiener schnitzel? That's what this drug does, instantaneously—it wipes away all the games and roles and bullshit society's imprinted you with, tabula rasa, and starts you out all over again, newborn. You're a baby, Fitz. An infant. My infant."

Tim let the notion hang there a moment. The deserted building, dense in its stillness, crepitated with the smallest noises, the forcing of heated water into the radiators, the hum of the fluorescent lights in the hall, an undefined ticking as of a clock hidden in a drawer somewhere—or maybe it was the sound of their own blood trickling through the resilient valves of their hearts. "You imprint on the one who gives you new life, gives you the drug for the first time"— he poked his breastbone, as if making a joke of it—"which in my case was Crazy Juana, the *curandera* down in Cuernavaca summer before last. But the point is, all of you—Ken, Fanchon, Charlie, the whole in-group—are opened up to your own inner selves now and not what society imposed on you. And if I'm the mother goose, so much the better. Or the male goose, what do you call it?"

"Gander?"

"Right, the gander. I'm the gander. Honk, honk." Tim's glass was empty too, a state of affairs that seemed to take him by surprise. He lifted it to his lips and rapped it with one long finger to get the last drop to descend, then he set it down on the desktop, took a drag off his cigarette, and stared into the null frame of the window as if it opened on a view only he could see. Was he drunk, was that it?

"Of course, that does mean I've got to fuck every woman who comes into the house because they fixate on me—and the drug, of course. I'm the source of the drug—and the fuck too." He grinned, rolled his eyes. "What we have to do in the name of science, huh, Fitz?"

What could he say? He was having private time with the icon himself, the young Turk of psychology, the man who'd admitted him to the inner circle, and if he was still cautious, still unsure of his direction or what it all meant, he couldn't help feeling the privilege of the moment—the prestige—and he grinned back and said something fatuous like, "Yeah, oh, yeah, I hear you."

They were both grinning now, as if it were a ritual, and they both held their grins for what seemed a beat too long, a beat that began to make him uncomfortable all over again, until Tim asked, out of nowhere, "You know the term 'entheogen'?"

"No, I don't think so."

"From the Greek, meaning 'generating the divine within.' *Éntheos,* full of the god, inspired, possessed, plus *genésthal,* to come into being. That's what we're talking about here. We're empiricists, we're rational, we're scientists, Fitz, but psilocybin—and *LSD, Fitz, LSD*— is opening up parts of the brain nobody even dreamed existed. This is where religion came from, mystical cults, the Eleusinian mysteries— tripping, that's all it is. Did you see the Light?"

"No."

"You believe in God?"

"No."

"Me either. But I believe in *something*—call it brain chemistry. And you know what, Fitz?"

"What?"

"Next time we'll up the dose."

Yes, Tim was unorthodox, but that was the whole attraction, wasn't it? How could you be an iconoclast without tipping over statues, stepping on toes, holding office hours whenever you damn well please? "Yeah," he said, in answer to Joanie's question or assertion or whatever it was meant to be, "of course he is, but most profs barely give their students the time of day and he truly goes out of his way, he does. But I really don't have to defend him, do I? You saw him, you met him, you tell me."

She dropped her chin and gave him a sidelong look, a jet of smoke issuing from her nostrils and her eyes catching the light of the neon sign so that they seemed to glow from deep inside her skull. "Did you talk to his girlfriend? Brenda?"

"Not really."

"If you ask me, she doesn't have a whole lot up here," tapping a finger to one temple. "But Fanchon's nice. Ken too. And smart, both of them."

"Our kind of people?"

She smiled. "I don't get a whole lot of stimulation stacking books at the library five days a week, if that's what you mean. I liked them. I liked the whole, what do you call it, *vibe* Saturday. It was good to get out of the house, good to go to a party for a change . . ."

"But it wasn't a party. It was a *session*."

"Tell me about it."

He reached across the table to take her hand again and give it a squeeze. He felt himself stiffening. "Right, you're right, you're always right—it was a session and a party too and a whole lot more. You know what Tim said? He said he'd up the dose next time because we just barely scratched the surface."

"You're kidding? If that was scratching the surface . . . But I thought you said you wanted to take it slow?"

"I'm not talking like next Saturday or anything—I mean, in a couple weeks, maybe. Or spring break. Maybe spring break. I mean, I'm intrigued, aren't you?"

She let her thumb rove over the back of his hand, so soft, skin to skin, tracing a series of concentric circles that radiated all the way down to his groin. "Oh, yeah," she said, "absolutely," and then Corey was there, burning up with excitement, telling them the astonishing story of how he'd won two free games, his high fluting adolescent voice like a new kind of music created in that very instant while the pinball machines provided the beat and the counterman—Joey Carbone himself—called out their number, blessed forty-two, to say their pizza was ready, and all the while the neon sign blinked bright and cool and bright all over again.

3.

The weeks fled. Winter got grimmer and grimmer. Half the time the car refused to start, no matter how much dollar-twenty-five-cent ether it ate, and eventually it just sat there in the driveway like a hulking steel sculpture that had no function at all beyond bad art. So it was the bus for both him and Joanie, the pocketful of change that was always running out or insufficient, nickels when you needed dimes, dimes when you needed quarters, and it was the same students, the same courses, the same desk in the same library and the wooden rack of a chair that remade his lumbar region every time he sat down in it. If the weekdays were dull, the weekends were even duller—to have variety, to have *fun,* you needed money, and money was a commodity they were chronically short of.

It was February, then it was March, and if he'd stayed away from Tim's sessions it was only because he was trying to exert a little discipline in his life, even if it meant tarnishing his status as one of the shiny new spokes of the inner circle's wheel. Which is not to say he didn't drop in on Tim's office hours every so often or take lunch with Ken and Charlie or some of the others, but still he kept his distance from Tim's house on Homer Street, which existed for him as a kind of seraglio of the mind, a temptation, and if he found himself nodding off over a case study and blinking his way into vivid fantasies of Brenda Maxxon and Fanchon with their clothes off and their focal points glistening, that was just harmless wish fulfillment. And safe. Safe all the way round. Better to be bored than distracted.

Then one afternoon he was coming down the steps of the library and there was Tim, head down, chugging up the stairs as if in a hurry, his overcoat flapping open and his scarf knotted awkwardly round his throat. "Tim!" he called, "hi," but Tim just gave him a quizzical look as if he didn't recognize him, which was odd and disconcerting and hit him right where his confidence lived. Tim was a blur. He was up at the top of the steps now, already reaching for the library door, and Fitz couldn't stop himself from calling out again, louder now, calling "Tim!" in a voice that nearly broke on the wind rushing in off the river. A pair of undergraduates gave him a look and Tim paused at the door to cast a glance back down the steps at him, the wire of the hearing aid as vivid as a groove cut into his cheek. "What?" he said in a shout that drew all the white condensed breath out of him. He looked irritated. Impatient. Looked as if his customary bonhomie had deserted him.

"It's me, Fitz," he heard himself call out. "I just wanted to say, to say . . . *hi*."

The undergraduates moved past him, their shoulders rollicking in the grip of their peacoats. The sky was the color of gravel. The wind dug at him. It was an early March day on the steps of Widener and Tim was all the way up at the top, looking down at him and frowning—was he frowning?

"All right, then," Tim said, producing a halfhearted wave with one hand while pulling open the door with the other. "Hi," he called, then the door swung shut and he was gone.

That might have had something to do with it, the way Tim had dismissed him, and whether Tim was distracted or not or whether it was a slight or just an oversight or any one of ten other excuses a psychologist might have been able to console himself with, the next night he presented himself at Tim's office, if only by way of clearing the air. It was past eight by the time he was able to get there (after helping Joanie with the dishes and reading Corey a chapter of Jules Verne), and at that hour the building was deserted, his footsteps echoing in the stairwell as if he were alone in a mine shaft. He heard laughter as he came down the hallway, thinking some of the others must be there, the ongoing party in progress, scotch whiskey, Tim the impresario. But there was no party. Only Hollingshead, perched atop the filing cabinet like some gaunt carrion bird, and what was that all about?

There were rumors, of course, and they had to do with imprinting as much as anything else. Word had it that Hollingshead was the one who'd introduced Tim to LSD back in the fall, after Hollingshead, who'd held a hazily defined position in New York as part of some sort of cultural exchange, came to visit on the pretext of an introduction through a professor at Cambridge, who, as it turned out, had nothing to do with psychology or psilocybin research and had died a year before the date under the letterhead. Oblivious, Tim invited him to lunch at the faculty club, where the Englishman waxed enthusiastic over Tim's research into the clinical uses of psilocybin, at the same time delivering a pointed message as to the infinitely more profound reach of LSD, to which he could personally attest. Apparently—and this was to become confirmed among the cognoscenti of the inner circle as time went on—Hollingshead had convinced an M.D. acquaintance to get him a full gram of LSD from Sandoz Laboratories, synthesized by Albert Hofmann himself, for use in medical research. As it turned out, there was no research, apart from Hollingshead's own self-experiments, which, from all appearances, had put him out on the far burning edge of transformative experience.

Soon thereafter, Tim discovered that Hollingshead was all but indigent and invited him to stay in the rented house on Homer Street, along with Hollingshead's wife and child (who left, permanently, ten days later), and if Tim had been content to this point with his psilocybin research and reluctant to move beyond it—especially with a drug that was two to three thousand times more potent— Hollingshead eventually wore him down. Hollingshead had mixed the entire gram of Sandoz LSD with distilled water and confectioners' sugar in a sixteen-ounce mayonnaise jar, enough for five thousand doses, which he'd brought with him when he moved up from New York, and one night—after his wife and child had left and Tim's own children, Suzie and Jackie, were in bed—he produced the jar. And a spoon. Tim watched him dig the spoon into the sweet paste, then lick it clean, and then Tim took the spoon and dipped it in the jar and within the hour fell under the grip of the most powerful mind-altering substance humankind had ever devised. He said later of that first trip that it was like hopping down from the seat of a buggy and climbing onto an Atlas rocket. Psilocybin was a toy compared to it. And really, there was no coming back, not once you'd been there.

That was the scenario. That was what Hollingshead was doing there in the office that night and the reason he was there every night, because if Fitz had imprinted on Tim—gosling and goose—then Tim had imprinted on Hollingshead. Of course, Fitz didn't know how much of this was true or not as he came down the hallway, just the lineaments of the story and what he could glean from the hints Tim kept dropping about the new possibilities out there, the need to *graduate* from psilocybin, as he kept putting it, mysteriously, and sometimes not so mysteriously. He was feeling uncertain of himself and his status and beyond that the whole course of his studies and his degree and his plans for the future because now more than ever Tim was the key to it all and Tim could shift his allegiance, stall him, drop him, and while he told himself he was reading too much into a random moment on the steps of the library, he felt he needed a little clarity all the same.

Don't press, he'd counseled himself on the way over in the car, *be*

casual, but his intention was to bring himself back into Tim's orbit
and if possible steer the conversation around to Saturday night and
the next session at Tim's house. (Tim's *and* Hollingshead's, that is,
because whether he was paying rent or not, which Fitz doubted, it
was Hollingshead's house now too.)

Tim had his back to the door, the chair swiveled round so he could
see Hollingshead, whom he'd been chatting with in the absence of
any of the students, though when Fitz gave a formal tap at the doorframe, Tim—who was either clairvoyant or had caught a glimpse of
his reflection in the windowpane—said, "Come on in, Fitz." And
then, swinging round, added, "Long time no see. What's up?"

The room was overheated—all the rooms were, a feature of academe he'd first noticed as an undergrad, as if higher learning was as
much a function of the sweat glands as the brain—and he was wet
under both arms as he came through the door and shrugged out of
his coat. "Oh, nothing in particular," he said. "I just wanted to, I
don't know, touch base?"

He saw Tim exchange a look with Hollingshead, who had nothing
for him, not a hello or even a nod of the head. "Touch away," Tim
said. "You can even steal second if you want."

Hollingshead seemed to find this funny, though he couldn't have
gotten the reference. Fitz hadn't known many Englishmen, but as a
tribe they seemed supremely indifferent to baseball—or any American sport for that matter.

He was about to invent something, an imaginary problem he was
having with the heavy Skinnerian emphasis of the required text for
the Psych 101 course he was teaching, when Tim stood abruptly and
lifted his coat down from the hook on the wall behind his desk, an-
nouncing, "Michael and I were just about to take a little stroll down
to the Square for a drink." He paused as Hollingshead slid down off
the filing cabinet, buttoned his sports jacket (a houndstooth tweed,
like Tim's) and reached for his own coat, hat and muffler. It was an
awkward moment and Tim kept him in suspense for the length of

it, which only made him sweat the more, before adding, almost as an afterthought, "You're welcome to join us—if I'm not keeping you from anything. You did want to talk, didn't you?"

At the bar—raucous with students, rattled by the jukebox, suspended in smoke—Tim put an arm round his shoulder and told him to order anything he wanted and not to worry about it. "It's on me, Fitz, because you don't have to tell me what it's like to have to live on a student income, and with a family too—been there, done that. Suzie came along when I was doing my doctoral work at Berkeley, did you know that?"

He hadn't known. All he knew of Tim was gossip—the suicide wife, the heroic struggle, the peripatetic scholar with the two motherless children to raise and the shining aura of the crusader glowing round him with every breath he took.

"Marianne dropped it on me like a bomb." He winced, mugged for Hollingshead, then laughed aloud. "But I survived it and you will too, believe me. Right, Michael?"

Hollingshead leaned into the bar, his bloodless face looming into Fitz's line of vision. "My wife's a bitch," he said. "There's no surviving that."

"But not Joanie," Tim said, his smile turned up to full power. "Joanie's the soul of the operation Chez Loney, I can see that." He lifted his glass—he was having a martini and Fitz was following suit; Hollingshead was drinking beer. Like an Englishman. "Here's to Joanie," he said. "You're a lucky man, Fitz."

"I am," he said, ducking his head. "And she wanted me to tell you how much she enjoyed, you know, the last time at your place—?"

Tim was on his left, Hollingshead on his right. They were both watching him.

"And she was wondering, we both were, when you were planning on holding another session, because we'd both like to, or we feel we need to, really—"

"Saturday night, sevenish," Tim said. "You're always welcome, you know that, Fitz."

There was no babysitter this time—they'd learned their lesson on that score—but right up to the minute they left the house he couldn't help imagining the various disasters that were sure to unfold in their absence. What if Corey got hungry and decided to cook something on the gas stove, a can of soup, anything, and forgot to light the burner? What if he took it in his head to play with matches? (*He's never played with matches,* Joanie countered when he brought it up for the third time. *He's not that kind of kid, you ought to know that.*) What about the door? What if somebody, some salesman, some pervert, came knocking? Or the park. What if Corey snuck off to the park with some of the neighborhood roughnecks, like Nicky Bayer and whoever? (*So what if he did?*) Well, they'd get drunk, wouldn't they? And then get run over in the street, or—

Joanie told him he was being ridiculous. Corey had a bag of potato chips and a quart of root beer and the Saturday night TV lineup on CBS, which was as dependable a hypnotic as you could ask for, *Jackie Gleason, The Defenders, Have Gun—Will Travel, Gunsmoke,* and after that he'd be in bed, asleep, where no one or nothing could harm him. He was going to be fourteen in a month. He was a steady, dependable, level-headed kid who'd never given them or anybody else any trouble. It was time to let go.

At quarter of seven he was still fussing over the last-minute details—obsessively, he'd be the first to admit it—and she was at the door in her heels and a tartan plaid skirt and nylons that showed off her legs, saying, "Come on, Fitz—you're the one who's going to make us late this time," and then she started in on a mini lecture about how anal-retentive he was, because really, didn't they have the right to go out and *enjoy* themselves once in a while without making a major production

of it? Implicit in this, of course, was the promise of sex, the kind of
unbounded primal sex they'd skyrocketed into the last time and hadn't
even come close to replicating since, and that was a mighty persuader,
so that when he did finally usher her out the door the merest touch of
her sent an electric jolt through him. Everything was settled, everything was fine. They were going to Tim's. For a session.

The problems with the car were beyond counting, but he'd sprung
for a tune-up and a new battery and with the coming of warmer
weather the thing had started up more often than not, as it did now,
gratifyingly. A rumble, two quick blasts of backfire, and they were
off. Joanie insisted on stopping at the liquor store for the same label
of wine they'd brought last time—low end, but French at least—and
he didn't fume over being late as he sat at the curb with the engine
running and the black budless trees waving in the breeze because
he'd seen how casual it all was at Tim's, a party, a session, pairing off,
the inner depths. Or heights. Definitely heights.

This time they didn't bother with the doorbell, just walked right
in as if they belonged. They slid out of their coats and dumped them
without ceremony on the pile in the entranceway, then went on into
the main room beyond, Joanie cradling the wine and he pausing to
light a cigarette (not that he was nervous, he told himself, but just
to have something to do with his hands). Chatter flew round the
room. Everybody was here, though it was a bigger crowd than last
time, and there were several faces he didn't recognize. The fireplace
was going—actually, he saw now that there were three fireplaces, all
ablaze—though the day had been fine, with temperatures reaching
into the mid-fifties. Was it too hot? Maybe. He felt a prickle under
his arms, drew in the smoke to calm himself.

There was jazz, not Coltrane this time, but something else altogether, something he liked a whole lot less: a hyperactive horn, a big
band, Stan Kenton? Or no: Maynard Ferguson. Word had it he was
a friend of Tim's, and why not? Ferguson had no doubt given him
the album, one amigo to another, and what was he getting in return?

The same thing they all were, a session, the chance to participate in an experiment with an agent that broke down the barriers and opened you up to yourself and the universe in a way that redefined consciousness. Fitz had no complaint with that, though if it was his choice he'd stick with a combo, absolutely.

Joanie crossed the room to set the wine on the sideboard and immediately a man he didn't recognize took it up, applied a corkscrew to it and poured out two glasses, one for her, one for himself. Fitz was just standing there observing all this and trying to decide whether he should go to the bar for a drink or seek out Tim, who was all the way across the room in conversation with Brenda—or no, it was another blonde, not Brenda at all—when he felt a tug at his arm and turned round on Fanchon.

"Oh, good," she said, her accent elongating the vowels, "good you are here. We missed you the last time. Or times, more than one, isn't that right?" A wide smile. "Too busy studying?"

"I guess," he said lamely. She smelled strongly of something, not perfume, something familiar, homey, and what was it? "I like the scent you're using," he said.

"Oh, this? It is just vanilla extract, that is all. Do you like it? Cheaper than Chanel—plus, in a pinch, you can drink it."

"Maybe I should let Joanie know."

"Good idea," she said, taking a sip of her drink (a martini, from the pitcher on the bar that was only a pitcher and nothing more, at least not yet). "Always prudent to save on money, especially when you are a student and you have to live like a peasant, no? She's looking nice tonight, by the way. I like how she did her hair. And her skirt, I love her skirt. *Très chic.*"

He didn't know what to say to this, but he took it as a kindness: if Joanie looked good, so did he.

"But"—and here Fanchon dropped her gaze so the light caught her lashes and the black feathers of mascara at the corners of her eyes—"you had better watch out."

"What do you mean?"

"For her."

She lifted her eyes to his and he gave her a puzzled look. "I'm watching," he said.

"You know who is this man pouring the wine?"

He looked over the stranger again, a man of his age or so, well built and dressed in a form-fitting suit, his hair brushed forward in a shag crew cut reminiscent of Marlon Brando's in *Julius Caesar*. "No, we haven't been introduced yet."

"It is Maynard Ferguson—you know, the trumpeter? He is staying for the weekend with his wife."

The news didn't move him much one way or the other. This wasn't Coltrane or Miles or even Gerry Mulligan or Herbie Mann, but still, he'd never been in the presence of a celebrity before, and there was something arresting in that. Ferguson was a big name. He toured all over the country. He got write-ups in *DownBeat* and the *Times*. And there he was, across the room, sharing a glass of wine with Joanie as if it were the most ordinary thing in the world. But really, he thought, you had to hand it to Tim: no matter what anybody said, he was no ordinary professor.

"But you do not want a drink?" Fanchon asked, lifting her glass in emphasis. "Not even one—to put you in the mood?"

He was watching Tim and the new blonde, who was every bit as striking as Brenda, maybe not as tall or busty, but she definitely had the goods, and wondering if he should go over and butt in because he really did need to talk to Tim or at least show himself so Tim could appreciate that he was here—and willing, a loyalist and a follower and a member of the inner circle whether Maynard Ferguson qualified or not.

"A drink?" Fanchon repeated. She was wearing a black cocktail dress that left her arms bare. She'd pinned up her hair in back and teased out her bangs so they floated and bobbed with every movement she made.

"Yes, sure," he said, "sounds good, but I can—"

"No, no," she murmured, putting a hand on his arm, "I will get it for you. A martini? Yes?" Her smile was tight and self-satisfied and it came to him that she was burning to tell him something, which she wound up doing in the next breath. "You know," she said, "I am the hostess now."

The trumpet flared and then the drummer came in, too heavily, making a stampede of the tune thumping through the speakers, and because he was distracted—*he needed to say hello to Tim*—he just said, "Sure," but when she didn't drop his arm, he appended a question, "What do you mean?"

"Tim has no wife," she said.

He looked to Tim again and now somebody else was there with him and the blonde—Ken—and he felt he'd lost his chance because he should have just walked right up to him and said, *Hi, Tim, thanks for the invite,* and gotten it over with. "It doesn't seem to be slowing him down any," he said, watching as the blonde, the new blonde, took his hand in hers and coiled herself under his right arm.

"No," Fanchon said, "this is not what I mean." Again that look, as if she had the latest news and could hardly contain it. She arched her back, balanced on one foot as if she were commencing a yoga exercise, then squared up and looked him in the eye. "What I mean is that I am the mistress of this house now. Didn't you hear? Ken and I, we moved in. See the stairs there, at the top, first door on the right? That is our bedroom."

The news came at him like a sack of stones flung out a window and he didn't have time to duck or even wince before he was asking, "Why?" when the answer should have been obvious. But if it was obvious, then that gave rise to a whole new set of questions beginning with, Why Ken and not him? Did it have to do with Fanchon? Were Tim and Fanchon—? But Tim had all the women he could want and here was the new blonde to prove it—no, it had to be Ken, Ken as factotum and alter ego, the little Tim who would walk in the master's footsteps, sing his hosannas, kowtow and brownnose and spread the word like the disciple he was. Still, no matter how you figured it, students didn't live with their professors—that just wasn't done. There were ethical considerations, weren't there? An academic code? Fitz was dumbfounded. And jealous, instantly jealous. Which made him lose any semblance of tact he might have brought into the room with him. "Why?" he repeated, his voice a register higher than it should have been. And then, when she just stared at him, he dropped his voice. "Okay, well," he said, "I guess that's great, really great. What's he asking for rent?"

The martini—and he was going to have one only, just one— loosened him up so that after a while he began to feel elastic on his feet, almost as if he wanted to dance, though he hated dancing. Dancing wasn't his cup of tea. It was for show-offs and he most definitely was not a show-off. Somebody changed the record to Miles's *Kind of Blue,* the antithesis of Ferguson, and he found himself nodding his head to the beat while Fanchon chattered on about what a saint Tim was because he was offering them the room gratis and how now they would finally be able to make ends meet ("Is that how you say: 'ends meet'? Or is it 'meet ends'?"). He liked her attention, liked her lips, liked the way her eyes searched his, and he felt his insecurity falling away, only to be replaced by, what—impatience?

He glanced at Joanie, who was apparently spellbound by the celebrity in the room, the man who at that moment lifted the bottle and refreshed her glass, and then at Tim, who'd been joined now by Charlie and Charlie's girlfriend, the redhead, and he kept thinking it was like the last time all over again, a party, an excuse for a party, and where was the science in that? But then immediately he felt like a hypocrite, because what was he doing here himself? Was it really the science that attracted him? The need to kiss up to his professor? The high? The sex? The sex was what it had been about last time, hadn't it? His mind—and Joanie's too—had expanded into regions they'd never even dreamed had existed, sure, but in the end their trip had come down to the most elemental act there is, the act shared by all animals, whether their consciousness was expanded or not or for that matter whether they could be said to have a consciousness at all. A term came to his lips unaccountably, the name of a flatworm he'd studied in biology lab a thousand years ago: *Platyhelminthes*. Now there was a consciousness. He said it aloud—"Platyhelminthes"— and Fanchon, looking puzzled, said, "What?"

What? Yes, that was the question. He stood there a moment swaying on his feet and blinking his eyes as if he'd been gassed. He seemed to have another martini in his hand, delivered to him by who? Suzie, the fourteen-year-old who was morphing into an adult and slipping unobtrusively through the room like the hired help, a tray of glasses cradled in her arms. But he had to talk to Tim, didn't he? Or show himself? Or—but then the music died and Tim was clapping his hands for attention and it was just like the last time and here was Joanie coming to his side and Fanchon crossing the room to her husband.

"We're about ready to begin," Tim announced. "Everybody get comfortable and I'll be coming to each of you in turn, so be patient. Tonight," he added, "will be a little different, as many of you already know, because the laboratories have finally sent me an adequate sample of Delysid, which, believe me, will enrich and extend the sort of experience you've had during the Psilocybin Project—which we're not abandoning, not by any means, just expanding."

Everyone in the room was focused on Tim. It was so quiet Fitz could hear the hiss and snap of the fireplaces and, somewhere in the distance, the faint moan of a siren. "It's one pill only this time, standard dose, two hundred fifty micrograms, the merest fraction of the psilocybin dose, but this drug—lysergic acid diethylamide—is far more potent. And revelatory. As you'll see."

There was a sudden thump overhead and in the next moment

Tim's son, Jackie (slim, dark, the generic crew cut, Keds, blue jeans, twelve and a half years on this earth) was pounding down the stairs, across the room and out the front door and into the night while thirty pairs of eyes watched him go. The door slammed and everyone turned back to Tim.

"That was Jackie," he said, "off on an urgent mission," and he paused, grinning, to show that this was a joke and give people time to reward him with a rueful chuckle, the icebreaker, but Fitz wasn't laughing: he was frozen in place by what he'd just heard. *LSD*? He'd barely had time to absorb his impressions of the last session and now Tim expected him—*them*—to try something infinitely more powerful, no matter how small the dose? The thing that had made Hollingshead Hollingshead? And where was *he* anyway? You'd think he wouldn't miss this for the world.

"All right," Tim said, "is everybody with me? As usual, I'll be here throughout the session as your guide, and Walter—Walter, where are you?" Fitz saw now that Pahnke was there, all the way in the back of the room, wearing his leather motorcycle jacket and looking less like a licensed M.D. and Ph.D. candidate in the Divinity School than a juvenile delinquent, as if that would inspire confidence. Of course, he did drive a motorcycle, but to Fitz's mind the jacket and engineer boots were less about practicality than affectation. And ridiculous too, as if he were embracing academia and rejecting it at the same time. "And Walter's here also to act in that capacity in case any of you should experience any rough patches—and you will, or you might, who can say, but my advice is to ride them out, that's all, because you are in for the experience of your lives."

He paused, glanced round the room at the expectant faces, couples holding hands, the shimmer of the cocktail glasses catching the light, everything ticking down to the moment of release, then added, "The questionnaires, please, as usual. And I'd appreciate your reports within the next forty-eight hours or so." Another pause, the grin holding steady as if to say everything's just fine, copacetic, and enjoy the trip. "While your impressions are still fresh, *entendu?*"

If to this point everything had been familiar, right down to Tim's showing him the pill bottle and even the cardboard box it came in—DELYSID (LSD 25), it read across the label, PHYSICIAN'S SAMPLE, and below it, in capital letters, *POISON*—nothing beyond that felt even remotely recognizable. The lights dimmed. Tim switched the record to some sort of repetitive Indian music—a raga, somebody said— which was nothing but a nagging presence that went on nagging for what seemed an eternity, and then the drug began to come on, rolling through him like waves mounting successively along an infinite beach. Joanie was there and then she wasn't, vanished into her own world. Things began to move, but in no delicate way, not the way it'd been the last time, but violently, in screaming ribbons of color, all of it slicing at him till everything visible was sucked down inside him in a free fall that would not and could not end. There was no sex. No touching. No bodies. He was all mind and his mind was a very rough customer, pounding his consciousness into submission, stingy with the glory, stingier with the heights, showing only what he'd suppressed all his life for the very good and excellent reason that to see it, know it, feel it in his innermost being, would destroy him. Images slammed down like heavy sashes shutting one after the other only to open up on the next and the next after that, control a joke, personality a hoax and schizophrenia the only realistic outcome because they didn't call these drugs psychotomimetics for nothing, did they? Of course, of course. He was losing his mind and what other result could he have expected?

He was scared, only that. Terrified. And if someone was there pushing down on him—Tim, with hands of stone, Tim murmuring *Don't fight it, just let go, it's going to be all right, all right, all right*—it meant nothing to him. There was no God—that was the bedrock certainty of everything he knew—but he prayed to Him now, *Our Father who art in heaven,* the cant of his Catholic youth come back to him till he was staring into the slit eyes of the Devil, some devil, all the devils, and the void that preceded consciousness and would ineluctably snuff it out absorbing him into its pure black nothingness whether his eyes were open or not. Somebody said that he'd been outside, running, that he'd stripped off his jacket and pants and slammed so hard into the inanimate world that there were bruises up and down his legs and a gash just above his right hip that might or might not need bandaging, but he didn't believe a word of it because when he thought about it very hard, when he really concentrated, he knew he hadn't been there at all.

4.

One bad trip, Fitz, don't let it throw you—it happens to us all.
The point is revelation and there's no promise of that—or
that it'll be all milk and honey either. Read Huxley—you
know Huxley? Sometimes it's heaven, sometimes it's hell. It just comes
in its own way and of its own accord and our job is to be patient and
follow it where it wants to lead us."

Tim was talking as he walked, striding across campus with his
arms swinging jubilantly and his hands rising and falling to frame
his words. He himself was trying to keep up, trying to make sense
of what had happened to him on Saturday night, trying to fit in and
stay focused at the same time. "So was it some kind of breakthrough,
is that what you think?"

Students milled, assembled, drifted past in groups. They didn't
know anything, couldn't imagine. Those were real bruises on his legs
and this was his mind taking him through the day, sharper and clearer
than it had ever been in all his life. It was as if he'd had a tune-up, a
mental tune-up, and all his cylinders were firing for the first time. The
trees were like people, the people like trees. The sky ached. A voice
shouted, "You just wait!" and another shouted back, "I'm still waiting!"

"The Catholic game, Fitz," Tim said, the wind ruffling his hair like an unseen hand, "the priest-haunted past letting go. You don't think I went through the same thing, all that Sunday morning gibberish and my mother and my aunt May sitting rigid in the pew beside me, murmuring the old rote incantations, *believing*?" He juggled his hands, gestured at the sky. "It's hard to let go, hard to *evolve,* but that's what we're doing here, that's what the project is all about. We're explorers, right? Going where nobody has gone before."

"Except Crazy Juana. And the Greeks at Eleusis."

Tim stopped so suddenly he almost collided with a bicyclist who'd swung out to pass them on the left. "Correct," he said, giving him an appreciative look, a fraternal look, as if he were reassessing him moment by moment. "But they didn't have Albert Hofmann and Sandoz Laboratories to provide for them. It's a new world, Fitz, and you better believe we're going to map it all out, right down to its core. And if *that's* God, then so be it."

Just as suddenly, he started off again and Fitz had to jog the first few steps to catch up with him. For a moment they were silent, matching each other stride for stride, before Tim swiveled his head round to search out his eyes. "Walter wanted to bring you back down with a shot of Thorazine, did I mention that?"

He felt as if he'd been slapped. "What do you mean?"

"It was an intense experience," Tim said, never breaking stride. "Which is fine, which is okay, just what we want, really."

"Was I that far gone? Did I, I mean, I didn't—do anything, did I?"

"I nixed it. And Dick, Dick was there—did you see Dick? Dick agreed with me, one hundred percent."

He had no recollection of Alpert being there, or he hadn't until this very moment. Now it came to him, a shimmering image of Dick with his arm around a beautiful young man, the two of them appearing there in the firelit room just as the drug was coming on. Both were grinning and looking down on him and Joanie as if they were subjects in a lab somewhere. It gave him an odd feeling to recover the memory now because he'd never studied with Professor Alpert and barely knew him and because Professor Alpert was known to be a homosexual. He'd never encountered a homosexual before and the whole concept of men wanting other men was alien to him, and while he'd read case studies and Havelock Ellis and Freud (*it is nothing to be ashamed of, no vice, no degradation*), he didn't know how he felt about it down deep, especially at a time when he'd been so vulnerable, so open and defenseless and uncertain. And Pahnke too. Yes, it was a comfort to know he was there, a medical doctor, but he was also a fellow student—a competitor—and to think Walter had even considered sticking a needle in him, of violating him, made him feel ill.

"It was our feeling that you should work through it," Tim was saying, "because it's the only way to really open up and strip away all those layers of societally imposed crap—I was right, wasn't I?"

"Tell you the truth, I don't really have all that clear a recollection."

"You got out into the backyard for a while there, dropped an article of clothing or two"—a laugh—"nothing essential, just your jacket. And trousers. But Walter and I were there with you and we got you back inside and settled in front of the fireplace and that seemed to do the trick. Your wife? She was fine, by the way. Just went deep and didn't move a muscle all evening. She did write up her report, didn't she?"

"Yes. And I've been meaning to get it to you. My report too, but I don't know how coherent it's going to be—"

Tim's hand rose and fell in dismissal. "Don't worry about it, I'm sure it'll be fine. As I say, it's all part of the catalog we're building." They'd come to the end of the walk and Tim stopped again. "I'm heading this way," he said, pointing to his left. "A meeting. But we've got a date for Saturday night, right?"

"Saturday? I don't know, I was going to, I don't know—Corey, my son? I promised to take him to a movie."

"Fitz," he said, shaking his head, "you have to realize you've started something here, you've embarked, and you can't just jump off the boat in the middle of the deep blue sea. Especially since you're coming off a bad trip, and it doesn't make the least particle of sense to leave it there. Saturday," he said. "Seven. You with me?"

The wind chased a scrap of paper across the dead yellow lawn. Fitz hunched his shoulders and put a hand to his throat to pinch his collar shut. He'd wanted Tim's attention and now he'd got it. Ken and Fanchon were living in the house on Homer Street, along with Hollingshead and Dick Alpert and maybe the new blonde—Peggy, her name was—and who knew who else? It was a club, an exclusive club, and he was a member. He was going to say, *I'll ask Joanie,* when Tim forestalled him. "Jesus, I hate this weather," he said. "You know what I find myself thinking about, all the time, day and night?"

"What?"

"Mexico, Fitz. You ever been to Mexico?"

The next morning there was a note from Tim in his departmental mailbox. Tim wanted to know if he'd stop by his office around four, if that was convenient, because he had a proposition for him—what the proposition involved was left unsaid. Throughout the day, though he was so busy with his classes and his own office hours he barely had time to think beyond the next sixty seconds, the mystery of that summons kept haunting him. Proposition? What did that mean? Did Tim want him to go out for drinks again, help him type up session reports, book tickets on the next liner to Veracruz? He couldn't imagine. And what made it even more mystifying was that Tim had never dropped him a note before. Tim was his adviser, yes, but he'd been strictly hands-off to this point, and since Fitz was still at least a year away from coming up with a thesis topic there'd been no pressing need to confer—in fact he'd sought out Tim on his own initiative just to make the connection, and, of course, for the comfort of knowing Tim was there to provide guidance if the need should arise.

When he arrived he was surprised to see Walter Pahnke sitting there across the desk from Tim, his legs stretched out casually before him and crossed at the ankles. "Fitz," Tim said, rising from his swivel chair, "you know Walter, of course? And, Walter, I think you know Fitz."

Walter wasn't in his motorcycle regalia—he was wearing a blazer and button-down shirt like anybody else. He looked like a student. He *was* a student, Fitz reminded himself. Walter didn't bother getting up. "Thanks for coming," he said, and that only deepened the mystery—why was Walter thanking him when it was Tim who'd asked him to come?

"No problem," Fitz said. He was going to say "My pleasure," but whether or not it was a pleasure depended on exactly what the expectations were here. And of course there was the complicating factor of Walter having witnessed his moment of crisis the other night, whether he'd viewed it with medical sangfroid or felt compelled to ply his hypodermic or not.

"Well, listen," Tim said, "I'll leave it to you two," then he lifted his coat from the hook and slipped out the door and down the hallway.

When his footsteps were no longer audible, Fitz, still standing there in the middle of the room, looked to Walter. "So what's this all about?"

In that moment and that light, Walter bore an uncanny resemblance to Maynard Ferguson, same haircut, same features, same eyes even, and Fitz found that somehow unsettling, though why he couldn't have said. Walter glanced up. "An experiment," he said, leaning back in the chair so that his cuffs rode up to expose the tops of his shoes—desert boots, and why was everybody wearing desert boots? "But why don't you have a seat?" He gestured to Tim's chair, and feeling awkward, Fitz obliged. "This'll only take a minute."

Walter was younger than he was and already an M.D., which gave him a gravitas none of the other grad students could begin to match. And the way he was lounging there, legs outstretched, as if this were his office and Fitz the petitioner, only seemed to emphasize the gulf between them. "Good," Fitz said, "because I really—"

"We're all busy, I know that," Walter said, waving away the objection. "And I appreciate this, Fitz, I do—but yours was one of the first names Tim brought up, along with Ken's and Charlie's. And Dick's, of course. And there's no obligation, none at all—"

"Okay, okay," he said, impatient suddenly. "Just tell me what you want."

Walter held his gaze, let a beat go by—he wasn't going to be rushed. "What I want, what I'm asking, is for you—all of you—to act as guides in a psilocybin experiment I'm putting together for my thesis in the Divinity School; you know I'm not in the Psych Department, right?"

Fitz nodded.

"Okay. Good. So I'm trying to arrange a session at Marsh Chapel for twenty students from the Andover seminary, who presumably are more attuned to religious experience than students of psychology or history or whatever discipline. What I'm interested in is the religious aspect of the psychedelic experience—that is, whether or not these drugs, psilocybin in particular, can facilitate the kind of transcendence or agape the saints and mystics experience. Sadhus, yogis, priests, the Vedantists, Joan of Arc. I mean, Tim goes so far as to claim all religion derives from pharmaceutically assisted visions, whether it be from ergot, peyote buttons or psychoactive mushrooms."

"But I've—I'm not qualified, really. I've only had two experiences, two *trips,* and you saw, well"—he felt the color rise to his face—"what happened the other night."

Walter wasn't listening. He was staring past him now, focused on the wall, as if working through a problem. "What I'm saying is people claim this is a shortcut to religious awakening, as if God is just a function of the neurons, a presence in our own brains and not some overarching deity, and if that's the case, what does it say about our world religions, all our gods, our need for them, for explanation, for purpose?"

The Light, that was what this was about. After that first session, Tim had asked him if he'd seen the Light. But of course he hadn't, because there was no Light and there was no God. "Listen, Walter, I'd like to help but I'm really just an amateur at all this—I'm following Tim's lead, is all, and I'm curious, I am—"

"That's just why I want you. You've had the experience but you're not biased one way or the other, am I right?"

"You want the truth? God is the least of my concerns."

"Okay, good. That's just what I want to hear because, after all, this is my thesis, not yours. And the fact is I've never taken the drug myself, though Tim keeps pressuring me, insisting that I absolutely have to in order to know what it's like for my subjects, that somehow I'd be inauthentic, even dishonest, if I didn't. But I disagree, absolutely. I want to go into this—and it's going to be a double-blind experiment, so neither the subjects nor I will know who's getting the psilocybin and who the placebo—without even the slightest hint of bias for or against, you understand?"

Yes, he understood and he understood too how persuasive Tim could be, but his instinct was to say no. Walter had said it himself—it wasn't *his* thesis, so what was in it for him? Why should he care even? But then Tim was the one who'd put him forward, and if Tim was on board with this, maybe he'd better be too.

"So, Fitz"—Walter drew up his legs and leaned into the desk— "what do you think?"

"I don't know—when is it? In case I have a conflict or anything—"

"Next month, April twentieth, Easter break." Walter was watching him carefully now, as if the point was won and any further objection all but useless. "It's Good Friday, actually."

Joanie didn't like the idea. She thought Tim was manipulating him, *using* him, and didn't he have enough obligations as it was? Wasn't he always complaining about how overworked he was? And what about her? What about Corey?

"But it'll only be that one morning—and afternoon. And all I have to do is be there, really, in case anybody, I don't know, has a bad reaction or something."

They were in the kitchen, moving around each other, sharing a quart of Budweiser and working cooperatively to put together the evening meal, which was going to be spaghetti and meatballs, with a side salad. Joanie was molding meatballs in her cupped palms and dropping them one by one into the pan on the front burner; he was dicing carrots and onions and deconstructing a head of lettuce. In the living room behind them, Corey was sunk into the couch, doing his homework and watching a western with the sound turned low.

"Like you, you mean? Like the other night?"

He looked up, then away again, focusing on the knife, the vegetables, the cutting board. "Yeah," he said, "I guess so. But I won't be taking the drug, or not necessarily—"

She turned to him now, poised over the pan, the meat sizzling, the windows steamed over. From the other room came the muted sounds of gunfire and galloping horses. "What do you mean, what are you talking about?"

"The chances are fifty-fifty, because half of us, of the ten guides and the twenty students, that is, will be getting the placebo, which is nicotinic acid—and by the way, I heard both Ken and Charlie have already signed on, because this could wind up being an important study, I mean, groundbreaking, and everybody wants to be in on it."

"You've got to be kidding me. You mean the *guides* take it too?"

"Well, yeah, you know how Tim feels about cutting through the doctor/patient game—"

"Tim," she said. "It's all about Tim, isn't it?"

"No, it's about science. About psychology, *clinical* psychology—

you know, like the whole idea of what we're doing here in Cambridge?"

She didn't answer. The aroma of the cooking meat and of the gar-
lic, oregano and seasoned bread crumbs she'd suffused it with filled
the room and made him realize how hungry he was. He set down the
knife and took another sip of his beer.

After a moment he said, "I'm really thinking of saying yes, if
only for my career. It'll be a learning experience and it'll make Tim
happy—and Walter too, one hand washes the other, right? And
maybe, who knows, I'll pick up some ideas about my own thesis—or
how to go about it anyway. It's not a big deal. Really."

"After what you went through the other night? You told me it was
pure hell—you were out in the yard, Fitz, out in the yard in your
underpants, slamming into things, and you tell me you're going to
be a guide? What if you get the drug, which by the way, I resent, because I'm not invited, isn't that right?" She shoved the pan angrily to
one side, all elbows, and set a pot of water on the burner with a stark
clatter of metal on metal. For a moment neither of them spoke. He
watched her go to the sink to rinse her hands, then take up her glass
and drain it in a single swallow. "And if you do get it," she said, "and
you have a reaction like the other night, what then? Who's going to
be *your* guide?"

"I don't know, Tim, I guess. Or Ken or Walter or anybody. Besides
which, it's only going to be psilocybin and only thirty milligrams—"

"Jesus, you sound like a chemistry major. 'Only thirty milligrams'—
isn't that more than what we got the first time? A full third more?"

"*If* I get it," he went on, "which is take your pick, roll of the dice,
fifty-fifty chance, and even if I do, I can handle it, I'm sure I can—"

"Oh, really?" She glanced beyond him into the front room to make
sure Corey wasn't listening. "The way you handled it the first time?
There won't be any women there, will there?"

"No. All men."

She was right there now, right at his elbow, and he didn't want to

look up at her or prolong this or get into a wrangle over nothing—
he'd already made up his mind. It was *his* profession, *his* obligation,
and when you came down to it, what business was it of hers?

"All men," she said, and gave a low growl of a laugh. "Great," she
said. "And so who are you going to screw then?"

As it turned out, they skipped the Saturday session—he'd made a
promise to Corey, and he and Joanie took him to the movies, as
promised. He was tied up all day Monday, as usual, and didn't have
a chance to see Tim and offer up an explanation, which he felt he
owed him—especially after their talk the previous week. And while
he wasn't avoiding Tim, or not exactly, it wasn't till Tuesday evening
that he finally ran into him, and not on campus but on the Square.
It was half-past five, he was on his way home, juggling his briefcase and an armful of books and trying to remember what Joanie
had asked him to pick up at the store, when he spotted Tim, Dick
and Hollingshead coming up the sidewalk toward him. They were
all three wearing dark glasses, though it was overcast, and from all
appearances having an animated discussion. Dick seemed especially
wrought up, throwing out his hands and twisting his torso jerkily,
first to make a point to Tim, then Hollingshead, then going back to
Tim again. The minute Fitz saw them, he felt intimidated, felt guilty,
and he almost ducked into the nearest doorway, but then he told
himself he was being ridiculous.

In the next moment they were on him and he almost thought
they were going to pass him by without even noticing, but Dick
snapped his head around and said something to the other two and
they all pulled up short. Tim, in overcoat and scarf, slid the glasses
down the bridge of his nose and peered at him out of enormous
black pupils. "Oh, Fitz," he said finally to the accompaniment of the
blatting exhaust of somebody's Spitfire careening down the street,

"is that you?" To Hollingshead he said, "Look, it's Fitz," and then, turning back to him, "what a surprise, I mean, fancy meeting you here. On Harvard Square. Imagine that."

He was high, or drunk, or both. All three of them were. "I'm sorry about Saturday," Fitz said, "but it was, you know, a family obligation really, and I—"

Tim waved him off. "The deep blue sea, Fitz, the deep blue sea."

And then Alpert, all the blood gone to the visible portion of his face beneath the sunglasses, focused on him. Rangy, tall, his crew cut severer than Tim's, he was two years younger than Fitz and already a professor. Which just made everything all that much harder. "You are aware of the meeting on the fifteenth, aren't you? Day after tomorrow?"

Hollingshead turned to Tim and intoned, "Beware the ides of March, Caesar."

The moment hung there, pregnant with the evening and the pigeons and a snatch of the hit of the week—*Bop shoo-op, a bop bop shoo-op*—drifting to them from the open window of a passing car, before Fitz could bring himself to ask, "What meeting?"

"Psych Department. Thursday, four P.M.—you be there, because believe me we need all the reinforcements we can get."

"They're going to crucify Tim, *Agni immolate*." Hollingshead's grin was a ragged tear across the bottom portion of his face.

"Kellard," Tim muttered. "Rooney. Mortenson. And all the rest of them too, all the dinosaurs who teach word for word from the notes they took as students from the professors who dictated them from their own student notes going all the way back to the Middle Ages." Mugging, he put his palms together as if in prayer and raised his face to the sky. "Mea culpa. Lord have mercy on my soul."

"They're putting us on trial," Dick said. "The whole project. And why? Because of jealousy, that's why. Because of fear of the new, because—"

Hollingshead cut him off. "Do not go forth today; call it my fear," he said in a thin falsetto plaint, at the same time reaching up to pull Tim's palms apart, and then, as if this were the original gesture, high comedy, the commencement of the farce, the three of them broke down in laughter.

5.

The Psilocybin Project had been an ongoing feature of the Center for Research in Personality since shortly after Tim inaugurated it on his return from Mexico two years earlier, and in that time he and Dick Alpert had collected data from more than four hundred subjects, including not just students and faculty, but also poets, intellectuals and musicians like Allen Ginsberg, Aldous Huxley, Robert Lowell, Charles Olson, Maynard Ferguson and Charlie Mingus. And he'd originated the Concord Prison Project, in which he took his researchers (Ken Sensabaugh, Charlie Millhouse and Rick Roberts among them) into the prison to conduct psilocybin sessions behind bars with the goal of re-imprinting habitual offenders and reducing recidivism once they were released. It was a radical idea and it paid off, at least as far as prison officials and the inmates were concerned, but Tim hadn't yet written up the results, let alone published them, though the project had concluded before Fitz had even enrolled. That was one strike against him. That and the rumors surrounding the sessions at the house on Homer Street, which, Fitz had to admit, could have been more rigorous and maybe just a hair less festive, though in truth the research was a work in progress since

there'd never been anything like it before. There were no precedents
to draw from, no previous studies, and Tim, like any pioneer, was
creating a new methodology as he went along. Set and setting. The
fireplace, the music, the aura of safety, harmony, mutual support. And,
really, what else were you supposed to do—dose people in sanitized
white rooms while psychologists in lab coats hovered over them with
clipboards? That would defeat the whole purpose.

Even worse, from the point of view of his colleagues, Tim had cha-
risma to burn, which the rest of them most definitely lacked ("dour
lab rats," Tim called them, "paper shufflers and pea counters"), and
there was a whole contingent that resented him for it. Not to mention the fact that his classes were oversubscribed while the numbers
in their own courses steadily dropped. No surprise then that they
were out for his blood.

The meeting that Thursday took a while to get under way because
additional chairs had to be brought into the room, and Fitz, who
was there with Ken, Fanchon and Charlie to lend support, was surprised to see how many people had shown up for what under normal
circumstances would have been the usual dull hour featuring one
prof after another droning on about the finer points of departmental
business. He tried to do a quick head count but gave up when he
reached fifty, distracted by Fanchon, who was squeezed in beside
him, exuding her sweet vanilla scent and something else too, something more private, a whiff of perspiration from under her arms and
between her legs. She was talking in a throaty confidential whisper,
giving a running commentary on the professors in the enemy camp,
which, as it turned out, was practically all of them. "That one. The
one in the suit that is the color of a dog's turd? He is Kellard, no?
Look at him, his eyes, just look at his eyes—he is clearly what do you
say, repressed? A"—and here she leaned into him and dropped her
voice—"a limp dick, no?"

It was ten past the hour by the time Professor McClelland, who
as chair of the Center had been responsible for hiring Tim two years

back, called the meeting to order. Tim was sitting in the front row, one leg casually crossed at the knee, Dick beside him. Dick looked grim, as if he expected a fight; Tim was nonchalant, turning round in his seat to greet people with a smile or an abbreviated wave. The minute hand of the wall clock shifted forward. A pair of professors ducked in the door at the last moment. Conversation fell off.

Professor Kellard was the first to take the floor. He was in his thirties, a lecturer in social psychology, and while Fitz had yet to study with him, he was currently taking Foundations in Clinical Psychology from the man seated to the right of him, Professor Lewiston. Lewiston was older—old, actually—and so soft-spoken his lectures were all but inaudible unless you were in one of the front two rows, where Fitz always made a point of sitting. As he watched him now, Fanchon murmuring, "Look at that *vieillard,* how do say, that *graybeard,* and who does he think he's fooling?," he was recalling the meeting he'd had with him a month or so back, at the professor's invitation. "Mr. Loney," he'd said, coming up to him after class one day, "why not drop by my office for a cup of tea? Let's say, Tuesday afternoon? So we can become better acquainted?"

It was a kindness on his professor's part, one he extended to all his new students, and Fitz had been touched by it. The tea was lukewarm, the cream turning and the sugar bowl so fissured and encrusted with residue it wouldn't have been out of place in a museum, but they wound up talking for nearly an hour, which essentially involved Fitz telling the older man his life story, or at least the salient points—Joanie, Corey, working as a school psychologist to pay the bills, earning his master's at night and finally coming here to fulfill his ambition of completing a Ph.D. and teaching at the college level. At some point Lewiston had asked how he was getting on with his other professors and he'd said, "Fine," and then, after a moment of silence, Lewiston—softly, so softly—asked, "And Professor Leary? You're getting on well with him?"

"Well, yes," he'd said, "but I haven't—I mean, he's my adviser, but

I haven't actually taken a course with him yet, though in the fall I intend to, or hope to."

"But"—and Lewiston's gaze never left his face—"you are part of the Psilocybin Project, or so I hear?"

"Well, not officially, but I, well, I suppose so—"

"Tell me," the professor said, folding his hands under his chin and leaning into the desk on both elbows, "because I'm curious about the new techniques—just what do these 'sessions' entail?"

Now, as Kellard rose to speak, Fitz saw his professor slip him a page of handwritten notes, and he understood in that moment that he was no friend of Tim's. Not that Fitz had given up much—he'd been circumspect, emphasizing the positive aspects of the research, trying not to let his bias show and consciously avoiding any talk of the oneness of being or hallucinations or the subject of sex and heightened gratification—but he couldn't bring himself to be anything less than forthcoming either, detailing the dosage, the duration, the setting, strictly the facts, and yet he saw now how even those same facts could be manipulated by someone who was an enemy of the project. As Professor Kellard clearly was.

"This meeting has been a long time coming," Kellard began, brandishing the sheaf of notes in his right hand. "For several months now I've been disturbed by reports of what I can only call improprieties in the conduct of Professors Leary and Alpert's research project, which definitely merit looking into." He paused, brought the notes to his face, then dropped them to the desk as if they were contaminated.

"What am I to make of coming into my morning class—at nine A.M.—and seeing a full one-third of the students wearing dark glasses?" Kellard asked, raising his head to sweep his gaze over the room. "Is this salutary? Is this conducive to learning? Well, I think not. In fact, I think that these students, under the influence of Dr. Leary, have been up all hours—at his house on Homer Street in Newton Center—conducting psilocybin 'sessions' with very little control or scientific rigor. And not, for the most part, on a randomized sample of subjects, but on themselves. Repeatedly." He let out a grating laugh. "The sad fact is there are twice as many researchers as there are subjects and that these drugs—dangerous drugs, prescribed only for experimental use under controlled circumstances—are being abused, over and over, by the same coterie—cult, if you will—of grad students under the auspices of Professors Leary and Alpert."

Dick rose to object, but the chair—Professor McClelland—gently admonished him. "Professor Kellard has the floor, Dick," he said. "Your turn will come."

"Furthermore," Kellard went on, "the whole program has an anti-intellectual bent, valuing pure experience over any sort of collection and interpretation of data, so that it has, in essence, become a quasi-religious sect bearing little resemblance to any form of scientific inquiry I've ever heard of. Even worse, students are being pressured to take these drugs—which have been shown in study after study to have potentially adverse effects on vulnerable subjects—as a condition of their acceptance into the program in the first place."

"But this is not true," Fanchon said, her voice rising above a whisper so that several people turned round to give her hostile looks. Three of them Fitz recognized as grad students who were most definitely not part of the inner circle and another as an assistant professor who sat very comfortably beside them, as if they were part of a team. They were no doubt wondering just who Fanchon was and what she was doing here at a department meeting with her pouffed-out hair, hoop earrings and tremulous bangs, and by extension what relation she bore to Fitz and Ken, who sat on either side of her. Ken leaned in to hush her and she shook her head defiantly. "You tell me to hush?" she threw back at him under her breath. "When it is all lies? Like, like . . . McCarthyism!"

This last caused more heads to turn and Professor Kellard himself to pause and look up to see what the disturbance was before McClelland rapped his knuckles lightly on his desk and intoned, "Go on, Herb, you have the floor . . ."

Kellard snatched up his notes as if he were going to quote aloud from them, then set them aside again. "I know of at least one case," he said, "in which a student of mine—one of a handful of holdouts who continue to stand for their rights and refuse to legitimize the taking of drugs for any purpose, let alone as an *academic requirement*—was finally pressured into participating and wound up having a psychotic episode, a real crisis, and believe me, no matter what anyone tells you there is no medical supervision here whatsoever."

A second professor—Mortenson, another of Tim's enemies—rose to say that he'd spent the morning in the medical library reviewing the published research into psilocybin studies, none of which had been generated by the Harvard Psilocybin Project, incidentally, and found that there were grave concerns about administering the drug outside of a controlled medical setting. He had his own sheaf of notes and he waved it like a gauntlet in Tim's direction. "In fact, there is evidence here of several cases of disorientation continuing for weeks after a single dose of these substances, of subjects being admitted to emergency rooms, of psychotic reactions in apparently normal people and increased suicidal ideation. You are not a medical doctor, Professor Leary, we're all aware of that here, and so I ask you how you can in good conscience administer these drugs without medical supervision or, as far as I can see, even an awareness of these medical issues?"

It was a no-win situation and Tim just had to sit there and take it. Fitz felt his stomach sink. He couldn't have explained what it was or exactly how it had come about or what it meant, but at that moment, more deeply than ever, he felt a bond with Tim, with Ken and Charlie and Fanchon and all the rest of the crowd he'd shared the experience with—Joanie, of course, even Maynard Ferguson—a bond that excluded everyone else in the room. They were wrong, he saw that clearly. They were misguided and shortsighted and protective of their own little fiefdoms no matter the cost in terms of academic freedom or the advancement of knowledge, and what was supposed to have been an equitable airing of concerns had turned into an all-out assault on the new, on Tim and Dick and by extension on himself too.

When Mortenson was finished, he sat heavily, slapping his notes down on the desk and pointing a shaking finger at Tim. "I'd be interested to know, Professor Leary, just what you have to say for yourself."

All the while Tim had been sitting there looking unconcerned, as if all this was to be expected and there was no way he was going to play the penitent's role for them or have his knuckles rapped or conform in any way to their expectations—these people, all of them, were squares, after all, the unenlightened, the uninitiated, and he, alone among them, was in possession of the truth. His smile was florid, his shoulders square, his tie perfectly knotted. He was about to respond when Dick rose beside him and in a voice so choked with outrage he could barely get the words out, blurted, "I can't believe what I'm hearing here. Let me remind you, Professor Mortenson—and you too, Herb—that this is not an inquisition, that we are all colleagues and there is nothing more or less at stake here than the issue of academic freedom itself. We're not answerable to you. We're conducting research about which you, as can plainly be seen, have little or no knowledge, dynamic research that's at the forefront of the field today, and we—I—very much resent the tone of these proceedings." His glasses flashed under the glare of the overhead lights. "So much so that I think you owe us an apology—no, I demand an apology."

The room fell silent. Everyone looked to McClelland, but before he could even so much as clear his throat, Tim was on his feet. "Thank you," he said, scanning the room and smiling broadly, at the same time putting a restraining hand on Dick's arm so that Dick, his face flushed, sank back into his seat and the tension eased. "And thank you, Herb, for your input, and you too, Lloyd"—nodding at Mortenson—"but I do have to say that your fears are unfounded. I admit mistakes have been made, but we are feeling our way here in

the research—let me remind you that this is a pioneering study—
and I'm confident we are well on our way to ironing out the kinks."

It was a revelation to see Tim in action, how he so quickly and
fluidly took control of the situation and changed the whole tenor of
the meeting. He was conciliatory and respectful but at the same time
he stood his ground, reasserting the vital significance of the research
and citing the dramatic success of the prison project, in which the recidivism rate was less than 25 percent among the sample he'd worked
with as compared to something in the vicinity of 70 percent among
the general prison population. He talked for ten minutes, persuasive,
charismatic, charming, and if he'd left it there, Fitz felt, he would
have won the day, but then he made a fatal misstep.

"Well, I can see I've held the floor too long," he said, "forgive me,
but I just want to make one more point." He looked to Mortenson
then, smiling serenely on him as if they were not simply colleagues
but the best of friends. "Lloyd, I want to thank you again for bringing up the medical issue," he said, "but let me assure you that we
are taking every precaution." He paused to glance round the room;
everybody's eyes were on him. "The fact is that we are working closely
with a distinguished psychiatrist at Massachusetts General Hospital,
Gerald Klinger, who is acting as adviser to the project."

At that moment, there was a sharp squeal of chair legs on the
linoleum floor and suddenly a small man with a receding hairline
and an overcoat slung over his right arm was standing in the rear of
the room, crying out in a shrill voice, "What is this? What are you
saying?"

Tim, taken by surprise, let his smile waver. "I'm sorry," he said,
"and who are you exactly?"

The man had come forward two or three rows now so that he was
standing directly in front of where Fitz, Ken, Fanchon and Charlie
were sitting, and he seemed worked up over something, his chest
heaving and his glasses slipping down the bridge of his nose. "I'm
Gerry Klinger," he said, and then looked round him as if he didn't

know where he was or how he'd gotten there. "And I've never laid eyes on you before in my life."

Afterward, Tim couldn't seem to stop laughing about it. "The joke's on me, I guess," he said when they were all back at the house on Homer Street and the first round of martinis was already circulating, because if ever they'd been needed they were needed now. "I mean, really, who would have thought Klinger would be there—did you see him? Just another lab rat like all the rest of them. Klinger! Jesus! Are you kidding me? He looked like he got off the bus at the wrong stop."

It was ten past six and the sinking sun was throwing trembling patterns on the wall behind him. Everyone was gathered round in an extended circle. Ken had lit a fire and Charlie put Coltrane's *Lush Life* on the stereo, the music meditative and warm and creeping in under the conversation in a consolatory way. Not that Tim seemed to need consolation—no, he was absolutely lit up with a kind of frantic joy, the life of the party, irrepressible, unbowed, and so what if a stake had been driven through the heart of the Psilocybin Project? What was it to him? Yes, McClelland was calling for all psilocybin samples to be turned in to him so he could monitor them and dole them out as he deemed necessary, but it was no secret to anyone in the room that the psilocybin phase of the research had been laid to rest when Hollingshead had showed up with his mayonnaise jar.

"They're all lab rats," Ken said, standing tall beside Tim, a band of light flickering across his chest, the branches in motion outside the window and making a shadow play of the wall. "I hate to say it but it's the truth."

Charlie joined in, his voice narrowed to a plaint: "They don't understand, that's all, they just don't understand."

"You can say that again," Tim crowed, clinking glasses with him.

Then he raised his own glass and everyone looked to him. "A toast! To the lab rats—may they stay mired in their mazes forever!"

"Hear, hear!" Fitz cried, the blood rising to his face. He felt exhilarated, vindicated, as if he himself had been on trial. It was all right. Everything was all right. Lewiston wasn't his mentor or even his friend, or Kellard or McClelland or any of the rest of them. No, Tim was—Tim and Tim alone.

After the second round of martinis, somebody mentioned pizza. It was getting late and no one had eaten, let alone Suzie and Jackie, who were immured in their rooms and presumably getting by on the sort of junk food adolescents preferred (in Corey's case it was Cheez Doodles, M&M's and red licorice whips), and so everybody tossed a few bills on the coffee table, preferences were noted and Ken and Charlie volunteered to go pick up the pizza. The door slammed. The record changed. The wall went gray and then it went dark. Tim was deep in conversation with Rick Roberts, Dick and one of the blondes—not Peggy this time, but Brenda again—and Fitz found himself thinking about Joanie, who he really should call to tell her he wouldn't be home for dinner, but Fanchon was right there beside him on the couch, and Alice, who'd mysteriously appeared, was beside her and everything began to feel so absolutely tranquil after the tension of the meeting he couldn't help pushing it to the back of his mind.

Fanchon was sitting with one leg folded under her and the other stretched out on the carpet. She'd been talking about a film she'd seen recently—one he hadn't seen and had already forgotten the title of—when she shifted closer to him and dropped her voice. "Tim is thinking of holding a session tonight, for all of us, because—well, because the time is right, *n'est-ce pas?*" She let out a soft purring laugh. "And I, for one, am more than ready. What about you, Fitz?" And without waiting for an answer, which was going to be no, definitely no, because he had a ten o'clock class in the morning and he had to go home to his wife and his son, she turned to Alice. "And you, Alice? What about it? You don't have work in the morning, do you? It is

Friday, end of the week, no? What do you say, T.G.I.F.? Or E.F.? Is it E.F.?"

Alice, her hair catching the light of the lamp in streaks of individuated color, red, red-gold, strawberry, blonde, said she didn't know. Then she laughed and said, "Make that a strong maybe. I actually don't have to be in tomorrow till half-past ten—"

"And you, Fitz?" Fanchon said, shifting her face to him now and casually laying a hand on his thigh, just above the knee, as if his thigh were the arm of the couch and not his thigh at all, not at all flesh and blood and susceptible to touch, pressure, suggestion. "Tonight is a special night—call it a what, a graduation ceremony?"

He looked into her eyes, then away again. The room was different than he remembered it, more cluttered, messier, as if the research didn't extend to anything as earth-bound as housecleaning. There were pill bottles scattered around—on the mantelpiece, the side table, even a few on the floor. And the wall behind the couch now sported a decoration done in careful vibrant orange brushstrokes, and what was it? A square with four openings and a circle in the middle.

Fanchon saw him studying it. "You like it?"

He didn't know really. It was carefully done, not an errant drip of paint, but somehow it offended his sense of proportion because this was an old house, a beautiful house, the sort of house he envisioned himself living in one day, and now the wainscoting was ruined—or desecrated anyway.

"This," Fanchon said, and her hand lifted from his thigh to gesture at the design and then float back down again so that he was all the more conscious of it, conscious to the point of feeling himself begin to stir, "is my handiwork. It is copied from a book of Tibetan patterns. You know what it is called?"

He didn't have a clue.

"A mandala. The circle inside a square is meant to represent the universe. Isn't that lovely?"

He supposed so, though to his mind a period print, Degas, Renoir, even Currier and Ives, would have been more appropriate—and less permanent. Fanchon was searching his eyes. "Yes," he said. "Very nice."

She clapped her hands, delighted. "And there," she said, pointing across the room to where Tim was seated on the floor now, in the lotus position, as were Rick Roberts, Brenda, Dick and one of Dick's young protégés, the five of them hunkered over their drinks and cigarettes. "You see that boring, boring wall behind Tim? I am thinking the same pattern there, but maybe in a shade of canary, or how do you say it, this *jaune* fruit from Hawaii, very prickly on the outside?"

"Pineapple," Alice put in.

"Yes, yes! This is it exactly!" Fanchon exclaimed. "Pineapple. What do you think?"

At some point the pizza arrived, four square boxes that might as well have had mandalas painted on them too, though there was no need because all you had to do was flip back the lid of each and there were the pizzas revealed, each a perfect circle inside a perfect square, the universe laid out on a slab of hot dough. The smell was irresistible—it was pizza, after all—but after drifting into the kitchen to take a look at it, he resisted. Tonight was special. Tonight—Fanchon had called it—was a kind of graduation, another graduation, and it didn't take him long to make up his mind. He was going to stay on, come what may, and whatever Joanie might have been thinking or what Corey might have wanted faded away into the fumes of the gin rising from his second martini. So what if he'd had a bad trip last time out? He owed it to Tim—to himself—to push beyond that and discover what the others kept talking about, the Light, the vision, the melting away of the ego and the awakening of the innermost mind. The boat had been rocked, the project attacked, but here they were—here was *Tim,* unfazed and unyielding, more determined than ever to push the boundaries. Fitz couldn't go home. Not now.

And so the pizza went untouched—he didn't want anything on

his stomach to weigh him down. Actually, hardly anybody seemed to want any, except Tim's kids and Ken, who fed slice after slice into his mouth before excusing himself ("Big day for me tomorrow") to mount the stairs to his room. Fanchon went round lighting candles and flicking off the lights. Charlie laid more wood on the fire. Then an unseen hand changed the record and Tim got up and circulated the Delysid samples. "Great, Fitz," Tim said, standing over the couch where he'd settled himself back down beside Fanchon and Alice. "Great," he repeated, handing over the pill as if it were a sacrament— and it was, it *was*—"because this is the true path to enlightenment and enlightenment is something you have to work at, right? No fears, no worries. Just sit back and relax."

Fitz swallowed and watched Fanchon and Alice do the same as Tim looked on, smiling his unflagging smile. "Great," he repeated again.

"What about the questionnaires?" Fitz asked, gesturing vaguely in the direction of the sideboard. The music—another raga, or maybe the same one—jumped and whined and tap-tap-tapped through the speakers.

"Oh, I don't know," Tim said, grinning down at him, hands on hips. "I don't think we're going to need them tonight, do you?"

This time, though the drug took hold of him with the same propulsive rush of color and image as if a movie were playing in his head at double speed—two movies, three—he wasn't afraid, or not primarily, but just . . . expectant. There was the first phase, people laughing, everything convivial, hilarious, Fanchon leaning forward to light a cigarette and the smoke spinning her head round on her shoulders as if she were riding a carousel—as if she *were* a carousel, a human carousel, whirling and whirling—and he laughed at the sight of it, laughed aloud, and Fanchon laughed right back at whatever she was seeing in him, and Alice . . . there was Alice way out there at the end of the couch that was like the far end of a pier, and she was laughing along with them.

Then it was the second phase, the phase that could go either way because the laughter died and the shared experience too and everybody went deep, the drug like a firm hand at the back of your neck, pushing you deeper, and all he could think about—all he could see—were the depths at the bottom of the lake back at home after he'd left the diving board and driven himself down into the cold and the blackness, ever deeper, yet it wasn't mud down there, not today, but a whole glittering gilded city, faces in the windows, carnival time, a cheer rising—for him, for him!—and then he was coming up for air and there was a woman right there beside him, flesh to flesh, arm to arm, thigh to thigh, and she was exquisite, insuperable, soft and hard at the same time, and he was feeling her, running his hands over her, and she was feeling him and she parted her lips and found his tongue and he went diving all over again.

There came a point when he found himself alone on the couch. He was fully dressed, his tie still knotted, his wallet in his left front pocket, the car keys in his right. The candles had burned down to stubs. There were shapes scattered about the room, people there still—or some of them—but no one was moving. He was thirsty suddenly and so he pushed himself up through all the whirling lariats of color and made his way to the kitchen, where the light blinded him as if it weren't a sixty-watt bulb but a klieg light fixed overhead. He couldn't find a glass and so for a long while he just ran the faucet over his cupped palms and bent to drink, until finally—the waves receding—he heard a sound behind him and turned round to see Suzie there, Tim's daughter, in a pair of flannel pajamas decorated with the figures of ponies and cowboys and prickling green cactus. She said, "Oh, hi," and went sleepily to the cabinet to extract a glass, pour it full of clean white milk and shuffle back out of the room. He returned her greeting—"Hi"—but she was no longer there.

Sometime later—minutes, hours?—he made his way out the front door, into his car and down the street that took him to another street and another until he was home.

When he woke in the morning, Joanie and Corey had already left. The house was utterly still, the curtains drawn and the sun just barely making the faintest inroads. He was wrapped up in a tangle of sheets and a comforter that smelled of Joanie's perfume—or no, the Noxzema she used to remove her makeup—and the instant he opened his eyes, he knew everything there was to know. Joanie, far from being angry, or demonstrating it anyway, had evidently tiptoed around him in the morning, and Corey, his model son, had gone his way without thumping around the living room and slamming the outside door behind him. There would have been dialogue, sotto voce: "Is Dad still asleep?" "Shhh, yes, he had that meeting last night." Of course, when he'd finally got in it was past four in the morning, but he'd been stealthy about it, barely breathing, and who was to say he hadn't come in at ten or eleven? Not from the meeting, which had been over by five-thirty, but the post-meeting, which—and the words were already forming on his lips—was really a kind of ad hoc strategizing session because the idiots in the Psych Department were all but shutting down the Psilocybin Project, can you believe it?

He had cold cereal for breakfast—Corey's Froot Loops, which were 97 percent sugar and stuck to his teeth—and a cup of warmed-over coffee Joanie had left behind. Maybe he was a bit tired, a bit sleep deprived, but he felt fine, better than fine—energized all over again. His trip had been glorious, heaven, all the heights, and only temporarily infested with what Charlie had begun calling "downers," or negative thoughts and associations. He'd felt exceptionally close to Fanchon, and that was certainly a help, though he was fairly certain that whatever had passed between them fell into the category of mutual stimulation, of kissing—making out—and not anything more involved than that. Though really, all that was hazy, the least part of the experience, and there was no reason to mention it when he gave Joanie his rundown of the evening, which she was sure to demand when she got home. He spooned up the cereal, sipped the coffee. Unfortunately, he saw by the clock built into the stove that he'd missed his ten o'clock class, but if he got himself moving—and he felt chockful of energy suddenly—he'd make his noon class easily.

He dressed in a hurry, grabbed his briefcase and stepped out on the porch in a rising inferno of light, the sun somehow positioned perfectly to blind him though he turned his head aside and shaded his eyes as he went down the stairs and headed up the street to the bus stop. Joanie had the car weekdays because there was free parking for her at the library and her hours were more demanding than his, which was fine with him. She put in a lot of hours, never refusing overtime, and if it weren't for her income—and what they'd put away for school the previous few years—he'd never have been able to afford the luxury of being a full-time student. He pictured her then, in her work clothes—skirt, blouse, flats, maybe a scarf or pin to lend a little color—and he saw the library too, hushed, reeking of floor wax, dust motes hanging in the air, and for an instant, just an instant, understood how dull her life must be, but then, gazing out the window as the bus lurched toward the next corner, he noticed a Rexall wedged between a shoe store and a diner and on an impulse pulled the cord and got out.

The sun was blinding. It wasn't especially warm, forties maybe, with a breeze, but the sun seemed intolerable, blazing down on him as if it were mid-July instead of mid-March. Just inside the door of the drugstore was a rack of sunglasses, a miniature oblong mirror set in it at eye level. The first pair he tried on—Ray-Bans, with metal frames and teardrop lenses—made him look vaguely insectoid, and clearly that wouldn't do. Plus, even under the weak illumination of the fluorescent lights, he could see that they made no provision for light coming in from the sides, only the front. Wraparounds, that's what he needed. And the next pair he tried on—Polaroids, black plastic, *all* black—made the world go away. He wore them up to the counter to pay. And when he stepped outside, out on the street with its rush of bicyclists and pedestrians and the metallic glint of the passing cars, the sun really wasn't a problem anymore.

6.

He stayed home that weekend, though Tim was holding the usual Saturday night session—just two days after the graduation party, as they were all calling it now—and he spent most of it catching up on his work. If he felt any guilt about Thursday night it was only because he hadn't exactly been forthcoming with Joanie, giving her a blow-by-blow account of the faculty meeting and all the high drama it involved, yes, but glossing over the details of its aftermath at Tim's, particularly—and most damningly—the fact that he'd taken the drug without her, the new drug, the one that was remaking him even now. He told her about the martinis and the pizza and how vital it had been for him to be there because the whole future of the project was at stake and by extension his place in it and the first stirrings of an idea that had come to him for a psilocybin study that might fall somewhere between Tim's prison work and Walter Pahnke's upcoming experiment with the divinity students. Saturday night they ate macaroni and cheese and watched *Gunsmoke* together and on Sunday afternoon they took a picnic lunch to the park and he played catch with Corey, who, though his loyalties lay with the Yankees still, was skyrocketing with excitement over the upcoming baseball season and the prospect of seeing the Red Sox at Fenway. All he could talk about was Frank Malzone and Carl Yastrzemski and how they were going to smash homer after homer and really challenge the Yankees—and wasn't that something, Dad, wasn't it?

Already he was so used to the dark glasses that when Joanie kidded him about them—her bare legs stretched out before her on the blanket, bologna sandwich in one hand, bottle of Bud in the other—he had to reach up and feel the frames to know whether they were there or not. "Jesus," she said, laughing, "you're really a member of the club now. Or gang. It's a gang, isn't it, like in *West Side Story,* us against them? Jets and Sharks, right?"

"Right," he said, picturing the actors circling each other and waving their knives. "And we're the Jets because the rest of the department, McClelland and Kellard and the rest, they're Sharks. Definitely Sharks."

Corey was a hundred yards off, a moving shadow flinging the ball up as high as he could and then running to catch it, over and over. The sun was a steady presence, promise of the season to come. There were birds, squirrels, children, couples with picnic baskets and transistor radios.

"You ought to get a pair for yourself," he said. "You're part of the gang now too."

"Absolutely," she said, raising a hand to shade her eyes. "I really do need something to hide behind."

"I'm not hiding," he protested, swiping the glasses from his face and immediately regretting it. He felt as if he'd just stepped out of a closet.

"Speaking of which," she said, drawing her knees up to her chin and at the same time reaching down to slip off her sandals, "shouldn't there be another session coming up?" She paused to rub the bridge of one foot, looked beyond him to where Corey was chasing after the ball, then dropped her hand and raised her eyes to his. "If we're part of the gang now, shouldn't we act like it?"

They went to Tim's the next three Saturdays in a row. There was no hesitation, no awkwardness—as soon as they stepped in the door they felt a sense of belonging, of *rightness,* that superseded everything. This was where they were meant to be and these people, the inner circle—the gang—were their closest friends on earth because they shared in a communion no one else, least of all the stiffs in the Psych Department, could begin to imagine. And if their weekday routine was dull the Saturday night get-togethers let them blow off steam—and more, much more, to open their minds to all of creation, to get loose, go deep, inject a little adventure into their lives. Joanie needed it even more than he did. And he'd held out on her, which only made him feel bad, as if he'd betrayed her, and he hadn't, or not that he could remember.

Joanie was outgoing, creative, bright, as bright as anybody he knew—probably, IQ-wise, brighter than he was—and she needed more engagement with life than sitting in a gloomy back room typing out cards for the catalog and filing the same books on the same shelves day after day, as she'd let him know on a regular basis over the course of the winter ("Christ, Fitz, work bores me to tears, you know that?"). He hadn't wanted to hear it—better for him if she just put her head down and brought in the paycheck until he got his degree—but he could see that now in a way he couldn't before, as if the drug had opened his eyes. She'd been a mother since she was nineteen and motherhood didn't allow for much sowing of wild oats or even social life. And, of course, he'd been in the same boat, forced to grow up the instant she came to him at the beginning of their sophomore year and told him she was pregnant. It was life lived in the traces, nose to the grindstone, everything in abeyance till the goal was achieved. That was why they went to Tim's, that was why they were there week after week, stepping across the threshold into a new life that made the old one seem like so much worn carpeting.

Tim wasn't there the second weekend—he was in New York with the other blonde, Peggy, who aside from being beautiful was heiress to some sort of staggering fortune, the rumor of which had just begun to sift down to the inner circle—but the session went on without him, Dick and Hollingshead presiding. It was an act of defiance really, since not only had the department slapped their hands and shackled the project, but the press had got hold of the story, which was reported first in the *Harvard Crimson* and then jumped to the *Boston Herald,* a disaster all the way around. The *Herald* was the worst sort of rag, interested only in selling copies and distorting the truth, and the headline it ran—HALLUCINATION DRUG FOUGHT AT HARVARD, 350 STUDENTS TAKE PILLS—was not only inflammatory but inaccurate and an embarrassment for the department and the university. Tim laughed it off. Dick got angry. People began to look over their shoulders, but the sessions went on.

And while Tim might not have been there that weekend, Maynard Ferguson dropped by, along with his wife, Flora Lu, and her pet monkey. The monkey—a rhesus macaque, same as the ones used in research—had a rhinestone collar and a little leash and she dosed it with a few grains of psilocybin and called it Thelonious Monkey. Which would have been a bit much—excessive, really—but for the fact that she was one of the most stunning women Fitz had ever laid eyes on, a celebrity's wife who traveled in celebrity circles, leagues ahead of Joanie or Fanchon or practically anybody else, and it was a certifiable fact that whatever a stunning woman did or said was intrinsically fascinating. And right. And correct. And inarguable.

The trips—three trips, three weeks running—were as powerful and transformative as the ones that had come before, though God remained elusive, at least for him, even if He did play a prominent role in Charlie's and Alice's experiences, and to hear her talk of it in the aftermath, Flora Lu's as well. For her part, Joanie seemed to negotiate her own trips with equanimity, never experiencing any strong negative reactions (Charlie was calling them "freak-outs" now, a whole new vocabulary replacing the standard Freudian lexicon) and if she climbed the heights or embraced the Light, she kept it to herself. And there was no sex, both of them gone so far inward their bodies were no more than afterthoughts. Husks, just husks.

"So what was it like for you?" he asked her after the second Saturday, the one on which the monkey tripped with them.

"I don't know," she said, "it's hard to put into words."

"Ineffable, right?"

She smiled, a soft compression of her lips. "Isn't that the whole point?"

There was no session scheduled for the fourth week, though by now Tim wasn't so much presiding as participating and on any given day someone at the Homer Street house would likely be tripping, so Saturdays didn't hold quite the significance they formerly had, at least not for the members of the inner circle. In this case, though, the Saturday party was upstaged because of Walter Pahnke's Good Friday experiment, for which Fitz intended to live up to his promise to serve as a guide though Joanie had been unhappy about it when he'd first mentioned it to her and was just as unhappy now. There were two complicating factors. The first was that Joanie (who hadn't, thankfully, found out about his post-meeting trip and the essential part Fanchon had played in it) was becoming increasingly possessive over the drug experience and resentful of anyone's excluding her. The second was that the experiment, by design and of necessity, excluded her. It was science, he kept telling her, it was controlled, academic, a study, and she wasn't a grad student and she wasn't a prof and, as he'd told her from the beginning, this would involve males exclusively. Which, of course, only made the situation worse.

"What've you got against females?"

"Nothing."

"Aren't there any women in the seminary?"

"Apparently not."

"All right. Great. Then you tell Walter—and whoever, *Tim*—that when they want to do a double-blind psilocybin experiment on librarians, I'm their girl. Or woman. I'm a woman, aren't I?"

"Yes," he said, "all woman, a hundred percent," and he'd tried to take her in his arms but she pushed him away.

The day of the experiment—Good Friday—dawned clear, though a chance of rain was predicted for later in the day. It was balmy. It was spring. The air was dense with the scent of flowers, and the animal world, from pigeons to squirrels to house sparrows and the ducks and geese on the river, was busy processing hormonal urges in a flurry of wings and blurred paws. Which didn't mean a whole lot to Fitz, who'd had to put up with Joanie's silence at breakfast and actually left the house half an hour early just to get away from her incinerating gaze. He sniffed the air, registered springtime, slammed into the car and shot up the street, irritated by the fact that the muffler seemed to have developed another perforation and the gas tank was all but empty.

Everyone had agreed to meet at ten A.M. at the Andover Seminary in Newton Center, not far from Tim's, where the ten guides and twenty theology students would be given identical envelopes containing a powder that was either a 30-milligram dose of psilocybin or a like dose of nicotinic acid. Each envelope was stamped with a code number, and no one, not even Pahnke himself, knew which contained the drug and which the placebo. Just before noon, once the drug had had a chance to come on, they would all be driven to Marsh Chapel on the B.U. campus for the Good Friday mass featuring a sermon by Reverend Howard Thurman, the thesis being that those under the influence of the psychotropic drug would be more likely to have a religious experience than would the control group, with the further implication that divine states—religious ecstasy— could be achieved chemically, just as Tim theorized and a number of the inner circle had begun to discover for themselves.

Though it was Walter's experiment, it was Tim who greeted him at the door (and Tim who'd obtained the drugs, sidestepping the department's new strictures and churning through his ever-widening circle of acquaintances till finally a psychiatrist in Worcester supplied him at the last minute). Fitz greeted Ken, Charlie, Dick, Hollingshead and the other guides, then went round to each of the Andover students, most of whom were younger than he and understandably a bit ambivalent as to what to expect, and said a word or two of encouragement, feeling very much the veteran. Which in itself was odd. He'd had all of six trips while Tim had had well over two hundred and Hollingshead—who knew how many he'd taken? Still, he *was* experienced, on a whole other plane of consciousness from these students, who were, after all, to borrow a phrase from Tim, squares.

Walter and Tim passed round the envelopes, Walter recording the number of the envelope beside each name, then everyone dissolved the contents in water, and after a brief prayer, ritually drained the glasses and settled in to wait for the effects to take hold. Half an hour later Fitz began to feel a familiar stirring or buzzing, as if his body were hooked up to an electric current, but he couldn't be sure yet whether this was the effect of the drug or the placebo. He'd been seated on a bench in the back of the room with Ken, talking, of all things, about baseball (Ken was a Sox fan and convinced the team was going to have a mediocre season; he himself didn't have much to say about it except that his hometown Yankees were the ordained power and Ken should just get used it), when all at once he felt restless and got up to pace round the room. His skin began to prickle. He felt hot, so hot in fact that he pushed through the door and went out into the fresh air, depressed all of a sudden because the overheating and prickling were indications that he'd got the nicotinic acid when what he wanted—what he'd been craving, he realized—was the real thing. If he was going to give up his morning and afternoon in a good cause—and this was an eminently good cause, not just for science or Tim or Walter or the project, but for him too, as a participant, as a *guide*—then he figured he might as well enjoy the experience.

He was standing there on the lawn in the shade of an oak glistening with minuscule new leaves when all at once the leaves turned to scales and the oak wasn't an oak but one of the dinosaurs from Wells's fantasy and he knew he'd got the real thing. It was only a glimpse—the tree was a tree again—but it made him laugh aloud. He was at the beginning of a journey, just strapping himself in, and now there were the colors too, so intense he had to reach for his sunglasses, which didn't help at all. He was wondering about that, enjoying himself by pushing the sunglasses up and down the bridge of his nose, now you see it, now you don't, when he heard a voice call out behind him and turned round to see Tim standing just outside the door of the seminary. "Hey, Fitz, time to go," Tim said, and here was the whole group filing out the door and into the cars parked along the street.

Was he okay to drive? Nobody asked, the presumption being that half the drivers would be feeling the effects and half wouldn't—and at this juncture no one could tell the difference. He climbed into his car along with Ken and the four students whose trips the two of them would be responsible for monitoring and though Ken didn't say anything about any subject other than baseball the whole way over, Fitz could see that he too was one of the lucky ones. As for the students, he'd forgotten their names the minute he'd been introduced to them, and they all seemed to look alike too, but for the one in the middle of the backseat whose eyes were like black sinkholes and who seemed strung together with wire, everything tightened to the breaking point, even the navy-blue tie he wore like a noose. *Okay.*

Here we go. The car knew the way, the drug subsided and rose again in a roil of foaming waves, Ken talked of nothing but Yastrzemski and the students, clutching their Bibles, never said a word.

F or evident reasons, Walter had arranged for their group to be sep-
arated from the Good Friday churchgoers, who would be seated in the main chapel in the presence of Reverend Thurman, while they would have the smaller basement chapel to themselves, the sermon to be piped down through the loudspeakers in the corners of the room. They arrived in a convoy of six cars and parked in the spaces reserved for them. Fitz pulled up to the curb with a blast of exhaust and shut down the engine, his shoulders squeezed between the door and the student who'd sat up front with him and Ken. "Well, here we are," he said, stating the obvious.

In the next moment the doors gaped open and the students climbed out, squinting against the sunlight, while up and down the line, the guides clapped on their dark glasses. He had to smile: this was called *experience* and if Professor Kellard were here he would have told him as much. What do we gain from experiments? Knowl-edge. What's the opposite of innocence? Experience. Simplest thing in the world, Professor. Meanwhile, they were out in the full blast of the sun and everyone's shadow stood upright as they milled around, trying to gather themselves, and the congregation—all those women in bonnets and pearls, the men in their dark suits and the children polished like apples—climbed the steps to the main chapel and the air grew fulsome with the downward drift of perfume.

They were following Walter and Tim up these same steps, with the difference being that they would descend to the basement im-mediately on passing through the main doors, when Fitz caught sight of Walter's wife and daughter picnicking on a bench in the stippled shade of a tree not a hundred feet away, and that made him think of Joanie. Here was Walter's wife and his little girl on hand to wait out the experiment and no doubt join in the festivities afterward at Tim's while Joanie was stuck at home, brooding. And what were her plans for the day? She hadn't said. Hadn't said anything, in fact.

A dank odor rose to his nostrils as he followed Walter and the students down into the basement chapel, a big spacious room that featured a single stained-glass window and a statue of Jesus holding an open Bible with the legend AND YE SHALL KNOW THE TRUTH AND THE TRUTH SHALL SET YOU FREE inscribed beneath it. There were pews, an organ, icons of one saint or another. Someone had set a vase of flowers on the altar and he could smell them now, lilies, Easter lilies, a scent to drive down the smell of mold and the Clorox used to combat it. The students shuffled in and took seats, a few of them making a feint at genuflecting and crossing themselves. Most were utterly calm—they were divinity students, after all, and this was their natural habitat—but a few, including his charge in the navy-blue tie, seemed agitated, jerking their necks around and darting their eyes to and fro, as if seeing things the others weren't. *All right,* he said to himself even as the statue of Jesus began shape-shifting before him, *I'll have to keep an eye on that one.*

The service began on the stroke of the hour with a distant organ roll and a disembodied female singing in a dragged-down lugubrious contralto that was like a heavy dose of codeine cough syrup, and then the music faded away and the reverend came in with his basso profundo that sent up corresponding vibrations in the long boards of the pews. It was a voice you felt first in your buttocks and thighs and then in your gut and finally in the space between yours ears, each word offered up like a hymn in itself. Fitz did his best to resist it—he was a scientist, not a worshipper, and while Walter and his students might have been susceptible to all this calculated claptrap, he wasn't, not at all. Or so he told himself.

The reverend intoned the old Bible stories, Jesus and his temptation by the devil—*Be gone, Satan! For it is written, "You shall worship the Lord your God and Him only shall you serve"*—and slowly worked his way through the Easter passion to his thundering climactic injunction to *Go out in the world and tell everyone you meet, "There's a man, a man on the cross!"* All of which would have been fine—it was nothing to him whether the statue of Jesus came to life over and over and the organ sounded and Thurman's voice dug in and clung to him like a parasite—except that the student with the blue tie, the one he and Ken had especially to watch, was on his feet now, waving his arms and delivering a counter-sermon in a language he seemed to be inventing on the spot.

All right. Clearly, he was one of those who'd gotten the drug, and so was this other one two pews up—one of Charlie's wards—who rose suddenly, stared wildly round him and charged the altar, halting ten feet from the statue of Christ and flinging something (which later was discovered to be his dental retainer) at Jesus himself, whether as an offering or an act of violent discord no one could say. Another student went to the organ and began playing spontaneously while Tim, who as it turned out, had gotten the nicotinic acid, gestured to his guides to let him go because whatever he did, short of harming himself or someone else, was all part of the experiment.

Time drifted. Fitz felt himself sinking into a state he didn't like at all, a nightmare of childhood, the Roman church, his mother, her veil, the priests like twitching beetles with their crosses and their censers and stoles and chasubles and tall peaked beetles' hats, and he wouldn't believe, he wouldn't, he couldn't, the trip turning sour on him now until suddenly the agitated student in the blue tie, who'd gone round trying all the doors, finally found one the janitor had neglected to lock, and in a blinding flash of light vanished into the world outside. It was a shock. Had he seen what he'd seen? A quick count of heads—no Blue-Tie. Suddenly Fitz was on his feet and moving, though the colors came at him like an assault and he couldn't even begin to shut them down, and where was Ken, why wasn't he tracking this guy, this pilgrim, who was clearly having a severe reaction to the drug and was outside now, out on the street where he could climb a tree or walk into traffic or get himself arrested? In the next moment he was out the door himself, groping for his sunglasses and scanning the pavement, which gave onto Commonwealth Avenue and a mad flashing hurtle of traffic.

Everything Tim had worked for, everything he'd worked for himself, was at risk—this was a crisis and make no mistake about it. If the student came to harm—got hurt, got *killed*—the newspapers would have a field day, HARVARD DRUG FATALITY; HARVARD EXPERIMENT GONE WRONG; DRUGGED STUDENT RUN DOWN BY BUS. He looked but didn't see. Big block letters clung to the lenses of his sunglasses. He smelled newsprint. And blood, blood too. His mind jerked itself away and snapped back again.

But where was the guy? There, walking briskly up the sidewalk to some destination only he could fathom. In the next moment Fitz broke into a trot—he had to catch him, had to stop him—and at the same time he spotted Eva Pahnke, where she was sitting with her daughter still, reading to her from a children's book with a cover that caught the light and flashed it back at him as if it were a signal from some unknown realm, something deep, some deep message he had no time for now, and he shouted out to her to go get Walter and pointed frantically at the wavering form of the pilgrim in the blue tie, who'd halted now to look around him as if to get his bearings. And where was he going, this pilgrim? Right out into traffic, right there, gliding between two parked vehicles and . . . suddenly Fitz had him by the arm and the student swung round on him with a look of outrage. "Hands off!" he shrieked, jerking away and flinging himself back up the sidewalk. "There's a man!" he shouted. "A man on the cross!"

Fitz was in no condition. Yes, as he was discovering, it *was* possible to fight down the drug in an extreme case, an emergency like this one, but set and setting had gone radically wrong, and this guy, Blue-Tie, the pilgrim with the mad staring eyes and the limbs made of wire, was plunging him down into the depths of a very bad trip, the worst. He was in a panic. He could see the very air he was breathing and it wasn't air at all but the blue fire of a blowtorch. "Wait up!" he shouted.

The pilgrim, not running, but walking stiff-legged, moving along like a competitor in the Olympic event, suddenly swung right—away from the traffic, thank the Lord—and up the steps and through the door of B.U.'s School of Theology, as if that was what he'd been looking for all along. Fitz caught up to him on the second floor and for lack of a better plan snatched him by the arm again, and again the man swung round on him, crying out as if he'd been stabbed. The problem—the further problem—was that the building was populated. That was what buildings were for—to be populated. And now, accordingly, there were people up and down the hall peering out their doors. Someone—a man with a face like a raised axe—barked, "What's going on here?"

It was then, everything scrambled and no sense at all to anything whatsoever, that Walter arrived, hustling down the hallway, his black bag in hand. "It's all right," he said to the faces gaping from the doorways, "I'm a medical doctor," and in the next moment he had hold of the pilgrim's other arm and he was cooing to him in the most soothing and reasonable tones. "Julius," he cooed, drawing out the syllables, "it's me, Walter. Everything's all right, everything's fine. Shhhh!"

Julius tried to pull away, but the two of them held fast. "There's a man," he said, his eyes black and staring. "A, a man—"

"It's all right," Walter whispered. "I know."

"But, but"—looking now to Fitz—"what about him?"

"He knows too."

That seemed to satisfy him and things might have settled down right there with no need for further intervention, but for the fact that the mailman happened to come down the hall at that moment, a registered letter for delivery to the main office clutched in one hand. As he passed by, Julius suddenly jerked his arm out of Fitz's grasp

and snatched the letter away, which the postman, with a look of in-
credulity, tried to snatch back, tug-of-war. Julius, still staring, still
tense as wire, began making a keening noise in the back of his throat
and then he was swinging wildly in place, the letter clutched in one
hand, even as the postman—middle-aged, graying sideburns, startled eyes—held fast to his end. What ensued was a wrestling match,
three against one, but even so the outcome was in doubt because
Julius was in a panic, and the panic flooded his veins with adrenaline, giving him all but superhuman strength. He grunted and spun
and held fiercely to the letter, shouting "A man on the cross!" even
as the three of them finally managed to wrestle him to the floor and
Walter, no choice in the matter now, plied his syringe.

After the service, which stretched out over the course of three
and a half hours, they all climbed back into their cars and
drove to Tim's house, feeling exhilarated. The experiment had been
a success—they'd pulled it off—despite Julius's breakdown and the
fact that it was immediately apparent to everyone just who had gotten the drug and who the placebo. No matter. The first public experiment with psilocybin had gone off with barely a hitch and the
students who'd received the drug were radiant with God, gushing
enthusiasm, their eyes on fire, eager—burning—to get their experiences down on paper. All except for Julius, who never uttered a word,
sitting as before in the middle of the backseat, his tie still rigidly
aligned but his eyes unfocused and his shoulders slumped, no doubt
an effect of the Thorazine. Fitz, his own trip waning, made a mental
note to ask Walter about that, not only how Thorazine worked physi-
ologically but also neurologically. Would it erase God or the Devil or
whatever Julius had seen? Or would it consolidate it, would it make
the vision concrete, a block of perception that could be kept intact or
shattered and removed like a bad tooth?

Eva Pahnke and her daughter, a child of three or four in pigtails and a pink dress, were waiting for them, along with Alice, Peggy, Suzie and Flora Lu and her monkey, the grill on the back patio already sending up a powerful gland-clenching aroma of hamburgers and hot dogs. Tim handed out beers, stirred up a pitcher of martinis. Dick was aglow. And Walter—Walter was the star of the moment, his thesis all but written and the degree all but bestowed, and so what if he looked like Maynard Ferguson, who was off somewhere with his band, Fitz forgave him that. He felt aglow himself, the crisis averted, his bad trip blooming into something ecstatic in the moment, not God, not a drug high, just grace and light and the deepest penetrating love for everybody present, everybody in the world, even Kellard and Mortenson, the fools, the poor deluded fools . . .

He drank a beer, then another. In his hand, a hot dog bun, split down the middle like a woman's private parts, and here was Suzie, her eyes tearing from the smoke, taking up the tongs and laying the phallic frankfurter right in the slot created for it, then heaping up the chopped onions and piccalilli relish to smother it and chase the image away. Elated, he compared notes with Charlie, with Tim and Dick and the students themselves, moving easily from one group to another, the sun a sacred glowing disk in the sky and the air as sweet and fresh as if it had been created on the spot. The only casualty was Julius, sitting slumped in a lawn chair at the edge of the patio, his eyes vacant and hair mussed, an untouched soda clutched in one hand and his shoes untied, as if he'd tried to get them off and given up. But what was one compared to all the rest? Counting the guides, fifteen had gotten the dose, and only one had broken down (though admittedly the one who'd flung his retainer at the statue might have gone through a rough patch or two). Par for the course? Worth the risk? Yes. Sure. Of course. They'd all gone through it, they'd all suffered, but they'd gloried too—and so would Julius, if given another chance.

He was standing there with Charlie, jabbering on about anything that came into his head while Charlie jabbered right back, feeling unconquerable, feeling like Superman, when an unseen hand took hold of his earlobe and gave it a twist and he swung round on Flora Lu and the monkey perched on her shoulder. The monkey was grinning—or showing its teeth, in any case—and Flora Lu, in a tight red dress and a shade of lipstick to match, pursed her lips as if she were going to blow him a kiss and said, "Don't mind Thelonious—he just likes to make human contact, that's all. Or monkey contact, I mean. Or monkey-human." She turned her face to the monkey, their noses inches apart, and crooned in falsetto, "Doesn't he, naughty monkey? Huh? Huh?"

Charlie—was he leering at her?—said, "Hey, it's only natural. Who doesn't want a little contact?"

They both looked to him now and he said, "You won't get any argument from me." He was watching her, the huge liquid eyes and high cheekbones that were like Audrey Hepburn's, and saw that her eyes were dilated and wondered if she were off on a private trip—and if so, how she could possibly tolerate the brightness of the sun.

As if reading his thoughts, she lifted her sunglasses—which she'd been holding casually in the hand braced against one hip—and fitted them to her face, where they gave back his own reflection for all of five seconds before the monkey snatched them away, bit down on them inquisitively and flung them into the bushes. "Craziest thing, he likes to see my eyes, can you imagine?" She blinked rapidly. "I must go through five pairs a week."

He was about to say he didn't blame the monkey or some such, to compliment her, flirt with her, when out of nowhere she asked, "Where's Joanie?"

"Home," he said. "With Corey—our son?"

"No," she said, "I mean now."

He was puzzled. He looked to Charlie, then back to her again. The monkey was no longer grinning, but it was still perched on her shoulder, toying with a strand of her hair, its legs dangling and its testicles on display. "Home," he repeated.

Flora Lu let out a laugh. "Then she must have sprouted wings, because I was just talking with her and Fanchon not five minutes ago—in the house?"

"Really?" he said, trying to cover his surprise. "I thought, well, I didn't realize—would you excuse me a minute?"

He crossed the patio to the back door and eased in past a scrum of divinity students with sodas in their hands—and Dick, with a beer, who was chatting them up—and went on into the deserted living room, which now featured mandalas on all four walls and even one on the ceiling. There were the familiar chairs and sofas, a scatter of pillows and blankets in the corners. Dirty glasses, dirty dishes, ashtrays crammed with butts, apple cores and walnut shells. If Joanie was here, where was she? And who was watching Corey? He had an impulse to call out her name, but resisted it, feeling foolish.

Just then the front door flung open and Jackie came hurtling in, a perpetual motion machine, and he saw with a jolt that Corey was with him, right on his heels, both of them already charging up the stairs, Jackie ignoring him and Corey throwing a quick greeting over one shoulder—"Hi, Dad!"—before vanishing round the corner on the second floor. He felt something then he couldn't have described, the faintest drawing-down of the exhilaration that had guided him back from the service, back from what Tim was already dubbing "the Miracle at Marsh Chapel," and he didn't know why exactly. It was just the surprise, that was all. Joanie was here. And Corey.

Well, all right. It was a cookout, wasn't it? And it was high time Corey got to know Jackie and Suzie—and Tim too, for that matter. But how had she gotten here—the bus? He was picturing it—she and Corey studying the route map, mounting the steel steps, sliding into the worn vinyl seat and pulling the cord at the intersection of Homer and whatever the cross street was—when he looked up and there she was at the top of the stairs. Fanchon was right behind her, just closing the door of her room, and as they started down the stairs together he could see that they were both high, giggling and making an elaborate game of holding on to each other as if they were afraid of falling, which would have been the most hilarious thing they could imagine, falling like that, teasing out the principles of gravity, cause and effect, body mass and flexibility. Fanchon was in a dress and heels, Joanie in pedal pushers and a yellow blouse he didn't recognize, her lipstick dulled and her hair in need of brushing.

He wanted to say something witty and breezy to show how unsurprised he was, how happy that she was here, but when they reached the bottom of the stairs, both of them grinning like clowns, all he could say was, "Hi."

Joanie's eyes focused on him, then went wide. "We, Corey and I . . ." she began and trailed off.

"You took the bus?"

This was hilarious, both of them breaking down in giggles, laughing so hard they had to hold on to each other all over again, and that was somehow sexy and disturbing at the same time because Joanie was his wife and Fanchon wasn't and now his wife was tripping— obviously tripping—without him. And worse: he was coming down, *had* come down, and she was just taking off. A thought he'd entertained more times than he could count flew in and out of his head: he wanted to see Fanchon naked. Or no, he wanted to fuck Fanchon.

"No, no, no," Fanchon said through a new storm of giggles, "I have picked her up. So she can, you know, *join* the party. After all"— and here she gave him an unreadable look, all mobile mouth and overblown eyes—"it is only fair, no? While the husband's away, the wife will play. Or does play—isn't that it? Does play?"

"What about Corey?"

Joanie put her lips together, then drew them apart. She was looking right through him. "He's fine," she said vaguely and held a hand up in front of her face as if she could see the image of their son playing across it. There was a burst of laughter from the patio, the barking of a dog. This was a party, a celebration, and he had to remind himself of that. Joanie was tripping and he wasn't, or not anymore, and he would take care of her if anything happened, that went without saying, but he couldn't help wondering what it would be like to trip again on the dregs of the chapel trip, to soar right back up there, soar even higher on the LSD Joanie was on as if he were lighting one cigarette off another.

But no, he told himself. He had work to do, a degree to flag. And Corey was here, seeing whatever there was to see. No, he had to straighten out, take charge. Somebody had to do it.

On the way home in the car, the windows black and the headlights as rigid as if they were fastened like boards on a catwalk running all the way to the apartment, Corey, in the backseat, kept up a nonstop disquisition on every subject that came into his head— *Those were the best hamburgers I ever had; Can you believe Jackie doesn't like baseball, doesn't even root for a team?; They've got more comic books than any kids I've ever seen, and not just* Superman *and* Donald Duck *but* Classics Illustrated *and* Mad Magazine *and everything else because there's this used comics store on, I think, Brattle Street, and everything's a nickel*—but Joanie was unresponsive. She was having a bad time. Not as bad as Julius, maybe, or not as violent, but bad just the same, her teeth gritted and her eyes wild, and she kept uttering little cries and whimpers. Corey talked around her—she never said *Uh-huh* or *That's nice* but just stared out the window—and Fitz tried to assuage him with elaborate (and heartily false) responses until finally he just put the radio on and tuned it to the baseball game.

Later, after Joanie had gone in to lie down, he asked Corey if he was hungry, but Corey said he wasn't.

"Do you want a story, then?" They were on to *The Invisible Man* now and Corey couldn't seem to get enough of it, pestering him each night for just one more chapter. Corey liked to envision himself having his way with the world, and who could blame him? Wasn't that the story's appeal? You want to watch women undress? Go right ahead. You want to slap your enemies with impunity? Get rich? Steal? Eat anything you want?

Corey was sunk into the couch. It was nine-thirty at night on Good Friday, the long weekend and Easter break only just begun. He glanced up from the pile of comics he'd brought back with him from Tim's. "Nah," he said, "I don't think so."

Fitz found himself feeling jittery suddenly and he couldn't have said why, whether it was an aftereffect of the drug or the result of too much of everything, so he went to the cabinet and poured himself an Irish whiskey, no ice, just for the taste of it, a luxury he rarely allowed himself. After a minute he came back into the room, settled into the easy chair with his drink and picked up the newspaper. There was a listing of Good Friday services, now all over with, at the top of the back page, and as he scanned the column, whatever he'd been feeling—this post-trip malaise, Corey, Joanie, Tim, the shock of Julius breaking madly for the street, Fanchon—began to dissipate and everything became usual again. He was home. Joanie was in bed. The paper felt heavy in his hands. It was past Corey's bedtime.

"Dad?" Corey was looking over the cover of his comic—Batman, with his black mask and bat's ears.

"What?"

"What's wrong with Mom?"

"Nothing. She'll be fine. She just—well, I think she had maybe one beer too many and that made her sleepy. You know how that is—remember your grandpa that time?"

Corey didn't say anything, but he didn't go back to his comic either. After a minute he lifted both his feet to the coffee table, which he wasn't allowed to do, and set the comic aside. He seemed to be grinning—or maybe it was a grimace. The tightest smile, and then a pucker of the lips. "That's not what Jackie said."

After Corey had gone to bed, he went in to check on her. The room was cold, unnaturally cold, and it took him a minute to realize the window was open—not just cracked, but open all the way on the night and the two-story drop to the yard below, where the moon drew shadows from the trees and silvered the lids of the garbage cans lined up against the fence. He didn't want to turn the light on, leery of waking her (or if she was awake still, of startling her, because when he'd checked half an hour earlier she'd been lying there rigid, staring at the ceiling), so he tiptoed to the window and eased it shut. That was when he glanced over his shoulder and saw with a shock that the bed was empty. His first thought was that she must be in the bathroom, but he'd just been in the bathroom himself, brushing his teeth, and he'd gone directly from there into the bedroom, so how could that be? A tic of fear pulsed in his temple: he should have seen her through this, he realized that now, but he'd been thinking of Corey, of shielding him, of propping up the pretense that nothing was out of order.

But where was she? He stood there dumbly, staring out into the yard and the puddles of shadow that could have been anything, Corey's bicycle, a wheelbarrow, the sprawled form of a human being—a female human being—lying there as still as death. He called her name softly, almost involuntarily—"Joanie?"—then went to the light switch and flicked it on. The room was empty. She wasn't in the bed, wasn't sitting in the armchair in the corner she liked to heap with her clothes and nest in when he and Corey were in the living room watching baseball, wasn't—he jerked open the door—in the closet either. "Joanie?" he repeated and held his breath until the faintest moan came back to him in response, as if she'd dematerialized or shrunk down and crawled into the space between the walls.

He found her under the bed. Trembling. And when he took hold of her as gently as he could and tried to coax her out, she wouldn't come. He was on his hands and knees, peering into the gap beneath

the bed that was curtained all around with the satiny sheen of the
bedspread and smelled of dust, of dust and her, crooning to her in his
best imitation of Tim: "It's all right, it's okay, I'm here, don't fight it,
just give in, Joanie, give in . . . You hear me? Joanie?"

It seemed to take forever, as if they were a thousand miles apart,
but he kept on whispering and crooning and drawing her out of
herself until finally she said, "Fitz?," and he said, "Yes."

And then he slid her free and had her in his arms and he was pressing her down into the bed with the weight of his body, just holding
her. He wasn't aroused, or not at first, but she was—oh, yes, she
certainly was.

7.

Things began to cool down after that. It was as if they'd reached some sort of meridian, halftime in the game they were playing, the game to neutralize all games, as Tim would say, the only game that wasn't a game at all. Work had begun to pile up. There were end-of-term exams, both for Fitz and his students. Joanie was busy too. One of her coworkers came down sick with something that might or might not have been pleurisy and Joanie covered for her, picking up still more hours, which was a good thing because they were undecided about what to do for the summer—stay and pay rent or go to the Jersey shore with her parents—and the extra money would come in handy either way. They kept away from Tim's the next two Saturdays and that was all right too because the rest of the group was feeling the same end-of-term pressures he was and because Tim had decamped with Dick and Peggy for an exploratory trip to Mexico, with the intention of finding a place where he could set up a summer research project, with or without Harvard's blessing.

The Yankees came to town the second week of May and he took Corey to see them play. Despite a powerful lineup featuring Mantle, Maris, Berra, Skowron and Howard, the Yankees were crushed, 14-4, and Carl Yastrzemski was the hero for Boston, with a home run and three RBIs, which seemed to suit Corey just fine. They had hot dogs, Cokes, peanuts and ice cream, and Corey, who'd brought his mitt along, almost caught a foul ball that wound up coming down in the row just behind them, where a loudmouthed clown with a beer belly reached over Corey to catch it barehanded. Not that it mattered. What mattered was that he'd gotten a chance to spend time with his son, special time without Joanie, who'd begged off on the grounds that she didn't really care all that much about baseball and it would only be wasted on her. Which was just fine with both of them—it was a men's thing anyway, wasn't it? And after that night at Tim's, he found himself trying to reach out more to his son, not that he felt guilty, or not exactly—it was just that the research was all about interiority, and interiority by its very definition was exclusive, selfish even. You could take your son to the ballpark, but you couldn't take him inside your head.

Tim came back with a suntan and a two-month lease on the Hotel Catalina in Zihuatanejo, an isolated spot north of Acapulco on Mexico's west coast. Fitz had to look it up in the atlas at the library and then, wasting time when he should have been studying, he found an old *National Geographic* article illustrated with photos of scalloped white beaches, coconut palms and a scatter of beach huts roofed with palm fronds—*palapas*—running up and down the shore just above the tide line. A fishing village—that was what the article called it. Very remote, very tranquil. The fishermen came in each evening to sell their catch and people gathered there by the shore, drinking beer, strumming guitars, grilling shrimp and lobster over an open fire. He'd never been to the tropics, never even been to Florida, and he couldn't help lingering over the pictures, wondering what it would be like to walk those beaches to the sound of monkeys and parrots in the trees, to swim, snorkel, lie there on a towel and watch the sun vanish in the sea while sipping a—what?—rum and Coke. Or no, a margarita—wasn't that what they drank down there?

He gave Tim exactly two days to reacclimate and then stopped by his office after classes on Tuesday, coming up the stairs to the strains of a radio playing bossa nova—Stan Getz and Charlie Byrd, the hottest thing going—and voices, the usual voices, raised in merriment. Tim, who'd missed a week of classes and should have been contrite about it or at least pretending to be, wasn't holding office hours—he was holding a party. Fitz smelled Fanchon's perfume before he rounded the corner and saw her sitting there cross-legged on the floor in a pair of shorts and a yellow blouse identical to the one Joanie had been wearing at the Good Friday party. Which meant Joanie must have borrowed it for some reason—dressing up? Trying on clothes as if she and Fanchon were sorority sisters? Or maybe Joanie had spilled something on her own blouse, maybe that was it. Or—and here a sudden image of Joanie and Fanchon, naked and locked together, kissing, grinding, flitted in and out of his head.

Fanchon glanced up. She had a bottle of beer in one hand, a paper cup in the other. "It's Fitz," she cried out, "and not a minute too soon!" The shorts were very short. She was wearing sandals, as if it were mid-summer, and she'd painted her toenails. "Look who's here," she called, leaning into the interior of the office on one arm so that her near thigh rose at an angle from the linoleum, the flesh reddened where it had been pressed to the floor.

Ken was there, as was Charlie, sans Alice, and Rick Roberts too, but no Dick and no Hollingshead, which was a surprise, but the biggest surprise was Tim. He looked, as usual, as if he'd just stepped out of an ad in a men's fashion magazine, with one exception: he was wearing a sombrero, a great towering elaborate thing with a brim the size of an extra-large pizza trimmed with bright blue balls of thread. The effect was—well, ridiculous—but this was a joke, this was Tim in high spirits, reveling in thumbing his nose at everything academic, everything Harvard. He was a Mexican now, and as he would soon announce, he was bored with the science game because the science game was too confining and had no place in it for pure experience.

What else? There was a bottle of tequila on the desk, along with a cutting board, some wedges of lime and a salt shaker. A Styrofoam cooler containing ice and bristling with the amber necks of beer bottles sat on the floor beside Tim's chair.

"Fitz," Tim said, "well met. We were just wondering where you were." He gestured at the desk, tipped back his sombrero. "We're getting acquainted with Mexico tonight, Fitz—you ever been there? No? Well, no matter. We're having a little tequila party here in honor of the lease I signed last week on this hotel, eighteen rooms cooled by the sea breeze, and right on the ocean. Very isolated. No roads—you have to fly in, Fitz, can you imagine that? And the manager, the most admirable Swiss in the world, is letting us have it all summer because summer is his slow season in any case and he'd just as soon see us set up our research project there as have the place sit empty. You see what I'm saying?"

Fitz was standing just inside the door, trying his best not to step on Fanchon's white, white thigh or the place where her calf was tucked under it. He was grinning. Everybody was grinning. He gestured at Tim's sombrero and said the first thing that came into his head. "So you're going native now?"

"Damn right I am." Tim stood, a bit uncertain on his feet, and poured a double shot of the tequila into one of the waxed paper cups on his desk and handed it to him. "You know how this is done?"

He didn't. He'd never tasted tequila, barely knew it existed. Before he'd gotten serious about life, when he'd been living with Joanie and his infant son in a little dump of a town on the Hudson River and doing a less-than-credible imitation of a school psychologist, it had been well-brandy and a beer back, and if he felt adventurous maybe a screwdriver. He lifted the cup to his nostrils and took a tentative sniff. The odor was strangely soapy, as if this wasn't liquor at all but a concentration of the stuff the janitors put in the dispensers in the men's room.

"Don't be afraid of it, Fitz, it's not going to bite you—but wait, here, this is how you do it."

He watched as Tim poured salt on the webbing of his left hand, licked it off, drained his own cup and bit into a lime wedge. "Woo!" Tim hooted, his eyes watering, "that's the ticket!"

Everyone was watching, loopy grins on their faces. "You ready, amigo?" Tim asked, already pouring, which mooted the question. Fitz hadn't planned on drinking anything—it was midweek, he was behind in his work and he'd only stopped by to welcome Tim home and hear the gossip, the gist of which had already reached him in bastardized form—but he poured the salt all the same, licked it off, threw back the liquor and sucked the juice out of a wedge of lime as if he'd been doing it all his life.

"Pancho Villa!" Rick Roberts crowed. He was perched on the filing cabinet in Hollingshead's spot. He was drunk, his collar open and tie askew. "Remember the Alamo!" he added, then broke down in giggles.

Ken was slumped in the chair beside the desk, a frozen grin on his face, and Charlie sat on the floor at his feet, cradling a beer. "Badges?" Charlie said. "We don't need no stinking badges," and then Ken lifted his eyes to the ceiling and started singing "*La cucaracha, la cucaracha, / Ya no puede caminar,*" and everybody—even Fitz, though he was shy about it—joined in, "*Porque no tiene, porque le falta / Marijuana que fumar!*"

There was another round of tequila and then Tim hushed everybody and said, "All right, let's get serious here a minute, because this is a commitment we're making—we've already made—and I want to know who's on for this." He paused, looked pointedly at Fitz. "And who's not."

Tim went into his spiel then, selling the place like a real estate agent, rhapsodizing over the weather, the sun, the crystalline sea that was warm as a bath and completely untouched so that the snorkeling

was as good as you could find anywhere in the world. He was talking
to the room, but kept breaking off to address him directly. ("Have
you been snorkeling, Fitz, really snorkeling? And I don't mean in
the ice tank off Martha's Vineyard, because the fish, the colors, the
shapes, the whole thing down there is a trip in itself, believe me.")
He talked about what they could achieve too, free of constraints, free
to vary dosages and just lie back and trip as often as they wanted in
order to see if they could attain a kind of group consciousness like the
communards in Huxley's new novel ("*Island,* Fitz—have you read it?
No? Read it. Now. Tonight") who developed higher powers through
the use of moksha, a kind of next-generation psychedelic.

The sombrero shaded his face, but his teeth gleamed in the grip
of his closer's smile. After a while, it became apparent that not only
had the others already heard Tim's appeal but had come to a decision, all of them, Ken and Fanchon, Charlie and Rick—and presumably Charlie's and Rick's wives and kids too. They were going
to Mexico for summer vacation. They were going to live an idyll
right out of a Huxley novel. And further the research into the bar-
gain.

Ten minutes later, Tim seemed finally to run out of breath—or
change tactics. He leaned into the desk, poured more tequila all
around—for Fitz too, even though he tried to put a hand over his cup
and say no—and then he raised his cup to propose a toast before apparently thinking better of it. "Wait, wait," he said, the thread balls
writhing and dancing under the brim of his hat. "We can't really
toast the summer camp until we have unanimity here. Right? What
do you say, Fitz?"

He wasn't caught by surprise because he could see all along where
this was going and he didn't draw back because what he was hearing
was irresistible and so very, very right. To hell with the Jersey Shore
and the way Joanie's father looked at him as if he were a form of
light entertainment ("Psychology? Don't you have to be certifiable to

study that?"). Mexico was a shining dream. The whole inner circle was going. How could he say no? How could he even think of it? But then, even as everybody's eyes fixed on him and Tim held the cup at half-mast, he thought of finances—reality, that is. "But," he stammered, "I'd like to—nothing I'd rather do. I'm flattered, I am, but we can't afford—I mean, the whole summer?"

Of course, Tim had anticipated this too. "All you have to do is get there, Fitz—the rest, room and board, three meals a day—is only fourteen-forty per diem. It's Mexico, Fitz, cheap as dirt. And if you can't afford that"—a wink for the room—"there's always the IFIF scholarship."

"The what?"

"The International Federation for Internal Freedom. Dick and I are founding it—for obvious reasons. The science game is falling short and we're not going to be held back by it any longer. But the point is, Peggy's rich—she and her twin brothers are heirs to the Mellon fortune—and if you didn't know, Dick's from a well-to-do family too. We'll underwrite you, Fitz—you'll be the first scholarship recipient, what do you say to that?"

"Come on, Fitz," Fanchon purred, canting her head to look up at him. "It will not be the same without you."

"But Joanie—her job?"

"Fitz, Fitz, Fitz," Tim said, shaking his head in a whirl of little blue balls, "you are just too rigid—"

"Uptight," Charlie put in.

"Which is all right, I'm not criticizing," Tim said, "but a library job? Joanie's worth ten times more than that and I'll bet you anything she'll get whatever she wants in the fall, I mean *whatever*, so you really have no grounds to stand on here, amigo. None at all."

Tim lifted his cup and Charlie, Ken, Fanchon and Rick followed suit. "To Mexico!" he cried, and Fitz, riding a sudden swell of joy that sank the library, his cramped apartment and the psych building from sight as if the pellucid waves had already closed over them, raised his too.

He was a bit foggy the next morning—and he had a headache, the first tequila headache of his life, which, he noted dully, was a novelty in itself—but he woke to a vision of frothing surf, white beaches and a sun parked overhead. Joanie was already up—he could hear her in the kitchen, rattling the pot she soft-boiled her morning eggs in, then padding across the floor to slip into Corey's room and whisper him awake. Some mornings, depending on her mood, she rattled out, "You gotta get up, you gotta get up, you gotta get up in the morning!" as her waking anthem, but today she just whispered, as if to spare them all.

She'd been asleep by the time he got in, so he hadn't had a chance to broach the subject of Mexico to her, though in the car on the way back from the bar they'd all retired to after Tim shut up his office, he'd begun to marshal his arguments. He hadn't been in much of a condition to drive, but he drove anyway, talking aloud to himself the whole way home on the dark familiar streets, foreseeing and countering Joanie's objections in the way Tim had countered his own. The fact was, it wasn't going to cost anything, or hardly anything, and it would be good for them all, for Corey especially—he could see a new part of the world and maybe even pick up the language, which would be a real advantage in school. Weren't they offering Spanish now? Wasn't it taking over from French and German? Wasn't it the language of the future?

She was reading the newspaper she'd propped up on the napkin holder and hovering over her eggs when he came into the room (runny eggs, with flecks of partially cooked albumen in a mucilaginous goop that very nearly made his stomach turn), but he managed to right himself, call out a soft "Good morning" and go to the stove for a cup of coffee. Her hair was damp still from the shower, her face smooth and pale without her makeup. It was a relaxed face, pretty, the most familiar face in the world to him, a face at the kitchen table at the very center of his life. To see her there like that, her ordinary self, struck him with a force that took him by surprise, and he felt a surge of sentimentality, of love, rush through him. Of course she'd want to go to Mexico—why wouldn't she? She could see her mother anytime—and the smell of that place on the Jersey Shore, the mold, the damp, everything clammy even in August . . .

Before he could think, he said, "Tim rented a whole hotel down in Mexico. Right on the ocean. For the summer. The entire summer."

She lifted her eyebrows, held the fork suspended over the plate. "Really? A whole hotel? Isn't that overdoing it a bit?"

"Not just for him—for everybody. He's calling it his summer camp, but you know Tim—he likes to make a joke out of everything. Actually, it's going to be for conducting research without having to worry about any limitations Harvard or McClelland or anybody else might impose. Think about it: there couldn't be any better setting and set too, no schedules, the beach, the sun? Everybody's going."

"What are you saying? You're not thinking—?"

"It won't cost anything—less, actually, than staying here. Peggy's underwriting it so all we have to do is get there and the rest—room and board, three meals a day, prepared by the hotel staff—is all free. Tim says he'll give me a scholarship. What do you think?"

Her face, sans makeup, showed the nicks and creases of time, the fine striations at the corners of her eyes, a pale rectangular scar pressed into her cheekbone and another just under her left ear, souvenirs of her girlhood in upstate New York. She grimaced and it all flattened in the light through the kitchen window. "I think you're nuts," she said. "What about my job? What about the apartment? What about *Corey*?"

And now he called up the lines he'd rehearsed in his head, how the experience would broaden Corey's perspective and contribute to his language skills, how Rick Roberts was bringing his two kids and Royce Eggers too—he had three, didn't he? And Tim's kids, of course. It would be like a mobile classroom, really. And fun—a real summer break, for once.

"What about my mother?"

"We'll see her when we get back. And we'll go to the shore next year, okay, I promise—it's not as if we haven't been there every summer for as long as anybody can remember . . . but don't you see, this is the chance of a lifetime."

She looked dubious. Looked the way she had when he'd applied to Harvard, when they'd pulled up their roots in New York and moved here towing a trailer behind the car, and it wasn't as if she was trying to hold him back—she wasn't like that, not at all—just that she was cautious. And so was he. More cautious, really, than she was. And he'd already made up his mind.

"What about the car?" she said. "It's a long trip, isn't it? How many miles—thousands? And you really mean we're going to accept charity from whoever—Peggy Hitchcock? That's one thing we've always agreed on, right—never be beholden to anybody?"

He waved her objections away. "You're just making excuses. We could take the train, put the furniture in storage, anything—if there's a will, there's a way." He was watching her, the fork poised, the eggs congealing, each successive thought sparking in her eyes till he could see Mexico taking shape there, palm trees, beaches, margaritas.

Her voice was small, ruminative. "I don't want to be beholden."

"So don't be. We can pay our own way." He was standing at the sink, sipping coffee, his headache dissolving on the ascent of the caffeine. "Though even at fourteen-forty a day it'd be a stretch, I admit it—but we'll save on rent. And groceries. And what, utilities?"

She shrugged. Gave him a smile. Then she deliberately set the fork down across the plate as if eggs didn't matter anymore or breakfast either or work or anything else. "So maybe being beholden isn't so bad after all, is that what you're saying? And Tim did say it was a scholarship, right?" She paused, her lips pursed round the tip of her tongue as she worked out the fine gradations of the ethics involved. "A scholarship's different," she said. "It's legitimate. It's something you earn—and you've earned it, right?"

"Oh, *sí*," he said. "*Sí, sí, señora. Claro que sí.*"

As the spring semester drew to a close, Tim was in constant motion, teaching, advising, floating a prospectus for the International Federation for Internal Freedom and planning for the summer institute in Zihuatanejo, all the while continuing to conduct weekly sessions at the house on Homer Street, which was looking the worse for wear, it seemed, every time Fitz and Joanie stepped through the door. Fanchon, apparently, wasn't much of a housekeeper, nor was Hollingshead or Ken or anyone else living there aside from Dick, who did his best to bring order to chaos, but with the traffic and the parties and so many people seeking internal freedom at the same time, it was a thankless task. Suzie helped. She was dutiful, driven, trying her best to please her father and be accommodating to the adults, and she always seemed to be trooping through one room or another with a private smile and a tray of dirty dishes and glasses. Jackie stayed out of sight, appearing only to gaze into the refrigerator from time to time or make his way through the torrent of pizza that poured into the house most nights. He got a dog—or Tim got him a dog—a mutt with floppy ears and Airedale whiskers that just seemed to add to the confusion. It was always darting between somebody's legs and it didn't seem especially interested in doing its business out on the lawn when there were so many much more convenient carpets spread throughout the house.

Tim's plan was to fly down to Zihuatanejo a week in advance of everybody else by way of getting established and making arrangements with the staff, who would stay on through the summer, though the manager himself—the admirable Swiss—would be gone, taking a busman's holiday at an inn in Gstaad or some such place. One morning, a few days before Tim was set to leave, Fitz came in to find a note from him in his departmental box. On a sheet of notepaper, folded once, Tim had scrawled, *Pls come to my office, 4:30, need ask favor,* and then added, in a looping hand, underlined twice, *Mexico.*

It had been raining all day, the air dense and tropical, the sidewalks strewn with earthworms giving themselves up to ecstasy—or trying to keep from drowning. He stepped round them, careful not to track anything in on his shoes, and started up the familiar stairs of the psych building. Fitz could hear the ding and rattle of Tim's typewriter as he came striding down the hall, rhythmically rapping his still-dripping umbrella against one calf and floating so high on the euphoria that set in each year at the end of the semester he actually found himself whistling. Summer break. Was there a happier term in the dictionary? He'd been going to school in one capacity or another since kindergarten and no matter how long the slog or how dreary the year, summer was always there before him like a shining promise.

He remembered one year—he must have been ten or so, younger than Corey anyway—when he spent the first morning of summer vacation playing ball with a dozen kids from the development, then went off into the woods by himself to sit up in the crotch of a tree, wash down his peanut butter and jelly sandwich with a Coke from the service station and indulge in a little philosophy. The morning might have been gone, he remembered thinking, but it was just the first in a long succession that stretched so far into the future he couldn't really wrap his mind around it. He was safe, he was free, it was summer. Right: And where had that summer gone? And all the rest of them too? He broke off in mid-whistle and laughed aloud. He'd have to tell Corey about it, because there was a lesson there, though Corey wouldn't get it, couldn't get it, he supposed—not till he was in his thirties too.

The door was open, but Tim was so absorbed he didn't even turn round when Fitz knocked. The keys tapped, a cigarette fumed in the

ashtray. From down the hallway came the odd sound of a door creaking open, footsteps, indistinct voices. Fitz knocked again, a bit more
sharply this time, and all at once the strangest thing happened: Tim
seemed to blur into a geometric array of neon colors and then refor-
mulate himself like a deck of shuffled cards. It took him a moment
to realize he was having a flashback, as Charlie and Tim called the
experience, a brief neural replay of a moment randomly selected from
a previous trip, nothing to worry about, nothing more than a trompe
l'oeil of the mind, and he wouldn't even have remarked it except that
it was his first. When Tim finally did turn around, the first thing Fitz
said was, "Weird."

The automatic smile, the laughing eyes, the hair grown ever so
slightly longer so that it didn't really qualify as a crew cut anymore
but more the kind of shag Maynard Ferguson favored. Tim. In his
glory. Smiling. "What's weird?"

"I think I just had a flashback, if that's what you call it."

"Welcome to the club," Tim said, opening his mouth in a yawn
and locking his fingers to stretch his arms before him. "It's an interesting phenomenon, isn't it? You know what it says to me? It says it's
time to dive in again—when's the last time you had a session?"

"Two weeks, three, I don't know. I've been so busy with school—
and packing—I've barely had time to come up for air."

"Tell me about it—it's an ordeal, isn't it? But you're all set, right?"

He was. Or nearly. Since their lease was up the first of August, he
and Joanie had arranged to put the furniture in storage—and they
were close to settling on a new place for September. Joanie had given
notice at work. He'd brought the car in for servicing—tune-up, oil
change, lube, radiator flush—and sprung for four new tires, or almost new. Charlie gave him a well-worn road atlas and Joanie found
an ice chest at a yard sale so they could take sandwiches and drinks
with them and not have to stop if they didn't want to. As soon as he
closed out the semester and Corey finished school, they were off.

He hadn't let himself dwell on it—there was too much to do—

but Mexico was never far from his thoughts, nirvana glowing on the horizon of the too-familiar campus and the dripping trees. Joanie was right there with him, poring over every guidebook she could find ("You realize how cheap everything is down there, Fitz? Those embroidered dresses and the cute white peasant blouses with the blue trim, the beadwork, silver, turquoise, all of it?"). And Corey—Corey was lit up like a rocket—he couldn't stop talking about the beach, about snorkeling and diving and whether or not they'd have Aqua-Lungs down there and all the fish he was going to spear, dorado and amberjacks and snappers and triggerfish, and who else was going, Jackie and the Roberts twins and who again?

"Yeah," he said, "I think so."

"All right," Tim said, "good, good, good. Have a seat, why don't you?"

He sat, propped the umbrella up against the desk. "I'm really looking forward to this," he said. "Mexico, I mean."

"You don't know the half of it, Fitz—this is going to be the biggest adventure of your life, of all our lives, and we're really going to have a chance to assess the potential of these chemicals, not simply for clinical use but for mind expansion. Do you believe in group consciousness—I mean, that it's possible?"

"Truthfully? I don't know."

Tim let out a laugh. "Always the scientist, right? But we're going to find out, Fitz, that's for sure. Now, I wonder if you wouldn't mind doing me a little favor?"

A little favor? Tim could have asked him anything—sprint to Mexico and back, jump out the window, strangle McClelland, Kellard and Mortenson in their sleep—and he would have done it without question. "Sure," he said, "what is it?"

"It's the house. It's gotten a bit out of hand, really, and Professor Sokoloff's coming back from sabbatical next week and I won't be here to give him the key because I'll be down in Zihuatanejo—setting things up for everybody. You understand? I'm going to need someone to deal with that. Oh, Ken and Fanchon are going to tidy up, but they've got to be in Connecticut for his sister's wedding and my kids aren't going to be there—they'll be staying with Royce Eggers and his wife till they fly down first week of July, so you see my predicament?"

"Sure," he heard himself say, "sure, I'll take care of it. No problem."

From the outside, the house looked fine. It really was impressive, a three-story Georgian revival mansion crowning a hill with a series of stone steps leading up from the street. The lawn was ragged and there were branches and leaves scattered across the expanse of it, but the shrubs were in bloom and the flowers in the neglected beds were pushing through the weeds to lend a little color and scent the air. Inside, it was different. The house held the chill of the night and the pervasive odor was of the cold ash that lay six inches deep in the fireplaces—that and the urine the dog had been so conscientious about depositing on the carpets. And something else too—was that marijuana or just the stale reek of cigarettes? Cigarettes, he decided as he pulled the door shut behind him, because Tim forbade marijuana on the premises, for the very good reason that marijuana was illegal and the last thing he needed—any of them needed—was to give the police a reason to come knocking at the door.

Fitz remembered one session when Tim's New York contingent was there, Maynard and Flora Lu and a couple of others, along with a few of the subsidiaries and hangers-on who were increasingly showing up to make the scene, as they called it, and a beatnik in beard and beret with a bota bag slung over one shoulder extracted a marijuana cigarette from his shirt pocket, casually lit it and began puffing away. Fitz had never seen Tim so angry—had never seen him angry at all, actually. In any case, Tim snatched the thing right out of the man's mouth, flung it into the fireplace and read him the riot act. Which really didn't help as far as mind-set was concerned, or at least not for that particular individual. But Tim was right—psilocybin was legal, LSD was legal, but marijuana was not.

The professor, who was driving up from New York, was due in the late afternoon, which really didn't give Fitz a whole lot of time to try to make things presentable, and he kicked himself for not getting there sooner. It was a Saturday, just past noon, and he'd spent the morning dealing with his own exponentially multiplying obligations, taking Corey to Little League practice, making a run to the storage unit with a bunch of odds and ends—crap—stuffed in boxes, scrubbing stains out of the sink and toilet with an eye to getting his deposit back at the end of the month. That was something he could exert some control over, but Tim's place was a disaster. Worst of all were the mandalas, which could only be painted over—either that or all the paneling would have to be stripped and refinished, and how could he hope to accomplish that short of waving a magic wand? As much as he owed Tim—and he owed him everything at this juncture—it really wasn't his problem. His problem was to pitch in as best he could, haul trash, sweep up, vacuum—air the place out, for Christsake. Whatever came next was between Tim and Professor Sokoloff, who was going to be keeping the deposit no matter what, that was for sure.

He was in the kitchen with a sponge and a can of Ajax, working on deglutinizing the burners on the stove, when he heard a dull thump behind him and turned round to see the professor himself in the doorway, jerking his fists up and down and kicking the wall with one of his heavy black brogans. The professor—he was an expert in Soviet law, as it turned out, and just off the boat after a year in Moscow—looked to be in his forties, clean-shaven, tall and fit, with a pair of Trotskyite glasses pinched over the bridge of his nose. Fitz had never laid eyes on him before. In fact, he was so far removed from all this he'd still been back in New York, in Beacon, wrapping up the school year when the professor had set sail for Leningrad. "You!" the professor snapped. "Who in hell are you?"

"I'm, well, I'm—" Fitz began, momentarily at a loss. He had a bucket in one hand, sponge in the other, and his scalp was prickling as if he'd just stepped out of the shower. He wanted to itch it, but his hands were encased in wet rubber gloves—grease-smeared wet rubber gloves—and so he compressed his neck and rubbed the back of his head against his collar, which was dirty. Everything about him was dirty. "A student," he said finally.

"A student!" the professor threw back at him as if it were the most preposterous designation in the English language and a lie and a calumny to boot. "Of whom, I'd like to know—Leary? *Dr.* Leary? The man I—*entrusted*—this house to?" He kicked the wall once more with a dull booming vibration that rattled all the way down the kitchen counter and into the cracked and mounded dishes on the drainboard. "Where is he? I demand to see him this minute!"

"He's not here, he's—in Mexico. And he asked me to give you the key?" He stripped off one glove and began digging in his front pocket until he retrieved the dull brass key and held it up in evidence.

A woman had appeared beside the professor now, elegant, mid-thirties, wearing a fur coat though it was summer. Her eyes were full, her makeup runneled with tears. "Oh, my sweet Jesus," she wailed. "This is beyond outrageous, it's, it's—*vandalism.*" She turned to her husband, who hadn't taken his eyes off Fitz, not for a second. "Marty, who is this, what's going on?"

And now the son came into the picture, a child of five or six who wore a version of his father's face and looked as if he'd just been thrust into a lifeboat as the ship went down. He seemed to be crying too, caught up in the emotional storm of whatever he imagined was going on here, and Fitz had a fleeting vision of the room at the top of the stairs where he'd gone so deep with Joanie that first night—hadn't there been children's posters on the walls? A teddy bear on the shelf? *Dick and Jane?*

The professor had come right up to him now. "Don't you try to pass that off on me!" he shouted. "Don't you dare!" And with a sudden jerk he slapped the key from Fitz's hand so that it went clattering across the floor, the only sound in that vast reverberating echo chamber of a house.

For a long moment, nobody said anything. The professor glared, the wife suppressed a sob, the child bowed his head as if he were the one being chastised, and they all looked to the key, where it had come to rest against the grill of the refrigerator. If Fitz was anything, he was dutiful. He paid his debts, got his work in on time, stood as a comfort and support for his wife and son and gave loyalty where loyalty was due. But this was too much—he didn't have to take this. He stripped off the other glove, dropped the sponge in the bucket atop the stove, turned his back on the professor and strode out of the room.

But the professor wasn't done, not yet. He caught up to Fitz as he was heading for the front door, his voice gone high in his throat, shouting, "The walls, what *is* this on the walls?"

Fitz swung round on him, calculating—he'd had enough, but the professor outweighed him and had the force of moral certainty on his side. Still, for all that, Fitz had been pushed to the limit. He was ready to take a punch for Tim, to give as good as he got come what may—expulsion, a broken jaw, a lawsuit—but in the end he just answered the question. "Mandalas," he said.

"Mandalas?" The professor's eyes jumped behind his glasses. His face twitched. His mouth hung open on a set of graying Soviet-patched teeth.

"Drug parties," the wife's voice keened in the background. "They had drug parties here, Marty, just like the Wheelers said—"

"Mandalas?" the professor repeated. "What in hell are mandalas?"

"India," he said. "Tibet. Look it up in the encyclopedia."

The professor was right there, right in his face. "Are you getting smart with me? Because if you're getting smart with me—" A breeze came up then, mercifully, to cool the sweat on Fitz's brow and under his arms, sweat he'd worked up for Tim—and for this man, this jerk he'd never seen before and would never see again. "I mean, do you have any idea what it's going to cost to, to—"

Fitz cut him off. "No," he said, "I don't. I told you, I'm just a student." And he turned and walked out the door and down the stone steps to where his car was waiting, thinking of one thing only: *Mexico*.

I t was overcast and muggy the day they finally stuffed the last of their things in the car, humping up and down the stairs like coolies, Fitz going back up six times alone to check if they'd left anything behind. "Aren't you glad now you never got that cat?" he said to Joanie as she settled into the front seat with the picnic hamper in her lap and Corey established himself in back with his comic books, baseball cards and the dollar and twenty-five cents' worth of Milky Ways, jawbreakers, candy buttons and red licorice sticks he'd been allowed to select at the corner store especially for the trip—and as a reward for his final report card, which was all A's and A minuses across the board. The reference was to the kitten Joanie had seen in the pet store window back in March and decided she couldn't live without, even attempting to enlist Corey on her side (who, to his credit, seemed indifferent to pets of any kind except tropical fish, his entire tank of which had gone belly up two weeks back because of some malfunction of the heater, which solved that problem). Fitz had talked her out of it, emphasizing the destructiveness of the animal's claws and the reek of the litter box—"You really want shit in a box under the sink with summer coming on? I mean, think of the flies alone."

Now she said, "We could have taken it to my mother's."

"Your mother's? I've got to clue you—we've got a five- or six-day drive ahead of us, if we really push it, and the last thing I want is to get hung up at your mother's house because you know she's going to talk us to death and insist we spend the night." He slid into the driver's seat and slammed the door, in high spirits, bringing up the cat only because it amused him to imagine it curled up in the lap of some other young housewife in another building in another neighborhood altogether. They were free. All the details, major and minor, had been settled, and if he'd forgotten anything it was too late now. "Mexico, here we come!" he cried, putting the car in gear and lurching away from the curb.

"What's wrong with visiting my mother?" she asked. "What if we did spend the night?—it'd save us on a motel room."

"No way." He gave her a smile, dodged round a fat man who suddenly flung open the door of a parked sedan and set one fat foot out on the pavement. "Didn't we say we need to make miles, drive straight through as long as we can stand it?"

"Sure," she said, crossing her legs and patting at her hair where the breeze through the open window whipped a loose strand across her lips. "I'm not disagreeing with you, Fitz. I want to get there as badly as you do—and Corey does too." She swiveled in her seat to face their son. "Right, honey?"

No answer from the backseat. Corey had his comics, comics he'd been hoarding for just this moment, and there was no distracting him, not yet anyway.

"I'm just saying," she went on, "it would be nice to see my mother, at least for a couple of hours, a pit stop, lunch, dinner, whatever—"

"We're going to Mexico," he said, "not Long Beach Island. *Mexico,* baby!" And he began singing "La Cucaracha," just as they all had that night in Tim's office, only altering the verse to drop the reference to marijuana because Corey was in the car and Corey had ears, comics or no. When he got to it, when he got to *"Porque no tiene, porque le falta / Marijuana que fumar,"* he substituted *"Dinero para caminar."* And then he turned to look over his shoulder and asked Corey if he knew what that meant and Corey said he didn't.

The car sailed on down the road, practically driving itself, and if a few spatters of rain began to tap at the windshield, what did it matter? They were on their way and there was no stopping them now.

"Money, Corey," he said. "The cockroach, he doesn't have the money to travel."

He let that ride a minute, the almost-new tires hissing now on the wet road and the traffic falling away behind them as he tapped the accelerator and felt the big V-8 engine surge beneath him. Then, thinking of Tim, thinking of Peggy, thinking of tamales and white sand beaches stretching as far as you could see and whatever else they had down there, he said, "But we do—we sure do."

PART II

Zihuatanejo/ Millbrook, 1962–1963

1.

The drive was an adventure, the adventure of her life, because she'd never been to the South or Texas or Mexico either, and they got through it with a minimum of trouble (if you except two blown tires and the six-hour delay in Hattiesburg, Mississippi, while a mechanic with an accent so thick he might as well have been speaking a foreign language replaced their water pump). She and Fitz took turns behind the wheel, with the intention of driving straight through so as to save on motels, one of them sleeping while the other drove in a fugue of radio static, blistering sun, inverted nights and sudden downpours, but in the end they wound up stopping twice out of sheer exhaustion—and for showers, merciful showers. When Corey wasn't buried in his comic books, he kept up a nonstop monologue about all the tropical fish he was going to catch in the jungle streams—firemouths, platys, swordtails—and all for free when they cost like fifty cents apiece in Boston—and snakes too. Did she know they had coral snakes in Mexico? With poison so potent it paralyzed your lungs so you couldn't breathe, which was like drowning on dry land? Neurotoxin, that was what it was called. And they had scorpions too, including one kind that was six inches long, and wasn't that cool?

It was. Just to see Corey so excited made everything cool, despite the heat that hammered them all the way down through the South and the Gulf Coast till half the time she was glued to the seat with her own sweat. Fitz was cool too, everything behind him now, exams, papers, his students, and when he wasn't fiddling with the radio or quoting *On the Road* ("I think of Dean Moriarty, I even think of old Dean Moriarty the father we never found") he was humming or singing off-key renditions of Johnny Hartman, Sinatra, Nina Simone, tapping out the rhythm on the steering wheel. Once they crossed the Mason-Dixon line, it was "Camptown Races" and "Dixie" and "Ol' Man River," and she joined in till the sound of their voices intertwined beat back the roar of the open windows. The road was blinding, mesmeric. Everything came at her in a blast of sensation, everything new every time she opened her eyes, and they didn't even think about the two doses of the sacrament Tim had pressed on them before he left because they didn't need them, or not yet, not till they got there.

They left the car at the airport in Monterrey, and no, they didn't have time for sightseeing, not even for the cathedral the guidebook was pushing or the limestone caves Corey was fixated on, because they were in a hurry now, a mad anticipatory rush to get to the Catalina Hotel—Tim's hotel—slip into their bathing suits, pick coconuts and just let go. The flight was on a Mexican air service nobody had ever heard of, but it was cheap, and if she had any reservations she just strapped herself in and swallowed them. There was the rattling dual-propeller airplane, the pilot who smiled through the heavy brush of his mustache as if this plane and this sky were the funniest things in the world, then the patchwork of the mountains and finally the dense green vision of Zihuatanejo and the blue transparency of the sea that hugged it close.

Ken was waiting for them on the dirt strip that served as an airfield, lounging in the driver's seat of the hotel's Jeep with a book in one hand and a beer in the other. He was tanned the color of a walnut and he'd let his crew cut grow out. The last time she'd seen him he was in chinos and a baby-blue button-down shirt, and now he was bare-chested, wearing nothing but his sunglasses, a pair of athletic shorts and the sandals they called huaraches, as if he'd already gone native. Which he had. They all had. And she and Fitz and Corey would too, just give them time, and wasn't that the whole point? As soon as the propellers stopped whirling and a pair of dark little men fixed the stairway in place, he sauntered across the field to greet them even as the door swung open and she was hit with a blast of heat that was like no heat she'd ever known, alien heat, Mexican heat that was propped up on a solid wall of sweetness and stench in equal proportions, jasmine, sewage, cookery, rot. Just to take a breath was a kind of synesthesia.

"Hey, amigo," he called out, taking Fitz by the hand and pulling him close for a back-thumping embrace. "*Bienvenidos a México*. This place is the real deal—paradise on earth, and you are going to love it, believe me." Then he turned to her and swept her up in his arms, whirling her around as if they were on ice skates. "Paradise," he kept saying in her ear, his breath like a hot salve, "really and truly and veritably!"

And then it was Corey's turn. Ken set her down and they were all grinning, everybody, even the Mexicans, and he held out his hand solemnly to Corey for a handshake. "And you know what else?" he asked, his voice riding up the register as if it could scarcely be believed, one marvel after another. "Richie caught a scorpion the size of a tamale last night. You know what a tamale is?"

Corey shook his head. "Like a *hot* tamale?"

"Yeah, exactly: a hot tamale."

"How big?"

Ken stretched out his hands as if he were approximating the length of a prize fish.

"You mean *Richard*?" Corey asked.

Ken shot her a look, still grinning. "Yeah, Richard—isn't that what I said?"

"You said 'Richie.'"

The smells seemed to intensify, reinforced now by the chemical assault of the airplane fuel. Richard was Ronald's twin brother and Corey's closest friend among the other children, and he was Richard, not Richie or Rick, as a way of distinguishing himself from his father, she supposed—and, given that, Ronald had had no chance of being Ronnie or Ron even if he'd wanted to.

Ken just smiled. "Same difference," he said, cuffing Corey lightly on the shoulder. "But listen"—his eyes found hers again, then Fitz's—"the important thing to remember is we've got a party to get started here, so where are your bags? And, oh yeah, as far as Spanish is concerned, the most significant term you're going to need to know in about, oh"—he checked his watch—"fifteen minutes, is 'margarita.' Can you say margarita?"

The hotel sat on a cliff above a crescent of beach and had been built in three rising tiers like a theater with balconies, so that all the rooms shared a view of the coconut palms and the thatched roofs of the beach huts and of the Pacific itself, which rolled on all the way to China in a blaze of roiling light. There was a pool, a bar, a courtyard of saltillo tile and a cable car down to the beach if you didn't want to negotiate the steps carved out of the dark volcanic rock—and you didn't, you definitely didn't, especially when you were tripping, the view from the cable car a whole trip in itself, as Charlie would say.

It was late in the afternoon when they arrived, the sun still fixed overhead because this was the tropics where it was hot year-round and the houseplants she'd known only as sickly stalks back in Boston could run riot, which was what amazed her most in those first few moments as they pulled up to the hotel: banana fronds broad

as shields, the jagged fingers of the palms, flowers sprouting everywhere, and the smells, the *smells*. No sewage here, no airplane fuel,
just a kind of saturate perfume that changed brands and scents every
ten steps you took. Ken, her suitcase in one hand, Fitz's in the other,
turned to her after he'd led them into the lobby and said, "Well, what
do you think? No worries about set and setting here, huh?"

She didn't know what to say. She was overwhelmed.

Behind her, one of the hotel staff, a teenager who didn't look to be
much older than Tommy Eggers, was helping Fitz and Corey with
the rest of their things, the light fracturing around them so it was as
if they were onstage in some fantastic play and she was here, in the
audience, trying to find the words to describe what she was feeling.
And then the words didn't matter because here came Fanchon in her
bikini, her skin glistening from the pool, to wrap her in her arms.

Within minutes she was in the pool herself, her clothes hastily
shucked in the room she'd barely had time to glance at (four walls,
double bed, ceiling fan, a cot for Corey), and everybody was gathered
round, the whole crew, laughing, chatting, smoking, drinking. They
might have been back at Tim's on a Saturday night, but for the pool
and the heat and the high hot Mexican sun. And the margaritas, an
example of which had magically appeared in her hand. Propping herself up on the coping of the pool, her hair gloriously wet and trailing
over her shoulders, her legs kicking lazily in the cool embrace of the
water, she sipped her exotic slushy drink that was sweet and tart all at
once, almost like a whiskey sour, only better, and when that one was
gone, there was another to replace it, and another, and before long
she was singing a ditty she made up on the spot, with a little help
from Carmen Miranda: "I'm Chiquita Margarita and I'm here to say,
margaritas are good for you in every way." And then Alice took it
up and Rick Roberts's wife, Paulette, and Susannah Eggers too and
they were all belting it out, making up the verses as they went along,
and what the hotel staff must have thought—or the kids, for that
matter—nobody really knew. Or cared.

At some point dinner was served poolside, a kind of fish and shrimp stew you sopped up with tortillas and washed down with cold Mexican beer. The talk, at least at first, was of the project, which was unconstrained now by any consideration other than pushing the boundaries to see what lay beyond them. They'd decided that people would rotate their trips so that on any given day a third of the group would be doing the sacrament, a third acting as guides, and the remaining third recuperating from the previous day's trip and writing up their experiences. There were thirty-three adults present that summer, meaning that on any given day ten or so would be tripping, and the lifeguard tower on the beach was reserved for those who wanted to withdraw from the scene and go deep with or without a guide. Climb up into the tower and it was yours, though most people preferred the *palapas* along the beach, where they could stretch out in the sand and feel the thump of the surf radiate through every fiber of their being, and wasn't that the true heartbeat of the earth?

"Your choice," Ken told her and Fitz. "Freedom, it's all about freedom."

And then Tim was there, wearing a pair of bathing trunks and nothing else because nothing else was needed. "Glad you kids could make it," he said. "Of course, if you'd got here last week like everybody else you'd have known all this already, because, really, we're making up the rules as we go along. But welcome to Freedom House."

Fitz, who was sitting on the tiles beside her chaise, his arms cradling his knees and a beer dangling from two fingers, grinned up at him. "IFIF, right?"

"Right. Internal freedom all the way."

"External too," Ken said, hovering over them with a margarita in one hand, a beer in the other, "because guess what—Kellard and Mortenson and all the rest of the drones are three thousand miles away."

"Where they belong," Fitz said.

Tim eased himself down on the patio, crossed his ankles and took a sip of his own margarita, of which there seemed to be a limitless supply. "I say good riddance. But really, can you imagine that stiff Mortenson in a bathing suit?"

"No way," Fanchon said. She was standing there beside her husband, her hip pressed to his, one arm draped round his waist and her hand casually inserted in the waistband of his trunks. "He is a real *limp dick*."

Everyone laughed at this, liberated now, not a care in the world, and what awaited them back at Harvard wasn't worth thinking about, not until this long paradisiacal summer played itself out and they all went deeper than they'd ever gone before, at which point it might not even matter anymore. She didn't have a job. She didn't have an apartment. What she had was this, the tropical night that trilled and resonated with the sounds of hidden things, magical things, frogs, cicadas, monkeys and the long sweet release of group laughter.

She thought of the pills then, the two pills Tim had given them for the trip down, and she leaned into Fitz and whispered, "You want to, you know, take the sacrament? Wouldn't that just cap things off, wouldn't it be great, I mean, our first night here?"

Fitz was leaning into the chaise, his back pressed to her bare legs, the flesh hot there, slick with sweat. He turned to her and she saw the way his mouth had gone slack at the corners, an indication he'd had too much to drink. The sun was setting now, the shadows thickening, and he reached up to slip off his sunglasses, his eyes floating there a moment, naked and unfocused. "Now? I mean, we just got here—"

Corey flitted across the patio then, chased by the Roberts kids and Nancy Eggers. Before they'd left Boston, Nancy had sent him a note in a scented pink envelope to tell him she liked him and was really looking forward to seeing him in Mexico, which was cute enough in its way, she supposed, but a kind of warning flag too. Nancy was developed, fully developed, an adult in teenager's clothing, and Corey

was a child still—he hadn't had his growth spurt (if he ever was going to have it, and that was a worry of hers, though Fitz dismissed it),
nor had his voice changed either. It was just a moment, the kids gone
as quickly as they'd appeared, replaced now by Brenda, Tim's girlfriend, who was making her way up from the pool, but it imparted
something to her she really didn't want to think about. She watched
Brenda cross the patio in her black spandex suit and wet flip-flops,
rotating her hips as if she were wearing heels, until she came up behind Tim and wrapped her arms around him in a way that made all
the men look up, Fitz included.

"Yes," she said. "Now. We waited all the way across the country—"

"Tomorrow," he said. "You heard Tim—everybody's on a schedule
here."

"I heard him," she said, and why did she feel so disappointed? She
could wait. It wasn't as if she needed the drug, not really, but the moment was perfect and it would enhance the experience, that was all
she was saying. "I also heard him say this wasn't the Catalina Hotel
anymore."

Fitz was slow on the uptake, even more saturated with tequila than
she was. "What do you mean?"

"I mean," she said, shifting her legs so she could get up from the
chair, find her way to the room and dig one of the smooth white pills
out of the bottle in the pocket of her suitcase, "this is *Freedom* House,
or didn't you hear?"

She tripped three times that first week, schedule or no schedule,
and the first two were seamless, Fanchon acting as her guide and
the visions coming so lucidly and in such a rush it was a kind of
ecstasy, Fanchon there for her the entire time, easing her along with
the tranquilizing touch of her fingers and the soft purr of her voice.
The third time she was on her own. Nobody knew she'd taken the

sacrament, or at least she hadn't told anyone, not even Fitz, and she'd weathered the blaze of the drug in one of the *palapas* on the beach, her body wedded to the sand, *become* the sand, fine grained and warm and eternal. Late in the afternoon, when she was coming down, she took the gondola back up to the hotel and sat out on the patio with a margarita while her friends' voices murmured around her and Dick's latest protégé, Martin Dugard, strummed his guitar and sang folk songs in a tremulous tenor that was as good as anything you'd hear on the radio (not that there was much on the dial down here beyond tinny Mexican music rattling through its endless verses like a carousel ride you couldn't get off of). Fitz wasn't there. He was up in their room, worrying over his notes and filling one lined yellow tablet after another in his graceful fluid hand. He'd been at it all week, trying to make his research congeal into a paper he could expand into a thesis that would pass muster and move him up the academic food chain, which was not to say he wasn't drinking as many margaritas as anybody else—and he'd tripped once, on schedule, with her and Charlie and Alice and some of the others—just that he was consecrating the daylight hours to his texts and charts and notes. She didn't mind—she had the sun and surf, the margaritas and the sacrament and the upwelling love of everybody there to sustain her.

Martin strummed his guitar. Pedro, the tame parrot with the clipped wings whose job it was to remind them all just what country they were in, waddled past, crying *"Disfrute!,"* whatever that meant, in his sandpaper voice. She was drifting still, as happy as she'd ever been, not really listening to Martin or the conversations rising and falling around her, when suddenly she was brought back to the moment by Fanchon, who let out a harsh choked cry that rearranged everything.

But what was it? Corey. Corey and Richard, trooping across the patio and dragging something behind them, something that might have been the branch of a tree weaving over the floor with a soft undulant swish and release. Only it wasn't a branch, it was . . . flesh, bleeding flesh, and the blood was scribbling its own message across the face of the tiles.

"Oh," Fanchon cried, "this is disgusting, is it dead?"

It took her a minute. She was coming down, yes, but this was a jolt, a hallucination in real time with scales and claws and teeth that made her heart seize. There was blood on her son's chest, his legs, his arms. "Mom," Corey was saying, "Mom, *look*!"

They were all on their feet now, except her—she was frozen there in the depths of the chaise, everything a horror all of a sudden, the blood, her son's face, Richard, who was showing his teeth in a grimace that was a smile, a killer's smile, and here was this animal the size of a beagle with an arrow thrust through the folds of its corrugated throat. She couldn't think. Couldn't speak. All she wanted was to be somewhere else.

"I killed it," Corey said. "With the bow and arrow from the hotel."

"What *is* it?" she heard herself ask, and it was as if she weren't even in control of her own voice.

"An iguana. A big iguana, the granddaddy of them all."

"*We* killed it," Richard corrected. He was shorter than Corey, squatter, with a sharp thrust of nose and two glittering eyes the color of pea soup. "I stabbed my knife right through its head." He held up the knife, rusted, chipped, brown with dried blood, in evidence.

"But why?" Alice asked in a thin voice. She was standing apart from the boys in a filmy Mexican wrap, the sun high over her and diminishing her shadow till all there was of it was a little puddle of shade no wider than her feet. She had a cigarette in one hand, a paperback book in the other. Her hair was piled up on her head, frizzy with the salt of the ocean that never seemed to wash out no matter how many showers you took.

"For meat," Richard said.

"Because it's dangerous," Corey said in the same moment, talking over him. "Look at its claws."

She looked. The thing was magnificently ugly, like a dragon, with a snake's slickness and a scaly beard and hackles down its back. And claws, the big hooks of its claws.

Corey abruptly dropped his end of the arrow, which had been thrust through the thing like a skewer, and that forced Richard to drop his end too, so that the carcass fell at their feet and Corey went on in a breathless rush to tell them all how he and Richard had gone up along the stream in the jungle out back, hoping to catch fish, when they'd seen the iguana clinging to a tree trunk and how lucky they were to have brought the bow and arrows along in case of snakes. "Wasn't that great?" he insisted, his voice leaping. "Wasn't that smart of us?"

Dick was there now, pushing through the circle gathered round her son, Martin at his side. Both of them were peeling across the back and shoulders and in a kind of scrim across their chests that looked like what was left behind when a tide pool dries up. "All right, then," he said, "let's give a shout for Carlos and have him make what, roast haunch of iguana? With a nice *salsa verde* and *patas fritas* on the side?"

Everybody laughed then and it was all right. If there was blood on the tiles, Carlos, chef and majordomo, could hose it off. Her son was fine, she was fine, they were all fine.

"Or what," Dick went on, "lizard tacos? Hey"—and he clapped his hands as if a light bulb had just gone on in his head—"anybody have a craving? I mean, get 'em while they're hot, ladies and gentlemen, your basic highly nutritious, supremely delicious and always-in-demand lizard tacos."

"Come on, Dick, that's disgusting," Alice said, squinting down the length of her cigarette.

"You think so? Tell it to the villagers around here. What about you, Corey? You want iguana tacos for dinner tonight?"

Her son flushed. His shorts were dirty, there was dried blood on his shins and his chest and arms were striated with a dozen cuts and scrapes she hoped weren't going to get infected, and maybe she should get up, maybe she should march him off to the room for a shower, or better yet, a bath. "Uh-uh," Corey said. "Shrimp."

"Or chicken?"

Corey shrugged. He was the center of attention, at least for the moment, at least until they all moved on and Carlos came out of the kitchen to clean up the mess. "I guess," he said.

"Okay, right," Dick said, "so we're just going to let all this meat go to waste? Martin, what do you think?"

Martin was as beautiful as an angel come down to earth, blond, perfectly proportioned, with a beatific face and lashes he emphasized with a touch of mascara. He was holding his guitar by the neck, the soundboard lightly poised against one leg. "Lizard tacos are the best, the very best—and you know what they taste like?"

Corey shook his head.

"Guess."

"I'll give you a hint," Dick said. "Cluck, cluck, cluck?"

Each day was more or less like the one that preceded it, people tripping or not, writing up reports or not, but everybody tanning on the beach and sipping cocktails by the pool come dinnertime. There was snorkeling, canoeing, fishing for the men and shopping in the plaza for the women, where in the stalls there you could get silver necklaces, pottery, Mexican blankets and embroidered peasant blouses so cheap they were practically free. She took advantage of it all. For the first time in as long as she could remember she wasn't expected to do anything, the food and cocktails prepared for them and the maids there to change the bedding and hang fresh towels on the rack, the kids vanishing after breakfast and reappearing only for meals, and always somebody to chat with or indulge in a game of cards or chess or checkers. She read. Relaxed. Tripped. And if anything happened at all, like the time the mayor of the village and five other officials dropped by with bottles of tequila and mescal to welcome all the Harvard researchers to Mexico, it barely caused a ripple. The Mexicans were courteous and soft-spoken and capable of drinking every bit as much as anybody at Freedom House, and if they knew about the LSD—or had an opinion about it—they never let on. Of course, she could barely understand a word of what they were saying, but it was a thrill just to be there to look into their darting black eyes and imagine the time of the pyramids and stelae and the mushroom cult that had sent its tendrils north to bring her here all the way from Boston, which was a kind of miracle in itself.

Toward the end of the summer Peggy flew down with her brother Tommy for a ten-day visit, and that did produce a ripple, though it was no fault of Peggy's. It was never clear whether Tim had miscounted the days or Brenda had stayed on longer than expected, but now both of them were there at the same time, and the first night, after a tense dinner during which Brenda sat off by herself in the shadows at the far end of the patio, tipping back shots of tequila and flicking one cigarette butt after another into the flowerbed, things came unglued.

At the time, she herself was immersed in a deep pool of calm. She'd spent the day as a guide, overseeing Alice and Paulette while they tripped in the lifeguard tower, and that had given her a kind of satisfaction and clarity that made her feel as if all this—the project, their mission—was the solidest foundation for human understanding ever devised. And good. Purely good. If she'd ever had doubts, she had them no more. Both women had gone deep and never experienced any sort of crisis that couldn't be cured by a gentle roll in the waves or the embrace of the sun, though at one point Paulette had become agitated by the shore crabs when she went down to dip her feet in the surf and saw them for what they were—monsters, that is, flesh-eating monsters—but that passed and she calmed down and slipped into an ecstatic state that lasted out the day.

After dinner Joanie went out to sit by the pool with Corey, trying to give him a little attention. He was fine, she kept telling herself, having the time of his life with the other kids, running from one thing to the other, catching fish, roaming the jungle, setting up an aquarium in a five-gallon pickle jar Carlos had given him and falling off to sleep each night as if he'd run a marathon, but still she felt the smallest nagging thread of guilt. And so she was sitting with him, drink in hand, the sun setting behind them, just listening to what he had to say.

"Did you see what I caught today?" he asked. He was drinking a Soldado de Chocolate, a kind of Mexican Yoo-hoo, and his lips were dark with the residue.

"No, what?"

"It's in the aquarium." A week earlier he'd hauled the pickle jar across the gleaming tile floor and positioned it on the big table in the center of the patio where everyone could admire it, and ever since he'd devoted himself to maintaining its contents, scraping the algae off the glass the minute it appeared, changing the water, adding or deleting specimens depending on what wound up in his net that day. "I mean, didn't you look?"

She shook her head. "I was guiding today."

And now—not for the first time—he asked what that was like, guiding, and if anybody had flipped out. "It was Alice, right? And Paulette?"

"Nobody flipped out," she said, "if that's what you want to call it. It was peaceful, beautiful, really."

He was silent a moment, swirling a dark fan of liquid round the bottom of the bottle. "What I don't get is why you have to do it at all. Dad keeps saying it's for research, so you can tell if the pills are going to help crazy people get better, right?"

"Not crazy. Just people with psychological problems, people in hospitals or undergoing analysis. It's a tool, that's all. A medicine."

"I know that," he said. "You already told me. But if you aren't crazy yourself, then how can you tell if it works?"

She laughed. "Maybe I am crazy. I have you, don't I? And your father?"

"Come on, Mom, I'm serious."

"It doesn't work that way," she said.

"What way *does* it work?"

The slush had melted in her drink and it was thin now and acidic. She lifted it to her lips and set it down again. "I don't know," she said. "It's hard to put in words."

"Is it bad for you?"

"Bad? No, not at all—just the opposite."

"You're not just saying that, are you?"

She made herself look into his eyes so he could see she meant what she was saying. "I would never lie to you."

There was a sudden sharp crash from the direction of the patio, which made them both look up. She didn't realize it yet, but that crash was the sound of the aquarium shattering on the tiles and sending five gallons of murky water and a spangled assortment of tropical fish out across the room in a miniature tidal wave. Somebody cursed, and then Brenda's voice rose up, harsh, shrill, shot through with rage. "You bitch!"

And then Peggy: "You call me a bitch? You're a tramp, that's what you are, a common tramp!"

In the aftermath, both of them appeared at the top of the steps to the pool area, shoving and snatching at one another, and there was blood on the tiles all over again, Brenda's blood, because Brenda, as it turned out, had flung the aquarium at Peggy and then, in the struggle that followed, wound up stepping on a fragment of shattered glass. Tim was right behind them, and everybody else too, and Tim was saying, "All right, all right, enough already," to no effect whatever. Brenda had Peggy by the wrists, trying to force her down the stairs and into the pool, but Peggy sidestepped her and broke free, and it was Brenda who missed her step and flailed backward into the water to come up sputtering an instant later while Peggy, her shoulders rigid and her teeth clenched, stalked off down the path to the beach.

Brenda was a bobbing dark spot in the pool, treading water and cursing. Tim seemed to be at a loss. He stood there at the edge of the pool looking down the path where Peggy had disappeared, until Brenda slashed her way to the coping and thrust both her elbows and her face up out of the water and in a low nasty voice demanded, "Are you just going to fucking stand there or are you going to help me out of here?"

The next morning, when she made her way down to breakfast, Brenda was gone. Fitz was already sitting at a table in the back corner of the patio, dressed in the shorts and unbuttoned Hawaiian shirt he'd taken to wearing day in and day out, Corey slouched beside him in his even more minimal outfit—shorts, period. They'd finished the huevos rancheros Carlos's wife, Reina, had served them and pushed away their plates, Fitz bent now over a dog-eared text called *Personality Psychology* and Corey absorbed in one of the Mexican comics Carlos had given him from his own personal supply stacked up on the shelves just inside the door to the pantry. "Good morning," she said, easing down across from them while gesturing to Reina to bring her coffee and a plate of the eggs. "Or should I say, '*Buenos días*'?"

"*Buenos días,*" Fitz said, without glancing up. Corey said nothing. His eyes never left the page.

"Well, okay," she said, "thanks for that enthusiastic greeting, you two. By the way, anybody hear what happened with Peggy? Or Brenda?"

Fitz glanced up. "Carlos drove her to the airport first thing."

"Who, Brenda?"

"Uh-huh."

"She's gone?"

"Apparently."

She paused to light a cigarette and watch a lizard no longer than her teaspoon appear over the rim of the table, then shoot across the surface and down the far side before Corey, his senses alerted now, could snatch it up and add it to the terrarium he'd already begun to assemble in the wake of last night's disaster. "That was sudden," she said.

"You can only have one girlfriend at a time," Corey piped up, looking from her to Fitz and back again. "Tommy Eggers told me."

"Really?" she said. "And why's that?"

He dropped his eyes to the comic. "Because you only have one dick."

"Don't talk like that," she said.

"I'm not. It's what Tommy said."

Fitz, far from supporting her, just laughed. "Maybe we should ask Tim."

As it turned out, Tim had taken Peggy up to his room shortly after the incident by the pool, and no one had seen either of them since, which indicated, at least to her, that they'd spent the night exploring the sacrament—and each other. At some point, Brenda had tried the door, but Tim had locked it and she was reduced to shouting accusations in the hallway till she tired of that and either went to her own room or not, nobody seemed to know. But Paulette, who was an early riser, had seen her getting into the Jeep with Carlos and her two matching pink suitcases for the flight that would take her to Mexico City and from there across the continent to Boston, a place that seemed as remote as the moon from this perspective. They'd all have to go back—and soon—but the thought was just a blip on her radar as the smell of jasmine drifted across the patio on a soft ocean breeze and Reina set a cup of coffee and a plate of huevos rancheros, salsa and tortillas before her.

"*Muchas gracias,*" she said, and then, trying out her Spanish, "*¿Cómo está usted?*"

"*Muy bien,*" Reina returned, showing her teeth in a bright pleased smile. She was in her mid-twenties but looked younger, with a bush of black hair she tied back in a ponytail. "*¿Y usted?*"

"*Muy bien.*"

Since that exhausted her Spanish, she just smiled back until Reina dipped her head in acknowledgment, scooped up the dirty plates and went back to the kitchen, at which point Corey, who'd been squirming in his seat during this exchange, folded back a page of his comic and held it out so Fitz, who did know Spanish, or a whole lot more than she did, could see it. "Dad?" he said.

Fitz looked up. "Yes?"

"What's a *mentiroso?*"

The comic—he angled it so she could see it now too—showed a pair of cowboys with wide-brimmed Mexican hats, neckerchiefs and holstered guns. One, who was quite obviously the good guy, had his hand twisted around the bad guy's neckerchief and was saying, "*Usted es un mentiroso, señor,*" which was surely some sort of insult or curse, but what exactly?

"*Mentiroso?*" Fitz said, setting his book down on the table. "That'd be a liar. Let's see if I can remember: *Miento,* I lie; *mientes,* you lie, familiar; *miente,* he, she or it lies; *mentimos,* we lie, and so on— *mienten,* they lie. You really should learn the forms of the verbs if you're going to pick up Spanish, I mean, that's the first thing . . ."

"And what's the second thing?"

"That's easy—the language of love. *Te amo, mi amor,* you know that one?"

"Not really."

"Go try it on Nancy—she's your girlfriend, isn't she?"

Corey didn't blush, though she expected him to. He just said, "Yeah, I guess."

On the weekend before they closed down Freedom House and headed back home for good, everyone agreed they should throw a party and trip as a group—no guides, no restrictions, no write-ups—just let the drug take them where it would. People dressed up for the occasion, but fancifully, almost as if it were Halloween, the girls in the bright flaring skirts, peasant blouses and silver necklaces they'd bought in the market stalls, the men in guayaberas and sombreros. Tim invited the mayor and his cohort and hired mariachis to provide music for the party, which started in the late afternoon with a lavish spread—*pozole, carnitas, chilaquiles, flautas con pollo,* shrimp, lobster, fish—for those who wanted it, though most of the inner circle wound up eating sparingly so as not to interfere with the sacrament, which they all took an hour before the guests arrived so as to be primed for the moment the festivities started in earnest. As for the kids, they would be on their own, which was just fine with them since the summer had set them free too and any sort of parental supervision wasn't much more than an afterthought at this juncture.

She was in their room, sitting before the mirror and doing her face for the party—false lashes, eye shadow, Mexican lipstick in a shade of red so bright it could have brought the dead back to life, and why not vamp it up?—when Corey slammed through the door in his bleached-out shorts and started rummaging through the backpack he kept under the cot. "Mom," he said, "have you seen my mask and snorkel?"

She lifted her eyes to him in the mirror and she asked, "Aren't you going to change for the party?"

"Change what?"

"I don't know, put on a shirt, for starters—and your other shorts, the ones you hardly ever wear? And wash your feet—when was the last time you washed your feet?"

Fitz was sitting on the bed in the pristine white guayabera she'd bought him in the market the day before and a pair of blue jeans she'd ironed so they'd have a nice crisp crease down the front of each leg. "Yeah," he said, "spruce up a bit, champ, get in the spirit of things. There's going to be dancing—don't you want to dance?"

Corey was on his knees, bent over the backpack, his feet splayed behind him. "I don't know."

"What about Nancy—she'll dance with you, won't she?"

"I don't know."

"Well, why don't you ask her and find out? But first, go into the bathroom and wash your feet. And put on a shirt like your mother says."

Fitz got up then, went to the closet for the sombrero she'd bought him, cocked it back on his head and asked, "How do I look?" He winked at her in the mirror. "Like a red-haired Mexican? Or no: an *Irish* Mexican?"

"You look fine," she said, and she was feeling good, not only in anticipation of the party but because she could feel the drug already beginning to work on her, the familiar crepitation in her bloodstream, the ever-so-subtle alteration in the frequency of the light, objects beginning to shift out of the material world and into another world altogether.

"What about you, Corey? You think I look Mexican?"

Corey studied him a moment, as if the question were in any way serious. "You look like my father."

"Okay, that's what I want to hear—so you must be Mexican then too. *Digame in español, mi hijo.*"

Corey said, "What?" and she said, "Just put on a shirt, that's all I ask."

The next day, their last day there, when all she wanted to do was lie on the beach and feel sorry for herself, Tim had arranged a softball game—*For goodwill, because we've got a two-summer lease on this place and we'll be back before you know it*—and they all had to pile into the Jeep and a pair of Volkswagen vans and go out in the heat and through the village and its stew of smells to a grass field adjacent to the airstrip and wade through the afternoon. Of course, with Tim (and Fitz and Ken and Charlie) everything was an occasion for a party, and the beer flowed and vendors were there to sell tacos and the whole town turned out to make it a holiday and say *adios* to the gringos from Harvard. She was surprised by the number of people there and it wasn't till later that she learned the reason why: the local newspaper had promoted the game as being between the local semi-pro team, Los Águilas, and Los Rojos de Harvard, as if the Crimson baseball squad had flown down from Cambridge for the event. The fact was, the party had gone on till dawn and Tim was lucky to be able to field a team at all, with Tommy Hitchcock on the mound, Fitz at shortstop, Dick at second, a very shaky Martin at third, Tim himself at first, Carlos pressed into service behind the plate, Ken in center field, Charlie in left and nobody in right.

She sat on a blanket with Fanchon, Alice and Susannah, sipping a beer and shading herself with a parasol Carlos had provided, and though she felt a bit queasy, whether from the heat or the excesses of the night before or a touch of *turista,* she didn't know. The party had kept on accelerating and accelerating, as if the earth were a big base-ball rocketing high into the deepest reaches of space, and what she'd done or where she'd been was a mystery, though she remembered Corey and Nancy popping up out of nowhere wearing big grinning lizard faces and the Mexicans throwing up pyramids block by mas-sive block till they were all buried under them and that she'd gone up to the lifeguard tower with somebody—Ken—and watched the full moon scrawl its icy script across the face of every wave in existence. Persistent waves. Waves that never stopped.

But this was baseball. All right. Fine. She liked baseball well enough, so that wasn't the problem. Fitz liked it too. And Corey lived and breathed it. She'd wanted Corey to sit with her but he preferred the company of the other kids, who settled in on their own blanket up the right-field sideline, where they were well supplied with Sol-dado de Chocolate, Naranja Crush and the *taquitos* one of the village women was selling for what amounted to a nickel apiece. The beer only seemed to make her stomach clench, but she finished the first and had Corey go get her another—another round for everybody—because she was here and this was their last day and she needed something to make her forget about the trip back to a place where she'd have to face the uncertainty of no job and no apartment all over again.

The visitors were up first. Tim led off himself, and while he cocked the bat over his shoulder and made a parody of menacing gestures, he never swung at all and wound up with a walk. The same thing happened with the second batter, Fitz, and then Ken, who was up third. Nobody swung at anything, but you could feel the intensity of their concentration, which Alice said was almost Zen-like, and here was another proposition: Did LSD enhance athletic prowess? Did it eliminate the psychological element and bring the randomness of the world under control? Maybe. Maybe so. Tommy Hitchcock—twenty-two, lean, boyish, quick as any lizard—hit the first pitch presented to him over the center field fence for a grand slam and suddenly she was on her feet, leaping and dancing and cheering as if she were in high school all over again. Baseball, they were playing baseball in Mexico, and wasn't that something? Alice shrieked, "Go, Crimson!" and everybody mobbed Tommy when he cruised across the plate.

It was eight to nothing in the bottom of the ninth inning, the Mexicans silent while she, Alice and Fanchon served as cheerleaders for the Rojos and the beer bottles made a pyramid of their own, when Tim called time-out and went to the mound to have a word with Tommy, who to this point had allowed only two hits. What he said to him, she didn't know, or not exactly, but it was apparent that in the interest of goodwill, not to mention international relations, he'd told Tommy to go easy, let them hit the ball, tie it up, win even . . .

Corey was outraged. When the Águilas scored their seventh run, he stamped across the grass and flung himself angrily down beside her on the blanket. "I can't believe this!" he said. "They're throwing the game!"

"They just want to be nice, that's all."

"Nice? Baseball isn't about being nice. Baseball's . . . *baseball*. It's about *winning*."

She looked out across the field, the colors so intense they were like living things, the green of the grass rippling with a cool fire, the faces of her players—of her husband, Ken, Tim, all of them—gone beyond the uniform white of Harvard and the Nordic races into another spectrum altogether and every dress on every woman in the crowd was as bright as the sun itself. It was a moment of release. She could feel it all go out of her like a long withheld breath. She was leaving in the morning, but she was part of this, part of the team, and she'd be back.

"No," she said. "That's where you're wrong. It's about playing the game."

2.

She'd never slept with another man until that first summer in Mexico when it had seemed like the most natural thing in the world. She didn't even think twice about it. She was tripping and so was Ken. Fitz wasn't there. Fanchon wasn't there. She and Ken were in the lifeguard tower together and the whole world was disarranged. Clothes—her two-piece, his bathing trunks—were encumbrances, worse than useless, the invention of a society they were no longer a part of, a screen designed to keep you from your authentic self. What mattered was touch. The touch of the sun on her face, her breasts, her belly, the touch of his fingers that sent sparks of fire through her so that she could see them as if she were riding through her own veins and jumping the synapses of her nerves till it felt so good she never wanted it to stop.

There was Charlie too and one of the other men, she didn't even remember who anymore, that first summer blurring with the second so that it was difficult to distinguish them except that during the second summer, when Tim had abandoned Harvard without even finishing out the spring semester and got himself fired in the aftermath, there were strangers there, paying guests of what Tim was now calling the Castalia Foundation after the fellowship of mystic scientists in Hesse's *Magister Ludi*. What he was thinking, and she couldn't blame him really, was that there was money to be made from this new field of psychedelic therapy, and if people wanted to come down to Mexico and pay the foundation two hundred dollars a week for the privilege of having guided sessions with him, all the better—he could pay the bills without having to rely on Harvard or Peggy or anyone else, broaden his base and get the message out to the larger society while pushing the research ever further. She saw the logic in it, but she wasn't really happy about it. They were harmless enough, these new people, poets, professors, businessmen, a psychiatrist from Berkeley and his wife and kids, but they were strangers too and the hotel felt less like their own transpersonative community where group mind could flourish (the synchronicity, the coincidences that weren't coincidences at all, knowing what somebody was going to say before they even opened their mouth) than the kind of impersonal place you could have found anywhere in the world, with people you didn't know and didn't particularly care about sitting across from you at breakfast.

The one incident from that second summer that stuck out—that was embedded in her brain, actually—was the one that ultimately brought the whole thing down and sent her, Fitz and Corey on a hellish premature trip across the brown back of Mexico, up into the featureless flats of Texas and on through the heart of the Deep South to the frigid waters of the Jersey Shore, where there were no palm trees, no margaritas and, worst of all, no sessions in the lifeguard tower, no sessions at all. It was a disaster and it broke her heart—and Corey's too, Corey's more than anybody's. He'd looked forward to Mexico all winter, talking about nothing but the fish, the iguanas, the tacos and *taquitos* and Soldados de Chocolate and laying out an elaborate schedule of what he was going to do on the first day and the second day and so on. And she was as eager as he was, the winter hanging like a gray sheet over Boston, her waitressing job not only exhausting but a humiliation too (they'd filled her position at the library and her supervisor was very sorry but they had nothing else for her at the moment) and their apartment even more cramped, drafty and depressing than the one they'd given up. She'd tried not to be bitter. She slogged through her days thinking of Mexico and only that. And then what? They no sooner got there than the whole thing came crashing down—and why? Because Tim was a jerk, that was why. Because Tim never listened to a word anybody said. Because he thought he was God.

The problem was publicity—too much publicity. If it was up to her, which it wasn't and never would be, she would have kept things quiet, contained, with access limited to the circle of people who really counted, but that wasn't the way Tim saw things. Restraint wasn't in his vocabulary. He was a promoter, an impresario, a showboat, giving lectures around the country on the benefits of mind expansion, writing articles, sitting for interviews, always talking, talking, talking. He hired a PR firm to publicize the summer sessions and roped Fitz into writing up the prospectus, and people responded, all the sessions fully subscribed, which would have been fine, just fine, but for the explosion of negative press, beginning with headlines like HARVARD DRUG PROF FIRED and PARADISE IN MEXICO—2 FIRED HARVARD PROFS OPEN COMMUNAL HOTEL and finally just devolving to DRUG HOTEL and TRIPPING ON THE BEACH. None of the articles mentioned science, therapy, the quest for knowledge, breaking set or lifting imprints, but only drug use, topless women and promiscuous sex. All of which was true, of course, but in a way the sensationalists could never have imagined.

Fitz mentioned it to Tim the day they arrived—in a cautionary way, as in, *Aren't you inviting trouble?*—but Tim laughed it off.

They were out on the pool deck in their bathing suits, sipping their first margaritas of the summer, and she'd just handed Tim a folder of press clippings they'd collected on the way down. Tim was stretched out on a recliner, his body deeply tanned, his hair bleached from the sun. He looked good, fit, much younger than his years, but then he always looked good. It was genetic. Some people aged more quickly than others, some went to fat, some developed cellulite and skin like an iguana's. But not Tim. Tim never changed.

Ken and Fanchon were there too, along with Charlie and Alice and two of the new people whose names she hadn't caught. Everybody was drinking margaritas except Tim and Charlie, who were doing the salt, lime, and shot glass ritual.

"Huge thanks, Joanie," Tim said, riffling through the clippings without seeming to take much notice of them. "Is that a new swimsuit? Yes? It looks great. You look great—doesn't she, Fitz?"

Her husband had painted his nose with zinc oxide and it seemed to draw in all the light till it gleamed like a hundred-watt bulb. His shoulders—good shoulders, strong shoulders—glistened with the tanning lotion she'd rubbed on them before coming down from their room. The hairs on his chest formed two broad wings around his nipples and they were the palest red, almost translucent. Everything about him glowed. The pool danced and shimmered behind him. They were in Mexico. In the sun. And it was glorious. "She does," he said, nodding in Tim's direction. "But when you have a chance, look at those articles, will you? Because some of them—"

"Will do," Tim said, bringing a hand up to shade his eyes, though he was wearing his dark glasses, "and this is great, thanks, but what were you going to say? Some of them, what? Attack us? Try to belittle what we're doing down here as if they knew the first thing about it?"

"Joanie and I were just concerned you might be attracting too much attention, if you know what I mean."

Tim laughed. "You hear that, Ken? Fitz is worried. Jesus, Fitz"—turning back to her husband now—"you sound like Dick. Dick's mantra is less is more and I've been hearing it till it's coming out my ears. Or at least one ear." He gave them a self-effacing smile and pointed to his bad ear, which was free of its hearing aid because hearing aids and swimming pools didn't make for a good match. "But you know what I say?"

He paused, grinning, and looked around at them one by one till somebody said, "No, what?"

The sun was like a hot iron and her back felt like the ironing board itself. In a minute, as soon as she finished her margarita and ordered another one, she was going to take a dip in the pool. Tim's question hung there until she really didn't care what he thought, one way or the other. He was a magician, *their* magician, and whatever he didn't like—bad press, the academic game, Harvard—he could just make disappear with a flick of his magic wand. *What, me worry?*

Tim dropped his eyes to the shot glass, poured himself another and went through the ritual of sprinkling salt on the webbing of his left hand, licking it off, throwing back the tequila as if he were snapping it out of the air and grimacing over the wedge of lime. "I say all publicity's good publicity, that's what I say." He reached out a hand, put it on Fitz's knee and gave a squeeze. "Right, Fitz?"

"Right," her husband said because there really was nothing else he could say.

"Okay, then," Tim said, giving everybody one of his stagey open-mouthed winks. "Let's drink on it."

The accounting came two weeks later. They'd barely settled into the routine—she and Fitz were planning on spending the full summer this time—and all she wanted out of life was more of the same, more living in the moment under a sun that never faltered, more sessions, more abandonment of the ego and tuning in to the group mind as if she were fine-tuning the dial on an FM radio, when what had seemed an unlikely, even paranoid, threat in Mississippi, Louisiana and Texas, a nagging worst-case scenario that would never come to pass, came to pass.

It was morning, post-breakfast. She was sitting in a wicker chair on the patio with a book and a glass of lemonade. Corey was out somewhere with the other kids, bodysurfing, scrambling up the cliffs, stalking through the jungle catching and killing things, whatever kids do, and she'd never seen him happier. Fitz was up in their room, working on his thesis proposal, which he was forging ahead with even though he no longer had a thesis adviser and would have to go crawling to McClelland or whoever when they got back in the fall. The only sound came from Pedro, who was on his perch by the fountain, preening his feathers and muttering to himself.

She wouldn't have looked up at all, wouldn't even have noticed the man, but for the noise his shoes made clicking across the tiles. That in itself was unusual because nobody bothered with footwear here except the hotel staff—and they all wore huaraches that barely whispered as they went silently about their tasks. She glanced up and saw the man coming toward her, a Mexican in his forties, dressed in a black long-sleeved shirt, pressed trousers and gleaming black boots, the pointed toes of which were decorated with silver chevrons that caught and released the light in a strangely hypnotic way. He stopped beside her chair and presented her with a wide ingratiating smile. "*Buenos días, señora*," he said, and without waiting for her to return the greeting, which she would have liked to do because she was trying to practice her Spanish as much as possible, he asked, "You are Mrs. Doctor Leary?"

She was so surprised by this she let out a laugh. *She* married to Tim? "Me? No, no: Tim isn't married. Dr. Leary, I mean. He's a widower."

The man gave her a puzzled look.

"His wife is dead," she said.

Still nothing.

"He has no wife," she said, carefully enunciating each word.

The man's smile returned. "I see," he said. "*Muy triste*, no? But"—he gestured to the chair beside hers—"do you mind?"

Before she could answer, he'd swiveled the chair neatly around so that it was facing her and lowered himself into it. "Excuse me," he murmured, "but I am Dr. Dionisio Padilla, of the Psychological Institute? A colleague of Dr. Leary? And you are—?"

"I'm"—she hesitated. What was she: a student, a friend, a fellow seeker? "One of his, that is, my husband is one of his grad students?"

"I see," he said. He was sitting too close to her, so close their knees were practically touching. "And your name?"

She gave it without hesitation, though she was beginning to feel uncomfortable and she couldn't have said why. The man seemed innocuous enough. A fellow psychologist. A colleague. But he didn't know Tim, that was obvious.

"And so," he said, smiling still and holding her with his eyes, "your husband is participating in Dr. Leary's sessions, is that it?"

"Yes."

"And you?"

"Yes, me too."

He was silent a moment. Pedro began rustling on his perch and let out a single shrill "*Caramba!*" before hopping down and strutting across the patio in his bow-legged gait.

"Tell me," the man said, "because this is of great interest—do you all, the whole class, that is, take the drug at once?"

"No," she said, "no, not at all. The idea is to stagger the days and limit the experience to once a week so the newcomers—the students— can adjust and learn. They attend seminars. They're assigned readings in the field. And they fill out questionnaires and write up reports of their experiences, which, of course, are different for everyone."

"And you—you are a student also? Or merely the wife of a student?"

The question took her by surprise. Again: What was she? What were Fanchon, Alice, Peggy, any of them? Why was she in Mexico? Why had she gone to Tim and Dick's house on alternate Saturdays throughout the fall, winter and spring? She was shaking her head very slowly. "No," she murmured, "I'm not a student." A beat went by. She stared into his deep unblinking eyes as if in a trance. "Just," she said, "a wife."

"I see," he said. "But then, if you are not a student of Dr. Leary, then why do you participate in his sessions? Why do you take this drug, which can be quite dangerous, you know that, don't you?"

She was thinking of the last time, two nights ago, when she and Fitz had gone up to the lifeguard tower and she watched the world peel away, layer by layer, as if she were deconstructing it herself and how when they'd had sex she was able to be both inside and outside her body at the same time and how they'd lain in each other's arms till dawn. She shrugged. "I don't know," she said. "For enlightenment."

He just stared at her. His smile had faded, but now it came back. "I see," he said. "Yes. That makes perfect sense."

Three days later, the man was back. This time he had another man with him and they were both wearing gun belts and holding black felt hats delicately in their hands, as if afraid of crushing them. She'd just taken a swim and was sitting on the pool deck with Alice, Fanchon and Paulette Roberts, while Tim, who'd been in the conference room working on updating *The Tibetan Book of the Dead* as a kind of guide to the psychedelic experience, had just come out for a smoke and a breath of fresh air. He was wearing a white cotton T-shirt, white shorts and tennis sneakers, as if to contrast with the two men in black, who had clicked across the patio and down the steps into the pool area. The one she knew—and knew now was no professor—called out, "Dr. Leary, is that you?" in a voice full of false heartiness.

She remembered Tim turning around then, his face lighting up with his usual anticipatory grin till he got a better look at the two black-clad men striding toward him and the grin faltered. He looked bewildered in that moment, as if he knew exactly what was to come and yet somehow didn't, as if he were immune to the hurts and persecutions of the world. But of course, he wasn't. And neither was she. Or Fitz. Or Corey.

Both men had reached Tim now and stood there at the edge of the pool, arms akimbo, until in a movement so graceful it might have been choreographed, they simultaneously reached up and positioned the hats on their heads. The one she knew introduced himself as an officer of the Federal Judicial Police and handed Tim a single folded sheet of paper. "What is this?" Tim demanded.

The man touched the brim of his hat, almost as if he were about to deliver a salute. "It is, Dr. Leary, a deportation order."

In that moment, Tim looked suddenly old, stricken, his shoulders slumped and his muscles gone slack. He was trying to find his grin but couldn't quite manage it. No one moved. The gurgle of the pool's filter grew louder and louder till it was unbearable. Before she could think, she was up out of her deck chair and coming toward him, a pulse of outrage flashing through her—and not just for this Judas of a policeman (*colleague:* yeah, right), but for Tim too, because how could he be so careless, so stupid, and what did this mean? *What?* That they were all to be deported too, as—as undesirables? Drug users? Criminals? Didn't these people know what this was all about? Didn't they understand?

"Deportation?" Tim echoed. "You must be crazy."

"You are a psychologist," the man said, the one she knew. "Look at me and then take a look at yourself engaging in all manner of degenerate behavior under the guise of science, and you tell me who is crazy. This is a Christian country, Doctor. This is a country ruled by moral principle."

She was right there now, right there beside them, and she reached out to pluck at the sleeve of the one she knew. "You," she said. "You lied to me. You're no *colleague*."

The man looked down at her hand on his arm and smiled softly, a smile of the lips only, as if all this was faintly amusing. The other man, who'd stood stiffly at attention to this point, now seemed tensed for action, and she realized, with a start of alarm, that if the one she knew were but to give the word, this one would show no restraint. "I am sorry," he said, still with that soft smile, then turned his gaze back to Tim, whose own smile had come back now, huge, toothy, titanic, as if to say everything was all right and always would be, nothing to worry about, just the smallest misunderstanding, that was all.

"On what grounds?" Tim said, smiling still.

"Read the order," the other man said, the one she didn't know. He was short, there were red flecks in his eyes and he regarded Tim steadily, as if he knew his kind—a perpetrator like any other, the lowest of the low—and wouldn't think twice about reaching for his handcuffs if that was what it would take.

"Running a business without a license," the first one said. "As an alien. That is the official offense, and the most convenient way to be rid of you. But if you'd really like to know it's because of this." And here he handed Tim a pair of rolled-up newspapers, which, as she was later to learn, accused them all of being a cult purveying "marijuana orgies, hairy women, black magic, venereal disease and profiteering." They were even tied to the death of a woman none of them had ever seen or heard of, whose body was found in a village more than a hundred miles away, which made for a front-page story under the headline HARVARD DRUG ORGY BLAMED FOR DECOMPOSING BODY.

Alice, who was right behind her, said, "But this is ridiculous. We have a lease on this property. We're scientists!"

Somehow, though, the claim itself seemed ridiculous, coming as it was from a barefooted woman in a bikini, and in that moment, Joanie saw the truth of it—they *were* ridiculous and all their beliefs and aspirations were laughable in the eyes of the authorities, of the stooges who ran things in a world of closed-off minds and seekers after nothing but more of the same. She took in the scenario—Tim in white, the *federales* in black, the women in a display of flesh—turned her back on them, dove into the pool and went all the way down till she touched bottom.

3.

The previous year, after they'd all got back from Mexico, Dick Alpert had bought a house in Newton a few blocks from the one Tim had leased from the irate professor of international law (who was suing him for damages). The idea was to keep the inner circle together, to keep the experiment of Zihuatanejo in full flower, and most of the core group moved in, including Tim and his kids, Ken and Fanchon, Charlie and Alice, Rick and Paulette Roberts and their two kids and an assortment of unattached grad students. She and Fitz had been invited to join them—expressly, both by Dick and Tim—but in the end, though they hashed it out over the course of three excruciating days, they declined. She'd wanted to say yes, an enthusiastic yes, because she'd re-imprinted on the whole group (her brothers and sisters, as she'd begun to think of them, her family, her true family) and it was so powerful, so far beyond anything in her experience, she couldn't imagine having her frame of reference reduced to three again. But Fitz, who'd been so jealous of Ken and Fanchon when they'd first moved into Tim's, was the one who nixed it. He needed to focus on his studies, that's what he said, that's what he insisted upon, and he was afraid he wouldn't be able to do it in an atmosphere where somebody was bound to be tripping no matter what hour of the day or what day of the week it was. "Look, Joanie," he pleaded, and he was pleading with himself as much as with her, "if I don't bear down here we're going to wind up back in Beacon—or worse."

"You can always go to the library," she said.

"It's not that—it's the evenings, the nights. You know how it is—a nonstop party. Which is great, I'm not saying it isn't. But what am I supposed to do? Lock myself in my room?"

Something sang in her head then, a snatch of one of the ragas Tim liked to play during sessions—an aural flashback, she thought: How about that?—and through the chiming of the sitar and the thump of the tablas she said, "We could try. And if it doesn't work out—"

"What? Go out and try to find a place in the middle of the semester? Are you crazy? We're talking about my degree here, Joanie, my *life*. I mean, do you really want to go back to being married to a high school psychologist?"

So they got an apartment that was like a prison cell and if it wasn't for the Saturdays at Tim and Dick's—every *other* Saturday, that is, as Fitz decreed it—she would have hanged herself. Sure. Fine. It was Fitz's decision because it was Fitz's degree—*Fitz's life*—and her life was reduced to cooking and cleaning and hustling for tips in a too-short skirt at a diner full of Greek and Italian immigrants who kept telling her how great she looked, how hot, how *sex-ee*. And now, after the disaster that was Zihuatanejo and an endless drive across country with a depressed husband and a withdrawn son (*You want to stop for a cheeseburger, Corey? I want a taco. How about clam strips? At Howard Johnson's? Your favorite, right? I want a taco*), they were right back in Boston and right back in the same boat. Only this time they didn't have the option of going to Dick's because Dick was done with Harvard and so was Tim and nobody really knew what to do since the rest of the inner circle was left out in the cold too.

Desperate, they went back to their landlord from the previous spring, but he had nothing for them, and then they tried the building where they'd had their first apartment only to find that it had changed hands and the new owners were renovating. They went through every listing in the want ads and dragged themselves from one place to another, but just about everything was gone by the time they got there and what wasn't was so shabby—no curtains, no blinds, no shower, refrigerators crusted in filth, silverfish, cockroaches, mouse turds scattered like rye seed across the kitchen counter and buried in the burners of the stove—she got a headache just walking through the door. In the meanwhile, they were staying in a motel all the way out in Waltham, living off what was left of their savings and the check her father had given her to tide them over when they left New Jersey, and clearly that wasn't sustainable.

And then it was the Labor Day weekend—ninety-two degrees, the sun like a hammer and the sidewalks burning right through the soles of your shoes. They could have been celebrating the holiday, picnicking in the park, flipping burgers on a charcoal grill and tossing a Frisbee back and forth like any other family, but they weren't. Corey was due to start school the next day, Fitz the day after that. She hadn't even begun to look for a job because there wasn't much point if you didn't have a place to live—and how could she leave a call-back number if she didn't have a phone? Her stomach was a vat of acid. She couldn't sleep. Mexico, if she thought about it at all, was just a cruel joke.

They were sitting in a deserted diner in Boston at half past one on Labor Day afternoon, she, Fitz and Corey, staring down at plates of the lunch special (macaroni and cheese with a boiled pink hot dog and pale green pickle triangulating the plate) while a fan on the counter shifted the air and set it right back in place again. She was sweating, her blouse stuck to her skin and the hair at the nape of her neck as wet as if she'd just stepped out of the shower. They'd spent the

morning tramping up and down stairs, going from one place to another, depressed, angry, willing at this point to take anything so long
as it had four walls and a roof, but either no one answered the bell
or some exhausted-looking middle-aged drone pulled open the door,
croaked "Already taken," and slammed it shut again. Just now, just
before they'd given up and slouched in for lunch—an iced tea, she
was dying for an iced tea—they'd gone back to the apartment with
the mouse turds, only to find that it too had been taken by somebody
whose level of desperation must have been positively Dostoevskian,
and now they were here, in the deserted diner, hating themselves and
each other too.

"I want to go back," Corey said, pinching his voice in a whine
of irritation. She could see he had no intention of eating the macaroni, which he'd separated into five ragged lumps surrounding the
hot dog, from which he'd cut a single slice after lathering it with
mustard, ketchup and piccalilli relish. He was slumped against the
cracked leatherette of the booth, a comic book in one hand, a cherry
Coke in the other. His mood, ever since they'd been deported from
Mexico and stretching through all of July and August at her parents',
had been poisonous. He barely spoke anymore. And where he'd once
reveled in the shore, in fishing, crabbing, boating, he'd spent most of
the summer sulking in his room. She'd begun to worry about him
and so had Fitz. But Fitz was so depressed himself he couldn't seem
to lift himself off the lawn chair in her parents' backyard.

"Go back where?" Fitz asked.

"The motel."

"You know we can't do that," she said, her tone flat and instruc-
tive. "If you want, we can drop you at the park and your father and
I'll go on looking. You don't have to come. Not unless you want some
say in what your room's going to look like, that is."

"I don't care," he said.

And then Fitz started in. "I told you we shouldn't have spent so
long in New Jersey."

"It was cheap," she said. "How was I to know everything'd be taken already? Last year—"

"We found a craphole, right? And we'd be head over heels if we could only get it back again. I mean, this is ridiculous."

"Last year," she went on, ignoring him, "we had our choice of places and the only reason we wound up where we did was because it was so close to Corey's school, if you remember. So don't blame me. I'm not the one who got us kicked out of Mexico—and my parents really went out of their way for us. Which was a blessing. And you know it."

Save your money, her mother would say every time she and Fitz offered to pay for groceries, and her father had been more than generous, especially when the car died and he just outright gave them her mother's station wagon. They had the beach, littleneck clams, sweet corn, their own room with a queen bed and a separate room for Corey. And all for free. It could have been fun, had been fun for all those years of the past, but it wasn't Mexico. And the depressing thing—the truly depressing thing—was that Mexico was never going to happen again.

"I'm not saying that." Fitz was bent over his plate, impaling the last few scraps of macaroni on the tines of his fork. "I'm just saying I wish we'd come back earlier. I wish we'd got our shit together instead of—"

"'Shit together'? You sound like Charlie."

"—instead of putting everything off and sitting there drinking gin and tonic like it was going out of style. And Charlie and Alice got a place, if you want to know. Two bedrooms, sixty a month."

"Where?"

"Roxbury."

"Roxbury? But that's in the ghetto?"

"They don't have to worry about school districts."

They both looked to Corey then, who still hadn't touched his food. He was staring fixedly at his comic book as if none of this concerned him.

"Hey, champ," Fitz said, "—if you're not going to eat that, do you mind?"

And Corey, without glancing up, just shoved the plate across to him.

They finally found a place within walking distance of Corey's school—a godsend, absolutely—and she picked up a temporary job as a receptionist at a dentist's office that would help tide them over till Fitz's teaching stipend kicked in at the end of the month. The apartment was on the ground floor of a brick building that looked as if it had been around since the Revolutionary War and could actually, from a certain angle and in a certain light, be described as charming. It had the requisite two bedrooms and an enclosed porch and was ten dollars a month cheaper than what they'd paid for their last apartment. The only problem was that the landlord had given the previous tenant—an old woman in a grimy neck brace who was headed to the nursing home—an extra two weeks to vacate, so they couldn't move in till the fifteenth. Which meant draining even more income on the motel (which did, thank God, have weekly rates) and eating out two meals a day, breakfast emerging from a cardboard cereal box and whatever she could manage to fix on a hot plate.

Was it miserable? Was it their low point? Was the group mind all but extinguished and higher consciousness to be replaced by the great shining hope of moving into a ground-floor apartment that would forever stink of old lady, not to mention her two cats? She tried not to think about it. Actually, she was scrambling so hard just to keep things together she didn't have time to think. What she knew was this: their clothes and furniture were in storage and on the fifteenth they would no longer be. On that day they would take them out of storage, make ten trips back and forth in the station wagon, arrange the furniture in the new apartment, stow the pots and pans under the sink and hang their winter clothes in the closets. Then she would go shopping for the essentials, fix dinner, and their lives would go on. That was it. And it was a whole lot better than nothing.

Then one evening, after the dentist had drilled and filled his last cavity of the day and she'd picked Corey up in front of the school where he'd been waiting for two hours, since none of the school buses ran as far out as Waltham, she pulled into the motel lot and saw, with a flash of irritation, that someone was parked in the spot reserved for their room and that all the other spots—what else?—were already taken. "Shit," she cursed, pounding the wheel with the flat of one hand. "Shit, shit, shit!"

The heat was relentless, radiating up off the pavement in a reek of tar and petrochemicals. Corey, slouched in the passenger's seat, hadn't said more than ten words since he'd climbed into the car, and he didn't say anything now. He just looked at her as if she were some previously unknown life-form he found only minimally interesting, Corey, who'd been the center of her life, whom she'd raised to be articulate and outgoing and who'd shared a special vocabulary with her—their own private language—until he'd stopped using it and she'd stopped too and it vanished without a trace, another of the lost languages of the world.

"What?" she demanded. "What are you looking at me like that for?" The car was in drive still and she had to fight down the impulse to take her foot off the brake and smash everything in front of her. "Shit!" she repeated. "Shit!"

He didn't answer. Instead, he gathered up his books, clutched them under one arm and swung open the car door.

"What are you doing?"

His face, in the hard hot light, was no longer the face of a child. He was fifteen. He was as tall as she was. He gave her a grimace, as if all this—the parking lot, the two hours waiting in front of the school, his *mother*—was too much for him. "Going in?" he said, making a question of it.

"You mean you're not going to help me?"

"Help you what?"

"Find a *spot*, for God's sake—I mean, is that too much to ask? And the groceries—what about the groceries?"

He slipped out of the car with the agility of an escape artist, slammed the door so hard the chassis rocked, then crossed the lot to their room, inserted the key in the lock and disappeared inside.

She stared at the door in disbelief, the anger rising in her, everything so petty, so futile. The heat slammed at her. The clock on the dashboard inched forward. Finally—these were the conditions of her life, this blistering lot, this obscenely ugly motel and more of the same, more, more, more—she reversed the car, the transmission whining, and made a slow circuit of the parking lot till a space appeared on the far side of the building, right next to the dumpster, the funk of which nearly made her gag. Gathering up the two bags of groceries, the newspaper and her purse, she started down the walkway, feeling as tired, angry and empty as she'd ever felt in her life. She didn't even want to think about dinner. Last night they'd had cheese sandwiches, washed down with a cheap rosé wine that tasted like aluminum and tonight would be no different, unless they went out to a burger stand. But she didn't feel like going out. She didn't feel like anything. She just wanted to crawl into bed, crank up the air conditioner and watch the TV that was bolted to the wall over the plasticized desk/bureau combo until she fell away into oblivion.

When she got to the door of their room, just as she was juggling the bags of groceries and her purse and trying to fit the key in the lock, she threw a glance at the car taking up their assigned spot with the number—19—painted right there on the pavement in white numerals nobody could miss, something arrested her, something clicked, and she saw that this car, a standard black VW Bug that seemed no different from a thousand others, was somehow familiar. Then she heard a shriek of laughter from within—Fanchon's laughter—and felt the burden drop from her.

Ken, Fanchon and Alice were stretched out on the queen-sized bed, their backs propped against the wall, feet bare, glasses of what appeared to be—what was—gin and tonic in their hands. The bottles stood on the end table, along with three limes, one of which had been cut in wedges and sat glistening in a puddle of its own juice. Fresh lime. The smell was enchanting—right, just right, perfect— and it drove down all the foul reek of the parking lot and flipped her mood as automatically as if a switch had been thrown. "My God!" she said, the groceries still clutched to her chest, "this *is* a surprise, I mean the best, the best surprise I could—my God, I can't believe it!"

In the next moment they were all on their feet, embracing, including Fitz, who'd been sitting in the sole chair in the room, grinning woozily over the rim of his own gin and tonic. Even Corey, who was propped up on the counter by the sink, digging into a bag of potato chips, seemed animated—this was new, this was different, and it had the distinct flavor of Mexico.

Ken—he looked better than ever, in a pair of tight white chinos and a navy shirt open at the neck so you could see the gold cross he'd taken to wearing in Mexico, in memoriam, he said, of a dead religion—squeezed her so hard he took the breath out of her. "Did you hear the news?" he chimed, leaning back from her as if they were dancing and he was about to execute a double dip and twirl her under one arm.

"News?" she repeated, gazing round at the grinning faces, everybody grinning, even Corey.

"We're celebrating tonight," Ken said. "We're all going out, my treat."

"Yay!" Corey crowed, jumping down from the counter. "Pizza. Let's go for pizza!"

"What is it?" she asked. "What are you talking about? Don't keep me in suspense—"

"It's Tim," Ken said, but before he could say more, Fanchon slipped an arm around her waist and said, "Tim has a new place, a new house—for us all!"

A new house? She was trying to get a grasp on the news, ready to commit—more than ready—and trying to fight back a wave of anxiety, because would Fitz allow it, would Fitz see how untenable their life was the way it was presently construed, even if they were to go ahead and take their things out of storage and move into the old lady's apartment? Would he see how much she needed this, needed Ken and Fanchon and Alice, needed *Tim*—and that he himself needed them too? "Where?" she asked. "Where is it?"

Nobody answered her, but she could feel their spirits soaring.

"Will it be—?" And here she looked to Fitz, who just smiled and lifted his glass to her. She looked round her giddily, everybody smiling, smiling, as if she were a child all over again and this were her birthday and the cake just about to be brought in, aglow with candles. "I mean, will it be big enough—I mean, for all of us?"

Ken shrugged, gave her his secret look that this time was meant to be public and publically appreciated. "It's a little place," he said. "Only sixty-four rooms."

That wasn't the shocker—the shocker was *where* the house was located. It wasn't in Cambridge, wasn't in Boston, wasn't even in Massachusetts. It was in Millbrook, New York, not far from Poughkeepsie, which wasn't far from Beacon, the very town they'd escaped from in the first place. The irony was stupendous. Or no, it wasn't irony—it was karma. If ever there was karma involved in their lives then this was it. "Can't you see, Fitz?" she said when they'd got back to the motel after a raucous dinner with too much beer and too much pizza and everybody talking at once and jumping up and down to feed the jukebox until Corey fell asleep in his chair and the owner of the restaurant came out of the kitchen to hang the CLOSED sign conspicuously on the front door. "It's meant to be."

Fitz was drunk. He'd been drunk when she got back with the groceries four hours ago and he was drunk now. She was floating herself, not just on the beer and the gin and tonics, but also on the lighter-than-air euphoria of escape, the possibility of getting out from under all this burden she'd been bearing like a mule and starting a new life where she belonged, with the best and truest friends she'd ever known—her brothers and sisters—and in a place that would be like a permanent Mexico, Mexico transposed to the U.S.A., where nobody could be deported, ever. Fitz said, "I don't know," which was better than no, which was what she was afraid he was going to say.

The fact was, Harvard was dead for them now—Ken had emphasized that. The department had disavowed the Psilocybin Project and anybody associated with it or any other form of psychedelic research. They'd fired Dick, ostensibly because he'd given the drug to an undergraduate when he'd sworn that only grad students would be involved, but that was only the proximate cause—they'd got rid of him because he was associated with Tim and Tim was an embarrassment not only to the department but the university as a whole. The upshot was that if you wanted to complete your degree, you'd better toe the line, and if your thesis was in any way related to psychedelic research, you were out of luck. And, of course, all the projects of the inner circle fell into that category, including Fitz's. Under first Tim, then Dick, he'd been developing a research project along the lines of Walter Pahnke's Good Friday experiment, substituting music students for divinity students and the concert hall for the chapel, the thesis being that the drug would facilitate creativity, opening them up to what down through the centuries had been called divine inspiration, with or without the face of God.

"You can work on a new thesis idea there, anything, some Skinnerian animal-in-a-box kind of thing, who cares—just to get the degree. Then you can go on and do any kind of research you want. And at Millbrook, you'll have both Tim and Dick there to guide you, like it was the best university in the world."

"They piss on Skinner."

"So somebody else, then—the point is, this is a chance to get them all off your back, start afresh, finish this thing, Fitz, once and for all. Don't you see?" She was sitting on the edge of the bed, removing her flats and stockings. Fitz was slumped in the chair. Corey, lightly snoring, lay facedown on the cot in the corner, an orange smear of pizza grease decorating the flange of his nose.

"What are we going to do for money?"

"It's rent free, you heard Ken. So that takes care of our biggest expense right there."

It was almost too good to be true: an entire estate, 2,500 acres, with ponds and fields and a turn-of-the-century mansion, and it was being given to Tim by Peggy's twin brothers, Tommy and Billy, who lived in another house on the property, for the sum of one dollar a year. And why? For the purpose of setting up the Castalia Foundation and conducting all the research he wanted without any academic constraints. "And I could work while you write your dissertation."

"Where? Poughkeepsie? *Beacon*?" Fitz's voice was thick and phlegmy, caught somewhere deep in his throat. He'd been drinking more heavily than usual, drinking all summer, though he'd vowed he was never going to sink to that level again. Which was all the more reason to get him out of here—and herself too. They'd already put down a deposit on the apartment haunted by the old lady and her cats, but she'd see what she could do to get that back.

"Sure," she said. "Anywhere. Face it, Fitz, this is a dead end here. And think of Corey—the schools have got to be better there, a little town like that surrounded by all these big estates. Rich people. Money. And there's a college there too, isn't there?"

Fitz said, "I don't know," and he wasn't referring to the college (Bennett, two years, all girls, which he knew every bit as well as she did), but this radical notion that had been dropped in their laps just hours before by Ken Sensabaugh, Fanchon and Alice at a time when radical change was just what they needed to keep from rotting in their shoes like all the other living corpses traipsing around the streets of Boston.

"It's the chance of a lifetime."

"You sound like a used car dealer."

"It's the exact same phrase you used on me, if I recall—about Mexico, the first time? Please, Fitz, *please*—we can all be together, don't you see? It'll be like Mexico all over again."

"Right," he said, and his voice had thickened still more, "but without the tacos. Or what, iguanas? But shhhh!"—he lifted a finger to his lips—"don't tell Corey."

She dropped her shoes to the floor, smoothed out the stockings and folded them over her forearm. He'd slept with Fanchon in Mexico, she was sure of that, and maybe Susannah too, though it didn't mean anything, not when you were under the influence, not when you were having a session, because jealousy was ego-dependent, a kind of disease of it, and the whole purpose of the drug was to enable you to let go of the ego and live in the moment. She'd had Ken. And Charlie. And that was nothing. Just brothers and sisters, just . . . tripping.

"I can still get the deposit back," she said, and her voice was thickening too. "I'll bet," she said. "I'll bet I can."

Someone flushed the toilet in the room next to theirs. There was the tattoo of pounding feet, the sigh of bedsprings.

"You know what I want to do?" he said.

"What?"

"Sleep on it."

In the next moment he was gone, his breathing coming slow and easy till it settled into a soft rasp that played counterpoint to their sleeping son's. She reached up and shut off the lamp behind her and for a long while she sat there in the chair, listening to the motel sink into the deep rhythms of the night. Sixty-four rooms. The Hotel Catalina had less than half that. And Ken said the big house—the Alte Haus, he called it—had a kitchen that in itself was bigger than their last apartment, with a walk-in refrigerator and an eight-burner range. The meals they could have, everybody together, the sessions, the clear skies, a lake for swimming in the summer and skating in the winter! How many fireplaces? How many floors? *Sixty-four rooms.* It was like a dream opening up to her one panel at a time, muted colors, movement, and then a vision of them all, Ken especially—especially Ken—gathered round a big stone fireplace while a raga played on the stereo and her mind drifted out to play along with it.

Tim *was* a magician. He *was.* And if she'd ever doubted him, she'd been wrong, because he'd really pulled one out of his hat this time.

4.

They made up a motley caravan, five cars in various colors and states of repair strung out in a gleaming procession along the clean white turnpike that sliced through the heart of Massachusetts. Before they even got going she'd already heard half a dozen quips about the Joads ("Don't call me an Okie," Charlie shouted, "I'm a Beantowner!" to which Alice added, "Ex-Beantowner," and Ken, clowning, cried out "Ma, Ma! Where's Pa?"). They'd gathered in the parking lot of a shopping center that was convenient to the turnpike at the appointed hour—eight A.M.—and stood around sipping coffee out of cardboard containers and taking delicate semicircular bites out of doughnuts until everybody was there. The last to arrive were Royce and Susannah Eggers, in a rust-spotted Pontiac with a pair of front wheels that let out an exasperated screech when Royce swung into the lot.

They were towing a trailer piled high with all sorts of junk—kids' bicycles, end tables, mattresses and bed frames, a birdcage, a basketball hoop and God knew what else, the intimate exfoliations of a life lived apart from the group. Though they had a trailer themselves, the smallest thing U-Haul offered because they'd got rid of practically everything and that was all the space they needed, Joanie couldn't help wondering what Royce and Susannah were thinking—they'd all be together soon, in the Alte Haus, which was furnished, or at least mostly so, and none of this stuff, this *junk,* would hold any meaning for any of them. It struck her then, as her friends milled around talking in quiet voices, lighting cigarettes, licking powdered sugar from their thumbs and forefingers, that this was the last time they'd appear as separate families, with separate vehicles and separate possessions, that they were finally going to come together as one and live not in the past but in the now.

Royce, mopping his bald head—he was sweating, though it was overcast and still relatively cool—kept saying, "Jesus, I hope it's not going to rain. I mean, I should've got a tarp to cover all this crap with, but you know how it is, everything right down to the last minute—"

"I hear you," Ken said, and he had something in his hand, pinched between two fingers, that wasn't a cigarette. He offered it first to her, and though she'd had little experience of marijuana and Tim's prohibition rang in her head (*It's illegal!*), she took it gladly, hungrily—she was high on the moment, as excited and sweetly expectant as she could ever remember being, and she figured why not be higher still?

She glanced up at Fitz then—he was just across the lot, not thirty feet away, where they'd parked to leave room for the others, since he'd insisted on getting here first. He kept circling the car, peering under it, checking the trailer hitch and tightening and retightening the ropes he'd secured their things with. He was nervous, she could see that, nervous about the whole business. He'd arranged for a leave of absence, telling McClelland how much he regretted having come under Dr. Leary's influence and pleading with him to understand that he was going to need time to reconfigure his dissertation—or, actually, jettison it altogether. In the interim, he told him, he was going to take a part-time job and really bear down on reviewing the latest literature in personality studies and come up with a dissertation proposal that would be acceptable to everybody in the depart-ment. And McClelland, relieved to be rid of Tim and Dick and any lingering influence they might still have, told him to take as long as he needed.

Now, seeing the expression on Fitz's face—he looked as if he were expecting war, not peace—she said to Ken, with a laugh, "I think Fitz needs this, really needs it," and after taking a furtive puff her-self, crossed the lot to their car, took hold of her husband and pulled him to her for a smoky kiss. "Mm," he murmured, "tastes good. But should we—I mean, I've got to drive, and it's not as if New York's just around the corner."

"Here," she said, after snatching a quick look over her shoulder—the nearest strangers all the way across the lot, Corey milling around with the Eggers kids and the Roberts twins, their heads down, dough-nuts and cartons of milk in their hands—she passed him the mari-juana cigarette. "Take this," she said. "It'll relax you."

And he did take it, his eyes masked against the smoke and his hair glowing in the soft filtered light just then beginning to seep through the overcast. He leaned back against the car, crossed his ankles, and took a deep drag and then another and yet one more, before finally handing it back to her.

After all the packing, preparation and anxiety over the final de-tails (Fitz's anxiety, in particular, which seemed to build on it-self with every item they stuffed into the trailer), the drive was a lark. Nobody got a flat tire, nobody got lost, and when they stopped for gas or a burger, they rolled into the parking lot like a traveling show, everybody on the same page, on the same team, and it was group mind that decided when everybody's stomach started rumbling or bladder sent out its urgent signals to the brain. They were together in body and spirit, that was how it was, they were off on a grand adventure and nothing could stop them now. She was so excited she couldn't seem to stop talking the whole way there, high on the trip and the marijuana too. Every hill and signpost seemed to remind her of something else, especially as they crossed the New York State line and took the Taconic south through the densely forested hills that were just beginning to show the first flames of fall color.

Her recollections of Millbrook were vague—she and Fitz might have visited it two or three times over the years, just to get out of the house for a Sunday drive and maybe stop for a sandwich at the diner there or a drink or two at the bar—but what she remembered, what she could see with her eyes closed, was the charm of the place, a prosperous little village of no more than maybe sixteen or seventeen hundred people that could have been set down in the Adirondacks or New Hampshire without anybody blinking an eye. Was there anything to do there? No. It was just a village, with a junior college for girls and not much else. If you wanted culture—or even a pair of shoes—you could buzz into Poughkeepsie, for what it was worth, but Manhattan was only two hours away if you really got desperate.

Of course, that wasn't the point. The point was to get away from everything and everybody and indulge what Tim called the Fifth Freedom, the freedom to explore your own mind without harassment or disapproval or even the knowledge of the outside world. Without the squares. The unenlightened. The mass of people who lived lives of quiet desperation and never suspected there was anything beyond work and sleep and what their blinkered senses brought them in a continuous loop from birth till death. But that wasn't her, not anymore. Or Fitz either.

The first thing you saw as you turned onto Franklin Avenue, Millbrook's main street, was a great towering five-story wooden structure straddling a hill in a sea of fussed-over lawns and flowerbeds. It was grim, institutional, and looked utterly out of place amid the farms and fields surrounding it. "What's that?" Corey asked from the backseat.

"That's the local insane asylum," Fitz said without looking over his shoulder.

"Your father's only joking, honey," she said. "That's the college—Bennett."

"No hope for you there," Fitz said, swinging easily into place behind Ken's VW Bug, as Charlie and Alice eased in behind him in their turquoise Chevrolet, followed by the Robertses' and Eggerses' bringing up the rear. "It's all girls. Or wait a minute"—now the glance over the shoulder—"maybe that *does* provide hope for you, after all. You do like older women, right?"

His face pressed to the window, Corey didn't answer.

"I mean, Nancy's what—four months older than you? Or did you throw her over when we left Mexico?"

Corey's voice was in the process of changing, and it got stuck a moment, so that when he did speak it came out as a croak. "This is it? You really mean we're going to live *here*? In this hick town? I mean, what does everybody do on Saturday night—ride cows?"

"They watch each other chew gum," Fitz said. "Especially the teenagers."

And she said, "Give it a chance, because just you wait and see where we're going to be living, which is just—it's at the top of this hill, isn't it, Fitz? At the T?"

Suddenly Ken had his blinker on and Fitz hit the brakes so hard she thought she was going to go through the windshield. Corey shouted "Ow!" and thumped heavily into the seatback behind her while everything on the dash—maps, her sunglasses, an empty soda bottle that was hard as a brick—came raining down on her. No one was hurt, just startled. And Fitz had managed to stop without plowing into the rear end of the VW, which was where the engine was, and who knew what kind of damage that would do. Fitz let out a curse, his eyes leaping to the rearview mirror, but fortunately Charlie and the others were far enough back to avoid a pileup, and following Ken's lead, they all rumbled up on the shoulder in a fan of dust. Dead ahead of them, rising up out of the pavement on the far side of the road, was a turreted stone gatehouse, three stories high. If they hadn't stopped they would have sailed right on through the intersection and barreled into the heavy wooden gate one after the other, the blind leading the blind.

In the next moment, they were all out of their cars and gaping up at the building before them, which might not have contained sixty-four rooms, but looked big enough for all of them.

"You think this is it?" Ken asked, and he was looking to her and Fitz, as the local experts.

"What else could it be?" Fitz snatched a look up and down the road, as if they might have missed something. "Dick said you take Franklin through the village till it ends and you're there. So this has to be it, right?"

"It looks like Disneyland," Corey said.

She said, "It does. And this is only the gatehouse. Imagine," she said, "just imagine what the big house is going to be like."

The others had begun to gather in a scrum around Ken's car, the adults alert and eager, the kids looking sheepish, as if they'd been the cause of some catastrophic loss and here was the evidence of it staring them in the face. She noticed Nancy Eggers in particular—she was the last one to emerge from any of the cars and she stood there in a slouch, gazing vacantly at the empty gatehouse, as if it had nothing to do with her. She was pretty enough, with her big eyes and the lipstick she'd begun to wear, her black hair cut in a pageboy and pinned up on one side with a barrette, but when was the last time anybody had seen her smile? You would have thought she was going off to prison instead of a new life that would make the old one in Boston look like something out of a Dickens novel.

"Where is everybody?" Royce demanded, his voice high and querulous. "I thought at least somebody'd be here to greet us or let us in or whatever. Should we try the gate?"

"Are you sure this is the right place?" Charlie had come up to stand there with the other men on the edge of the pavement, gazing dubiously at the gate. He was wearing blue jeans and a flannel shirt open at the collar, as if that was what rural life would expect of him. "I wouldn't want to see you get an ass full of buckshot, my friend. These are good country folk out here, never forget that."

Just then she became aware of the sound of an automobile coming up the road behind them and swung round expectantly. It wasn't Dick. And it wasn't Tim. It was a stranger in a battered station wagon, and when he pulled up to the stop sign she flagged him down. She took in his tortoiseshell glasses, the baseball cap, a face of angles and gouges and a straggle of hair the color of Fitz's. In the next moment she was leaning into the open window. "Excuse me," she said, "but is that"—pointing across the street to the stone turrets and mute gate—"the Hitchcock estate?"

"Private property, as far as I know," the man said, squinting up at her. He paused. "That's why they've got the gate."

"But we're expected." She looked to the others, everyone watching her now as if all the progress of their lives depended on this exchange. "We're guests. Actually," she said, and she couldn't suppress a flush of pride, "we're going to be living here."

The man just blinked at her. "I guess the Hitchcock boys'll have something to say about that." Then, sweeping his eyes over the whole group, he put the car in gear, added, "You take care now," and drove off.

Everyone looked to her—and why was her heart fluttering? "Yes," she said, smiling in relief. "This is it."

Ken and Fitz immediately strode across the street and tried the gate, but it was padlocked, and then the rain that had held off all day began to spatter the pavement and they all had to retreat to the shelter of their cars. "So near," she said, climbing in and slamming the door behind her, "and yet so far."

"I don't know why they couldn't have left the gate open," Fitz said, and though he rarely complained, he was complaining now. "I mean, it's not as if they didn't know we were coming."

"I'll go," Corey said, and before she could object—*But it's raining*—the door sliced open on a cool sweet smell of wet fields and moribund wildflowers and he was across the street and mounting the low wall at the side of the gatehouse. She saw him perched there a moment and then he was gone, racing up the drive through a scrim of rain.

"You think he'll be all right?" she murmured, turning to Fitz. The main house was a full mile from the gate, or so Dick had said, because that was the way the original owner, a German American industrialist named Dieterich, had wanted it, not simply as a show of elegance and the privilege that came with wealth but for privacy too. Which was ideal for Tim's purposes—for *their* purposes—as if they really were on Huxley's island. But still, a mile was a mile. And it was coming down hard now, ricocheting up off the pavement and churning in the gullies on both sides of the road.

"He's fifteen," Fitz said. "He's been wet before."

"What's the world record for a mile?"

"Just under four minutes. But give Corey ten—he's out of training."

The windows had steamed up, but she lit a cigarette anyway, just to do something. "What's the first thing you're going to do when we get there?" she asked.

"I don't know—have a drink, I guess."

"Yeah, me too. But no margaritas—something German, right? What do the Germans drink anyway?"

"Beer."

"And schnapps—what about schnapps?"

"I wouldn't count on Tim having a whole lot of schnapps in the cupboard," he said, smiling and laying a hand on her knee. "Going German does have its limitations, you know." He was in a good mood, she could see that—their troubles were over, or about to be. They both stared through the windshield a moment, as if to be sure the fairy-tale gatehouse hadn't vanished in a puff of smoke. "I'd settle for a martini," he said. "Actually, at this point, I'd settle for anything."

She was thinking about unloading the car and getting things settled and what a trial that was going to be after a long day on the road—she had a headache already—when the high whine and blat-blat-blat of Dick's little sports car came to them over the drumbeat of the rain on the roof, and then Dick was there and the gate was opening and Corey was sprinting across the road to them. Dick grinned, waved, then climbed back into his car and led the procession through the gate and up the long tree-lined avenue to the house.

So often, when you've built something up in your mind, the reality can't come close to the fantasy, but that wasn't the case with the Alte Haus. The minute it came into view, she was enchanted. Even through the rain-smeared blur of the windshield, she could see this was no ordinary house but a vision out of a storied past, the past of princesses, ogres and castles—and the myth, replayed a thousand times, of good conquering evil that every little girl in the Western world battened on. The style was late Victorian, though Tim was to describe it as Bavarian baroque, whatever that meant, and it was three stories high with towers on either side that extended it to four, and as they drove up in their procession, the spires that capped the towers seemed to take hold of the clouds and split them into long gauzy streamers as if the weather was just another facet of the house. "Wow," Fitz said and gave a low whistle. "Can you believe it?"

Inside, it was even better—all tapestries and rich dark wood hand-tooled by the German craftsmen the original owner had brought over to make gingerbread of the banisters and carve fanciful figures into the mantels of the outsized stone fireplaces that were tall enough to step into. Tim had greeted them at the door, his grin as big as the house, and he wouldn't hear of anybody unpacking anything until they each had a drink in hand and took a tour of the place. Martinis went round. Everybody seemed to be talking at once. And then Tim, pitcher in one hand, glass in the other, led them through the halls and up and down the staircases, pointing out the salient features in his crisp tutorial way.

Fanchon, in a pair of black toreador pants and a cardigan in poppy red that had to be at least two sizes too small, was full of herself, hanging on Tim and cooing over every detail, but all along she was looking to her main chance when it came to divvying up the rooms, make no doubt about that. As Joanie herself was (though, of course, as she had to remind herself, it wasn't a competition and there was plenty of room for everybody). Each floor, each hallway, offered up new possibilities, and while Tim presided and everybody gabbled at once till the excitement was a current running through all of them like a new kind of electricity, she was trying to decide what would work out best—ground floor, where you had access to the gardens and all that glorious acreage or second or even third floor, where you could take in the views?

Tim, gesturing with his glass, reassured them. "Nothing's permanent. Just pick whatever rooms strike your fancy, okay? If you don't like them, we'll switch them up, no problem. I want you all to be happy."

They were on the second floor, the windows pregnant with rain, everybody milling around as if they were on a museum tour—and in a sense they were, because that was what this was, a museum, though in this case it was one you could live in. The kids—Corey, the Roberts twins and the Eggers trio—had vanished the minute they'd come in the front door, off on their own more visceral tour under the auspices of Suzie and Jackie, who'd been here a week already and knew the odd corners and adolescent enticements of the house in the way no adult ever could.

"Is everybody happy?" Tim asked.

"Happy?" Ken echoed. "We're ecstatic." And here he looked to Fanchon. "Right, kitten?"

"It is awestruck," she said, and then corrected herself, "*awesome*. Times ten the size of Dick's house—and Homer Street? Not even the same page."

"Three cheers for Tim!" Rick Roberts cried, raising his glass, and they all joined in till they trailed off in laughter, delighted with themselves. They couldn't believe their luck, couldn't believe all this was theirs. Alice was crying, actually crying, with joy. Charlie's glasses flashed. Tim grinned his grin. Fitz turned and gave her a hug. It was a moment, maybe *the* moment all her life had been building toward.

They weren't the idle rich or the working rich or any kind of rich at all. They were students and student wives. They were used to cramped quarters and scrounging for rent and never having quite enough of anything. And here they were, gathered on the second floor of a mansion to end all mansions—and it was theirs for the duration, or however long it was going to be, brothers and sisters alike. And for now she really didn't want to think beyond that. She put the glass to her lips, inhaled the fragrance of gin, and took a small slow sip of her drink as if she had all the time in the world.

Even after they'd been led up and down the hallways and peered into every one of the sixty-four rooms and admired the views from both towers, Tim still wouldn't let anyone even think about unpacking. No, it was dinnertime, and Dick had spent the better part of the afternoon in the enormous kitchen, preparing one of his nonpareil marinara sauces, with meatballs and real Italian sausage from the deli in Poughkeepsie and enough vermicelli to feed the entire county. They had wine to drink, stories to tell, the moment to celebrate, and all these trivial details—choosing a room, lugging in suitcases, fretting over school registration and the next trip to the store for deodorant, toothpaste and shampoo—were nothing to worry over now. "Things'll sort themselves out," he said, as high on the moment as she'd ever seen him—and maybe high on something else too. "They always do, don't they?"

Dinner was served in the formal dining room and they all pitched in to set the table for twenty, which seemed to her the perfect number—twelve adults, eight children, the adults at one end of the table, the children at the other, but for Dick, who insisted on sitting with the children. Tim had music playing—the first thing he'd done on moving in was to set up the stereo, wired to play in several rooms at once, because, as he said, there could be no life without music. She recognized the first album—Miles Davis's *Someday My Prince Will Come,* their copy of which Fitz had played so many times it sounded as if an aerial bombardment were going on over the quieter parts— but then he put something on she didn't recognize, a flute rising up over a deep well of bass and piano till it felt as if a bird on very light wings was soaring round the room. Which was nice. Very nice. She was feeling pleasantly inebriated, what with the cocktails and the Chianti Dick had served with dinner, and she settled in, Fitz on one side, Tim on the other, and just let herself drift.

"Group mind," Tim was saying, addressing the table, "that's what we're going to get into here—and Mexico was just a foretaste of it. You remember Dick's toe?"

She did—and she had to smile at the memory. It was in Mexico, back in early June, shortly after they'd got there, and everyone was gathered round on the patio one evening, just as they were gathered now, when Dick, coming up the steps from the pool, let out a sharp cry, followed by a volley of curses. He'd inadvertently stepped on a scorpion and the scorpion had stung him in retaliation. In the next moment, here came Dick, hopping on one foot and cursing still, till she and Paulette rushed to him and each took an arm to support him so he could limp into the torchlight and sit heavily in the midst of them. It might have been comical, a Laurel and Hardy moment, except that his toe, red as a cherry pepper, had already begun to swell and somebody—Royce—said that of over two hundred species of scorpions in Mexico, only the *Centruroides* are really dangerous, and she asked, "Well, what does that mean?" and he said, "They're not going to kill you, most likely, but they do deliver a neurotoxin that can cause convulsions—and a serious inflammation of the pancreas, which is no joke. He really should have a doctor." And then, to Dick: "Did you get a look at it? Was it a pale brownish color?"

"You kidding me?" Dick said, clenching his teeth against the pain. "I barely saw the thing."

Somebody went for ice and a bar towel to use for a tourniquet and Corey and Tommy Eggers got a flashlight from the desk and went looking for the thing, as if it could possibly matter. Susannah telephoned for the doctor, but the doctor was off somewhere delivering a baby, and in the end they all just sat around watching Dick's face and the bright swollen afflicted toe till Tim said, "Why not just close our eyes—all of us—and think it away? Focus, people, just focus. On Dick's toe and on dissolving the negativity this little—what is it?, *arachnid*—has brought into our circle. Think healing thoughts, radiate outward, we are all one, *Om*."

By the time they went to bed, Dick was up and about—nearly paralyzed with tequila, maybe, and walking with a limp, but the crisis had passed, and when the doctor finally did come the next morning, Dick just waved him away.

"That's what we're capable of," Tim said. "And if we could do it then, in Mexico, with all those nasty little black shirts breathing down our necks, think what we can accomplish here—"

The mention of it made her breath come quick because she was sure he was going to propose a group session for tonight, their first night under the same roof, though of course that would hardly be practical since it was already getting late and they were barely settled yet. Earlier, during a break in the rain—and over Tim's protestations that they were spoiling the mood—Fitz and Corey had brought most of their things up to the adjoining rooms they'd settled on (in the north tower, second floor, looking down on the big rolling expanse of lawn that was the sea surrounding their island). She'd hardly had a chance to hang their clothes in the closets before Dick was banging the dinner gong, and what little time she did have she'd spent wrangling with Corey, who wanted to set up a kids-only room on the third floor—which was absolutely not going to happen because she could see that quickly devolving into a *Lord of the Flies* scenario, and Fitz had stepped in to back her up. "So what's the point, then? Corey had demanded. "I mean, it's just a joke. Group mind for the adults, and what—no mind for the kids?" And she'd said, "The point is we're your parents, okay? And you'll sleep where you're told."

Now, before she could turn to Tim and put the question to him—"When's our first group session going to be?"—Paulette called out sharply down the table to where the kids had somehow managed to substitute Coca-Cola for the milk everyone agreed they needed to drink first, for their bones and teeth and all the rest, nutrition, protein, vitamin D. "Richard," she snapped, "Ronald—you know better than that. All of you, all you kids—"

But the kids didn't say anything, either in accord or rebuttal. The milk—eight full glasses of it—sat untouched before their eight plates while the Coke bottles rotated from the table to their lips and back again. This was their celebration too. And it had been tough on them, being uprooted first from Mexico and then from their schools and apartments in Boston and Cambridge. The youngest, Bobby Eggers, who'd just turned eight, sat there blinking at her as if he were riding a balloon somewhere over the mountains and she'd just let the air out of it.

"Come on now. I'm warning you." Paulette clapped her hands sharply while the conversation died around her and everyone looked down the table to where Bobby, at least, picked up his milk glass and made a show of taking a swallow from it. "I'm not kidding—Nancy, boys, set an example, won't you?"

Susannah Eggers, who'd been tipping farther and farther back in her chair, plainly exhausted, came to life at the sound of her daughter's name. She righted the chair, snapped, "Nancy, behave yourself!" and gave the child a withering look, though she didn't seem to know what the fuss was all about. It was a general admonition though and all the children seemed to absorb it, even as Dick raised his glass high and cried, "Let them eat cake!" and the children, one by one, drained their glasses and began to slink off, whether to bed or some unscripted adventure that had nothing to do with unpacking or worrying over what to wear for the first day at their new school or even getting sufficient sleep, Joanie couldn't say. Or even imagine. She was occupied with her own drama, which at the moment involved Tim, who certainly wasn't going to let the festivities die, was he?

Eventually, as people got up to clear away the dishes—"I'll wash them in the morning," she heard herself offer—and Tim passed around snifters and a decanter of cognac, things settled into a familiar pattern, some drifting off, some staying on to extend the evening. The record changed and changed again. At some point Charlie put on a record by an English pop group called the Beatles that was a jangle of guitars and heavy obvious drumbeats and Tim, in the middle of a story about an animal he swore was a wolf loping across the face of one of the hills out back ("This place is *wild*, I'm telling you"), looked up with a pained expression and said, "Jesus, take that racket off, will you, Charlie?" and Fitz seconded him.

"Just listen," Charlie said, ignoring them both. "Because what you're hearing is the sound of the future. Hear it? Hear those harmonies? Tell me that's not catchy—"

"Give me jazz or give me death," Fitz said, draining his snifter and looking as if he were about to fling it against the wall. He was tired, she could see that. And drunk.

But the Beatles went on, singing about love, and Charlie danced around the room, snapping his fingers and mugging like a lounge singer. "Dig it," he said, leaning into Tim and mouthing the simplistic words—"Love, love me do"—and making a general ass of himself. "This is only available in England now—remember Pete Meister, my amigo who runs the print shop in Cambridge? He brought it back with him over the summer, so you are listening to the rarest of the rare. And mark my words—this is going to blow the lid off everything."

The Beatles—she would come to love them, but not yet, not now—drove everybody from the room except her, Fitz, Tim and Alice, and after ten minutes of them, Fitz pushed himself up from the table, hollered over the music so Charlie could hear him—"I hope they stay in England and die a quick death!"—and then hovered at her side a moment before saying, "I'm beat. I'm going up to bed. You coming?"

She really didn't feel like moving. She was too content, the music notwithstanding. "Give me a minute," she said, holding up the snifter in evidence. "Just till I finish this." Fitz's eyes were bloodshot. He wavered a bit, his eyes blunted in the candlelight. Then he shrugged and went off to find their bed in their new room in the house that was as big as the world.

When both sides of the album had played, Charlie went to the stereo, put on side one again and came dancing back across the room, snapping his fingers and rotating his hips. He tried to persuade Alice to get up and dance with him, but she just gave him a numb smile and stared right through him. Then he came to her and she pointed to her brandy glass and said, "This dance is already taken." Tim laughed. Then he raised his eyebrows and shot his eyes to heaven, and that was funny, so she laughed along with him. It was almost as if he were putting on a performance for her, Tim the academic, connoisseur of Bach, Mozart and Chopin, devotee of modern jazz, and here he was on their first night of living together tolerating this nadir of low culture in the service of group harmony, mutual support—and yes, as the Beatles so persistently had it—love.

"Listen," he said, and he leaned into her and cupped his hand to her ear to be heard over the music, "I know when I'm beat: let's abandon the field to the Beatles."

She pulled back from him to look him in the face, then shrugged and smiled. "Yeah," she said, "good idea," mouthing the words because she knew he wouldn't hear her with his bad ear—he had trouble hearing when there was ambient noise, and this was as ambient as noise got.

Then they were rising from the table and he was bending over Alice with the same offer of rescue and the two of them followed Tim out of the room, across the hall and up the stairs to the second floor while Charlie danced and throbbed in the dining room and the Beatles screamed out their love. "I've got a stereo up in my room," Tim called over his shoulder, "and it's pretty good quality, you'll be surprised."

She and Alice mounted the steps side by side behind him and she focused on the heels of his white tennis sneakers, which were as spotless as if they'd just come out of the box, one foot rising, then the next, tennis sneakers that were like tennis balls bouncing up the stairs instead of down, and she realized she was drunk—or exhausted. Or some combination of the two. It had been quite a day. Still, tired though she was, she wasn't ready for bed yet—she was too exhilarated, too full of the present and the future even to think about shutting her eyes.

"How you feeling, Alice?" she asked, putting a hand on her arm as much to steady herself as draw her attention. Was she woozy? No. She'd had—how many drinks? Two martinis, wasn't it? The wine with dinner, then the cognac. *But what about the marijuana cigarette?* a voice inside her asked and then immediately answered itself, *But that was hours ago, miles ago, all the way back in Boston,* which didn't even seem possible. Had she really gone from Boston—from the seedy discount motel in Waltham, actually—all the way here in a single day? It was too much, like going from one planet to another.

Alice—her face was a marvel, the smoothest unbroken complexion, the high forehead and thick-lashed eyes—just smiled and said, "Great. Never better."

Tim had the best rooms of all, a suite really, that looked out on the front garden and the fountain that had receded into darkness hours ago. He'd pushed his desk up against the window of the main room and there was a typewriter there and his books and papers were scattered about as if he'd jumped up from his desk in medias res when they'd come rumbling up the driveway. There was a couch, a pair of armchairs and an Oriental rug that took up half the room and a king-size bed in the adjoining room, the double doors to which were flung open.

"Sit down, make yourselves comfortable," he said, gesturing to the couch. "After all, every space here is everybody's space, because we've got to get over this possessiveness game, mine, mine, mine all the time. Spread your wings, ladies, put your feet up. As they say in Mexico, '*Mi casa es tu casa.*'"

They both settled into the couch and Alice said, "I can't believe this place, I just can't. I mean, I feel so lucky."

He had the cognac decanter in his hand still, another magic trick, and he produced three snifters and poured them each a drink. "I know what you mean," he said. "And if you think you're lucky, just look at me—hounded out of Harvard and Mexico and I—*we*—end up here? Is this the best of all possible worlds, or what?"

It was, and it was thanks to Peggy, but Peggy wasn't here. She was in Manhattan, where her apartment was, dining out, going to nightclubs, living her glamorous life among the other heiresses and jetsetters and all the rest of the people to whom money meant nothing. She wouldn't be here till the weekend or maybe the weekend after that, Tim wasn't sure. And Tim wasn't one to worry over it either—if Peggy didn't show up, someone else would. That was the way he operated, the ultimate bachelor, but his attachments and flirtations and his magnetism for women were all a cover for the guilt he felt over the suicide of his first wife—that much was as plain as day. And you didn't have to be a psychologist to see it either.

The way she heard it, from Ken and Fanchon both and what Fitz was able to piece together, Tim, no surprise, had been anything but monogamous when he'd been at Berkeley, drifting away from his first wife—Marianne—to be with the woman he was then having an affair with (and who would ultimately become his second wife, but that marriage didn't last either). It all came to a head on the eve of his thirty-fifth birthday, when he and Marianne came back from a party, drunk, and the other woman showed up at the house. There was a fight. The other woman left. And Tim and Marianne, drinking still, drinking more, passed out in bed together. When Tim woke the next morning, Marianne was gone. Sometime in the night she'd got up and baked him a cake for his birthday, which she'd left in the middle of the kitchen table before going out to the garage, starting up the car and letting it run till the fumes asphyxiated her. Ken said that in the moment of discovery, when Tim, panicked, flung open the garage door, both Suzie and Jackie—eight and six at the time—had seen their mother lying there across the front seat of the car in her nightie, as if she were sleeping out, as if she were having fun, but that detail was too much to hold on to and Joanie let go of it. She had to. It would have crushed her to believe it. Would have crushed anybody, of course it would, and what had it done to Tim?

When she looked up, he was at the stereo, his back to her. There was the static of the needle dropping, and then something soothing was playing through the speakers, something that wasn't the Beatles, that wasn't jazz, or not any jazz she'd ever heard—it was piano music, simple and unadorned, and it felt as if each note were a separate slow pulse matching itself to her own.

"What is this?" she asked. "I love it."

"That's Satie," Alice said. "Isn't it?"

"The *Gymnopédies*." Tim had turned back round now and when he did she saw that he had a cigarette in his hand—a marijuana cigarette, like the one Ken had handed her that morning. He crossed the room and sat between them on the couch, then made a show of lighting the cigarette, taking a deep drag and holding in the smoke before passing it to her.

"But, Tim," she said, grinning and taking it from him in the firm pinch of two fingers, the way she'd seen Ken and Charlie do it, "I thought you were against drugs—illegal drugs anyway. Or is this legal now?"

"You bet it is. We're on a space station, our very own space station. And we make the rules here, not the squares. Go on, indulge. It's good stuff—good *shit*, as Charlie and all the other hepcats would say; Ginsberg, have you met Allen? No? I'll introduce you; he'll be here sooner or later—and while it's not in a league with the true sacrament, it'll do for tonight, don't you think? Joanie? Alice?"

She passed the cigarette to Alice, who laid her head back on the arm of the couch, closed her eyes and drew deeply on it. She stretched out her legs and crossed her feet and Joanie saw that she'd shucked her shoes, because who needed shoes? This was a slumber party, one long slumber party. Joanie pulled up first one knee, then the other, and dropped her own shoes to the carpet, one thump, two thumps.

"And you know something else?" he went on, his voice coming from somewhere far off, as if he were a late-night disc jockey on the jazz station out of New York. "It's got the same aphrodisiac qualities LSD has"—and here he casually laid a hand in her lap and they both took a moment to study it there in a way that was both intimate and unbiased at the same time. "Though, of course, not as intense, but what I'm thinking is we don't really want to have a session at this hour . . ."

He trailed off. The piano music fell like a blizzard of soft warm feathers all around her. She looked into his eyes and smiled and he added, "Do we?"

5.

Things unfolded in a slow sure way, people dividing up the household tasks with perfect equanimity, everybody contributing for groceries according to their means, and no friction—or even the suggestion of it—over whether a family of five (the Eggerses) should put in more than a single couple like Charlie and Alice. She was going to have to get a job sooner or later, she knew that, but during that first month, as fall settled in and the trees turned color and the group sessions deepened their attachment to one another till they were like a single organism connected everywhere and at once by tendrils of perception and emotion and the deepest level of transpersonative harmony she'd ever known, she hardly gave it a thought. They had enough to get by—she'd recovered the deposit on the apartment and still had fifty dollars left out of her father's check. And they had their savings, or what was left of them. Of course, the biggest factor by far was rent—or the lack of it. Without the burden of rent, she felt solvent for the first time in her life, the roof over their heads no more a worry than the air they breathed.

She even made a joke of it one night, laying two dimes on the tabletop in front of Tim as they were sitting down to dinner. Every-one was there, making small talk, and Dick and Fanchon, who'd collaborated on a pot-au-feu, accompanied by a Caesar salad, fresh-baked bread and a selection of cheeses, had just set the serving dishes on the table. Tim made a show of examining the coins in the palm of his hand, slapped them back down and shot a glance around the table to be sure everyone was watching, and asked, "What's this for?"

"Rent."

"Rent? But we don't—"

Charlie cut in: "We don't pay no stinking rent."

All eyes were on her now, even the kids'. "Oh, really?" she said, bringing a hand to her mouth as if in surprise. "My understanding was that our bloodsucking landlords are demanding a whole dollar a year, isn't that right?"

Fitz was cracking up. Fanchon tittered.

"Well, if that's the case, then this is our share—for the three of us, that is, which comes out to fifteen cents." She slid the two dimes across the table to him. "You owe me a nickel."

Not to be outdone, Tim said, "I'll flip you for it."

"Sure," she said, "that's only fair," called heads and lost.

Tim held up the coins so everyone could see them, then shifted one hip and slipped them into his pocket, poker-faced.

"There," she said, "now we're even, right?"

And he said, "Till next year anyway."

After dinner most evenings they retired to the library or the big sitting room, the fire snapping and crackling merrily away while they played cards and board games, read poetry or Hesse aloud or listened as one of the men read from whatever paper or book he was working on, including Fitz, who had a beautiful speaking voice, his cadences so measured it was as if he were singing. Sometimes the children took part, but most often they went off on their own. They had homework to occupy them, of course, and one or the other of the adults would make an effort to supervise them and offer up help where they could. On weekends, the kids tended to drift down to the village to horse around, kick a ball in the park or sit giggling in a booth at the diner over egg creams or sundaes, and that was fine, utterly harmless, because Millbrook was as safe a town as any in the country. And while the kids were off exerting their independence and entertaining themselves and their school friends, the adults participated in regular Saturday night sessions, experimenting with mood and ambience, but always secure, no matter how rugged a given portion of a given trip might be, in the setting. Nobody had to drive home. Nobody had to deliver himself up to the external world. And nobody had to confront his demons alone.

Was it an idyll? Was she happy? Did she love Fitz even more because of the experience of Ken and Tim and Charlie and her sisterhood with the other women? Did she live in the moment as she never had before? Her days, from breakfast at seven and ushering the kids off to school to taking a morning walk around the lake and making her way through the household chores—gladly, gladly—were consecrated to experience. She'd never seen nature the way she saw it now, never before opened up to it like Thoreau or Siddhartha or the gurus Dick was always quoting, and she filled her days with it, ambling through the fields, hiking, rowing, meditating, watching the sun rise high to saturate the lake with its transformative power before peeling off her clothes and plunging into the water that was pure enough and cold enough to take the breath out of her. So yes, it was an idyll. And yes, she was happier than ever before. And yes, yes, yes, she loved Fitz all the more and Ken, Tim and Charlie too, her erotic life a dream of the flesh and the mind both.

Of course, by its very definition, an idyll can't last, and the first crack in the facade came the week before Halloween. Everyone was in a state of high excitement, from Bobby Eggers, their resident third grader, to the teenagers and the adults, especially Tim, the eldest among them and always the most enthusiastic no matter the program, whether it was a group session or a birthday party or a game of touch football on the lawn. This would be their first holiday together, a pagan holiday—and what could be better, more appropriate, more *trippy*, than that? Tim was planning a party for a hundred guests or more, Peggy and her set coming up from the city, along with Maynard and Flo Ferguson and Tommy and Billy and some of their friends too. She threw herself into the preparations, putting up decorations, sewing costumes, carving jack-o'-lanterns, running to the grocery and liquor store in the station wagon with Fanchon, Paulette, Alice and Susannah while the men split wood or sequestered themselves in their rooms with their books and papers and eternally clacking typewriters. She was distracted, that was it, living her own life in her own way for a change, and in retrospect she realized she could have—should have—paid a little more attention to Corey.

She went into his room one night on some trivial errand—underwear, did he have clean underwear for school?—only to find his bed empty. The sheets and blankets were mussed, but that didn't mean anything, since he never made his bed anyway and there was no maid service here, unlike at the Hotel Catalina. She checked her watch. It was past one in the morning—and on a school night, no less. Where could he be? Her first thought was that he must have fallen asleep in one of the other boys' rooms, most likely Richard's, because Richard was the one he was closest to. She went out into the hallway, then down the stairs to the first floor and along the corridor to the back of the south wing of the house, where the Robertses had their rooms, but no one was stirring, so she decided to try Tommy Eggers on the off chance Corey was there.

Royce and Susannah were also on the first floor but on the other side of the house, and they'd taken three rooms together, one for themselves, one for Nancy and another for Tommy and Bobby. Everybody shared and shared alike and they were all one, yes, of course, but there were privacy concerns too, especially with regard to the children's rooms, and she didn't really want to intrude, but after backing up to make a quick search of the public rooms (Dick and Alice were sitting before the fire in the library playing chess, and when she asked they said they hadn't seen Corey since dinner), she felt she had no choice.

Going down the lower hallway in a silence that was broken only by the soft frictive shuffle of her own bare feet, she kept picturing the worst—he'd got lost in the woods, drowned in the lake, locked himself in the walk-in fridge—while reassuring herself that there had to be some obvious explanation. It was a big house. He could be anywhere. He did tend to nod off wherever he was—and he'd been doing it since he was a child, one minute adamantly insisting he wasn't tired and had to watch just one more show on the television, *please, please, please,* and the next passed out at the kitchen table or in the depths of one of the armchairs. She saw movement at the end of the hall and caught herself till she realized it was a cat, one of the three cats currently inhabiting the place, the vanguard of countless cats—and dogs and a single monkey that had the destructive power of a whole troop—to come. The cat froze in mid-stride, one paw lifted delicately as if to put it down would cause the floor to detonate. It regarded her steadily a moment, then dropped the paw and vanished into the shadows.

It was then that she thought she heard music playing, very faintly—so faintly she had to hold her breath to be sure, but yes, somebody's stereo was going. She stood there a moment, listening, until she realized what it was—the Beatles, Charlie's group, their voices reduced to a squeak and the guitars lowered to an insectoid whine, only the insistent drum clearly audible—and that it seemed to be coming from one of the Eggerses' rooms. Which was strange, unless Charlie was with Royce and Susannah, turning them on to this new musical wonder—or, which was more likely, he'd loaned it to one of the kids, because really, no matter what Charlie might say, this was the most juvenile music she could imagine. When she got closer, she realized the sound was coming not from Royce and Susannah's room, but from Nancy's, which was two doors up from theirs.

She felt odd standing there, like some sort of spy—or what, music critic? What did it matter to her what sort of music Nancy or any of the other kids listened to? Suddenly, she felt a wave of exhaustion roll over her. She'd put in a long day and she'd have to be up in five and a half hours to fix the kids' breakfast, the whole mob of them, because the three mothers were rotating breakfast duties and tomorrow was her day on. She wanted to just turn around and go back up to bed—Corey was fine, she was sure of it, and it was time she stopped fussing over him; if he'd fallen asleep somewhere, even in one of the spare rooms, what difference did it make? Still, she was there, and in the next moment she moved to Tommy's door and eased it open. It was dark, darker inside than in the hallway, which was lit by a single lamp on a table at the far end, but after a moment—a moment in which the cat, or another just like it, slipped between her legs and into the depths of the room—she could make out the sleeping forms of Tommy and Bobby in their twin beds and saw that there was no one else there, no one stretched out on the floor or slumped over in the armchair. She pulled the door closed, but then thought better of it and left it open a crack for the convenience of the cat.

The Beatles. *Love me do,* they sang in a buzz of tiny chirping voices. She couldn't explain what she did next because it wasn't right and it wasn't like her to snoop, but on an impulse, she checked Nancy's door to see if it was locked. It wasn't. Very gently, wincing against the faintest protest of the hinges, she cracked open the door and peered inside. What she saw were four walls decorated with drawings and art posters, a bed, an armchair and a night table with a record player on it, the whole illuminated by a single night-light in the far corner. There were two heads buried in the pillow, the heads of two children—adolescents—and both of them were asleep. The record ended in a scratch of static, then there was the clunk of the mechanical arm cueing it up again—and again, once again and endlessly, the Beatles were singing. *Love, love me do.*

Y ou just can't behave like that," she told Corey when he got home from school the next afternoon. She'd been stewing about it all night and all day, angry, disappointed and fearful at the same time. He was too young for this. And so was Nancy. Fifteen was the age for first crushes, Valentine's Day cards and school dances, not a full-blown sexual relationship, if that was what this was—and, really, what else could it be? She'd fought down the impulse to stalk into the room and shake them both awake because that would only have made matters worse. Unnerved, she'd eased the door shut and retreated down the hall in confusion. She hadn't told anyone yet, not even Fitz—or Susannah, who really should rein in her daughter before something happened that was beyond the power of any of them to repair. Nancy. Nancy, with her eyeliner and lipstick—she was the one who should have known better.

"Behave like what? What're you talking about?"

She'd taken him aside the minute he burst through the back door and into the kitchen along with Jackie, Tommy and the twins, all of them flushed from the walk home in the chill breeze that was coming down out of the north to put an abrupt end to the Indian summer everybody'd been enjoying practically that whole first month. They'd been tossing a football around, roughhousing, and they were in high spirits, cuffing each other in the meat of the arm and throwing taunts and quips back and forth till the kitchen, big as it was, seemed too small for them. She told him she wanted to speak with him privately—*Right now, and don't give me that look*—and then she'd led him up the stairs and down the hall to her room, where he casually tossed his book bag on the bed and fell into the chair by the window as if he'd lost the use of his limbs. His face gave away nothing.

She looked at him, really looked at him, for the first time in weeks. He had her coloring, dark eyes and hair and not a trace of Fitz's carrot top, and he was growing so fast she saw he'd be needing new pants soon—and she'd just gone out and bought him the current pair not three months ago, at her mother's. His nails were dirty. His hair needed cutting. There was a crusted-over cut just below his left ear.

"I'm talking about Nancy."

She could see he was making an effort to keep his eyes on hers, holding his stare to maintain the pretense that he had nothing to hide. "What about her?"

"Last night," she said, and she was making an effort too, trying to keep her voice even, "you weren't in your room. I checked. It was one-thirty and I was worried, wondering where you were—"

"We were listening to records."

"You were in bed with her."

"What are you, spying on me?"

"I was worried," she repeated. She could hear the blood whispering in her ears, a sound like the wind rushing across a barren plain. "And I heard the music, so I pushed open the door a crack and there you were, in *bed* with her. I don't know if you realize how wrong that is at your age, I mean, what the consequences can be—"

"Consequences of what—listening to records? Records are bad for you now?"

"Don't get wise with me. You know what I'm talking about."

His face hardened. "No, I don't—why don't you explain it to me?"

She and Fitz had always been open with their son and they'd both sat him down when he turned eleven for the facts-of-life discussion— *You can ask me anything, she told him, anything, because sex, human sexuality, is nothing to be ashamed of*—and she'd thought that was that, the learning process initiated and all the rest to follow in its wake, adolescence, college, dating, marriage. Now she said, "Do you know anything about birth control—I mean, the first thing?"

He didn't answer.

The breeze, the autumn breeze that had a foretaste of winter on it, rattled the windows and she could feel the draft on her legs, which meant the house was going to be like a refrigerator come December. "You're too young for this," she said. "It's not just sex and the dangers of—well, you *do* know how girls get pregnant, don't you?—but the emotions involved, the hormones you can't even imagine making all these changes to your body. And your mind too. Ask your father. He knows. He'll tell you."

"Tell me what? You do it. You do it all the time. I saw you—" He'd pushed himself up now so that he was on the edge of the chair, poised there over his coiled legs, challenging her.

"Saw me what?"

"Kissing. Making out. With Ken, Charlie and who knows who else? Tim. Did you do it with Tim yet?" His voice had tightened till it was almost a snarl.

"That's different," she said, "*we're* different." One hand rose unconsciously to her hair to tamp it in place though it hadn't come loose at all. "We're adults. We're all in this together, this *experiment,* you know that . . ."

"Yeah," he said, "well, I'm different too and so's Nancy." He was on his feet suddenly, brushing by her and heading for the door, and it occurred to her in that moment that he was taller than she was, taller by an inch, maybe more, and how could she have missed that?

"I don't mean it that way," she said. "Corey, come back here, I'm talking to you—"

He turned at the door to give her a look. "No, you're not," he said. "Not anymore."

Halloween was on a Thursday that year, which meant that for all practical purposes the party was going to be a four-day affair, and the big question was how they were going to pace themselves. Fanchon argued for a group session on the night itself—"For the feeling of the spirits on the true date, the veritable date, no?"—and then maybe following it up with another session on Saturday, when the main influx of guests was expected. Charlie pointed out that a lot of people he'd talked to were coming for the weekend, which meant they'd be arriving on Friday and expecting the fullest efflorescence of Millbrook hospitality, and Paulette said, "That's fine. If they want to trip they can trip," and Tim, who was presiding over what amounted to an impromptu meeting in the kitchen over cocktails and the sweet sustaining scent of the bread Paulette and Susannah had been baking all afternoon, said, "Okay, that's it then—group consensus. We play it by ear."

The real problem at this juncture was the question of supply. Though LSD (the sacrament, as Tim called it, or, alternately, heavenly blue) was legal, it was almost impossible to obtain after all the negative publicity surrounding Harvard and Zihuatanejo and the way the drug had jumped out of the lab and onto the front pages of the tabloids. Sandoz backed off, no longer offering free samples, but charging now, as with any other drug. Tim and Dick, seeing which way the wind was blowing, managed to come up with ten thousand dollars, which Tim sent in the form of a personal check to the Sandoz affiliate in New Jersey, along with an order for enough doses to keep half the Eastern Seaboard seeing visions for the next five years, but Sandoz returned the check with a terse note indicating that the drug would henceforth be made available only in small quantities and only to qualified researchers, which apparently was a status Tim and Dick no longer enjoyed. The solution? Dick, who was an amateur pilot in possession of his own plane, flew to Canada, where the authorities weren't yet infected by all this negativity, and obtained what they needed—not through Sandoz but a Czech company that was producing its own iteration of the drug and didn't much concern itself with what Sandoz did or didn't do.

Which amazed her, the whole thing, beginning to end. That the government, the federal government, the FDA, Sandoz, whoever, would want to prevent people from exercising their right to the Fifth Freedom—their right to absolve themselves, become one with creation and maybe even look on the face of God—was simply beyond comprehension. Harvard had turned on them. The Mexicans. The press. Everybody seemed to be against them—and for no other reason but ignorance. As Tim said, they were like the mental midgets of Galileo's day who refused to look through the telescope when the evidence was right there staring them in the face.

But then there was Dick, the shining light in all this—he had all these revelatory facets about him, each one illuminating the other, right down to the core, which was as resilient as the core of a golf ball and would just bounce all the higher the harder you hit it. Dick the professor, Dick the advocate of mind expansion, Dick the guru and housekeeper who was more a father—and mother—to Suzie and Jackie than Tim was himself. And he was a pilot on top of it? He was. And that was all it took. Dick. In his plane. And after that?—the party was on.

All four of the older boys, Corey included, dressed as hoboes. This had the virtue of being simple—old clothes from the Salvation Army in Poughkeepsie and a few strokes of eyebrow pencil for whiskers—and it enabled them to present a group front as they went trick-or-treating in town. Bobby, the youngest, had his heart set on being Tigger, from the Winnie-the-Pooh books, so she helped Susannah sew him a playsuit out of an orange-and-black-striped pattern they found on the top of the back shelf at the fabric shop. She herself dressed as Jackie Kennedy, in a white skirt, white top, white gloves and a black pillbox hat perched on top of her sprayed-up hair as if it had floated down from the sky. Everybody had an early dinner—a dunch, as Fitz called it—and by the time it got dark and the kids trooped up the long drive and down into town to ring doorbells and smash pumpkins, Tim went around to each of the adults and delivered the sacrament, LSD-25, in 250-microgram doses.

They were in the library, lights turned low, the fire glowing in a bed of ash and one of Tim's eternal ragas on the stereo, just settling in, just waiting for the neural fireworks to start, when an unaccountable sound—a buzzing, it seemed like—began to intrude itself under the cascading flights of the sitar. She heard it and then she didn't. Heard it again and then didn't. She was sitting cross-legged on the carpet with Ken, Fanchon and Susannah in a little group apart from the others and they'd been talking about the Light, the ecstatic all-bright light that obliterates your field of vision and announces the presence of God, a light each of them in turn admitted they'd never yet seen, but were hoping to, maybe even tonight—when the buzzing started in again and she interrupted Susannah, who was saying that it wasn't the First Light you were ultimately seeking but the one it gave rise to, the Second Light, which appeared only to the very highest adepts and opened up God and the universe to them for all of time and the time beyond that. Which seemed to Joanie a dubious proposition, as if you could put God on order, and of course to do that would mean that He actually did exist, for which she'd yet to see the evidence—or intuit it. But anything was possible . . . wasn't it?

"Do you hear that?" she asked, interrupting.

"What?"

"Oh, wait," Ken said, "I hear it—a buzz, right? Or is that just the drug coming on?"

Something made her push herself up and go out into the hall to investigate. It was supremely interesting to be on her feet—she felt inexpressibly light, as if her shoes weren't touching the floor at all, as if there were no floor or ground beneath it either. There were shadows everywhere. Cutouts of witches on brooms ascended the walls and a pair of jack-o'-lanterns glowed on either side of the door. Jack-o'-lanterns. With slit eyes and pointed fangs. Inside them was molten lava, a whole volcano's worth, and suddenly it was pouring out all over the room and she realized that she was in the experience now, deep in it, except for that buzzing, which was . . . which was . . . the front door! Wasn't it? Yes. The front door. Definitely the front door.

No one had expected trick-or-treaters. Here they were all the way up at the far end of the village and with a mile-long drive to boot, but wouldn't it be a surprise—a treat, a *gas,* as Charlie would say—to see kids in costumes? That would be the ultimate. She would love that. She went to the door expectantly, took hold of the handle, which seemed in that moment to be melting under the touch of her skin, and pulled it open.

Standing there on the doorstep was a girl of Suzie's age or maybe a little older, who could tell, since the girls in this town all looked as alike as pennies. This girl was dressed in black, all black, in a skirt that fell to the ground and a tight black blouse unbuttoned partway down to expose a black brassiere and the tops of her breasts. On her forehead, centered precisely, was a third eye reproduced in acrylic paint, or maybe that was a hallucination too?

"Hi," the girl said, in a voice that had too much air in it, a kind of a squeak of a voice, "is Nancy in?"

"Nancy?" she repeated, as if she'd never heard the name before in her life.

"Nancy Eggers? She told me to meet her here at seven, I mean, if this is the right place?"

She was about to say something in response, to say yes, when the girl said, "Wow, I love your costume," making a gesture with one hand as if to indicate the whole picture, the doorframe, the jack-o'-lanterns, the white gloves and pillbox hat and the shadows warring beyond. "Jackie Kennedy, right?"

Despite herself, despite the fact that she was just beginning to feel untethered, she was pleased, as if she'd been transformed into a girl herself. "Yes," she said, and felt herself smile.

"Cool," the girl said, looking beyond her into the depths of the hallway before coming back to her. "As a goof, right?"

"Right," she said. "As a goof." Though that scrambled things further, because her intention hadn't been satiric at all—she admired Jackie Kennedy, the First Lady, the woman who'd brought some style to the White House after the relentless dowdiness of Mamie Eisenhower and the dreariness that seemed to radiate outward from her till it swallowed up the whole country in nonentityness, if that was even a word. But that didn't matter now. What mattered was getting back to the circle and the trip and the opening up of *all* her senses, including the ones she didn't yet know she had. "I think Nancy went into town with, with—"

"I'm right here," a voice intoned behind her and she turned round on Nancy, who was dressed exactly like the girl on the front steps, right down to the third eye, and looking not at all like the sixteen-year-old she would be in two weeks' time but a girl—a woman—already in her twenties. She was showing her bra too—and what it supported—and that was wrong, that was inappropriate, and before she knew what she was saying she said, "You look nice. What're you dressed as?"

Nancy gave her an even look. "Same as Lori," she said.

"Really?" The jack-o'-lanterns had begun to exude hot lava again until the whole house crackled with flames and the world beyond rushed away from her and then jerked back again till it was right there trapped inside her skull. "And what would that be—a witch?"

Nancy shook her head.

"Vampire?"

Lori—the girl on the steps—answered for her. "We're both Jackie Kennedy." She made a circular motion with one hand. "Just like you."

This time was different—deeper, more immediate, more powerful—and she had neither the leisure nor presence of mind to wonder whether the formula was skewed or if the dosage had been miscalculated in the lab or if it was just her. She went down hard and fast. She remembered sitting on the floor with her back propped up against the couch and Ken on one side of her and Fitz on the other and Ken saying *You are too perfect, and don't you know it, because, really, no joke, I've always wanted to make it with Jackie Kennedy—what about you, Fitz? You want to make it with her too?* Then she was locked up inside herself for the longest time, just feeling the music and the texture of the carpet beneath her as if it were the portal to the center of the earth and she was dropping down the molten sides of it over and over again, a thousand times, ten thousand, and everybody kept joking and calling her Jackie until she *was* Jackie and nobody else, Jackie presiding over a televised tour of the White House, Jackie smiling into the camera, hosting Girl Scout troops and sewing circles and all the foreign dignitaries and their foreign wives and all of them gabbling in their foreign tongues. At one point, Hollingshead showed up in a rubber mask and she was sure he was Nikita Khrushchev until he took it off and said, *Nyet, nyet, I am only Mickey Mouse,* and everybody was laughing and laughing until she had to go someplace quiet, all by herself—the bedroom, somebody's bedroom—and hold on tight to the wooden post there while all the trains in the world rushed by one after another, slamming at the air and then taking it all, every breath of it, away with them. She choked, she gasped, stroked the carpet—another carpet or was it the same one?—and fell down the very same hole again, right to the center of the earth, and yes, there was someone there with her, a man, a male *Homo sapiens,* representative of her very own species and a very good friend and true, somebody she loved very, very much, and Jackie Kennedy had the time of her life.

Maybe it was nine o'clock. Maybe Fitz was in another room with another person, with people, lots of people, and she was out in the hallway watching the front door pull open and shut on four hoboes and a very small tiger—a Tigger—with shopping bags that bulged and sagged and gave up their contents in multiform array (*You want some candy, Mom?*), until she was alone there once more with the taste of chocolate in her mouth and the door was opening again, this time on two girls, two young *women,* dressed like vampires, like streetwalkers, like *presidents' wives,* if presidents' wives were tramps.

6.

For days after the party—the main party, the big one on Saturday night—she kept running into people she'd never seen before in the hallways or the library or one of the twelve bathrooms, as if the festivities were still in full swing. It was disconcerting, to say the least. And annoying, that too. One couple (the man turned out to be a psychologist friend of Tim's who was dosing himself with LSD in the hope of recovering from an addiction to amphetamines and alcohol) seemed to have moved into one of the vacant rooms on the second floor with a steamer trunk and a dozen cardboard boxes of belongings, which they promptly scattered all over the house. They appeared only at meals, sitting passively at the end of the table among the children, waiting to be fed, and the thing was, both of them had long beaky noses and feathery hair so that they looked like nothing so much as baby birds in a nest—*nestlings,* that was what they were, and that was how she wound up referring to them for the first week or so, as in, *Anybody seen the Nestlings yet?*

And Hollingshead—it was clear he was here to stay as well. He'd brought a sour-faced woman with him who'd dressed as a pussycat at the party—or maybe it was a Playboy bunny—and he went around telling everybody he was with her for the sex only and that when you came right down to it, he didn't even like her. Well, fine. Nobody else liked her either. She was a complainer, nothing about the house or the food or the noise level or the frequency of the sessions or the quality of the marijuana or even the martinis quite up to her standards. Charlie called her a downer, another descriptor he dug out of his Beat dictionary, and the whole household had to put up with her nagging presence—three meals a day and right there in your face every time you turned around—till at the end of the week somebody drove her to the station in Poughkeepsie and she was gone, never to be seen again.

Twelve bathrooms. Somebody had to clean them and it wasn't going to be Hollingshead or the amphetamine addict or the amphetamine addict's wife or girlfriend or whoever she was. More food was needed too, which meant more money and more trips to the supermarket in the station wagon, which really—and she was being honest here—made her rethink, or at least put limits on, the concept of brother- and sisterhood. And while the rest of the hangers-on had eventually left once they saw that the party had played itself out and Tim wasn't the walking drug dispensary he appeared to be, one guest, if you could call her that, didn't seem to have gotten the message. That was Lori, Nancy's smart-mouth friend, who as it turned out was eighteen and not in high school at all—she was a freshman at Bennett, who should have been in her dorm room, should have been studying and joining the Thespians Club or whatever else she was meant to do, but seemed always to be sitting in a prime spot in front of the fire in the evening and at the breakfast table in the morning.

Joanie asked her about it one day, not meaning to be confrontational, or not exactly. She was just curious, because college life for her—at least until Corey came along and she had to drop out—had been very different, with a full class schedule five days a week and enough homework to keep her busy most weekends too. What was this girl thinking, that was what she wanted to know. How had she insinuated herself here? What did she expect? More importantly: When was she going to leave?

It was just after breakfast. Nancy, Corey and the other kids had left for school and she and Susannah had done the dishes and fed the animals and the house had settled into a profound morning silence. This was her favorite time of day, some people not up yet, others off in the woods or sequestered in one nook or another and all the excitement of the group experiment tempered in the simple routine of being alive in the world till it would build to climax again in the evening when there'd be dinner, discussion, music, sometimes a film on Tim's brand-new projector and on Saturdays the weekly group session everybody looked forward to. She found Lori in the library with Fitz and Ken, who'd started a fire there to take the chill off the room. They were all reading, Fitz and Ken absorbed in the newspaper, Lori in a book of what appeared to be poetry.

"Oh, hello, all," she said, settling into the couch beside Fitz but looking only to Lori, who was sprawled on the other side of him with one of the cats—a bloated tabby with a head the size of a cantaloupe—asleep in her lap.

Ken, who was occupying one of the armchairs in front of the fire, said "Hi" and Fitz murmured a greeting, but Lori said nothing.

A moment ticked by, the only sound the hiss of the fire. She picked up a section of the newspaper and scanned the headlines, only to set it back down again, the news of the outside world—a volcanic eruption in the North Atlantic, Malcolm X's speech, a train disaster in Japan and a coup in Vietnam—as remote and meaningless as if she really were on a spaceship floating in the void. But this was a private spaceship, wasn't it? She'd thought so. Except that now she had to adjust to the Nestlings and Hollingshead—and on top of it she had to see this girl slumped there on the couch as if this were her own house, as if she belonged, as if the inner circle were open to just anybody now no matter their age or experience. "So, Lori," she said, after the silence had simmered a moment, "how are you?"

The girl—unbrushed hair, chewed nails, skin as white and featureless as a sheet of Fitz's Corrasable Bond—just gave her a look and shrugged.

"I was just wondering how school was going?"

"Fine."

Fitz looked up, smoothed out a wrinkle in the newspaper and said, "Have we got any coffee left? I could really use a cup of coffee— anybody else? Joanie? Ken? Lori?"

No one answered him, so he pushed himself up and went off in the direction of the kitchen, pausing in the doorway to say, "Last chance," before Lori murmured, "No thanks," and he was gone.

"Because," Joanie said, taking up the conversation where she'd left off, "it's really none of my business, I guess, but shouldn't you be in class?"

Another shrug. Lori's feet were bare, her nail polish chipped and dull.

"And your dorm," she went on, "what about your dorm—and your roommates? Aren't they missing you, because it's been over a week now, or more—?"

"Susannah said I could stay as long as I want"—that little squeak of a voice, as if there were a bicycle pump inside her. "And Tim. And Fitz too. Is there a problem with that? Ken?"

Ken turned his head to look over his shoulder, his hair struck gold in the sun through the windows.

"Ken," Lori repeated, holding the book open in one hand and stroking the ears of the cat with the other, "do you have a problem with me being here?"

"No," he said, "no, not at all. You're—nice. A nice person. And it's nice to see such a beautiful smile around here, right, Joanie?"

To this point, Lori's face had been about as expressive as a stone, but now she did smile, on cue, and it was as if she were doing one of those toothpaste commercials you saw on TV, her lips pulled back to show off her healthy pink gums and flawless teeth. The smile invested her eyes, brought out a display of dimples, lit her up till she *was* beautiful and no doubt about it.

"Right," she heard herself say, but she said it perfunctorily because she was trying to get at something here. She turned back to the girl. "And maybe it's just me, but aren't you afraid of getting bad grades and didn't I hear something about your college president declaring the Hitchcock estate—us, that is—out-of-bounds for all you girls? Which isn't right, I'm not saying that, but—"

The smile vanished. "He's a jerk," she said.

"Well, that may be, but he's the jerk in charge." Something in the girl's face told her to stop, that it was none of her business, but of course it was, if she was *living* here now. Living here and influencing the other kids. And Fitz. And Ken. And Tim. "Maybe it's not for me to say—"

Lori's mouth hardened.

"I mean, I'm not your mother."

"No," Lori said, "you're not."

Tim was gone intermittently during that week and the next, traveling back and forth to New York to lecture on the psychedelic experience, sit for interviews and drum up financial support for the Castalia Foundation while managing both to play down and capitalize on the press hysteria over LSD, which seemed to be everywhere now, not just in the tabloids. The *New York Times* had done an article on Tim's and Dick's move to Millbrook (and, of course, their unceremonious departure from Harvard) and *The Saturday Evening Post*, *Newsweek* and *Esquire* ran sedately sensational stories about psychedelic drugs and the revolution they were fomenting not simply among psychologists but the general public as well. The big news? That the drug had escaped the lab and people were beginning to use it indiscriminately—not under a psychiatrist's direction or in controlled studies or for any purpose any reasonable observer could deem legitimate. And that they were courting trouble, like the group of college students who had stared so long and hard at the sun while under the influence of LSD as to scorch their retinas and become permanently blinded (a story that turned out to be untrue, ridiculous really, but stood in vivid testimony nonetheless).

Joanie didn't like any of this one bit. It just called attention to themselves and what they were trying to accomplish here—and what they were trying to accomplish demanded privacy because you didn't entertain visitors on a spaceship, did you? Wasn't that the whole point of blasting off into space in the first place? And look what had happened in Mexico. Did they really want a repeat of that?

She brought it up during a group meeting one night when Tim was back from New York and the martinis were flowing and the children, under Lori's and Nancy's direction, had prepared the evening meal of tuna casserole blackened around the edges and broccoli so overboiled it had the consistency of pudding, a meal everyone had felt obligated to praise, right down to the dessert, which was three pans of fudge brownies topped with cream cheese and walnuts.

"I don't know," she said, leaning into the table to address Tim, who, as always, was talking nonstop, and she waited till he paused and lifted his eyes to her before going on. "What I'm saying is I don't know how much good all this publicity is really doing us—"

"We need money," Tim said, giving her an even look. "If for nothing else"—he tapped his glass—"for gin alone. You have any idea how much gin we're going through here?"

"I'm serious, Tim. I mean, the kids are even hearing about it at school. The other kids are calling them names, mind-benders, freaks, astronauts—"

"Astronauts?" Ken said, grinning. "Hairy women I can understand, but *astronauts*?"

Charlie, seated across the table from her between Alice and Fanchon, cut in to say, "The proper term is psychonauts, and we ought to get them all to wear jumpsuits or sweatshirts or something with THE

PSYCHONAUTS emblazoned on them in big red letters, with maybe a red light bulb underneath it, shooting out rays, what do you think?"

"Perfect," Ken said. "I can see it already. The school mascot is just a big glowing bulb dancing around the field. Or no, a brain. Pink, of course. With all the convolutions pulsing."

"The Millbrook High Convoluters," Charlie said. "That ought to put a scare into the opposition."

What she thought was that they ought to get serious here a minute, just once, just for a minute, and was that too much to ask? She felt a flash of anger with Charlie, who always had to make a joke of everything. "Easy for you to say, but you don't have any kids."

"I do," he protested. "Every kid in this house is my kid." And here they all looked down the table to where the children had abandoned the field, all except for Lori, who didn't really qualify, though she slept in Nancy's room and always seemed to be slipping in and out of one doorway or another in the company of Nancy, Suzie or one of the boys. "And that's another thing," he went on, "—I just don't see how we can pretend to be so concerned about the kids, about us as a family, when we keep denying them the sacrament. It's hypocritical. Why shouldn't they have that experience, like Susannah said last time? Talk about school, it'll give them an *advantage,* that's what it'll do. And that'd shut the naysayers up faster than anything."

It was an idea that had been floated before and she was of two minds about it. On the one hand, she wanted Corey to have that advantage, to see through the veil, enrich his mind—and his IQ; she was sure it would boost his IQ even higher than it already was—but by the same token she was afraid for him, afraid of what a bad trip might do to somebody so young, whose personality wasn't fully formed yet. "What about Bobby?" she said. "He's only eight."

Fitz—he was sitting beside her, sipping from a glass of brandy—said there ought to be a cutoff age. "Just in terms of brain development—the stages of it, I mean. All the literature—"

"Literature," Hollingshead interjected bitterly. "Textbooks. Papers,

articles, *The New England Journal of Medicine*. All written by aca-
demics who wouldn't know transcendence if it bit them in the ass."

"I'll second that," Charlie said. They were beyond academia now,
into a new realm in which they were the pioneers and the mas-
ters too, not McClelland and Kellard or even the neurologists in the
medical school, who, as Fitz himself liked to point out, knew the
brain only as an organ, anatomically, but didn't have a clue as to what
thought was—or what it was capable of either.

Royce—he was Bobby's father, after all, and so it was his decision, his and Susannah's—tilted his head and gave Charlie a quizzical
look. "I don't know,' he said. "He *is* awfully young. Just a little kid,
really . . ."

"Hypocrisy," Hollingshead said, shaking his head, and Susannah,
who was seated between him and her husband, leaned forward so she
could look past him to where Tim sat in his usual spot, at the head
of the table, and said, "A microdose. A hundred micrograms or even
less. What do you think, Tim?"

Tim was beaming. This was the kind of question he lived for—if
they were going to get the word out to the world, it had to start right
here, at home. He tipped back his glass, looked round the table. "It's
all in the family," he said.

Ultimately it was decided that the following Saturday the entire
household would trip together, with the exception of her and
Fitz, who volunteered to act as guides, and Bobby, who was deemed
too young to process the experience, even if he was limited to so
small a dose it was barely viable. She saw the sense in that—what
was the rush? Give him time to grow into his body. And his mind.
With the other kids, it was different—they were all in their teens, and
she half-suspected Tim had dosed Suzie and Jackie at some point,
though the subject hadn't come up and nobody had seemed eager to
ask about it.

Whether that had ever happened or not didn't really matter—all that mattered to her was Corey. He'd been sleeping in his own room again, as far as she knew, and he was doing fine in school—no complaints there—but he felt excluded, she could see that. Every time she thought of the way he'd reacted when she'd confronted him over Nancy she felt as if she were being attacked all over again. He was an adolescent, yes, growing away from her and Fitz, testing the limits, but the depth of his bitterness had shocked her—and the way he'd judged her too, as if she'd done something to be ashamed of, as if giving herself over to the experience had somehow diminished her love for him and Fitz, when nothing could be further from the truth. But then how could he understand what this was all about if they kept him from it? And that was true of the other kids too. It was time. Past time. But still, *still*—and this was why she and Fitz had volunteered to abstain and guide him through the process—she was worried about him. How could she not be? She was his mother. She'd always be his mother. And as much as she gave of herself to all of them, to everybody at Millbrook, adults and children alike, that would never change.

She waited till the morning of the session before saying anything to him. She could have broached the subject earlier—or Fitz could have, but Fitz was so wrapped up in his books and papers he was barely present half the time, and she hadn't wanted to burden Corey unnecessarily or build up his expectations or even to make the session sound like anything out of the ordinary. He had school to worry about. And sports (he'd gone out for the soccer team at the urging of Tommy Eggers, who was the center forward, and to his own surprise—and hers—he'd made it). Better, she thought, just to mention it casually, as in *By the way, we're having a session tonight, like every Saturday, only tonight's going to be a little different.* So she stayed in the room, reading, until Fitz had gone off to get his coffee and a couple slices of the homemade bread he liked to dunk idly in it ("You want coffee?" he'd asked and she'd shaken her head no), then got up and rapped lightly at the door that connected their room and Corey's.

"Can I come in?" she asked, projecting her voice through the door.

"Who is it?"

"Me—who do you think?"

"What do you want?"

"Nothing, it's just"—and here she pushed open the door to see him sitting up bare-chested on the edge of the bed, though the room was like an icebox—"I wanted to say good morning. Pancakes for breakfast today. With those sausages you like—the links?"

"It's Saturday," he moaned. "I just want to sleep, okay?"

She noticed that the window was open and so she crossed the room to pull it shut. "God, it's freezing in here," she said, turning round on him and shaking her head, but fondly, and with a smile. "I guess you're just like your father, because he likes it cold enough at night to freeze Nanook himself. And all the sled dogs too."

His clothes, including his soccer things—jersey, sweat socks, jockstrap—were piled up in the corner, which gave the place a feral smell. The sheets could have been cleaner and she made a note to herself to ball everything up and stick it in the washing machine, though she'd been trying not to interfere. What he did in his own room was his business (as long as Nancy wasn't involved). On the dresser stood the twenty-gallon aquarium her mother had bought for him, and it was lit now and burbling and as clean and well maintained as the ones at the pet shop. Fish in every color imaginable rose and fell and darted in and out of brilliant green clumps of plants that rocked gently in the current generated by the filter. It struck her as intensely beautiful, a beautiful thing—a world—he'd created all on his own.

"The fish tank looks nice," she said. "How are they doing—the fish, I mean?"

He shrugged. "All right."

"Listen, you can sleep in if you want. I'll set aside a plate for you. We can heat it up in the oven whenever you want, okay?"

"Yeah, sure," he said, and he drew up his legs and got back under the covers.

"All right, then." She made her way back across the room, pausing with one hand on the door before turning round as if she'd just remembered something. "Oh, I wanted to say we're having a session tonight. Just us. No visitors coming up from the city, as far as I know."

He said nothing, just stared at her, his head propped up on the pillow with its beige pillowcase that could have been cleaner.

"We—we've all been discussing it," she said, fumbling over the words. "And everybody thought it was time you kids joined in—all of you except Bobby, that is."

"Yeah," he said, "I know." She must have looked surprised because he added, "Everybody knows. Lori told us."

"Good," she said, "fine," trying to cover herself though she felt a jolt of anger. *Lori.* What business was it of hers? "I just wanted to tell you, that's all, because it's going to be special, you'll see, and there's nothing to worry about, because your father and I'll be right there the whole time."

The room held its odor. The tank gurgled. His voice, when he finally spoke, was so soft she barely heard him. "You're not going to do it?"

"No," she said. "Not this time. This time is for you."

They had their big meal in the afternoon, a pair of overstuffed tom turkeys with all the trimmings—it might have been two weeks yet till Thanksgiving, but who could resist the sale price, turkey flesh so cheap they were practically giving it away? Afterward they all went outside to take advantage of what turned out to be a fine clear high-toned day with barely a trace of a breeze. Nearly everybody, herself included, participated in a touch football game that went on, with various substitutions and a wildly fluctuating score that had one team up by three touchdowns only to end in a tie or a draw or whatever you wanted to call it, until it was too dark to see the ball, after which they showered, changed clothes, stoked up the fireplace and settled in with martinis while the kids had hot chocolate and turkey sandwiches and Tim put on the MJQ to get everybody in the mood for what was to come.

A few visitors did show up—Peggy and her brother Tommy, who'd been initiated in Mexico and was as enthusiastic as any of them about the ongoing experiment they were all committed to and sometimes spent the weekend in his own house on the property in any case, so he wasn't exactly a visitor—but Tim had let it be known that this particular Saturday session was going to be a family affair, and so they were spared the influx of guests the weekends had been increasingly attracting. Which was fine with everybody. This session, above all, was for the dedicated members of their little colony—and their offspring, because without the next generation, where would you be?

At seven, Tim and Dick went around dispensing the drug, the adults to get 250 mics, which had become the standard dose, the children a beginner's dose of 100. The adults, seasoned voyagers all, just threw back their pills and went on waving their martini glasses and chattering away as if this were just another session, which in a sense it was, but the children, especially the Roberts boys and Corey, seemed solemn—or maybe even a little frightened. "It's okay," she kept saying, "it's going to be fun," but they just stared at her. Corey, especially, seemed to be holding himself in, as if he were resisting what hadn't yet happened. Which was all wrong, because if you went into this with a negative mind-set you were just looking for trouble, she knew that as well as anybody.

It was Tim who came to the rescue. He saw right away what was happening and took over, just like that. He spent a few minutes with each of the kids, calmly explaining what was happening and what to expect and how marvelous it was going to be, how right and necessary and enduring. "Any of you worried about higher math?" he asked. "There is no higher math than this. Just don't tell your teacher, that's all—he'll say you've got an unfair advantage."

Half an hour later, Corey was in the nook beside the fireplace, sitting on an Indian blanket spread out over the floor, with Richard and Ronald on one side of him, Nancy and Lori on the other. They had their legs pulled up to their chests and were staring vacantly into the flame of a big columnar candle Lori had dipped and scented herself with vanilla extract she'd borrowed from Fanchon's limitless supply. The other kids—Jackie, Suzie and Tommy Eggers—were sitting in front of the fire with Tim, Dick, Peggy and her brother, while Bobby was hunched over the coffee table, absorbed in building a shiny silver robot with the Erector set Royce had picked up that morning to occupy him.

The music (no Beatles, though that was what Corey would have wanted or would have thought he wanted) segued from the brittle tinkling of the MJQ to Ravi Shankar, master of the extended raga that beat on in your brain till your brain was all the way across the world in India, perched high on a palanquin on the back of an elephant framed against the white peaks of the Himalayas. Which was a funny image—a brain riding an elephant—and she had to step back from herself a moment and give out with a little laugh that no one seemed to notice, and just as well. They were tripping, or soon would be, and she wasn't. What she was doing was sipping her second martini and watching the kids furtively from her perch on the couch alongside Fitz, Ken and Fanchon, already beginning to regret her resolution.

But the kids. They were in another world now, intense, expectant, their faces just beginning to register what was happening inside them, the relentless beat drawing them in degree by degree, Richard tapping his foot, Ronald drumming on one knee, Nancy suddenly up on her knees and drawing circles in the air with both hands as her mind rushed off to explain something her tongue couldn't keep up with. And Corey. He wasn't musically inclined, not as far as she could see, and he'd told her and Fitz more than once that jazz was boring and that you could take the boredom to the third power with Indian music, but he was beginning to nod his head in time to the beat, if ever so marginally. Richard—his hair grown out and worked up into a pompadour since school began—said something that got them all laughing and then Corey said something and Nancy took it up and they kept on laughing till they were rolling on the floor in sheer abandon and then sitting up to clap along with the music and laugh some more. They were opening up, even Ronald, the quiet one, and she could see the excitement in their eyes.

For a while, an hour so in, Lori and Nancy got up and started dancing in place, doing a kind of modified Twist they tried to time to the skittering beat, but none of the boys would join in and after ten or fifteen minutes of gyrating their hips and pumping their arms like cheerleaders they gave it up and sank back down to the floor. Where it felt safer. Closer. Solider. Where they could fold their legs under them and give themselves up to the all-embracing force of gravity that would hold them in place so their minds could roam free. And so what if Nancy took hold of Corey's hand and intertwined her fingers with his and held on to him as if she owned him, as if they were ten years older and married and stretched out on their own bed in their own house somewhere in a future existence neither of them could begin to fathom? So what if every day of her life she regretted getting pregnant at nineteen and missing out on college and was determined to spare Corey that sort of burden? It was all right. Nothing was going to happen between Nancy and Corey, not while she was here. ("Is she on birth control?" she'd asked Susannah the morning after she'd found them in bed together and Susannah had said, "Are you crazy? She's fifteen," and she'd said, "My point exactly.")

She was watching. Right here, watching. Sipping and nodding her head to the music and trying to sink into the mood of the room on the fumes of alcohol alone. Which wasn't happening and wasn't going to happen. Not as things stood. Fitz sat with her a while after Ken and Fanchon had gone into the library to commune with some of the others—the ones who were tripping instead of sitting there straight as arrows—and they both watched the kids, but the kids were quiet now, deep into their own minds, and really, it couldn't have gone better, they both agreed on that. Still, she wasn't satisfied, not in herself. And when she let her gaze fall over the room to see how tuned-in everybody was, she felt even less satisfied. She wanted to be there with them—with Corey, with Fanchon and Ken and everybody else—and it came to her that there was no good reason why she had to deprive herself aside from paranoia and her own ego that just wouldn't let go even if she swilled a gallon of gin. *So why not?* she thought. Really, why not join the party?

By this point, Fitz, who'd had too much to drink, was sunk into the couch, his chin pressed to his chest, snoring lightly. She didn't consult him. She didn't need to. Everything was as fine as fine could be. She got up and made her way across the room, dodging people laid out like corpses in the flickering shadows, nobody talking now and the only sound the airy repeated figures of Ravi Shankar's sitar and the ceaseless tapping of the frenetic little drums.

She found Tim in the far corner, stretched out on his back in a heap of pillows with Peggy beside him, her head resting on his shoulder and her hair so disordered it looked as if she'd been out in a windstorm. She had one hand inside Tim's shirt, dreamily massaging his chest, her hand flexing and releasing over and over again. Tim's eyes were closed, but he was seeing things, that was for sure: if everybody else had taken 250 mics, he would have done double that or even three times it, because he'd tripped more than all of them combined and needed larger and larger doses to get him where he wanted to go. Which, after two martinis that had had no effect on her whatsoever, was where she wanted to go too.

"Tim," she whispered, standing over him as the candles flickered and the music thumped and rattled on.

His eyes flashed open, two dark gouges in the shadowy architecture of his face. He saw her, or seemed to see her, and smiled.

"I've changed my mind," she said.

He didn't ask why or what had taken her so long or say yes or say no—he just said, "My right front pocket," and in the next moment she was bending over him and slipping her hand into his pocket like a thief. Or a lover. She had been his lover and would be again, all in the family, but not tonight. Tonight—and here she shot a look around the room only to see that nobody was stirring, let alone watching her—she was going to shake one pill from the bottle . . . no, two. Why not two?

7.

Fall exploded in color and then left them, so that by the third week of November it already seemed like mid-winter, the trees stripped bare, the grass dead, the flowerbeds withered and the fountain transformed into an ice sculpture. The jack-o'-lanterns had long since collapsed on themselves and the dozen or so uncarved pumpkins on the front porch were frozen through till they were like so many cannonballs stockpiled against an invasion. Mice thrived in the house, legions of them appearing and disappearing like phantoms, and the cats, which could have earned their keep, just seemed bored by the whole spectacle. What else? The furnace burned fuel like a battleship at sea and it didn't seem to make much difference, since the house was inhumanly cold in all its sixty-four rooms except in the kitchen and within ten feet of one of the fireplaces. The women shopped at the A & P, cooked, cleaned and took the sacrament one night a week. The men typed, read, split wood and took the sacrament with them, though some began to feel that the regimen was too confining. Why not two nights a week? Three? Why not (it was Charlie who proposed this, only half-jokingly) every day?

For the children—the teenagers, the offspring—who'd passed their test with flying colors, it was to be once a month like an infusion of vitamins. Lori was the exception, though Lori wasn't a child and wasn't one of their offspring either. She was a presence, already becoming a fixture, serving as an intermediary between the other teenagers and the adults, and she pitched in with the housework and the cooking too, as did both the Nestlings once they came out of their haze. After a while, nobody asked her about school anymore or wondered what she was doing there among them or who exactly had invited her or why. She did seem to have money though (rich parents?) and she never failed to make a weekly contribution to the grocery pool, which was more than could be said for some—all the men, except Dick, were hurting, deprived of their salaries and stipends, and none of the women worked outside of the house. Something had to give. And so at the next meeting, when Tim and Dick revived the idea of conducting psychedelic seminars, just as they'd attempted to do in Zihuatanejo before the black shirts descended on them, what had once sounded so intrusive began to sound better, much better, salvatory even.

"What are we going to charge?" Rick Roberts wanted to know.

"Seventy-five dollars apiece," Tim said. "As a donation, a *minimum* donation. More if the spirit moves them." He was at the head of the table, as usual, the dinner dishes cleared away, candles burning, wine and beer flowing, a pair of marijuana cigarettes—joints—making their slow way from hand to hand. He'd thought everything out. He was in charge, guru and impresario both, as capable as anybody of finding a way to profit from the inner life, and that was all that mattered now—they had to keep things going. They had to. And while Joanie hated the idea of strangers intruding on them—more strangers—what was the alternative?

"We'll start," Dick was saying, "with maybe twenty couples—"

"Which will net us a nice clean three thousand dollars," Tim said, giving a glance round the table. "Which, I think you'll all agree, is a nice weekend's work, no?"

She was stunned. *Three thousand dollars.* That would solve a lot of problems, one of which was that she hadn't even begun to look for work yet, though their nest egg was just about gone and she was feeling increasingly guilty about it. Corey needed a new winter jacket. Needed boots. Christmas was coming up. Would she get a share? Would they all? Or maybe a salary—the Castalia Foundation could pay out salaries, couldn't it?

"What are we going to feed them?" Paulette wanted to know. She was slumped in her chair, glassy-eyed. She'd lost weight, which was evident from the way her sweater hung from her in long depleted folds. And her hair, which had lightened so prettily under the Mexican sun, seemed to have lost its sheen. She looked exhausted. Of all of them, she put in the most time in the kitchen, so it wasn't just an idle question.

"Same thing we eat," Tim said, "only more of it."

"Much more," Charlie said.

"All that's wonderful," Susannah said, "but this isn't a hotel. Who's going to do all the cooking, clean the rooms—they're going to expect clean rooms, aren't they?"

"We'll all pitch in," Dick said. "It's worth it, isn't it? I mean, three thousand dollars? And it's not as if we don't have all the names and addresses of the people who joined the IFIF and now the Foundation— all we have to do is send out letters and watch the money roll in."

"What about the heavenly blue?" Fitz asked. He was propped on both elbows, his cigarette fuming in the ashtray, his drink—brandy, more brandy—squared up right beside it as if he were sitting in a bar someplace. "We need it for ourselves, isn't that right? For our *own* sessions? Isn't that what this is all about?" He was irritated, the lines in his brow compressing like waves crashing one atop the other. He looked directly at Dick. "Unless you're planning on buzzing up to Canada in your Cessna every other week."

"We're going to do it without drugs," Tim said.

"Without drugs?" Charlie could barely contain himself. "How

can you have a session without drugs? That's like, like"—he snatched up the first thing that came to hand, Fitz's drink—"brandy without a glass. Or, or—"

"A pigeon without wings?" Tim said. "A Girl Scout without a uniform? An ocean without water?" He held up both palms for silence. "We are going to give them exactly what we promise: lectures, meditation, group mind. Just the way Gurdjieff's people do it. Think of it as a retreat, a weekend in the country away from the madhouse of the city, leave your ego at the door, thank you very much. In fact, the first night, the way Dick and I see it, we dress everybody in robes so as to eliminate status symbols, and that goes for jewelry too, even watches—and we forbid them to talk, not a word, till the morning of the second day. Silence. A strict code of silence."

"Right," Dick said. "No 'I'm a stockbroker' or 'We live in Scarsdale' or any of that nonsense."

"They're going to want drugs," Charlie said.

Fanchon, silent to this point, said, "But of course. This is what we all want, is it not?"

And Tim, serene, above it all, had every angle figured out: "They're not going to get them. As Fitz points out, we've got our own supply to worry about—thanks, Dick, for all your efforts on our behalf, by the way, and don't think we're not supremely grateful—and the way the press is stirring things up, not to mention Lori's dear old college prez, we don't really need to attract any *official* attention here, do we?" He looked round the table. "We give them illusion, perfectly legal, noncontroversial and totally habit forming."

"Hocus-pocus," Charlie said, and everybody laughed.

"Now you see it," Tim said, pulling an imaginary card out of his sleeve, "now you don't."

It was amazing what the promise of money could do. Everyone pitched in to clean the place up, which was long overdue, and because Tim felt the atmosphere was too staid—too bourgeois—they went around painting mandalas and third eyes on the walls and then sawed the legs off the furniture so as to reduce everything to floor level, Arabian Nights style. Or Japanese. (It was around that time they'd all piled into a couple of the cars and driven up to Bard for a showing of Kurosawa's *Yojimbo,* which really took Tim's fancy— "That's the way to do it," he said, "go minimal, sit right on the floor and all you need for a table is a block of wood. Right?" he said. "Right? Which, by the way, is also your pillow.") She did her part and more, though she knew in her heart it was all wrong, that they were selling out, constructing some ersatz version of the life they'd chosen in a way that would be hard to shake off, as if the artificial were the real and the real the illusion. Still, it was better than going back to work at some shitty job, waitressing in a café or typing up index cards in some tomb of a library in Poughkeepsie or Newburgh.

Then, just as they'd gotten focused, the bomb hit: in a single day, President Kennedy was assassinated and Aldous Huxley, their animating spirit, died. Huxley's death wasn't unexpected—he'd been ill with cancer for some time and Tim had recently flown out to Los Angeles to pay his last respects—but it was a blow nonetheless. With Kennedy, it was different. Nobody had expected that, least of all her—and she must have been one of the last people in the country to hear about it. She'd been out for a long ramble through the woods that afternoon and when she got back—late, the sky already beginning to close up—she was puzzled to find no one in the sitting room or the library, not even the dog or one of the cats. Puzzled, she sank into the couch in front of the fire, which had burned down to coals, something that was unusual in itself—there was always somebody around to throw a log on. One of the satisfactions of a house with a fireplace, as opposed to the chintzy apartments they'd been stuck in the past two years, was to build a fire and plant yourself in front of it to absorb the heat and watch the play of the flames that were a whole trip in themselves, whether you were high or not. She always liked to picture the primeval men and women—cavemen, Neanderthals— staring into their bonfires and leaving their bodies for hours at a time while the stars rained down on them and the wind howled and the mammoths and musk oxen and all the rest of the ice-bound creatures curled up in their fur.

When she got up to fetch wood from the porch, still wondering where everybody was, she thought she heard a noise from the kitchen and stopped a moment, listening. There was a crackle, a whine, then a mechanical voice—*the radio*—and went to investigate. Pushing through the double doors, she was stunned to see everybody there, the entire household, right down to the Nestlings and little Bobby Eggers, crowded round the kitchen radio and sitting on every available surface, the counters, the table, the kitchen chairs, the chopping block. No one said a word, no one even glanced up at her. For one wild moment she thought she was in a *Twilight Zone* episode and everyone had been transformed into automatons, but then, her heart fluttering, she asked, "What is it? What's happened?"—and Fitz looked up at her and said, "Kennedy's dead."

"What do you mean dead?"

Corey shot her a look. He had tears in his eyes.

The announcer, in a lugubrious voice, was progressing through a slow drumbeat of detail, *Dallas, 12:30 P.M. Central time, motorcade, shots fired,* which didn't make sense at all. The president dead? But no, that couldn't be—he'd been shot, that was all, and they'd just patch him up like in the westerns, where the heroes got shot all the time. Then somebody, one of the kids, said, "Turn on the TV," which didn't make any sense either. Nobody had a television here. They'd come to Millbrook for the inner life, not commercials for potato peelers and Oscar Mayer wieners. She looked wildly around her. "TV? What are you talking about?"

In the next moment, everybody was filing out of the kitchen in solemn procession and heading down the corridor to Royce and Susannah's room, where Royce was already bent over the rabbit ears of a big maple TV cabinet that must have been buried in the trailer they'd towed behind them when they left Boston and had sat there all these weeks awaiting just this moment. But it was on now, humming to life: a flicker, an adjustment of the dial, a new announcer, his voice shaken and hollow. Then the first image appeared, and it was devastating, the real world, the world of hate and pain and horror, slamming right into her like a clenched fist. She saw a casket being lowered from an airplane, and behind it, the president's wife—Jackie—in her pastel suit, which was steeped in her husband's blood, following numbly in its wake.

No one said a word. She squeezed in beside Fitz, who was pressed up against the wall, one arm around Corey, and for the longest time she held on to them both, her eyes fixed on the screen and the figures moving there in shadowy procession. *Jackie Kennedy, right?* Lori had said. *As a goof, right?* All at once she was crying too. It was her fault. All her fault—if she'd only dressed as somebody else, a witch, a cabaret dancer, a sea hag, this would never have happened. It was karma, all karma, and she'd been wrong, she was deluded, and she was guilty, guilty, guilty, of this and everything else.

She glanced round the room and saw that everybody was huddled in separate groups, husbands and wives and children together, Tim, Peggy, Suzie and Jackie, the Nestlings, the Robertses, the Eggerses, the Sensabaughs, as if everything to this point had just been playacting and once the world sank its talons into them, they were ready to give up the pretense. This was no family. This was just a collection of strangers united by one thing only and that thing was a drug, just a drug . . .

That was when Tim crossed the room to the television—*This is a tragic day for America,* the announcer was intoning, *for the whole—* and flicked it off. "I guess this is as bad as it gets," he said, bowing his head. "We've lost a president—and I've just learned that Aldous passed away this afternoon out in Los Angeles. Two gone in one day," he said, shaking his head. "But what we're going to do is hold a vigil, a candlelight vigil, for both their souls." He nodded to Dick, who was standing in the corner beside Lori, stone-faced. "We'll gather by the fire in ten minutes for meditation, and for those who want to commune with them, Dick will be passing round the sacrament."

People began pushing themselves up from the floor, patting down their pockets and looking around them absently as if they'd forgotten something. Still nobody said anything, not even the kids, not even Bobby.

"By the way," Tim went on, "if it will make any of you feel any better, Aldous at least went peacefully. Laura gave him two intramuscular injections of LSD-25 in his final hours, just as he'd requested when I last saw him. His body might have failed him, as all our bodies will fail in time, but his mind soared—and if we focus, really focus as a group, I don't have the slightest doubt we'll feel those emanations tonight."

He paused. The dog, which had been lying on the floor beside Jackie, got up and stretched himself, then gave his head and shoulders a good shake so that his collar rattled and chimed in a way that seemed to bring the whole room out of its trance. "And Kennedy's too," Tim added. "Maybe even Kennedy's too."

They held the first of the consciousness-raising seminars three weeks later, which gave everyone a little breathing room after the national tragedy (and here Tim was thinking of the paying guests especially). Forty participants, mostly couples and mostly middle-aged, signed up and sent in their registration fees in advance. They began arriving on Friday afternoon in the face of a cold northerly wind and intermittent snow showers, and the first problem, which no one, incredibly, had anticipated, was where they were going to park. She was in the kitchen, working furiously over the dinner preparations—forty more mouths to feed, above and beyond the daily demands of the household—when Tommy Eggers burst in the back door, shouting, "They're here! They're here!"

Susannah and Paulette were with her, tucking the roasts in the oven and putting the finishing touches to the relish trays, and at the moment she was bent over the biggest pot in the kitchen, mashing potatoes. "Who?" she asked, looking up irritably. The guests weren't due till five—the instructions had been explicit on that score—and it was hardly past four yet.

Tommy was tall, narrow shouldered, seventeen now—or was it eighteen?—and his coloring was nothing like his sister's. He had her eyes, perfectly round and black as pitted olives, but his hair was a sort of neutral brown, whereas Nancy's was so unrelievedly black you would have thought she was an Indian. Or a gypsy. He was nice enough, she supposed, a good kid, but no one would mistake him for a genius. "I don't know," he said, looking to his mother, then back to her again, "—the people, you know, the ones we're like all supposed to hide from?"

"You kids don't have to hide," Susannah said, but they did. Nobody wanted to pay seventy-five dollars and upward for a mystic retreat and see a sneering contingent of adolescents slinking around. The kids were to stay strictly to themselves, out of sight, out of earshot. Tim had ordained it so and Dick had set them up in the house out back called the Bowling Alley, which had plenty of room for all of them and, as its name indicated, sported its own bowling alley in the basement to help keep them entertained.

Just then, a face appeared in the window over the kitchen table. She saw a man there, a stranger, mid-thirties, gray fedora, gray herringbone overcoat with the collar pulled up, white shirt, blue tie. He began rapping at the glass. *Where,* he mouthed, *do we park?*

She gave him an abrupt wave, then turned to Tommy. "Can't one of the men take care of it?"

Tommy—he was already picking at the relish tray, folding a piece of bologna into his mouth—just shrugged. "I don't know," he said. "Nobody's around."

"They can't be here already," Paulette said, all evidence to the contrary.

"All right, all right," she heard herself say. "I'll do it."

She went to the door, where somebody's jacket—one of the kids'?—was hanging on a hook there and she shrugged into it, all the while making conciliatory gestures to the man in the window, who seemed to be pressing his face to the glass now. She was just about to open the door when she realized that she'd have to talk to him, which would spoil the whole illusion, as if his seeing her there in the steamed-over kitchen mashing potatoes wasn't demystifying enough, and so she held up her palm to stall him while she ran out the other door and through the dining room to the front hall, where she snatched up half a dozen sheets of the instructions she'd typed up and mimeographed herself. There was no one around. "Dick!" she shouted up the stairs. "Fitz!" No answer. So she hurried out the front door, thinking to cut round the side of the house.

The day was blustery, stung with the cold. There were already three cars in the driveway, faces watching her expectantly from behind the silvered windows as she darted across the dead grass, the wind in her face, pellets of snow rattling off the jacket—which must have been Nancy's, she realized, too tight at the waist and short in the sleeves—and came up to the man at the window, who swung round on her, startled, and said, "Sorry, I just wanted to know where we're supposed to park?"

She held a finger to her lips.

He looked puzzled. "Is this the right place? This is where the seminar's supposed to be, isn't it?"

She nodded and handed him one of the sheets of paper, which fluttered in the wind as he tried to make it out. What it said, under the heading *Awareness* was that silence would be required among the participants for the first twelve hours, as a way of breaking set and eliminating role-playing. And then—Tim had dictated this to her—it got more explicit: *No one here is eager to play the game of "you" or the game of "guest" with you. There will be little interest manifested in your thoughts, opinions, accomplishments, nor in the history and com-*

plexity of your personality. You will find total acceptance but little verbal reassurance. "Good" is what raises the ecstasy count of all persons present and "bad" is what lowers the ecstasy count.

The wind snatched away his breath. Hard dry pellets of snow batted at him, whitened the brim of his hat. He read as if it were a Herculean labor, the first test in a long string of them. Finally he looked up at her out of eyes the color of his hat and she realized he was good-looking, solidly built, handsome in the way of the detectives in the old films. And eager too, she could see that. He wanted enlightenment just as she did, just as they all did.

"Right," he said, handing her back the flyer, "but where do I park?"

This was Tim's show, Tim's and Dick's, and she was window dressing—and hostess, of course, that too. And waitress. And pot scrubber. And chambermaid. Tim told her to dress in white, as much as possible, even though it was winter, and to look good, look her best and give everybody a mysterious smile. "You're good at that, Joanie—you're a champ." He was always doling out compliments, that was his way, that was his method, and the night they'd tripped together he'd told her she had the best figure of any woman—or girl—in the inner circle, Peggy included. And that from the minute he'd laid eyes on her, at that first session, that first night back in Newton, he'd wanted to trip with her. And fuck her. He'd wanted to fuck her—and what did she think about that? She'd thought nothing. She was tripping and smiling so hard she thought her face would split in six places and fall right off her. But he was Tim and Tim always got what he wanted.

Now, after all the guests had been settled in their rooms and the slowly accumulating snow swept off the front and back porches, she was in the kitchen with Paulette and Süsannah, putting the finishing touches to the meal. What they were doing—and the idea had been Michael Hollingshead's—was doctoring the dishes with food coloring. The potatoes she'd mashed were a bright Saint Patrick's Day green, the Chablis was black as coffee, the coffee pink and the meat glazed a bright banana yellow. Why? To disorient the senses, to make things seem what they weren't and break set for all the hushed guests who might have been wealthy, might have been powers in their own right, but were dressed indistinguishably in white robes, stripped now of clothes and jewelry and any other identifying ornaments and sitting solemnly at the big table in the dining room where candles flickered and a projector threw rotating globs of color against the far wall, precursor of the light shows Tim would begin to employ on the lecture circuit.

They'd been treated to an introductory lecture by Tim and Dick, in which they learned about meditation, transcendence, set and setting, the group mind and the importance of avoiding the imposition of their own jargon or experimental games on others. They would eat in silence, gather around the big fireplace in the sitting room for a meditation session led by Dick and then proceed by candlelight to their rooms. In the morning, after a breakfast featuring black milk, violet eggs and home fries the color of Christmas tree ornaments, they'd be allowed to converse with one another, but only if they avoided any sort of ego game whatever, beginning with a prohibition on using their names. If, for instance, someone wanted the person seated beside him to pass him something, he would say, *Please, brother (or sister), pass me the eggs or waffles or carnation-pink coffee, would you?*

Was it all a bit much? Yes, it was. Did she feel, in Charlie's words, like a sellout? Yes, again. Was it a violation of everything they believed in to hold a session without the sacrament, to trip without drugs? Was it even possible? Did she want to throw down her apron and go upstairs with Fitz—or *Ken*—take the sacrament and feel him inside her all night long while their minds soared and their bodies melded like the first animalcules in the progression of life, like protozoans and paramecia merging and budding and whatever else they were capable of? She did. But she understood the importance of what they were doing and what these anonymous strangers meant to them (money, just that, *money),* and as she bent over the elbow of a Park Avenue housewife and poured her another glass of Chablis the color of squid's ink—or the restauranteur from Scarsdale or professor from Columbia—she tried to keep that in mind.

And it would have worked, would have sailed as smoothly as things could possibly sail, both for her and the guests, if it weren't for Corey. Corey and the other kids were supposed to stay out of sight, strictly and absolutely, and they'd been lectured on that score by Fitz, Charlie, Ken and Rick; if she'd forgotten about him in the chaos of the guests' arrival, that was neither here nor there. He knew what to do. He was capable of entertaining himself, as were the rest of the kids. Royce and Fitz had lugged the television all the way across the yard and out to the Bowling Alley so they could watch *Million Dollar Movie* or *Route 66,* and she had personally gone out to the deli to select and purchase the sandwich things—capicola, Swiss cheese, salami, bologna, hard rolls—and the big bags of potato chips and bottles of Coke to go with them. She shared a joint with Fanchon in the kitchen, stirred food dye into the dishes, waitressed and hostessed and gave everybody her mysterious smile on cue.

It just happened—*karma*—that she was passing through the front hall on one errand or another when the doorbell rang. Thinking it must be some late-arriving guest, she went to the door and pulled it open, smiling in anticipation, until she saw the policeman there, the first of a whole succession of policemen who would descend on the house over the months and years to come, as if there really were no refuge from the outside world. Standing beside him, their shoulders slumped and eyes downcast, were Corey, Nancy and Lori. The porch light glistened on the snow sprinkled over their hats and the shoulders of their coats. Behind them, the night fell back in a riot of slashing snowflakes.

She was dressed in white, high on marijuana and Chablis, and her mysterious smile dropped right off her face like so much sloughed skin. There was one creaking infinitude of a moment during which no one said anything and the only sound was the sound of the wind, and then the policeman, his voice staid and automatic, was putting a question to her: "Do these kids belong here?"

She looked to him first—the cop, who was younger than she was and whose bloodless face was squeezed under a too-tight fur cap with the earflaps standing up like signposts—and then to Corey, who wouldn't meet her eyes. "Yes," she said, "they do." And then, finding an official voice herself, she asked, "What seems to be the problem?"

The policeman was wearing black leather gloves and unconsciously fingering his duty belt, the gun there, the nightstick, the bullets—were those bullets? He was about to say something, his breath held in pale suspension like the dialogue balloons in the comics Corey devoured by the dozen, but Lori, still not looking up, said, "It's bogus, the whole thing—we didn't do *anything*."

"They were caught shoplifting," the policeman—the cop—said. "Or this one was." He pointed to Nancy, whose hair projected in tufts from under the hood of the quilted jacket she herself had earlier found on the hook in the kitchen.

Nancy lifted her eyes now and looked her full in the face so that Joanie could see the plea there—and the guilt. "I was going to pay for it, I was—I just, I guess I just forgot, is all."

"A compact," the cop said, the snow rioting behind him. "Gary Kracik, the store owner? He caught them in the act."

"If it's a question of money—" she began but the cop held up a gloved palm to stop her.

"This is a quiet village," the cop said, lecturing her now. "We don't have any crime and we want to keep it that way. I don't know what you people do here, and as long as it's legal and it stays here, that's your business. But when you break the law there are consequences." The cop paused. He looked perfectly at home, as if he'd spent his entire life right there on the doorstep. He was watching her face to be sure she appreciated what he was saying, was heeding it, that is. "And who, exactly," he asked now, "are you?"

"Joanie—*Joan*—Loney," she said. "His mother." And she was pointing now, to Corey, who still wouldn't look at her.

"And you live here?" The cop peered beyond her into the depths of the house, where one of the guests in her shapeless white robe was crossing the hall for some reason—the bathroom? More wine? "Or are you just visiting?"

"Yes, I live here," she said. "With my husband and the other members of our"—and here she stumbled, everything drifting on her in a hazy float of movement that seemed to mimic the snow—"*research* institute."

"And these girls?" She saw now that he had a leather-bound pad in one hand, which he flipped open to consult. "Nancy Eggers and Lori Cunningham?"

"Yes, they live here too."

"And you're willing to take responsibility for them?"

She nodded.

The snow jumped and settled and gnawed at the sky. The woman in the white robe gaped at the little scene they'd put together for her there in the doorway but kept on walking till she disappeared down the hall. The cop said, "All right, then. Since Mr. Kracik doesn't want to press charges and the kids are local—Millbrook High, right?— we're going to let the matter drop."

There was a silence, then the cop was folding his notepad back into the inner pocket of his jacket and the three kids, still with their heads down and shoulders slumped, filed into the house. She took hold of the door, thinking to ease it shut yet feeling that something more should be said—*Thank you? Good night? Go home and die a quick death?*—but before she could speak the cop leveled a look on her and said, "I hope you understand this is a onetime-only thing. There won't be a repeat, correct?"

"I understand," she said, and then, as she was easing the door shut on a snowy dark sliver of the night, on the porch light and the cop's slick black patrol boots and his black uniform and puffed-up jacket, she paused to add, "Thank you. We're all very"—what were they?— "*grateful*."

L ater, after the guests had taken their white robes and flakes of group mind up the candlelit stairs to bed, she pulled on her boots and coat and went out to the Bowling Alley to confront Corey. She was seething. Angrier at the girls than him, but furious with him all the same. What was he thinking? He couldn't have said no? Couldn't have stood up for himself? She imagined the girls talking him into it—*Nancy, Nancy talking him into it*—so he could serve as a distraction, holding the store owner's attention while they stole things and nobody the wiser. That wasn't how she'd raised him. Neither she nor Fitz had ever been in trouble with the law in their lives, not even for a speeding ticket, and to have her son mixed up in this—brought home by a cop, no less—was just beyond the pale. And the project, the sacrament, the unity of the inner circle—didn't he realize how everything they were striving for was threatened by something like this? A cop on their doorstep? With all the notoriety the press had stirred up and what the other kids were saying in school and the way rumors must have flown around a stick-in-the-mud little hick town like this? And that was what it was too, a hick town, just as Corey had said right from the start. It was infuriating, so infuriating she barely noticed the snow she was kicking through or the wind beating at the flaps of her parka.

It wasn't far and she'd been there a hundred times, but somehow she got turned around, the snow transfiguring every feature of the landscape till it was unrecognizable, and before long she realized she'd gone right by the place. Angry at herself now—and her hands were freezing because she'd forgotten her gloves and why hadn't she at least thought to bring a flashlight?—she had to backtrack through the blow, getting angrier by the minute, till finally she stumbled across the stone steps and went up them and into the warmth of the house.

She saw that the kids had a fire going—the only light in the place—which was why she'd walked right past it. She smelled the sharp tang of woodsmoke and something else too: marijuana. She couldn't believe it—they were smoking marijuana after that little scene in the hallway? *Jesus.* And where were they? There, there they were, sprawled out on the floor in their sleeping bags though there were beds enough for them all, dark humps against the darker field of the floor and the shadowed walls. Humps. Dark humps. And so what if she was high on marijuana herself? So what?

"Corey?" she whispered.

No one stirred, no one answered. Gradually, as she stood there adjusting her eyes to the firelight, she began to distinguish one hump from the other—that was Tommy Eggers lying there in the corner, and the twins here in the middle of the floor. And that was Jackie, wasn't it? And Suzie stretched out on the couch? She wanted to flick on the lights, rage through the room, shake them all awake—shoplifting, marijuana, what were they thinking?—but she didn't. She just stepped around them, her arms flung out for balance, looking for her son, for Corey, because he was all that mattered.

She found him at the far end of the room, about as far from the fireplace as you could get, and he was in his sleeping bag, the down bag she'd bought him four years ago when he was in the Boy Scouts, but the thing was—and it took her a moment for it to sink in—he wasn't alone. No, Nancy was squeezed in beside him, the two of them there in a confusion of limbs that were like the protuberant bones of some exotic two-headed creature made of nylon, and before she knew what she was doing she had hold of the thing and was shaking it like a rug and the two faces there came instantly to life and her son—*her son*—let out a curse, a whole string of curses, and then Nancy was shouting and clawing at her arm and the whole room erupting in chaos.

Corey wasn't wearing a pajama top. He was naked, or at least as much of him as she could see, and she was tugging and tugging at the neck of the sleeping bag till she felt the zipper give and somebody was crying out "Who is it? What's happening?" and her son pushed himself up to a sitting position and he was fighting her too and then the sleeping bag slipped away and she saw Nancy there naked to her little gypsy waist. Corey shoved violently away from her, scrambling to his feet now—and he wasn't wearing shorts or pajama bottoms either—and she was slapping him, or trying to, and saying, *sobbing,* "What are you *thinking?* What are you doing? Don't you realize, don't you understand—?"

They were all watching, all the kids. Somebody had flicked on the overhead light so that the room flared up in her face as if it had burst into flame and she remembered thinking *They can all see her, see Nancy, and Nancy doesn't even care,* and then Corey, his face twisted, was shouting, "I hate you! Get out, get out, get out!"

Then she was back out in the snow again, furious, absolutely furious—they'd actually shoved her out the door and locked it behind her!—determined to put an end to this once and for all. She was going to go get Fitz—and Nancy's father too. And Susannah. And Tim—and everybody else. Enough was enough. She kicked through the drifts, one hand held up in front of her face to shield it from the wind-borne snow, which seemed to have changed direction, or—wait a minute, where was she? Was this right? Wasn't that the house over there?

No, no it wasn't . . . everything was different now. She wasn't high, not anymore, or not that she could feel, but she'd never had much of a sense of direction and with the way the wind was blowing she could hardly see a thing and her hands—her hands were freezing. The Alte Haus wasn't more than a couple hundred yards from the Bowling Alley, a big turreted fairy-tale palace you could see from a mile away, which no one could miss, even in a storm like this. But where was it? Usually it was ablaze with light like a ship at sea, but everybody seemed to have gone to bed by now—the guests, all the white-robed guests—and the night just held there, uniform, every which way she looked. But this was ridiculous. She kept walking, the night held, the snow kept coming. She was thinking about Fitz and what he was forever saying to her about her sense of direction: *Turn around and go in exactly the opposite way because you're always 100 percent wrong— the correct data's in there somewhere, but you've got a brain glitch. Trust me. Just go the opposite way.*

But what was the opposite way? She was so turned around she didn't know which way she'd come, and her tracks were filling as fast as she made them. And her hands were so cold. And her feet, her feet too. She backtracked, thinking to find the Bowling Alley again, just to orient herself. Problem was, she couldn't find that either. She must have gone off on a tangent—toward the lake? Where was the lake? She didn't have a clue. Everything was molded of snow. There was no moon. There were no stars. And the wind never stopped, not for an instant.

How much time went by she didn't know. But she couldn't feel her feet and she fell repeatedly so that the snow was worked up inside her sleeves and under the waistband of her jacket, which was wrong, and stupid, that too, and she'd forgotten about Corey now—or almost; she would deal with him in the morning—and she was so wrung out and exhausted all she could think was that she might just want to lie down in the snow for a bit, right here, just to catch her breath . . . when a sound came to her. It was sharp and sudden, a crack, a thump, a clatter, and then it repeated again, and again.

She went toward it. Ten steps, twenty, and there it was, the big house, revealed through a torn curtain of wind-shattered snow, and a light there, the light of the back porch and the shadow of a figure at the chopping block, a man raising a sledgehammer to drive an iron spike into a round of wood. Somebody out there splitting wood against the dwindling of the fire, which must have burned down to coals by now. And who was it? Fitz? Tim? She came closer, all in white, just as Tim had wanted, a bride of the night. Hurrying, she shuffled across the yard and into the pool of light and saw that it was Ken there, splitting wood for the fire that would blaze up in a minute and warm her all the way through, flesh and tendons and bones and her feet that were like blocks of ice.

In the next minute she was there, in his arms, clutching him to her. "Ken," she cried, "Jesus, *Ken*!"

"What is it?" he said, rocking with her. "But you're freezing. Where've you been?"

The wind threw a spray of pellets in her face. She couldn't feel her toes, her fingertips, her nose. Corey was in that house somewhere out in the darkness and he was having sex with that girl—fucking her—and he wasn't a boy anymore, wasn't her boy, and never would be again. Yes. All right. That was how it was. And where did that leave her? Free. Free to look after her own needs for a change, to soar and come down and soar again anytime the spirit moved her, and her own child could tell her he hated her and lock her out in the cold and it didn't matter one iota, not anymore.

"Nowhere," she said, shivering hard against him. Even through her jacket, even through the cold, she could feel the heat of him, and she wasn't crying, was she? "I'm fine now," she said. "I am. Really, I am."

PART III

Millbrook, 1964

1.

Everything was free-form that first winter at Millbrook, people drifting in and out, chores assigned and forgotten, shrines appearing in the hallways and alcoves and at the top of each flight of stairs. People cooked, washed dishes, split wood. There wasn't enough money, then there was. The furnace mysteriously broke down and just as mysteriously repaired itself. Mandalas flowered on the walls and Tim, Ken and Fanchon covered the downstairs ceilings in glittering gold paint by way of enhancing the view from the supine position. There were the pets. There were martinis. There was music. And above all, there was the sacrament.

Fitz tried to settle in, tried to move forward with his work, but outside the bubble of academe—outside Harvard—he was finding it increasingly difficult to focus, especially when everything seemed to revolve around group dynamics, group consciousness, group *being*. It was one thing to live as one big happy family in a Mexican hotel, where the hired staff took care of the necessities, and another when you had to divide up the responsibilities in a household that was overrun with guests on the weekends and now numbered twenty-nine full-time residents, including Lori, who'd just appeared one day and never left; Hollingshead, who never strayed far from the source of the sacrament; and Maynard and Flora Lu Ferguson and their five children, who moved in after the first of the year. With their monkey. Which, as far as he could see, wrought more destruction and chaos than all the children combined.

He had a cage, this monkey, but he was rarely in it because why should he want to be confined when he could run screeching through the corridors and smear the walls with shit? You could come across him anywhere, leering down at you from the chandelier, popping out from behind the toilet the minute you dropped your pants and settled down with the newspaper, snaking a leathery hand out from beneath the dining room table to filch your morning pancake or evening dessert. Fruit? Forget it. Nobody that winter ever ate an apple, orange, banana or grapefruit that didn't display the impress of a set of simian teeth.

He had to admit he'd never cared all that much for monkeys. As an undergrad, his work-study scholarship had required him to look after twenty of them in the primate lab, which meant he'd been regularly scratched, bitten and bombarded with monkey spittle, urine and worse. Monkeys were foul, mean-spirited and far too intelligent for their own or anybody's else's good and they belonged in a cage—or better yet, back in the jungle they came from. He tried to speak to Flora Lu about the situation, but in the end the monkey had his way because he could never quite bring himself to mention it. The fact was, he always seemed to be tongue-tied in her presence—she was an exotic, a celebrity's wife, and some part of him couldn't get past that no matter how many times she sat across the table from him at dinner, sipping, chewing and plying her fork like any other woman, like Joanie or Fanchon or Paulette.

What he wanted, what he fantasized about, was to get lucky in the Saturday night drawing and wind up paired off with her in the meditation house for a week of improvised activity. The only problem with that little fantasy was that she and Maynard—who was out touring with his band half the time in any case—declined to participate in the exercise, which only emphasized their difference from everybody else. They were part of the inner circle, but in the way of electrons orbiting the nucleus of an atom, part of it and outside it at the same time. In the end, she was Flora Lu Ferguson, and for all her communion with the sacrament, she never forgot it or let anybody else forget it either.

Which went against the whole rationale of the drawing in the first place. The idea was to break through the sexual jealousy game as a way of deepening the communal bond and transitioning from the individual ego to the group mind—or that was how Tim explained it. And once he'd explained it—or actually just broached the subject—there was little debate or even hesitation because they were psychologists and this was the new frontier and they could all participate in a way that was strictly clinical and disinterested and might well have the added benefit of providing data for future papers, articles and even books. Or at least that was what they told themselves. The way it worked was that once a week Tim would draw a pair of names from the sombrero he'd brought back from Mexico, and whoever's names came up would have to spend the next seven days in the meditation-house-cum-bowling-alley, relieved of all household duties and free to trip and engage in any activity they wanted, sexual or otherwise, without constraint. Two people, going deep.

The first drawing—Tim made a ceremony of it, as he did with everything—was held in front of the fireplace in the library at the beginning of one of their regular Saturday night sessions. There were no paying guests involved—that experiment, while profitable, had proved a nightmare, what with people's cars mired in the snow and various fender benders that tested everybody's equanimity and all but destroyed any meditative peace they might have found, and they'd decided to suspend the seminars till the weather improved. There were people up from the city, of course, friends, friends of friends, hangers-on and semi-regulars, but Tim had blessed them all with the sacrament they'd come for, then pulled the big doors shut on the library so that only the inner circle was gathered inside.

Everything was perfect, people's faces lit by the glow of the fire, the odd cat or dog lying there where you could reach out a hand and stroke an ear or pat a belly, the sacrament coming on and the monkey, for once, confined upstairs in his cage. It was the sort of scene Fitz had come to embrace, to love, really, all the mad rush of the world kept at bay and the people he most cared about gathered round him. This was what they were here for. This was what life was meant to be, and if the children were excluded this weekend and he and Joanie were all but broke and his thesis—*Aspects of Operant Conditioning: A Statistical Analysis of Recent Maze-Based Experiments*—stalled, so be it.

Joanie was right beside him, cradling her knees and smiling faintly, a smile that was more a genetic tilt of the muscles at the corners of her mouth than a sign of amusement or even engagement (what Tim liked to call her "mysterious smile," as in, *Joanie, light up that mysterious smile for us, will you?*). She was parting her hair in the middle now and had let it grow out till it trailed over her shoulders in the style of a folk singer whose music Alice had introduced her to, a woman who sang in a churchy soprano about farmers and coal miners and such, and what was her name? He couldn't remember. And it didn't matter. Because that sort of music meant nothing more to him than Charlie's Beatles, except that there was only one of her, which reduced the annoyance factor by 75 percent.

Tim waited till he was sure everyone was watching, then dipped his hand in the hat and with a flourish came up with the first slip of paper, which he carefully unfolded and smoothed flat in the palm of one hand. He made a show of squinting at the name written across the face of it as if he couldn't quite make it out, but of course he was just toying with them. "Joanie," he announced, glancing up at her and flashing his fluid grin. "Congratulations."

Everyone looked to her—they all feigned indifference but in truth everyone was on edge, as you could plainly see in their faces—and then a few people clapped and the whole group broke out in nervous laughter. "No potato peeling for you this week, you lucky devil," Paulette sang out. "And no dishes either. Queen for a day! Or no, for a week, a whole week!"

Before Fitz could even begin to sort out his feelings—Corey was the first thing he thought of, then himself, then whichever man might or might not be called next, and what if it was Hollingshead?—Tim was fishing in the hat again, and here came the strip of paper and the widening smile and in the next breath the announcement they were all waiting for. Which—and this was the nature of the game—came as a jolt of surprise because everyone had been thinking of a man, of sex, because that was the attraction here, that was the titillation, a kind of communal spin the bottle no matter the psychological rationale. Tim didn't call Ken's name or Royce's or Hollingshead's, but Fanchon's, and after a moment of stunned silence the applause started up again, along with the laughter and catcalls. "A woman's work is never done," Charlie piped up, and somebody else—it was Hollingshead, seated in back—added, "Or Sappho's either."

No matter—from Fanchon's reaction you would have thought she'd won the Miss America contest. She let out a squeal of delight and clapped her hands, applauding for herself. "Oh, this is so nice," she said, springing up from where she was seated at the edge of the carpet so everyone could see her, "my best friend!" She skipped across the room to Joanie and reached down a hand to help her to her feet and then, their hands entwined, raised them high in triumph. "We will have a vacation, no?" she cried. "Bon voyage!"

He was thinking of the first time he'd made love with her—in Mexico it was, that first summer—and how she'd come to him in darkness when he was in the lifeguard tower navigating his way through his weekly session. The sea thundered against the shore and everything smelled of the first life the earth had known and the three-quarters moon was making a light show of each rippling wave all the way out to infinity and suddenly there she was, Fanchon, in her two-piece, and she didn't say a word, just eased down his swim trunks and took him in her mouth. She was shorter than Joanie, more compact in her torso, and her breasts were higher and smaller but she was warm and wet and he slipped into her—deep, so deep—and hardly knew the difference.

"All right," Tim said, and he was on his feet too, "now that's settled, let's go in and join the party."

You're joking, right?" Corey said.

"No, not at all. Luck of the draw. I'll probably be next."

It was the following morning, Sunday, the house quiet—and cold, so cold you tried to stay in bed as long as you could, in Fitz's case with the *Times,* which he normally shared with Joanie, but that wasn't in the cards this morning because Joanie wasn't in bed with him. Joanie was in the meditation house with Fanchon, in bed or not, and Corey had come in without knocking and asked where his mother was because, as it turned out, he had a paper due the next day for history and she'd been helping him with the research.

"For the whole *week?*"

"It's an experiment. We all voted on it. It's a way of bringing us all closer together—"

"One big family."

"Right."

Corey just stood there, his loose-leaf notebook thrust under one arm, looking puzzled and upset. As fiercely as he asserted his independence, he was still a kid—not yet sixteen—who didn't seem to have much of an idea as to how clean underwear wound up in his dresser drawer or the food got from the supermarket to the stove to the table, and though he'd never admit it, he needed his mother. If not as his confidante—it seemed Nancy and Richard had replaced her there—then as the bête noire he could react against and at the same time test over and over with his multiplying needs. That night of the snowstorm, the night the kids had been shunted off to the Bowling Alley and Joanie had found him there with Nancy, was the turning point, though Fitz had been unaware of it at the time. Joanie hadn't come to bed at the usual hour that night and he'd assumed she was busy with the cleanup and preparations for the next day's meals and seminars, but when he woke at dawn there she was, sitting on the edge of the bed, still dressed in the white skirt and sweater she'd put on for the paying guests. "What's the matter?" he'd asked. "Are you all right?"

For a long moment she said nothing, her breath steaming in the cold of the room that might as well have been a tent in the woods for all the heat the radiators gave up. "Corey," she said. "I won't have it. I won't."

"Have what? What are you talking about?"

"He's going to get her pregnant, you know that, don't you?"

"Nancy?"

"Who do you think I'm talking about, Queen Elizabeth? You know what he did?" Suddenly, angrily, she was shoving the sleeve of the sweater up her arm to reveal a dark seep of discoloration in the crease of her elbow and a matching bruise on her forearm. "He pushed me out the door! Pushed me!"

He threw back the blankets and tried to pull her to him but she resisted. "No," she said, "no! I have to tell you this, I have to—he's too young, Fitz. Way too young. You've got to do something. Talk to him. And don't give me that boys-will-be-boys crap either . . ."

He had talked to him, back in the fall when they'd first discovered he wasn't sleeping in his room, and if he hadn't exactly laid down the law—that wasn't his method, and besides which, it made him feel like a hypocrite—they'd at least come to an understanding. As far as he knew, Corey had been sleeping in his room ever since—he even checked on him every once in a while, just to reassure himself. When he thought about it, that is, and he had to admit he didn't think about it all that often. Boys *will* be boys, that was how he felt, and girls will be girls, and the Alte Haus and the surrounding hills and fields featured a hundred places for private assignations, as he himself knew full well. Corey wasn't the little boy he used to read aloud to, not anymore. And it wasn't as if he was haunting dark alleys or taking the train into Harlem and soliciting prostitutes. Nancy was fine. Nancy was adequate. And Corey would outgrow her and go on to college—or she'd outgrow him. It was all the same.

But Joanie wouldn't hear of it. Her voice was bitter, her eyes burning. "I don't want him to wind up like us."

"Yeah," he said. "I wouldn't wish that fate on anyone."

"That's not what I mean."

"What do you mean then?"

She looked away in exasperation. She was trembling, angry still—and cold, that too. Again he reached out for her and again she pushed him away. "I mean he's *too young*."

Now, in the chill of the bedroom on the first morning of her exile, Corey slapped the loose-leaf rhythmically against his thigh and said, "I forgot to mention happy."

"Happy? What do you mean?"

He gave a little smile, and he was still a kid, still and always. "One big *happy* family," he said, and then he pulled back the door, slipped out into the hallway and was gone.

What went on between Joanie and Fanchon was anybody's guess and Joanie didn't say much more than, "It was peaceful." Apparently, they'd tripped every day, varying the dosages so that one day they took the minimum—the kids' dose—and the next the 500 mics Tim was accustomed to. They read, listened to music, consulted the *I Ching* and never left the house or saw anybody except in the moment their meals were delivered by Susannah or Paulette, who set a tray on the table just inside the door, rang the buzzer and hurried away so as not to interfere with anything they might be engaged in, whether it be interpersonal relations, soul sharing or pushing beyond the First Light to the Second Light 'and the all-encompassing embrace of the divinity and the threads of consciousness that knitted the universe together. Or a shower. Or a bath. Did they bathe together, one body as convenient as another? Was he jealous? Did he miss her, miss them both? The more he thought about it, the more he realized it didn't really matter because bodies were only envelopes of the mind and he was already picturing his own week in the meditation house—and not with one of the men, though that would be all right by way of *Blutsbrüderschaft* and all the rest, but with one of the women, like Fanchon or Alice. Or Peggy. Was Peggy in? And here he inevitably conjured up Flora Lu and felt a stab of regret.

The second drawing, to everyone's disappointment, paired two men—Hubert Westfall, the male half of the couple Joanie made a point of referring to as the Nestlings, and Ken. There was less excitement this time around, less frivolity, and though there was some grousing ("Why can't we use two hats," Charlie wanted to know, "—one for the men and one for the women?"), both the principals seemed to take it in stride and they went out to the meditation house, if not arm in arm, then at least shoulder to shoulder, and spent their week exploring what it meant to go free, the nights melding with the days and the days uncoupled from the rotation of the earth and the elegant elliptical orbit round the sun it took a full year to make, every year, from the beginning of time to the end.

Then there was the third drawing. Everyone knew, theoretically, statistically, that there'd have to be a male/female pairing not only in terms of the odds but because that was what this was all about, that was why it mattered, because possessiveness—I, me, exclusivity, the marriage game, the property game—was the enemy of group consciousness and harmony. Or at least that was what Tim proposed. And Dick seconded. And everyone seemed to agree was a good idea, a very good idea. He'd agreed too, but as the third Saturday rolled around he found he was having second thoughts. Maybe he was just out of sorts that evening, not angry exactly, but impatient with the whole tenor of the exercise, all of them sitting around waiting for the sacrament to take hold and yet at the same time wrought up with the tension of this game—a game that broke down the conventions, but a game all the same—and all he could think was that it wasn't right because it undermined the first principle of any session: mind-set. If you were wrought up you could hardly expect to soar. Set and setting. Wasn't that the mantra? He made a mental note to question Tim about that, to modify the game, neutralize it, maybe do a private drawing and simply announce the names the next morning, because what was the point of putting everybody through this week in and week out?

But then he was seated there on the carpet, a cognac in hand and the first stirrings of the drug coming on, and Tim reached into the hat and announced Lori's name. Lori. He'd never even thought of her, nor, apparently had anybody else, given their reaction—no one applauded, no one laughed or whistled. He looked to her—they all did—where she was seated on the floor, barefoot, the whiskery head of Jackie's dog in her lap and one shoulder propped up against Dick, who was seated, as always, in the lotus position. What was she wearing? A turtleneck, a black turtleneck that clung to her and defined her in a way a blouse never could have. He wasn't blind, and his eyes had followed her across one room or another a hundred times, but he'd always thought of her as a girl, as one of the kids, the teenagers, and how old was she anyway—eighteen? Nineteen? She reddened and let her smile transform her but she didn't get up to take a bow, mock or otherwise, or show herself off the way Fanchon had—she let her eyes jump to Tim's, then shot a quick glance around the room and went back to stroking the dog's ears. He did a quick calculation, he couldn't help himself: he was thirty-five and she was nineteen. Or eighteen. Which was sixteen—or seventeen—years younger.

Everyone exhaled. Lori had been chosen, and that was only fitting because Lori was one of them now and nobody could argue with that. Right? Duly noted?

Yes, but that was just the preliminary to the main event, because Tim dipped back into the sombrero, took a second to unfold the slip of paper in his hand, then looked straight at him.

The tradition, three whole weeks in the making, was for the selected couple to publically embrace or at least clasp hands, make a tour of the room to accept everyone's congratulations (and relief?), then proceed through the library doors and out into the currents of the party-in-progress while Tim led the way waving a censer of Tibetan incense and Charlie thumped out a slow funereal march on a pair of bongos clutched under one arm. It was no different this time, the anti-game become its own game already. Fitz barely had a chance to register Joanie's reaction—was she scowling or was that an ironic smirk?—before he found himself in the center of the room beside Lori, tiny Lori, Lori of the slumped shoulders and eyes that seemed always to be focused on something off in the distance, the drug coming on in a cascade of shattering reds and oranges and the carpet beneath him falling away as if he were in an elevator and present on every floor simultaneously. Lori moved into him, her hip pressed to his thigh, and gave him a noncommittal hug, the sort of hug she might have given her grandmother on the steps of the nursing home, and he felt as strange as he ever had. Then the bongos were bongoing and all the faces were parting and he was weaving out of the library and through the sitting room—more faces, grins, jazz like a horse collar—and down the hallway to the back door and the night, Lori at his side and her hand clutched in his as if she were a schoolchild on a class trip. But this was no class and she was no child.

The night air hit him like a bucket of cold water and he must have frozen there on the steps of the porch, everything cycling back inside him again, because Lori, who'd removed her hand from his to slip on her mittens, said, "Well, are we going or not?" and her words hung there in front of him, written on the air.

Behind them, behind the closed door, were the giddy faces of half a dozen people he loved as much as anybody alive (but not Joanie's, or Corey's, because Joanie either didn't care at all or cared too much and Corey was downtown, at the basketball game in the school gym, isolated with the rest of the kids). The next thing that hit him was clarity, as if the scene had shifted and he was right there behind a camera, directing it. "Sure," he heard himself say, "but watch out for the ice because these steps are—" and before he could pronounce the word his left foot went out from under him and he realized the movie he was directing was a Marx Brothers comedy, or no, Laurel and Hardy, and she was Stan and he was Ollie, and wasn't that the funniest thing in the world?

He didn't fall. And it wouldn't have mattered if he did—he was beyond hurt at this point, an adept, a master, and the universe existed for the sole purpose of orchestrating his needs and desires and preserving him from mishaps. She slipped too, in the very moment, and they both laughed but she was the one who shot out a hand to steady him—her tiny hand, electric, confident, sure—and not the other way around.

The meditation house was warm, hot even. The fire had been stoked, candles lit, there was a bowl of fruit set out on the coffee table and a joss stick burning in the ashtray beside it, steadily converting itself into a fine pale ribbon of ash. He unbuttoned his coat and looked round him for a place to put it, a hook on the wall, a closet, the back of a chair, but that wasn't really working for him so he just let it drop from his shoulders to the floor and eased himself down on the couch, facing the fire. She was there somewhere, Lori, just out of his range of vision, but he didn't turn his head because all at once he was fiercely busy deciphering the message of the flames that kept grabbing and releasing the belly of the log laid out there across the andirons that weren't solid inanimate things anymore but beings in themselves that never winced or complained no matter the heat or fury of the fire. At some point she appeared beside him, not on the cushions but on the floor, her legs drawn up to her chest and her back propped against the edge of the couch, and she wasn't wearing the socks or shoes she must have put on for the trek across the yard. Her feet were right there before him, naked and glistening in the firelight, an understated miracle of skin, bone and tendon, her toes gripping the carpet as if she were high up in the canopy of a tree, and where was the monkey when they needed him?

Neither of them said a word. Worlds collided, glaciers calved, civilizations marched across the landscape erecting temples and tearing them down and starting all over again. He heard voices though no one was speaking, watched the universe shrink to the size of a hard black rubber ball he could hold in one hand and then spit itself back out again. Then the images became the ghosts of images, the night deepened, the candles flickered out, the fire settled. And when he woke, at first light, she was curled up asleep on the couch beneath a knit comforter, her head resting on his shoulder as if they'd spent the night in a narrow seat on a Greyhound bus in the middle of nowhere.

He was trying to extricate himself without waking her when her eyes blinked open and she asked, "Did you see him?"

Her pupils were dilated still. She was inches from him. "Who?"

"God. Did you see God?"

He shook his head. He needed to piss, needed to find a bed—and what time was it anyway?

"Do you even believe in God?" She was sitting up now, her legs crossed beneath her, her voice echoing as if she were talking from the bottom of a very tall and very deep urn. "Or anything? Beyond this?" She swept her hand to take in the room, the cold ash of the fireplace, the morning at the windows.

"I believe in breakfast," he said.

"Don't talk down to me," she said. "Do anything, but not that."

"I'm not talking down to you. I'm just—it's early, that's all."

"What's that got to do with the price of tea in China? We've only got a week—we can't waste it." She drew the comforter up to her throat. It was very still. A framed picture on the wall concentrated the light. There were beams, high ceilings, vases of dried flowers. "So do you believe in God or not?"

He shrugged. "I don't know, what about you?"

"These drugs are entheogens," she said. "Did you know that? Do you know what that means?"

"Of course I do—I'm the one who should be telling you." He was beginning to feel irritated—rinsed clean, as after any session, but ready to move back into the world, move on, *recalibrate*. "I've been with Tim from the beginning, or almost the beginning, and you've been here, what, a couple of months?"

"Don't talk down to me."

"I'm not."

She shut her eyes, as if in concentration or prayer, and began reciting: "'I never saw a moor, / I never saw the sea; / Yet know I how the heather looks, / And what a wave must be. / I never spoke with God, / Nor visited in heaven; / Yet certain am I of the spot, / As if the chart were given.'"

The house was utterly silent. The fruit sat untouched on the table, free of imprints, simian or otherwise. He needed to get up, needed to piss, start the fire, see about coffee, but there was something here that hadn't been here before and the weight of it held him in place.

She smiled at him then and it was like a leap into another dimension. "You want to go deep?"

"Now? Again?"

Her eyes were scorched, cored out, the blackest eyes, the deepest. "Think about it," she said, "—we've only got a week."

She wasn't really asking and she didn't give him time to say yes or no or even get up to use the bathroom—she just rose from the couch with the comforter wrapped round her, drifted off to the kitchen and returned a moment later with two glasses of water and a bottle of the Czechoslovakian sacrament Dick had gone all the way to Canada and back to provide for them. Her eyeliner was blurred, her lipstick faded to pink. Her hair—she wore it like Joanie's, like the folk singer's—was a mess, shoved up in a tangle on one side, fallen loose to curtain her face on the other. As she came across the room to him he could see she was shivering—the house was freezing and what he had to do was get up and start the fire, make coffee, make sense of things, but before he could summon the volition she was handing him a glass of water and the pill bottle and settling back into the couch to study his face as if it were the text for the day.

"I don't know," he said. "It's crazy. Shouldn't we at least wait till tonight?"

In answer, she took the bottle back from him and shook two pills out into the palm of her hand, holding them there a moment so he could see them, register them, contemplate them—one for him, one for her. Was she trying to goad him? Challenge him? Make up his mind for him in an unrelievedly childish way, as if it were a dare? It was morning. It was cold. He didn't want to launch himself on another trip, not on the contrails of the last one, and yet the way she offered it, her nonchalance, her certainty, gave him pause. They were on a mission here—he was on a mission—and what did he have to lose? It wasn't as if he was going to spend the day typing up his notes or writing a book or comparing statistics on drug addiction in lab rats.

And yet, and yet . . .

That was when she showed him who she was. She wasn't offering, she was taking. In that moment she clapped her hand to her mouth, snatched up her own glass of water and swallowed. Both pills. Both of them—and on top of what she'd taken the night before. The shock must have registered in his face because she gave him a long slow smile and said, "What?"

"But that—you took both of them. That's five hundred mics."

She shrugged, shivered again. "I want to see what Tim sees."

He didn't say anything. He was shivering now too. He had to get up and start a fire and he had to make coffee and eat something— had Paulette or whoever dropped off their breakfast yet? Was that coffee he smelled? Or just the idea of it?

"Aren't you going to join me?"

"It's too early," he said.

She pulled her feet up on the couch, slipped them beneath the cushions and arranged the comforter over her legs with a brisk snap of her wrists. "You didn't answer my question. I mean, really? Because isn't this what we're supposed to be doing out here together? Pushing the limits, right? Making breakthroughs?" She paused, ran a finger across her lower lip. "And screwing. We're supposed to be screwing too, aren't we?"

"Yoni and lingam."

"Right," she said, and laughed.

He picked up the bottle and rattled it like a maraca and she laughed again. It was a strange moment in a strange cold house with this shivering girl right there beside him, spirit incarnate, her lips compressed and her eyes never leaving his face. He positioned the bottle over his palm, shook out a pill, lingered for just the fraction of a beat, and shook out another.

At the end of the week they both emerged, hand in hand. There was no welcoming committee, no applause, just Joanie and Susannah, who'd apparently delegated themselves to go bring them back and prepare the house for the next pair, to be selected that night. There had been a knock at the door, which he hadn't answered. Then the door had opened and there was Joanie, there was Susannah. He was sitting beside Lori on the couch, the morning at the windows again, and there was a tray in the front hall with breakfast on it, right next to the tray from the previous night and the previous afternoon and the previous morning. He'd been fasting—they both had—but it wasn't through any conscious choice because they weren't anchorites in the desert and they weren't abnegating the flesh, just the opposite. They were essential, clamped together, lock and key. He had no intimation that the week was up or that they hadn't been eating or sleeping or that there was a world, a material world, outside the door of the meditation house.

He remembered Lori peeling an orange, the way her fingers slid in under the shield of color to isolate and annul it, and he remembered the chessboard and the bowling alley in the basement, how she perched over the ball and the pins clattered and they kept score and battled for dominance and how it came to him that the game was a metaphor for life itself, the ball a planetary sphere hurtling through space and the pins emblematic of the flesh, of mortality, of the roar and crash of annihilation. It was bleak. It was naked to the dregs. And it wasn't a game, most definitely not a game.

Joanie's voice, his wife's voice, then Susannah's, new voices altogether that flitted and chased each other round the room, no sense yet, just sound. Then he was up and moving and the world was spinning back at him, the big black ball slicing across the gleaming strip of the alley under the lights that were too bright until it landed with a thump in the gutter and he had hold of her hand, Lori's hand, and she was moving too.

There was sunshine, right there, right on the front porch, and it was painful, so they fished out their sunglasses, and it was only then that they let go of each other because they needed both hands to pat down their pockets, dig out the glasses and fit them over their ears. Joanie, her eyes lit like holy fire, said, "Jesus, you look like shit. You both look like shit."

He didn't know how to respond to that because he wasn't quite back in his body yet and wouldn't be till he'd slept through the rest of the morning and the afternoon and found himself crouched over the carpet in the library with a sandwich in one hand and a beer in the other, waiting for Tim to dip his hand into the hat while the monkey screeched from somewhere upstairs and the next couple, the next voyagers, waited to discover who they were.

2.

What he learned from his week in the Bowling Alley was that nothing was absolute, not his attachment to Joanie or his son or the consciousness he'd inhabited all the way back to the oral stage of infancy. He learned that imprints matter and that theses (which, in a kind of internal mantra, he kept rhyming with feces) were just a distraction from the inner life, the only life that counted, and beyond that, from love. Erotic love and agape too, which were indistinguishable if you went deep enough. He came back to the Alte Haus and sat beside Joanie while Tim fished in the sombrero and paired Royce Eggers and Alice and he felt nothing but joy for them. When he went up to bed that night, back to bed, Joanie was there with him, but she felt strange, her body all wrong, the way she moved and spoke and how her consciousness ebbed and flowed without him. She'd taken the sacrament—it was Saturday night— and if she lay there in the dark all wrapped up in herself he didn't know it because he was asleep.

In the days that followed, he gradually came back to himself, back to the world of splitting and stacking wood, scrubbing pans, reading, writing, typing, talking, listening to Indian music, piano trios and jazz (and the Beatles, the inescapable Beatles, who seemed to be twanging and thumping through one speaker or another throughout the house from daybreak to the hour of the wolf). He put gas in the car, went to the bank, the drugstore, the diner, worried over the money he could no longer contribute to the communal pot for food and other necessities—brandy, scotch, gin—and how he was possibly going to find it. He drank too much. His personality shrank. His son was a ghost and his wife a cipher.

What was it? Nothing quite fit right, as if the world were a suit of clothes that had shrunk in the dryer and had to be pinched and tugged till it stretched back out again. Joanie didn't come to bed the second night he was back—or the third night either. He saw her at meals, in the hallway, on the staircase and around the fire at night, when everybody was chatty and expansive and the drinks and marijuana circulated and every subject imaginable was batted around, from women's lib to Johnson and civil rights to jazz and rock and roll and the eating of bush meat in Africa, including monkeys, which, according to Charlie, who'd been in Gambia for a week once, tasted just like monkey, but he didn't seem to have much to say to her because the essential thing, the thing the whole household had to understand, was that she wasn't Lori. Nothing against her—she was his wife, she was Joanie, and he loved her—but he wasn't imprinted on her, not anymore. It was Lori he wanted, Lori he obsessed over, Lori he needed to be with through every minute of every day.

Which was problematic on a number of counts. The first being that the fundamental purpose of the experiment was to dissolve sexual jealousy and exclusivity, not encourage it, and the second that Lori didn't seem to feel the same way about him, or at least she didn't make it apparent in any way he could see. There she was, just as she'd been before, slump-shouldered, dark, enigmatic, huddled at the end of the table with the other kids—with Nancy, Corey, Jackie, Suzie—or stretched out on the couch beside Tim, who, she'd confided, was her God, and accordingly had had her any number of times and ways. He'd learned about that in detail, about how she'd seen Tim's picture in a magazine and felt an instant connection—*karma*—and cultivated Nancy so she could get her foot in the door and get close to him, get close to them all, and to the sacrament. He'd learned too that the kids—no surprise—had their own forms and rituals, a society within a society, and that some of them (*Not Corey, not yet, don't worry*) kept pushing the limits. Jackie had spent two days locked in his room at the top of the south tower, tripping on an astonishing 1,000 mics, and she herself, along with Nancy and a guy she knew from Bard (*Toby Husted?*) had done more than half that up on Ecstasy Hill the weekend they'd all gone camping back in October.

And then there was Joanie.

She came into the room one morning—by his count it was the fourth day he'd been back—and without a word began gathering up socks, underwear, T-shirts and towels and stuffing them into the laundry bag while he sat there at his desk, puzzling over half a dozen sheets of graphs he'd drawn up in his previous life and wondering what he was going to do with them. He'd long since given up any notion of making his mark in the field—his thesis wasn't going to be revolutionary like Tim's, just workmanlike, a compilation and comparison of Skinnerian lab studies that was as yet searching for a conclusion or even an overriding idea. He just wanted to get through with it, that was all, wanted his degree, though it seemed to matter less and less as the days went on and the interpersonal became all there was.

She was making an inordinate amount of noise for somebody simply stuffing clothes into a bag, but he didn't turn around, didn't want to be distracted, though he was already distracted, had been distracted before she even came into the room. He heard her rummaging around Corey's room and a moment later she came back through the doorway with a second bag, flung it down beside the first and began stripping the bed—their bed—and balling up the dirty sheets in one of the pillowcases.

After a moment of this—she was exaggerating her breathing, sighing, grunting—she said, "I can't believe you," and now he did turn around.

"What do you mean?"

She was wearing sweatpants, moccasins and a tan cable-knit sweater three sizes too big for her, a man's sweater, and it wasn't one of his. "I mean, I haven't slept here the last two nights and you don't say anything about it? Jesus, did you even notice?"

"Of course I noticed."

"So why didn't you say anything?"

"I don't know, I thought you were"—a phrase of Charlie's popped into his head—"doing your own thing."

"I was. I am." Her hands jumped, the pillowcase swelled. "I've been sleeping with Ken. And Fanchon. The three of us. Just for a little"—and here her voice broke—"affection. Affection, Fitz, you know what that is?"

"Sure," he said, "of course I do," but he didn't get up from the desk.

"I'm in love with him."

He saw Ken's face then, the knowing eyes and ear-to-ear smile, the shaggy crew cut he'd grown out in imitation of Tim, the height of him, the power, and he saw Fanchon too, with her everted lips and her soft pink nipples he'd sucked till they were stiff and hard. He couldn't be jealous—they were beyond jealousy here and besides which it wasn't Joanie he wanted or Fanchon either, it was Lori, only Lori—but he was. "Come on," he said, and he was on his feet now, holding her, pressing her to him, "I did miss you. And I want you. You're my wife."

"You don't want me," she said, and she pushed away from him. "You want her, that little slut, that child, that infant—isn't that right?"

He could have said they were one big happy family, could have insisted it was a passing thing, the effect of the drug and nothing more, could have denied the accusation in no uncertain terms, but he didn't. He didn't say a word.

In the afternoon, in the wake of that scene and the living death of the work spread out on the desk before him, he pulled on his thermal underwear, slipped into a pair of jeans, a sweater and his hooded parka and went out for a walk. It was unforgivably cold, the twisted black branches of the trees rattling in the wind, the day low-ceilinged and sunless, a mockery of the memory of Mexico. He needed to clear his head, or that was what he told himself, but after his week in the meditation house, his week with Lori, the phrase had no meaning—he wasn't even sure if he had a head anymore. A skull, yes, calcium-rich bone with an integument of skin and hair pulled up over it, but the brain inside didn't seem to be his anymore, or not solely his. The wind blew. The snow crunched. The branches rattled. He walked, simplest thing in the world, one foot in front of the other, and before long, without intending it or even thinking about it, he was deep in the forest, where the snow, crusted and degraded, clung haphazardly to the trunks of the trees and the trees massed and thinned and massed again.

Tim had seen a wolf out here, though that hardly seemed possible, wolves having been eradicated a century ago, but then one of them could have migrated down from Canada—a whole pack of them for that matter, who knew? There were certainly enough deer around to feed them. He saw deer tracks everywhere, holes poked in the snow as if by phantom ski poles, and their droppings scattered like so many handfuls of raisins in the clearings. And what was that Russian story where the family in the sled was heading back home in the dark of night, the wolves right on them, and they flung their baby out into the snow to distract them and save themselves? Would he have flung

Corey out? Or no, Lori—would he have shoved her over the transom and whipped the horses on?

At some point he got turned around, the forest a maze in itself and he the animal seeking pleasure in the absence of pain, but the estate was bounded by county roads and there were any number of outbuildings to navigate by, including a farm on the east end of the property, so it wasn't really a problem. He was back before the kids returned from school, the house quiet, a rich aroma of communal cookery wafting through the gold-ceilinged rooms and the fire going strong in the library. Which was where he found Lori, all alone, crouched on her knees before the fire and feeding sticks into the flames—kindling—when what the fire needed at this stage were the split logs stacked outside on the porch. This was wasteful behavior, lazy really, the sort of thing you'd expect from a child, and no matter what Joanie said Lori was no child.

"Hi," he said, and she swung round, startled, her face small and pale. "Need help with that?"

She didn't answer, or not in a way that made any sense. She said, "'I'm nobody! Who are you? / Are you nobody, too? / Then there's a pair of us—don't tell! / They'd banish us, you know.'"

"You're quoting again."

"Yes," she said, and turned to poke at the fire.

"So we're two nobodies, huh?"

She didn't answer. Sparks jumped and floated across the flames like glittering insects.

He was standing over her now, feeling strange again, out of place, out of body, as if he were back in the meditation house. It was a moment—a flashback—and then it passed. "Are you all right? Everything okay?"

She got to her feet—her bare feet, her monkey feet—and put her arms around him. "I'm fine," she said. "Never better." Then she broke away and went to the couch, folding her legs under her and snatching up the comforter all in one motion. "Why, do I seem sad or sick or whatever?"

"I don't know. I just had a feeling, that's all. I mean, seeing you here all alone, wasting kindling on the fire that really could use a log, a couple of logs—"

"Are you criticizing me? Talking down to me? Again?"

What he wanted was to hold on to her, feel her beneath him, feel her move. "No," he said, and he was sliding in beside her on the couch now, "I would never talk down to you, never—you know that. What I want to do, the only thing I want to do, is go to bed with you. Right now." He put his arm over her shoulder, brought his face to hers. "Come on," he said, "let's go upstairs."

Her face—he leaned in to kiss her, but she shifted away from him—was the most perfect physical manifestation he had ever seen, the living presence, but her expression didn't match it. She looked— what? Frightened? Or no, no, worse than that: detached. "I'm coming down with a cold," she said. "I don't feel good. Really."

"Don't give me that crap—you just told me you were fine, *never better*. So what is it, what's the matter? Don't you know what I'm going through here?"

The small voice, the distant eyes, the pout: "I don't feel like it."

"I do," he said.

"Well, I don't."

"What is this, a debate? It's been four days—*four days*!"

She turned her head away, shut her eyes. "'The brain is wider than the sky, / For, put them side by side, / The one the other will include / With ease, and you beside.'"

"Jesus Christ! I don't need quotes, or what, riddles? I need you. Don't you hear me? Don't you care?"

Her eyes flashed open then and she wasn't looking at him but beyond him to where Tommy Eggers, six foot one, gawky, thin-shanked, his face red with the cold and a scarf wrapped like a noose round his throat, was edging up to the fire, his hands spread wide to catch the warmth. "It's colder than a witch's tit out there," he observed, glancing over his shoulder to where the two of them sat squeezed in at the end of the couch.

He heard himself say, "Yeah, and how do you suppose the witch's mother feels about it?" and it was nonsensical, a cover, something to say while he took his arm from Lori's shoulder and inched over on the cushion.

Tommy—he wasn't a bad kid, wasn't a kid who meant anybody harm—was watching his face for clues, but there were no clues to give up, only facts, and the facts were that he'd had his arm around Lori, the teenager, who'd just rebuffed him as if they barely knew each other, as if they hadn't gone deeper together than any couple in human history, and he was feeling poisonous. Tommy said, "Why don't you tell me about it, Fitz—tell *us*."

He was on his feet now and Lori was way down there below him, shrinking till she might have been a thousand miles away. "It's a long story," he said, looking not at her but at Tommy, only Tommy, "and it has a lot of cold tits in it. And you know what else? Cold cunts. Cold cunts too."

It was around that time—late February, early March—that he was pulled over by the village police for no apparent reason. He was coming back from Beacon, of all places, where he'd gone to have a cup of coffee with Dave Jacobs, principal of his old school, by way of catching up. He was the one who'd reestablished the connection, calling Dave at home one night and wondering if he might buy him a cup of coffee—or a drink, would he rather go out for a drink? Dave had seemed surprised to hear from him, but not unfriendly, just the opposite. "It's good to hear your voice, Fitz. We figured it'd be a long time before we heard from you again—how's Harvard treating you?" He told him Harvard was treating him great, but did he know he'd moved to Millbrook? To finish up his thesis? Yeah, Millbrook, what a coincidence, huh?

They met after school the next day, at a diner Fitz used to frequent in the old days of toil and trouble—toil and boredom, actually— and nothing had changed. The plasticized menus might have been a little grimier, a little more creased and dog-eared, but the offerings, from ham and eggs with a side of toast or pancakes (Breakfast Served All Day!) to the blue-plate special (Chicken Parmesan with choice of spaghetti or mashed) and the allegedly homemade pies, were the same as they'd always been, as were the prices and the specials listed on the chalkboard behind the counter. Dave was the same too, early fifties, crew cut patched with gray, suit, tie, buffed black shoes the size of cement blocks. They exchanged pleasantries, ran down some of the gossip on former colleagues Fitz barely remembered, even tried out the weather for a bit, till finally, scraping up the remnants of a slice of coconut cream pie with the edge of his fork, Dave asked, "So to what do I owe the honor?"

Fitz had ducked his head, grinned. "You could always read me, Dave."

"That's my job—hell, you're a psychologist, you ought to know that."

"What I wanted to ask is, have you got anything for me? Temporary, I mean, a day or two a week, help with the evaluations, IQ tests, whatever, even subbing—just to tide me over till the thesis is done and I can get back out on the job market."

What this cost him, in terms of self-worth, in sheer humiliation, was incalculable, but he was beyond all that now. All that counted now was bringing in a paycheck, any paycheck, something rather than nothing, because he'd never lived off anyone in his life and he wasn't going to start doing it at this point no matter how forgiving Tim and Dick might be. When he'd got accepted at Harvard, Dave—and all the rest of them, teachers, administrators, even the superintendent—had looked at him as if he'd been named to the president's cabinet or the Mercury space team, as if he'd won the lottery and hit a grand slam at Yankee Stadium on the same day. He'd relished that. The envious looks, the complicated handshakes and dry-throated congratulations—he was getting out of there, going on to something great and glorious, and they weren't.

Right. And here he was, begging.

Dave said, "Millbrook. That's where Leary and, who, Alpert, are now, isn't it?" The fork scraped, he took a sip of coffee. "Are you part of that?"

"I am. We're all engaged in the research together. It's—well, it's exciting. New frontiers and all that, you know?"

"We hear rumors—the stuff in the papers. It sounds pretty extreme."

He shrugged. "You know the papers—anything for a story. But listen, have you got anything for me?"

"You sure you want to make that drive? It's got to be forty minutes or more."

"At six in the morning? There'll be nobody on the road."

"Except the snowplows."

"It's only temporary. And it's mostly a straight shot down the Taconic, right?"

Dave played with his fork a minute, then set it down and stared right into him. "Sure," he said, "we can always use subs. All you have to do is register with the district." He gave him a thin smile. "We'll call you, okay?"

And then he got in the car, cursing himself, and drove through the slush to Millbrook, where one of the village's two cruisers swung out behind him and flashed its red lights. He was already upset enough—Lori, Joanie, Corey, *subbing*—and though he'd had nothing to drink but coffee and nothing to smoke but tobacco, the sight of the cruiser in his rearview mirror and the single truncated whoop of the siren made his heart clench. His hands were trembling on the wheel as the officer approached the car—a man of forty with an expressionless face he'd seen around the village a dozen times but had never acknowledged because they were strangers and there was no need to acknowledge him because they were on opposite sides of the divide that made Millbrook what it was and gave the police department its rights and prerogatives.

The man had a flashlight in his hand—it was dark now, a fine misting rain dancing in the headlights—and he shined it through the driver's side window, at the same time making a circular gesture with his other hand, indicating that Fitz should roll the window down. Which he did, the wet air a cold kiss on his face and throat. "License and registration," the officer said.

"But I didn't do anything—what's this all about?"

"License and registration," the cop repeated.

It was a simple request—unnecessary maybe, wrong, the heel of the boot—and though Fitz didn't yet know it, it was the first in a long unspooling skein of requests, demands, searches, seizures and routine harassment of everybody who passed through the gates of the Hitchcock estate, though what they were doing, *legitimately*, violated no laws. Or hardly any. He dug his license out of his wallet and handed it to the cop, then began fishing through the glove box, looking for the registration as directed, but the glove box was a mess, stuffed with tissues, crumpled burger wrappers, maps, pens, notebooks, a pair of sunglasses—the fact was the station wagon had become a kind of communal car and anybody could have been driving it last. Okay. Fine. But the registration remained elusive. He said, "It's right here somewhere, I know it is."

"You know why I stopped you?" the cop asked, bending down to peer through the window.

"No, no idea."

"You didn't signal back there—when you turned onto Franklin?"

"I didn't?"

The cop shook his head.

"I'm sorry, I thought I did. Everything's okay though, isn't it?"

The cop took a minute, the fine misting rain shining on his black leather cap. "You're up the end of the road, at the Alte Haus, right?"

He nodded.

"You live there?"

He nodded again.

"This license is a Massachusetts issue, are you aware of that?"

"Yes, but—I mean, we just moved in."

"New York State law requires residents to possess and produce a valid state driver's license at the request of a peace officer—and the law states that a new license must be obtained within thirty days of official residence. Are you aware of *that*?"

"No, I wasn't, but, as I say, we just got here—"

"I'm going to have to write you up, failure to signal, invalid license, no vehicle registration."

"Oh, come on, give me a break—I've never had a ticket in my life."

The cop took his time. He was smiling, actually smiling. "Well, you've got one now." He paused. "Actually," he said, "you've got three of them."

3.

I n the next month he must have made the drive to Beacon five or six times, filling in for teachers who were out sick or just sitting in front of a space heater in their pajamas with a book and a mug of coffee laced with bourbon, using up their paid sick leave. Each time, without fail, he was pulled over by Officer Salter, he of the stone face, or his younger colleague, Officer Albright, on one pretext or another, though he'd paid the fines and mailed a Photostat of his registration to the courthouse and was careful never to drive under the influence or fail to use his signal light. Did he know his license plate light was out? Did he realize he hadn't come to a full stop at the corner of Elm? Was he aware that the starburst crack in the lower right-hand corner of his windshield was technically a violation? Where was he going? Where had he been? He lived up at the Alte Haus, didn't he?

It wasn't just him, it was everybody. Dick was flagged for speeding, Fanchon pulled over for failure to come to a complete stop not twenty feet from the entrance to the estate and Tim himself given a lecture by Officer Salter over the distinction between a blinking yellow light and a blinking red. And then there were the weekenders.

The ones who didn't arrive by taxi were subjected to the same sort of harassment, which didn't bode well for the summer's Castalia Foundation seminars, and though no one was arrested on any charge, trumped up or otherwise, it certainly didn't enhance the Millbrook experience or improve anybody's mind-set. Tim sent a letter to the police chief in protest and Dick followed up with a letter from his well-connected father's well-connected lawyer and the police eventually backed off, though they'd served notice, and every transaction, every session, every high was tainted with the knowledge that they were out there, awaiting their opportunity.

For his part, Fitz couldn't remember a more depressing period in his life. Joanie came back to him, yes, and they were sleeping in the same bed and had one or two Saturday sessions where they melted into each other like before, but it couldn't touch what he'd experienced with Lori—and Lori, infuriatingly, didn't seem to want anything to do with him. She was always busy, reading, sketching, writing poetry in her big looping schoolgirl's hand, helping in the kitchen, wandering the hills with her shoulders hunched and her head down or just sitting there playing solitaire in front of the fire, and no, she didn't want company, and no, she didn't want to play two hands or pitch or hearts or anything else. Corey was no help. He was more distant than ever, and when Fitz tried to talk to him about Nancy and about what Jackie and some of the others—*Lori*—were risking with their massive doses of the drug, he got defensive, and after he'd got defensive, he denied everything. ("I never did it with Nancy or anybody else, I swear, not that it's any of your business—or Mom's either. And the only dose I ever take is a hundred mics, once a month—it's a sacrament, remember?") But the worst thing, the worst thing by far, was the Beacon School District. He was making thirty dollars a day, minus withholding and the cost of the traffic tickets, and to earn that pittance he had to endure overcrowded classrooms crammed to the windows with savage fermenting adolescents who saw him as a weak-kneed fraud and nothing more, and on top of that, every time he stepped out in the hall he was subjected to the unforgiving looks of his former colleagues. He wasn't at Harvard. He wasn't a Ph.D. He wasn't climbing the academic ladder or making advances in the field. No, he was back here in prison, the worst kind of recidivist, and no time off for good behavior.

"Hey, Fitz, I heard you were back," one of the English teachers, Ron Wiesenthal, said to him in the hall one day.

"Yeah."

Students—kids—flowed by them as if they were snags in a stream, which, in essence, they were. Ron had bags under his eyes. His suit was rumpled. He'd aged prematurely. He was nothing in the scheme of things and Fitz was—or had been. "So you're okay, then? Things are good?"

"Never better," he'd said, and then went on to give him the story everybody already knew, about taking time off to finish his thesis and make a few bucks just to pay the bills—he knew how that was, didn't he? Oh, yeah, he did—"I hear you, believe me"—and the subject of Millbrook, Timothy Leary and LSD never came up, but it was right there, front and center, in Ron Wiesenthal's baggy eyes and everybody else's too.

Still, the communal experiment went on, more devotedly than ever, Tim presiding, Peggy and a handful of her Upper East Side friends showing up most weekends, Maynard blowing in and out with his air of glamour and untouchability. This was America, wasn't it? What they were doing on their own property was their business and nobody else's. And Tim—Tim was never happier than when he was flouting one convention or another. As far as the local constabulary were concerned, Tim borrowed an expression from Hollingshead to convey his sentiments: *I piss on them from a great height.*

It happened that the vernal equinox fell on a Saturday that year, and so it was all but irresistible to throw a party—a big party, the biggest yet—to welcome back the sun and the promise of the lengthening days to come. Invitations went out—*Celebrate the Equinox, the*

Alte Haus, Millbrook, 7:00 P.M.—and by eight the party was running on all cylinders, Dick and Charlie having stationed themselves at the door to greet each of the guests with a three-and-a-half-ounce paper cup of the sacrament, in liquid form, mixed with cherry Kool-Aid. For his part, Fitz was ready to let go and travel where the drug—and the company—took him. He'd had an especially galling time the previous day, when he'd gone in to substitute for a history teacher and wound up losing it over some little shit of a kid who refused to take his feet down off the desk in front of him and had to be escorted out into the hall and pinned up against the wall before he came to appreciate the nature of the transactional psychology going on between them. What he was thinking was *I don't need this shit,* and he'd actually gone down to the principal's office to tell Dave Jacobs to forget it, thanks but no thanks, but Dave wasn't there, which just made it all the worse.

Now, with a glass of brandy in one hand, a joint in the other and the drug beginning to channel its familiar messages through his veins and into the gaps between his neurons, he began to feel almost normal, even if his fingertips were glowing like flashlights and people's faces took on a metallic cast, as if they'd been cast in bronze and arrayed round the room like so many masks in a gallery. The lights were low, the music strictly jazz (Coltrane reinventing the soprano saxophone on "My Favorite Things"), Joanie in a huddle with Fanchon, and Lori nowhere to be seen, but Flora Lu . . . right here before him, sitting on a mattress pushed up against the near wall, the monkey asleep on her shoulder. He didn't say *Hi* or *Mind if I join you?* but just eased down beside her, his back braced against the wall and his legs splayed out before him. "Thank God it's not rock and roll," he said, indicating the big KLH speaker not two feet from her, and she acknowledged the sentiment with a quick dip of her chin and a smile that melted the bronze right off her face and brought all her beauty rushing to the surface.

"Tell me about it," she said.

"Charlie's worse than the kids. It's all he talks about, the Beatles-this and the Beatles-that—"

"The juvenilization of America. Ed Sullivan. Can you believe that? He used to have *Maynard* on, real music, not this, this *crap.*"

She was vehement, and in her vehemence, she awakened the monkey, which leveled an evil look on him and immediately sat up and began furiously scratching its crotch before settling back down again, its monkey face nestled in the silk of her hair and its tail lazily twitching at her left breast.

"Charlie used to be all about jazz," he offered, "a real aficionado, you know? Not that he still isn't, it's just this teenage music seems to have taken over his brain like in *Invasion of the Body Snatchers*—you think he's had his body snatched?"

Flora Lu liked the idea. She laughed. "Yeah, sure," she said, "that explains it all—they've all had their bodies snatched, especially the Beatles, and who?—*Ringo.*"

He was thinking about taking her hand. There it was, curled casually beside him on the mattress, and he had an urge to experience the feel of the skin there, to engage it, stroke it, a companionable urge that had nothing and everything to do with the ascent of the drug, but then he felt the faintest tickle on the back of his own hand and saw that there was a flea there, a monkey flea, poised to bite him—or not just poised, it *was* biting him. He slapped at it, but it evaded him, making a mighty backward leap into its protectress's lap. "Your monkey has fleas," he said.

She grimaced. "I keep buying him flea collars, but did you ever try to keep a flea collar on a monkey?" She reached up and pulled the animal down from her shoulder, set it on the mattress and gave it an admonitory pat on the hind end. "Now shoo," she said. "Go spread your fleas someplace else. You hear me?" Another pat, this time a bit more forceful. And then, as if it were a huge spider, it scampered straight up the wall, across the top of the wainscoting and shot on up the banister to disappear in the shadows at the top of the stairs.

He was seeing colors, which was usual, and he could feel the brandy as a complementary force, putting the brakes on the wheel cranking round in his brain, if ever so tentatively. "You didn't have to get rid of him," he said. "I mean"—and now he was just talking to hear himself—"he wasn't bothering anybody."

"No," and she was laughing again, "just his fleas were."

"They chew their fleas, you know that, right? Groom each other, bite them between their teeth? Nobody likes fleas."

She gave him the full force of her smile. "The poor fleas. They're just misunderstood."

"Right," he said, nodding vigorously, and he was going to say "Do you want to start the Millbrook chapter of the National Flea Protective Society or should I?" when a wave crested inside him and the words washed up on the shore, each syllable broken and fragmented like so many shards of porcelain, which really didn't seem to matter because he wasn't looking into Flora Lu's eyes anymore—he was focused on an indistinct clump of shadow all the way across the room. Lori was part of that clump of shadow. He'd heard her voice—high, tinny, as if she were breathing Freon instead of oxygen—and now he heard it again and it made him rise to his feet in a confusion of pinwheeling shapes and colors and go right for it.

Lori was down on the floor, slumped in one of the low cutoff chairs, a blanket thrown over her legs. Her face was the face he saw every night when he closed his eyes, the face that had been revealed to him in the meditation house in a way no other face ever had, not even Joanie's, not even Corey's. He knew her. He knew her better than anybody, and now he was right there beside her, sinking into the floor, asking—and this was a routine between them, or had been—"You see God yet?"

"Oh, yeah," she said, and she wasn't looking at him but at the hunched-over shadow beside her, a shadow with a face, a guy—a boy—"we see Him all the time, right, Toby?"

Toby, predictably, said, "Right."

"And what does He tell us? He tells us, *I love you, yeah, yeah, yeah.*"
Toby laughed and she joined in, point/counterpoint.

"No, come on, be serious."

"Nothing's serious, man," Toby said. "We're tripping, okay? So lighten up."

For some reason, for every reason—the way she'd turned her back on him as if what they'd experienced together was nothing, his thesis, *Beacon,* Joanie and Ken and Fanchon, the way she leaned into this weasel-faced kid from Bard she'd tripped alone with up on Ecstasy Hill back in October when he himself hardly knew her—this rubbed him the wrong way. Suddenly he was angry, and nobody got angry on this drug because it was a leveler and it took you outside of all that, but this time was different. He said, "Fuck you."

And Toby, predictably, said, "Fuck you too."

He jumped to his feet, starbursts everywhere, then reached down a hand for Lori, to lift her out of the chair, take her someplace private, talk to her, hold her, love her, but Lori didn't give him her hand, she just gave him a quote, another quote, instead. "'There's a stake in your fat black heart,'" she hissed. "'And the villagers never liked you.'" What happened next he couldn't have said, but it was violent and it was between him and Toby, who was small and slight and didn't stand a chance, just like that little shit in the hall at Beacon High, and then there were arms around him, Toby fading into the depths and Dick's voice in his ear, "It's okay, Fitz, you're just having a bad trip," and Lori, glaring at him out of the two black pits of her eyes, finishing the deal. "'Daddy,'" she said, "'Daddy, you bastard, I'm through.'"

Looking back on it, he wasn't sure when the third-floor experiment began, but it must have been around then, because the weather was still gloomy and everybody was bored, whether they wanted to admit it or not. If Tim's idea of pairing people at random was meant to break down the last remaining barriers to group consciousness, it wasn't working, certainly not in Fitz's case, but for the most part not for the others either, because it abrogated the exercise of free will. You might want to open up to someone a given session had brought you closer to, to go deep with her (or him), but you had to wait your turn, if your turn ever came, and that was the essential flaw in the exercise. Of course, they were all free to do what they wanted by mutual consent, but this wasn't about individuals, it was about the group, and so the third-floor experiment was initiated as a way of addressing all that.

It was Royce Eggers who first brought it up. Everyone was sitting around after dinner as usual, lingering at the table to plug into the current of conversation that was always the best thing about Millbrook—and Zihuatanejo and Newton before it—when Royce, who'd been seen conferring with Tim earlier, tapped his glass with a spoon in order to get everyone's attention. "I have a proposal," he announced, as the conversation subsided around him. "And it has to do with the meditation house pairings—or it's the next logical step beyond them, by way of extending the familial experience here . . ."

As soon as he mentioned the meditation house, everyone's ears pricked up. It happened that Royce's wife, Susannah, was out there that week, in the company of Ken Sensabaugh, and there was all sorts of speculation as to what was going on between them, not simply with regard to sex—if there was any, and that wasn't a given— but with the larger notions of spiritual exploration and the fusing of personalities. They hadn't seemed especially close in the way of some of the others, men and women both, who seemed to seek each other out over meals or group activities or the bullshit sessions around the fire that went on till all hours every night of the week, and while Ken would have been ready for anything, Susannah was probably the most conventional of the women at Millbrook. She was the proto-typical housewife and mother of three who as far as anybody could see would have been perfectly content in her own kitchen in her own home if she hadn't been swept up in the revolution they were all living—and she was a bit older, too, at forty-one. She was attractive enough in her way, but she was no Fanchon. Or Joanie. Not to mention Flora Lu, who was another species altogether. Still, it wasn't looks that mattered, Fitz reminded himself—it was purpose. And if Royce had a problem with his wife being out there in the meditation house with Ken Sensabaugh, it was everybody's problem.

What Royce was proposing, with the backing of Tim and Dick, was to establish an improvisatory sleeping arrangement on the third floor, where most of the rooms were unoccupied simply because they were farthest from the center of things. Mattresses would be laid out and whoever chose to spend the night there was at least tacitly agreeing to sleep with whoever came along. Or not, no compulsion, of course—just openness.

Royce outlined the advantages of the arrangement in terms Tim might have employed (overturning taboos, casting off societally imposed strictures, strengthening the group bonds and driving a stake into the heart of the bourgeois games they'd been stuck playing all their lives), his voice pinched in lecture mode, his hands like white birds fluttering round his face. He'd had an awkward time of it in the meditation house during his week with Alice (she told Fanchon, who told Joanie, that she wasn't attracted to him and no matter how much of the sacrament they ingested or how much they saw of each other, that wasn't about to change). Instead of growing closer, they seemed to have lost any sympathy they might have built up for each other over the past two years. They barely acknowledged each other, and invariably, at meals, you'd find them sitting at opposite ends of the table.

When he was through, no one responded at first because they were all privately assessing what it would mean to them personally, vis-à-vis interrelationships—sex—and Fitz was no different. He was sitting beside Joanie, but he wasn't looking at her—he was looking at Lori, who was giving nothing away, just doodling in her sketch pad as if all this chatter was meaningless to her.

Tim said, "We don't need it to be anything formal—the more informal, the better, really. If people want to get together, with or without the sacrament, well, here's the opportunity. No fuss, no hassle, the kids all tucked away and the rest of us up there peeling back the layers whenever the mood takes us." He paused, glanced round the table. "Everybody in?"

Lori looked up from her sketch pad, then pushed back in her chair and raised her hand as if she were in one of her classrooms at Bennett, where she hadn't set foot since October as far as anybody knew. "When do we start?"

Tim shrugged. "Whenever we want—again, the whole idea is to make it second nature."

"How about now—is now good? Tonight, I mean?"

Another shrug. "Why not? All we have to do is drag some mattresses up there." He paused, flashed his grin. "Lord knows there's enough of them around here."

Fitz could see where Royce was going with this—he was feeling low because Susannah was out in the meditation house, and this was a way of declaring himself ready and willing without having to approach any of the women and risk a rebuff—but Lori? Lori didn't have to play any games. All she had to do was give the signal and Fitz would find a way to be with her—she knew that and that was her power over him. She didn't need more men in her life, she needed less, or, actually just one—him. And here it was again—jealousy, sexual possessiveness—when the whole idea was to get beyond it.

Joanie turned to him and said, "I'm tired. I'm going to bed. You coming?"

"I don't know," he said. "It's early."

And she, lowering her voice even as the conversation started up around the table again, "Don't you even think about it."

"I'm not," he lied, and took a sip of the brandy from the cocktail glass that was as much a part of him these days as a supernumerary limb.

Joanie pinched her features so that her eyes were slits and the two grooves above the bridge of her nose went rigid in the candlelight. "I want you in bed," she said. "With me. Me and nobody else."

This was a theme she'd been playing over the course of the past few days. He'd come into the bedroom one afternoon and saw that she'd been crying, her eyes reddened and a scatter of balled-up tissues on the night table beside her. He was going to his desk on some internal pretext or another that had little to do with the work that had become a kind of joke and when he saw her there like that his first instinct was to turn around and walk right back out, but instead he picked up one of his notebooks and began riffling through the pages as if there were some point to the whole charade. "I don't like this," she said, in a voice that wasn't much more than a whisper.

"Don't like what?" he asked, though he already knew.

"Tim," she said. "Millbrook. This isn't any kind of life. It's a delusion, Fitz—we're all just deluding ourselves, don't you get it?"

He didn't want to talk about it. He was entrenched. And she was so very wrong: this was the *only* kind of life, even if he had to whore himself out to the Beacon City School District to keep living it. "I don't know," he said, "you seemed just fine with it till Ken and Fanchon started locking the door on you."

"Don't."

"Don't what? It's the truth, isn't it? Didn't you say you were in love with him? And her too, right? Her too?"

"I only did it because of you, because you're obsessed with that girl, that little bitch who won't even give you the time of day—"

"She will."

"She won't. You're too old for her—and she's got a boyfriend, what's his name, and every other man in this house too, and you know it. She's mentally unstable, which you, of all people, should recognize. I mean, sleeping around just for the hell of it, quoting poetry instead of making sense when you try to get anything out of her." (This was a reference to a fraught scene in the kitchen a couple of weeks back between her and Lori in which Joanie said some harsh things and Lori just started quoting Sylvia Plath and Emily Dickinson until they both ran out of breath.) "Face it, Fitz: she doesn't want you."

"She doesn't know what she wants."

"She's nineteen, Fitz."

"I don't care if she's ten, she's a whole lot more than you give her credit for."

"And how do you know that—because you spent a week with her blasted out of your mind?"

"Because I'm a psychologist, okay? That good enough for you?"

Now, in the aftermath of Royce's proposal she took hold of his arm, dug her nails in—Was anybody watching them? No, they were all abuzz with possibility, the conversation cycling through the third floor and back again—and repeated herself: "Don't you even think about it."

He wound up pouring himself another drink—she wasn't going to tell him what to do, not now or ever. And he didn't just dampen the bottom of the glass, he poured it full by way of demonstration. She was far from sober herself. She'd had a martini to kick things off while they were sitting around the fire earlier and she'd been drinking Mateus ever since, and of course there was a joint circulating, the eternal joint, and things were convivial in the way they always were after meals. A couple of people had got up to clear the table— Paulette and Diana Westfall—and several of the others, including Lori and Royce, went off to see about the third-floor accommodations. They would need mattresses. Bedding. And candles—candles would be as essential to the operation as bodies themselves.

Charlie, the joint in one hand, a cigarette in the other, was going

on about summer and how great it was going to be, how *stoked* he
was, and how it was never too early to start making plans—"Beyond
the seminars, I mean. Are we going to do anything for May Day, the
summer solstice, the Fourth . . . Or what, Flag Day?" Fitz was watching the smoke fume round Charlie's face, a kind of rippling effect
that might or might not have had anything to do with flashbacks—it
was the light, the movement of the smoke, the transformative nature of the world of appearances, *I see, therefore I am.* Out of the
corner of his eye he saw Joanie lift the wineglass to her lips, drain it
and set it back down again, and he felt her eyes on him and turned
to look at her. It might have been the drink—his glass was already
half empty—but he saw something unconquerably sad in her eyes,
his own wife unhappy, deeply unhappy, and whose fault was that?
"You've had your drink," she said. "I'm going up to bed."

And what did he say? "Sure. Okay. Great. I'll be right there."

But as soon as she left, as soon as she'd pushed back her chair and
weaved through the room and out the door without saying a word to
anybody, he reached for the bottle and topped off his glass, and by
the time it was empty there were only three people left at the table—
Charlie, Alice and Diana—and he realized he hadn't heard a word of
the conversation because Alice was asking him something and he had
to say *what?* twice before he could respond. The question was about
Ken Kesey's first novel: What did he think of it?

"I don't think anything," he said. "I haven't read it."

"Oh, you've got to read it—it's amazing. Like nothing else you'll
read this year. Especially for a psychologist." Alice leaned into the
table, her elbows planted, her hair aflame. "Plus, rumor is he's coming
out with a new one this summer and it's going to be huge. I mean,
I've got a copy of *Cuckoo's Nest* up in my room—actually Lori gave
it to me, because, I mean, everybody was talking about it when we
were up in Cambridge, but somehow I never got around to it. It's
top-notch, isn't it, Charlie?"

"Yeah," Charlie said, "yeah, absolutely. Top-notch."

He wasn't really thinking—he was drunk, Joanie was waiting up-stairs for him and Lori had tipped his boat over and he was flounder-ing in the darkening waters, picturing her up there with Royce, down on her knees tucking in the sheets and fluffing the pillows—but if he was, or had been, he would have wondered why Alice and Charlie were so keen on his literary education all of a sudden.

"I'm sorry," he said, getting up from the table with an assist from both hands, "I guess I'm a little out of it tonight."

"You know Kesey's doing the sacrament, don't you?" Charlie said. "He's got a whole coterie out there in California, just like us—is that *interesting* or what? I mean, the word is *out*."

"I'm sorry," he repeated, shaking his head till his ears began to ring, and what had happened to Charlie? He'd been a Ph.D. candi-date, a scholar, a seeker after wisdom, and now what was he? Kesey? Who cared? What mattered was right here before them, right in this room, right in this house. "I don't know anything about it, but—but thanks anyway." He made a vague gesture and started for the door.

"'Night, Fitz," Alice said.

"Yeah," he said, and then he was out the door and passing by the group gathered round the fireplace, thinking only to climb the stairs and fall into bed beside Joanie, maybe read a bit—yeah, read a bit—but when he reached the second floor he kept on climbing.

There was a big open room at the top of the stairs, then a hallway with bedrooms branching off it—and the towers at the far ends. When he got to the top, his legs gone heavy on him all of a sudden and his lungs like liquid fire (he had to cut back on his smoking, absolutely, and drinking, drinking too), he saw that someone had turned on the lamp in the far corner of the room, which smelled of cats, and something else beyond that, something feral, something you couldn't keep a flea collar on. Had the monkey been up here? And if so, what about Flora Lu? Maynard was off on tour, and just

because she'd rejected the meditation house experiment didn't necessarily mean . . . but no, he was only deluding himself. There was
nobody here, at least not in this room, which served as the third-floor
sitting room and an informal dormitory for the weekenders who'd
given in to the demands of gravity after one party or another. In any
case, it was nothing special. A few odds and ends of furniture stood
forlornly against the walls—a mismatched pair of easy chairs and a
couch from the thrift store he himself had helped haul up the stairs
in the enthusiasm of those first few weeks—and there were half a
dozen sleeping bags scattered about, none of which seemed to be occupied.

He wasn't sure how much time had passed since Lori left the table,
but it must have been an hour or more anyway, plenty enough time
for her to get settled, if that was what she was going to do. And the
others too, whoever they might be. He was curious, that was all. This
was the new experiment, the new freedom, and he told himself he
just wanted to see who was taking advantage of it—disinterestedly,
in his role as a psychologist who might just write some of this up
someday, but as an interested party too because this was his house,
his community, his stew of limbs and bodies and minds. Would Ken
be here? Hollingshead? Paulette? Fanchon? And what about Tim?
Would he be in one of the back bedrooms, inaugurating the festivities? Peggy was in New York, and whenever she was away Tim
let his libido guide him—on any given day he might show up with
somebody he'd met at a party or one of his lectures or a socialite
from Peggy's set, and how Peggy felt about it was anybody's guess.
Certainly Royce would be here—he was the one who'd brought it
up, he was the one with the need. But then he had a need himself
too, didn't he?

He started down the hallway and saw that some of the doors stood
open, like in a brothel, not that he'd had any direct experience of
brothels, just that he'd read novels and seen movies and that was the
way it was, the doors open so the customers could browse and the

girls inside (they were always girls and they were always gorgeous with their sprayed-up hair and cover-girl faces and great bleeding eyes) could lure them in. The first room stood empty or at least that was how it appeared, and no, he didn't want to turn the light on because if anyone was in there he'd feel like a voyeur—but then they were all brothers and sisters, weren't they? He thought of Dick then, Dick and his friend Martin. But where was Dick? He'd seen him by the fire, hadn't he? Or no, maybe he hadn't—everything was a bit out of focus because he'd had too much drink. Which was all because of Joanie. And Lori. And where was *she*?

There was somebody in the room across the hall, a candle flickering, shadows there, and when he paused in the doorway, a woman's voice called out to him—"Fitz? Is that you?"—and it took him a moment to realize it was Paulette and that she was alone and lying there on a mattress, advertising her availability, and in the next moment he was thinking of Rick and where he might be, which, inevitably, made him think of Lori.

"I was just—" he said, and broke off. "Where is everybody?"

Paulette—she was a brunette, with a mass of kinky hair and a dark trace of it under her arms too—was someone he hadn't really thought of in this particular connection. She'd raise her arms on the beach in Zihuatanejo or when she was wearing a halter top in summer and he'd catch a glimpse of the private hair there and it stirred him, absolutely, he had to admit, but she wasn't really his type. She was Rick's wife, that was all. But then, if you followed the logic, she was everybody's wife. She said, "I just thought I'd try this . . . tonight. Seemed like a good idea, what do you think?"

He was leaning against the doorframe. It wasn't just his legs that felt heavy—it was his torso too, his arms, his shoulders, his head. He wanted another drink. He didn't want another drink. "Are you tripping?" he asked.

"Uh-huh," she said. "Some of us just felt like it after the meeting, you know—Royce, Lori, Tim—but not Rick. Rick's downstairs. He's already asleep." Her face was washed of expression in the candlelight. "It's just coming on," she murmured. "You?"

"No, not tonight. Tonight's just brandy and maybe a little pot— just enough to get fuzzy around the edges." It was a school night and school nights kept him tethered. If the phone rang at six A.M., he'd have to get up, put on a tie and drive down to Beacon to endure another day among the adolescents. Brandy he could handle, pot even, but not the sacrament—the sacrament required a whole lot more space, an infinitude, really. And God, God too. Or at least the promise of Him.

He became aware then of a faint murmur of voices coming from down the hall and an even fainter drift of music rising from somewhere below. The doorframe dug into his shoulder, but he didn't move.

When she spoke again, her voice was caught deep in her throat. "Do you want to join me?"

It was a delicate moment. There was nothing about her that was seductive but the question itself, and it wasn't so much a question as a plea. She lay there motionless atop the covers in the flickering light, fully clothed, with her hair splayed out over the pillow and her legs crossed at the ankles. If her feet had been bare, that would have been one thing, but they weren't—she was wearing a pair of thick white socks because the room was as cold as a cave, and he couldn't help thinking how much easier all this would be if only it were summer and it was like it was in Zihuatanejo, everything free and easy and no worries about anything, not even socks.

"Well, actually," he said, searching for the right tone, "the truth is, I was just curious, that's all—you know, to see how this was going to go? But really, I have to get up in the morning. Or might have to. That's the bitch of it with subbing, because you never know."

She was silent a moment, and then, her voice tightening, she said, "If you're looking for Lori, she's with Royce, I think, down the end of the hall, last room on the left."

So he extricated himself and found a use for his legs again. The hallway was a conduit, a tube, and he made his way down it, guided by the murmur of voices—or no, it was a single voice now, Lori's— until he found himself leaning into another doorframe and peering into another candlelit room. Lori was there. On a mattress, propped up on one elbow beside Royce, an unzipped sleeping bag thrown over them both. Lori was reading aloud from a paperback—*Steppenwolf;* he recognized the cover, with its mysterious shadows and the figure of a brooding man, the thinker, the traveler, the one who goes deeper than anyone ever has and finds not enlightenment but nothingness— and Royce, his eyes closed and his head thrown back, was listening. Or not. His eyes were shut, his baldness gleaming in the candle- light. "'Yes, and he who thinks, what's more, he who makes thought his business,'" Lori read in her strange canned whoop of a voice, "'he may go far in it, but he has bartered the solid earth for the water all the same, and one day he will drown.'"

He didn't know what to do. He wanted to clap, give her a lit- tle applause for her effort, but instead he said, "Storytime," and she looked up and saw him there where she hadn't expected him to be or anybody else either. Her face gave nothing away. Was she glad to see him? Irritated? Was this what she'd thought the third-floor experi- ment would be like—reading aloud to a deep-diving bald-headed thirty-something man while another thirty-something man, the one she knew best, stood looming in the doorway?

"Oh, hi, Fitz," she said, without missing a beat. "You want to join us?"

When he didn't say anything, she went on, the words coming in a nervous rush, which tipped her hand: she wasn't made of ice, after all. "We were just reading to each other, like our favorite passages, Royce started off and then I got into it and it's, it's"—she waved a hand, searching for the word—"*amazing.*" She patted the bed beside her. "Come on. Sit down. Do you want to listen?"

It was a narrow mattress, full-size or maybe even a single. He could have squeezed in beside her on the floor and that would have been better than nothing, and he saw that she was wearing a sweater, her black turtleneck, which was all right, which was fine, but the sleeping bag was pulled up to her waist and whether she was wearing her jeans or not, her *panties,* he couldn't say and because he couldn't say and because he was drunk, he said, "I don't know. Do you want me to?"

She shrugged. And Royce, responding to the sound of his voice from some faraway place, flashed open his eyes, looked directly at him and said, "Wow," then closed them again.

Fitz hadn't moved, though everything was so heavy inside him now. He said, "This is crazy," and his voice cracked. "Look at yourself," he said. "Look at *me*. I mean, what are you *doing*?"

Her eyes were open but whatever she was seeing, it wasn't him. Finally she said, "Living. Living, Fitz. On the planet Earth. Or no, that's not right: the planet Millbrook." She smiled then, her big smile, the one that transported her from the plane of the conventional to the exalted. "How about you, Fitz? What are *you* doing?"

4.

A June morning, the air heavy as a wet sock and the sun hanging unencumbered overhead. He was right out in the middle of it, mowing the lawn, aware only of the roar of the mower, of the way it sparked and rattled when it chewed up a handful of pebbles or took a long wheezing breath over the hidden twigs and branches the kids were supposed to have raked up and tossed on the pile for the solstice bonfire. Everything in his field of vision had taken on a hard white edge, as if traced in light, the sun glorious and reigning supreme, the trees in freeze-frame, the house a stage set. He was wearing tennis sneakers, a pair of shorts and a T-shirt he'd sweated through an hour ago—and his sunglasses. They were the essential piece of equipment here. He'd taken a microdose after breakfast—everybody had—to get him through the task at hand, to *enliven* things a little as the twigs jumped and the mower roared and the sky bore down on him.

What they were doing, collectively, was sprucing the place up with two goals in mind: the renewal of the weekend seminars and the big blowout Fourth of July party they were planning for some two hundred guests, which was to feature a barbecue pit, clams on the half shell and Maynard Ferguson's fifteen-man band set up under a white circus tent on the front lawn. Tim and a few of the others—Charlie, Alice, Paulette—were crouched over the rounded stones lining the long driveway with wet brushes and buckets of white paint, trading Tom Sawyer jokes. Ken and Fanchon were overseeing the weeding and replanting of the flowerbeds and Suzie, Richard, Ronald and a couple of the other kids were taking clippers to the mad growth of shrubbery that was threatening to engulf the house till Tim had begun to joke it was like the Beast's castle in the Cocteau movie, which, as Charlie pointed out, was a whole trip in itself.

He pushed the mower into the high grass and it sputtered and choked and spat out the two halves of a tennis ball in a slurry of yellow-green weed and he tipped back the mower to clear the blades, then dropped it and pushed again. He could feel the strain in his shoulders, but that was good, that was what he wanted—pain on his own terms—because otherwise he was left to face the fact that Joanie wasn't there on the lawn with him and she wasn't painting stones or planting flowers either. No, she was on the other side of the house, dressed in pedal pushers and a halter top and with her hair pinned up like the housewife of the month, making one trip after another up the stairs to their bedroom and down again to the car.

This process, brisk, efficient, up and down, the two suitcases, the steamer trunk, was the end result of a series of reversals and misunderstandings that had reached the tipping point just over a week ago. He'd been up early that day, long before the alarm, and he'd slipped out of bed without waking her and gone down to make himself a cup of coffee and sit by the phone, fervently hoping Dave Jacobs would call—he needed the thirty dollars—while just as fervently hoping he wouldn't. Sitting there in the hall in the soft trembling light, sipping yesterday's warmed-over coffee and lighting his first cigarette, he felt something come over him, not a break with reality, but a slippage, certainly a slippage, so that what had seemed so definite—wall, table, glass, cup, sun—was undermined by a whole new presence seething beneath it. He saw himself as from a distance, a partially dressed great ape with a tube of tobacco in one hand and the concentrated residue of a caffeinated plant in the other and knew that he knew nothing whatever of this or any other world. It wasn't a flashback. It had nothing to do with the drug. It was a glimpse of something else, something numinous that underpinned the cardboard cutout that was the world he pretended to know, and it made him feel such a surge of joy it brought him up out of the chair, to his feet, to the window, to the light. The phone rang. The phone rang again. And again. And he let it ring till Dave Jacobs gave up and the house fell back into silence.

At some point he became aware of a noise behind him, a faint rustling—one of the dogs, the cats, the monkey?—and turned round to see Lori standing there, perfectly still, just watching him. She was wearing cutoff blue jeans and one of the embroidered peasant blouses the women had got for a song in Mexico, which somebody must have given her—or she'd appropriated. Because she was like that: if she saw something she wanted, she took it. No matter, because it looked good on her, a canvas for the deep tan of her face, throat and limbs. She didn't say hi. She didn't quote a poem. She said, "You see what kind of day it is out there?"

He was at the window, everything shining, and he'd just gone out of his body without the assistance of Albert Hofmann or Tim or anybody else. "I do," he said, and then he said it again, because this was the glory and the kingdom too: "I do."

"You want to go for a walk? Before everybody gets up and spoils it?"

"Sounds like a plan," he said, and she crossed the floor to him, took his hand and led him out the door and into the soft warm glow of the morning.

The grass was high, in need of cutting, and it held the dew so that his cuffs were wet through before he'd gone fifty feet. She had no such problem—she was barefoot, bare-legged, the blades of the grass swiping at her ankles and calves like brushes at a car wash, and she held fast to his hand, the first contact they'd had in weeks, which only made him float all the higher. Neither of them said a word—they didn't have to. They were out in the morning, just that, and it made so much sense to him he wondered why he hadn't been out here every day since the sun had come back, but that was complicated in a whole host of ways—Beacon, Dave Jacobs, late nights, late mornings. Joanie. His fecis.

Where were they going? Toward the lake. Of course, the lake, which was a sacrament in itself, spread out before them in a glaze of light. Soon they were out of the deep grass and on a path just wide enough for two that led down to the dock where the rowboat was tethered, and the minute he saw it there he knew what they were going to do as clearly as if it had all been planned in advance, as if lakes and rowboats had been created for just this moment. "You want to go out?" he asked, and she just nodded, let go of his hand and skipped down the length of the dock to drop into the stern of the boat and sit there looking up at him as he paused to roll up his pants and kick off his shoes.

"I love this," he said, easing into the boat and feeling the lake tremble beneath him. "No school for me," he said, taking up the oars and shoving off, everything clean, perfect, still. "Not today."

"Right," she said, "let's play hooky together," and whether that made sense or not, since she was playing hooky on a permanent basis, didn't matter. He took it for what it was—a gesture, a pleasantry, an invitation. She was back, at least for now, and now was all that mattered.

There was the smell of the water, fresh-turned under the oars, a smell that took him back to the time before he'd met Joanie, when water skis sustained him and his parents were young and psychology just a word in the dictionary. Mist rose, dissipated. Sparrows hopped along the shore, a crow called from the top of a pine. The boat glided on a string. Behind them, in the distance, was the house, where people would be stirring or not. It was the final week of school and the kids, Corey included, had been going in selectively, and aside from Susannah, and sometimes Joanie, depending on her mood, nobody really bothered much about them anymore—they could feed themselves and they were adept at exercising their powers of ambulation through the simple expedient of putting one foot in front of the other. Let them go to school, let them stay home: it was all the same. In the next moment the house dropped out of sight and he felt himself expanding till he could have absorbed the entire lake and the hills beyond it like some fantastic amoeba of the mind, and all was well, all was very, very well.

She was right there facing him, inches away, her legs tucked under the seat. The oars were extensions of his arms, the waters parted and the boat slipped across the surface, trailing its wake behind them in a continuous pattern of loops and folds that sparked under the sun. It was a big lake, deep, clear enough at this time of year to see twenty feet down. He rowed till they were out in the middle, far from the sight of the house or any of the other buildings, then shipped the oars and let the boat drift. "This is nice," Lori murmured, leaning back, her face to the sky. Then she stretched her legs, lifted her feet in tandem and eased them down in his lap, all the while watching his eyes to gauge his response. "You mind?"

In answer, he stroked her ankles, her feet, her slim tanned calves. The boat drifted, the water lapped. After a while he said, "You're up early this morning—I mean, that was a surprise."

"I don't know," she said, "I've just been wanting to do that, get up early, I mean. You know, embrace the day, all that?"

He didn't ask her where she'd slept, though he'd heard she'd given up on the third-floor experiment and gone back to sleeping in the room she'd appropriated in the back of the house. Instead he asked, "You get anything to eat?"

"No. I wasn't hungry. And the kitchen's always such a mess—I can't really sit down to eat if everything's all over the place. You?"

"The whole schmear," he said. "Coffee, black, and a cigarette."

She laughed and then she went quiet. "Just as well," she said after a moment. "Because I brought something along"—she patted the pocket of her cutoffs—"that really goes better on an empty stomach."

He could have drawn back, could have thought of Dave Jacobs, Joanie, Corey, putting some money in the pot instead of living off the goodwill of everybody else, seeing to his thesis, improving the minds of the rudderless students of the Beacon School District and all the rest of the shit that was pinning him down till he felt like he was chained inside a cage sinking into the depths of a cold dark sea, but he didn't. He just said, "You're a real altruist, aren't you?"

Before he knew it, the sun poked through the tops of the trees, then sprang clear of them, rising steadily till it took command of the sky. He was feeling no pain, only bliss. He watched Lori rise and dip with the motion of the boat, watched the trees dance across the shore behind her. When he felt thirsty, he leaned over, cupped his hands to the water and drank. After a time he became vaguely aware of the heat of the sun, his forearms prickling and the skin stretched tight over his face, and when she said something about it he picked up the oars and rowed them through sheaves of blistering color to the far shore, where he tied up in the shade of a willow and they both stripped down and plunged into the water. They swam. They lay in the grass. They swam. They lay in the grass. Then the wheel of the day took another turn and they wound up stretched out flat on their backs in the bottom of the boat, watching the clouds roll on overhead while the breeze took them wherever it wanted.

It was late afternoon by the time they got back. Rowing, he kept glancing over his shoulder to home in on the dock, and as the dock grew larger he saw that there was someone there, a woman in a sundress and floppy hat he at first took to be Susannah, but wasn't Susannah at all. It was Joanie. Wearing Susannah's hat—or one just like it. He was free of the elation now, coming down off the drug and the glory of the day, his shoulders ached and he was starving and badly sunburned, especially in those places where the sun didn't ordinarily reach. He felt something squeeze tight inside him.

Why his wife was there, he couldn't imagine—unless something had gone wrong. His first thought was for Corey—had he got hurt, been in an accident? But no, that couldn't be, because she was just sitting there tranquilly at the edge of the dock, a book open in her lap, her feet dangling in the water. All right, fine: his wife was there, enjoying the day, and it had nothing to do with the fact that Lori was his obsession and he hadn't gone to Beacon and marriage *was* possessiveness no matter what Tim said or how much of the sacrament you took. He maneuvered the boat in and dropped the oars, letting it glide till he reached out a hand and took hold of the dock. Lori hopped out, secured the painter to the near post, and then, without a word, walked right past Joanie and headed up the path for the house.

He couldn't make out his wife's face beneath the brim of the hat, and that was just as well because he was unprepared for whatever this was or might be, not to mention a bit awkward getting out of the boat, which lurched away from him at the last minute so that he had to snatch at the post to steady himself. The dock trembled down the length of it; the boat shot out and jerked back again. "Jesus," he said, more to himself than her, and then he was standing over her, conscious suddenly of how red his feet and legs were.

She looked up at him now, her face tight with anger. "I hope you had a nice time," she said, and that left him without an opening, because he was going to say *Hi,* say *What are you reading?,* say *What a day, huh?*

"Yeah," he said, "it was great. We just happened to come down here and see the boat—and it was such an amazing day . . . I felt like I was twelve years old again, like Huck Finn out on his raft."

She didn't bother to respond. She said only, "We're going to New Jersey next week. As soon as school's out."

"New Jersey? What about the party, what about the Fourth?"

She spun round, put her legs under her and came up so fast he had to take a step back just to get out of her way, and there she was, right in his face. "*Parties.* I've had it with parties. With everything. With this whole place. It's destroying us, Fitz, and it's destroying Corey too. Jackie's a bad influence, and you know it. *Nancy,* for Christ's sake—"

He wasn't thinking clearly, but what she was saying was wrong, so very wrong. This wasn't about Corey or Jackie either—it was about Ken, it was about Fanchon, it was about Lori. He said, "I'm not going."

And that was it, that was the moment that led inevitably to this one, to the buzz of the lawn mower as it tore at the tall grass and the downed branches that weren't supposed to be there while Joanie, all the way across the yard and up the stairs in the shadowy theater of their room, put things in suitcases and paper bags and carried them down to the station wagon that was going to take her and his son to the Jersey Shore. For the summer. Just for the summer. And he didn't really need to say goodbye to Corey at this point because he was busy now and everything in the world was very bright and present and he'd already done that three nights in succession and assured him he'd be there as soon as he could get away—after the party, after the party for sure—and that they'd go crabbing and take his grand-father's boat out to fish for stripers and blues the way they used to.

He was running sweat. He could taste the salt at the corners of his mouth, his own salt, the salt his body took in daily and daily expelled, and felt the sting of it in his eyes. Grasshoppers arced across his field of vision, the grass flattened and yielded. He kept going, kept pushing, working furiously toward a self-imposed terminus, which would coincide with the moment the station wagon rolled off down the drive and disappeared through the gate, and he wasn't going to look up, he promised himself that, because if he looked up it would confuse things in a way that was going to be hurtful to all parties concerned. He and Joanie had already said what they had to say and he'd made his pledges and taken his vows and gotten a reprieve at least for now, at least till the party was over, and then he'd catch a train or a bus or get Charlie or Rick to drive him . . .

His back was to the house and if somebody was calling his name he couldn't really hear it over the racket of the motor, but then he felt a hand on his shoulder and he swung round, startled, to see Corey standing there in a mad explosion of sunlight and the car, the station wagon, idling in the drive behind him. He shut off the mower, and all the sounds of the day—his coworkers' voices, birdsong, the drone of an airplane high overhead—came rushing back to him. "Dad," Corey was saying, "Dad, we're leaving now."

He was looking into his son's face but he couldn't see anything there beyond the impact of the moment—was he frightened? Distraught? Upset over leaving his father, his friends, Nancy?

"Listen," he said, pausing to wipe the sweat from his hands on the damp seat of his shorts, "you be good now, okay? And I know Jersey isn't exactly Mexico, but it's the beach, right, and at least you'll be out of this heat—"

Corey didn't seem to have anything to say to this, which was just talk, after all.

"And the summer'll be over before you can blink twice, right?"

Corey's voice was deep now, the adolescent croak all but gone, and lately, whenever he spoke, Fitz found himself momentarily baffled, as if some stranger had assumed his son's shape and form. Corey said, "I just blinked twice. And look, here's another one."

He told himself it was all for the better—a little break, that was all—and there was no need to get emotional about it, but he was getting emotional, feeling all the air go out of him as if his lungs had suddenly deflated. Never once since his son came into the world had he been away from him for more than a day or two at a time, and this wasn't just a day or two, it was a summer, or part of a summer, and even as the thought came to him he knew he wasn't going to go to New Jersey to sit there sweltering in that cramped house while

his father-in-law baited him and his mother-in-law presided over a
sheaf of newspaper clippings about Tim and Millbrook and the evils
of LSD.

"Okay," he said, rocking back on his heels, "you take care now,"
and he held out his hand and Corey took it and maybe he would have
hugged him if he wasn't so sweaty but then Corey dropped his hand
and looked back to where the station wagon sat idling at the curb.

"Aren't you going to say goodbye to Mom?"

He could make her out behind the wheel in shadowy silhouette.
Things sparked at the edges of his vision. He was too wrought up,
too sweaty—maybe he was dehydrated, maybe that was it. He almost
waved, just let it go, just *wave*—they'd had their talk, and if he knew
one thing, if he knew anything at all, he knew she'd be back—but
then Corey started walking and he found himself following along,
just like one of Lorenz's geese.

Joanie didn't get out of the car. Her face was very small and very
white and clenched like a fist. He leaned in to kiss her, but she didn't
give him her lips, only the hard slanted bone of her left cheek. "Okay,
well," he said as Corey slid into the passenger's seat and slammed the
door, "I guess this is it, then. Have a good trip, okay?"

She didn't say anything. Just put the car in gear and headed up the
long drive lined with painted stones till she reached the gatehouse,
looked both ways and turned west on Route 44.

The party was the biggest yet, and if that presented a problem for
the village police, it really wasn't Tim's concern. The guests had
been forewarned, everybody adhered strictly to the speed limit and
no one parked on the public streets, but that was as far as he was willing to go, because this was America and not some police state, right?
Still, as a concession, they'd stationed a couple of the kids in the
driveway waving Tibetan prayer flags to guide the cars through the
gates and out onto the lawn, which had at least been cut for the occa-

sion, thanks to Fitz, and it hadn't rained in the past few days so that
the various ruts and cross-hatchings were more or less negotiable.
People arriving by taxi proceeded directly to the front door, a few appeared on foot and one party of six came all the way from the station
on bicycles. By noon, there were people all over the property, some
familiar, some not, but every one of them in a state of bliss over the
beauty of the day and the unfolding of the sacrament and whatever
else the Castalia Foundation had to offer by way of emollients, which
included an open bar and what people were passing hand to hand.

For the past two and a half weeks he'd been focusing on the preparations in a way he never had before. There were trips to the supermarket and the liquor store, the acquisition of paper plates, plastic
utensils, charcoal briquettes, the rental of folding chairs, Canadian
fireworks purchased on the sly, acrylic paints for the mandala he was
decorating his bedroom door with and the mural he was contemplat-
ing for the ceiling over his bed, and there was always a car available
and somebody who wanted to tag along. If he was sleeping alone,
if Lori was elusive and back to spouting poetry and he was going
deep more times than he could count, that was all the more reason
to plunge in here. Joanie was at her parents' house, at the shore, and
Corey was there with her as if none of this had ever meant a thing
to them. He'd spoken to her exactly once, long-distance, for exactly
three minutes, and it hadn't been a pleasant experience. The Castalia
Foundation was $50,000 in debt according to the latest accounting
and nobody was supposed to use the phone except for local calls, and
Paulette, her face set, had let him know as much. He'd had three
minutes of expressing himself in full sentences while Joanie replied in
monosyllables, and no, Corey couldn't come to the phone because he
was out somewhere with his fishing pole. *Love you. Yeah, love you too.*

He was wandering the halls and drifting out across the lawn and
back again, a coffee mug of brandy and soda in one hand, a cigarette
in the other, enjoying himself—enjoying the spectacle—when Maynard and his fourteen bandmates started up with "Blue Birdland,"

a tune he'd heard before and disliked on principle, a flabby tune, a tune that had nothing to do with modern jazz and everything to do with what was unhip and uncool and tied to a dying era, and he realized the afternoon was getting on and it was time to drop his tab of acid (as people were referring to it now, verb and noun) so he'd be soaring for the fireworks.

Two hundred people. The old guard was there, longtime friends of Tim and Dick, and a younger crowd too, a couple of the men wearing their hair long and swept across the brow, Beatles fashion. And there were girls everywhere, half of them fresh from the pool and sauntering around in bikinis, an illustration of the flesh that brought home to him all over again the fact that he was sleeping alone and hadn't laid eyes on Lori all day. Which was maddening. This was the biggest party of the year—she knew that as well as anybody. For the past hour he'd been asking people if they'd seen her and he must have gone down to her room looking for her half a dozen times already, everything a muddle, the dogs underfoot, the monkey screeching from some hidden perch, everybody grinning in his face and pumping his hand. And Maynard. Maynard wailing away.

He was just about to go up the steps and back into the house to check again, when he caught himself: two young women were coming up the walk, arm in arm, striding in perfect sync as if they were working the runway at a fashion show. They were wearing dresses, stockings, heels, though this was an outdoor party, a country party, with steamed corn and paper plates, but then maybe they hadn't gotten the message—or didn't care. And why should they? They were exquisite. And if they wanted to get down and dirty out on the back lawn, they could always take their shoes off, right? That was what he was thinking, if he was thinking at all, because he was mesmerized. One of them, the taller of the two, had a dog with her, a Pekingese with an elaborate hairdo done up in ribbons and bows, tucked like a muff under her arm. She was blond, five nine or ten even accounting for the heels, and every bit as stunning as Flora Lu, or maybe even more so—definitely more so—and she gave him a big melting smile as she passed by and strode up the steps and onto the porch, where Charlie, who was just emerging from the house, held the front door for her and her companion, then threw him a look as if to say, *Did you see that?*

What neither of them realized was that this very tall girl with the Pekingese tucked under one arm and the flawless face and figure was in fact a fashion model, one who was already famous for impersonating a Viking princess standing at the prow of a ship coming up the Hudson in a television ad for Erik cigars, and that she posed a greater threat to Millbrook than all the cops in the county combined. Within minutes she would latch onto Tim, the verified celebrity among them who'd had his picture in the papers even more than she had, and within the hour they'd be doing the sacrament together, privately, in his bedroom, while Peggy pretended to be absorbed in the band and the party went on without them, and two weeks later would announce their engagement with plans for a December wedding and a six-month honeymoon in India, which left the inner circle . . . where?

But that was the future. That was a set of circumstances he didn't know of and couldn't imagine as he stood there on the steps in Nena von Schlebrügge's wake, momentarily distracted from the fact that Lori was missing and he wanted her more than all the blond fashion models in the world stacked up one atop the other till they reached the troposphere. He needed another drink. He needed the drug to come on. He needed Lori and he needed the Light—even the merest glimpse of it, because he'd settle for that if he could have Lori just for the afternoon. And the evening. And the night, especially the night.

She wasn't in her room. He verified that, both audibly and visually, then slipped inside, pulling the door shut behind him. The room showed hardly a trace of her, as if it were a cell in a convent. She kept her clothes in a blue nylon backpack propped up against the wall inside the closet next to a cheap straw hamper for her laundry, and no, he didn't sift through it for the scent of her—he wasn't that far gone, or at least that's what he told himself. The bed was neatly made. There were a few books, poetry mostly, on a bookcase she'd constructed of cement blocks and three naked planks of pine. From beyond the window, which didn't afford a view of the side lawn or the circus tent or the smoke of the barbecue, he could hear Maynard's trumpet rising over the blur of the other horns and the eggbeater of the drummer's snare and tom-toms. At some point, he couldn't say when exactly, the exhilaration he'd felt all day began to seep out of him and he pulled back the comforter and lay down on the bed. He didn't sleep. The drug wouldn't allow that. He just lay still, staring at the ceiling as the ceiling went through its permutations, maps there, cities, roads, trunk lines, spur lines, housing developments, trees, canals, tunnels, bridges, New York Central, B&O, and plaster, plain opaque plaster that didn't want to give up its secrets except in the stingiest little packets.

Then the door swung open and Lori was there. All she had on was a bathing suit. Her hair was wet and she clutched a towel in one hand, as if she'd just come up from the pool. She didn't seem to see him, or not at first, and she dropped the towel at her feet and went straight to the window to shut the blinds, her movements jerky and uncertain, as if she were dancing with an unseen partner. She was muttering to herself—or singing, maybe she was singing. Or reciting, that was it—she was reciting one of her poems, though the words were piling up so fast he couldn't make any sense of them. He called her name then, softly, and she spun round on him in a panic, her eyes like holes drilled in her face, and said one thing only: "No!"

The drug was coming up on him and if he'd begun to feel dissociated from her, from the shadows of the room and the grid of light trapped in the slats of the blinds, her voice brought him right back. This was a party. They were having a party. And here she was, at long last, right where he wanted her. He got up and tried to wrap her in his arms—to hug her, just to hug her—but she pushed away and he saw her face then, the look there, and it was the look the divinity student had given him back in Boston, Julius, the one who'd come unhinged and run out onto the street. That gave him pause. Sobered him. Lori was having a hard time, Lori was flipping out, hurting, hurting badly, and Walter Pahnke and his syringe were hundreds of miles away. "It's okay," he said, though he knew it wasn't, and he reached out for her a second time, fighting through the pulsations of the drug that cut everything in half and then halved it again, but she dodged away from him, tore open the door and ran out into the hallway, screaming, "No! No! No!"

There was a couple just outside the door, leaning against the wall sharing a cigarette, a hepcat with a fringe of goatee and a skinny girl in a white beret, and the guy said, "Hey, what's going on?" and tried to grab hold of his arm, but Fitz ran right through him, down the hall and across the front room with everybody standing around levitating cocktails and beers and somebody—Charlie—calling, "Where's the fire?" Lori never hesitated. She darted through the crowd, shot out the front door and down the length of the porch till she was out on the lawn and past the tent and Maynard and the seismic heave of the band building to climax, and Fitz didn't hesitate either. He was afraid suddenly, deeply afraid, great jarring blocks of the world thundering down before him, and what if she got to the lake, what if she tried to swim, what if the water took hold of her and never let go?

Sure enough: she was heading right for it. And though he ran as hard as he could—and harder, still harder—he was no match for her. She hurled herself down the path, shoulders rotating, arms pumping, the dirty soles of her feet flashing like shuffled cards, flew across the slats of the dock in full stride and careened off the end of it and into the dark pall of the water, only to emerge an instant later, tearing the surface in a smooth coordinated crawl that already had her fifty yards out by the time he hit the water himself, his shirt and pants and shoes gone heavy in the instant, and what was the problem, why the panic, why was he chasing her? Because she wasn't herself. Because she'd done some astronomical dose and was right there in the place Julius had been before—and Julius was only on psilocybin, a plaything compared to this—and he was afraid for her. Terrified. What if she hurt herself? What if she drowned? Could people swim on LSD? Had there been any studies? Rats, what about rats?

He paused, treading water, to rid himself of the shoes, the pants, his shirt, the grip of the lake so cold and unforgiving, so, so . . . wet . . . and saw that there were people on the dock behind him, tranquillized people, partygoers, sacramental people, and they were all smiling and waving as if this were part of the entertainment, but where was she? There, straight out, the slash of her arms and kick of her feet and everything exploding all around him, and he was swimming now too, focusing on that distant perturbation of the water and the slick black bulb of her head that kept dipping and rising and moving farther and ever farther away from him.

The sky went gray, then black, and then there were stars. He was flailing, chilled through, Lori lost to him and the shore receding in every direction till there was no shore, only night. Dog paddle, backstroke, breaststroke, crawl. He gulped for air. His ears were clogged and he couldn't see where he was going, the stars there only to mock him. He swam in circles, rested, shivered, and then, just as he was descending into the core of his being, mind and body interlocked once and forever, no sacrament now, no God, no nothing, the sky sliced open and the silhouette of the shore materialized right there in front of him. There was a concussive blast, more light, color, the rockets—Canadian rockets—arcing overhead to snuff themselves in a rain of sparks. That was the very moment he felt the bottom rise up to take hold of him, weeds grappling with his legs, the suck of the mud, and then he was heaving himself up the bank and into the night so he could shiver in his mud-stained underwear and see the death's heads grinning all around him because Lori was dead, dead and drowned, and the sacrament was flaying the flesh from his bones.

He went toward the light, limping over the stones, and there was the dock, the path, the house, the bonfire. The first person he saw— the tallest one there, the one who stood out, who always stood out— was Ken. "Ken!" he shouted, "Ken!," clutching at his arm now while the two women Ken was chatting up gave him big blissful smiles. "The police—we've got to call the police."

Ken took a step back as if to get a better look at him. He was soaring too—they all were. "You been swimming, Fitz?" he asked, giving the women a sidelong glance. One of the women let out a short sharp bark of a laugh, the one with her hair cut close and the figure of a boy; the other one, busty and thick-limbed in a pink sundress that glowed and shimmered as if it were on fire, didn't laugh at all, just stared. Fitz had never seen either of them before and he couldn't understand what they were doing here or how they'd become part of this long howling interval that kept echoing and echoing inside his head.

"No, you don't understand—"

"You're shivering, Fitz—don't you want a towel or something? Or here, come on"—taking him by the arm—"come closer to the fire."

He snatched his arm away, shivering violently, and stamped in place to bring himself back to the now, to the *situation*.

"The police?" the boyish one echoed, tailing it with a laugh. "I didn't know they were invited."

"It's Lori"—and here his voice broke. "She's out there in the lake. I think she—she was out there in the lake and I tried to, to—"

"Come on now, it's all right, Fitz, it's okay," Ken said, and then, sharply, to the woman in the sundress, "could you find us a towel or a blanket or something? *Please?*"

"Julius," he said. "She was like Julius, remember Julius? She's dead, Ken." His voice rose, he couldn't help it: "Dead, you get it? Lori's dead!"

Ken didn't move. He just smiled at him, and it was a condescending smile, the sort of smile you'd give to a child or to a friend and colleague whose wife you'd shared mutually and was showing every sign of hallucinatory derangement. "Hey, come on, old buddy," he said, "calm down, everything's all right—I just saw her five minutes ago. She was right here." He turned to the boyish woman. "The dark-haired girl in the black bathing suit? The one who was a little out of it?"

"Oh, yeah," the woman said, "yeah, of course, she was right here," though Fitz was no longer listening. He just watched her lips move and her lips told him nothing he didn't already know.

In the next moment he had hold of Ken's arm and was insisting that he come down to the lake with him, because if he didn't he was going to go into the house and call the cops himself, an ambulance, the fire department, people to dredge the lake, because he'd seen her, he'd seen her go down, and she was dead, she was dead and drowned and everything was so narrow and constricted, so foreordained, so wrong.

"Okay, okay," Ken said, and here was the woman with the towel and Ken was wrapping it around his shoulders, "but only if you promise me you'll get out of those wet Jockeys and put some clothes on, all right?"

"Later," he said, his teeth chattering, "I'll do it later," and he was already moving and Ken was beside him and they were off into the night, the two women tagging along. The light of the fire receded behind them but somebody—Ken—had a flashlight and here was the path revealing itself as a pale line drawn down the center of a field of dark ragged grass. The crickets roared. Fireflies hung in the air. He was shivering, his feet were killing him, and Ken kept saying, "I swear it, Fitz, I swear I saw her, isn't that right, Melanie?" And

Melanie—the one in the sundress—kept saying, "Yeah, absolutely. She's around here someplace."

The lake was black. The dock hung pale above it. The other woman said, "God, it's beautiful out here—isn't it great to be out in the country?"

"Tell it to the mosquitoes," Melanie said, slapping her forearm with a sharp percussive crack that echoed out over the lake.

They were on the dock now and there was something in the water, definitely something in the water, and it was no hallucination because they were there with him and they saw it too and if he snatched the flashlight out of Ken's hand it was because he was in the grip of a dread beyond anything he'd ever known. The beam ricocheted off the surface, running every which way till he steadied it and focused it on what was there in the water, bobbing facedown just off the end of the dock.

"Oh, my God," one of the women said, and it was the worst moment of his life, of anybody's life, till the other woman said, "What *is* it?" and what had been Lori, what he was sure was Lori, transmuted itself into something else altogether, a primate, yes, but one that was so much smaller, one with fur and a tail and hands like fine leather gloves.

"Shit," Ken said with real vehemence. "Oh, shit." The beam wavered. He felt his throat clench. "Who's going to tell Flora Lu?"

5.

ori was at breakfast the next morning, barefoot, in a blue terry
cloth robe, spooning up cornflakes as if nothing had happened. Her hair was snarled and her eye shadow so smudged
she looked as if she'd been squeezed through a tube, but she was
alive and whole and the sight of her there at the table surrounded by
party guests who'd never left and in some cases hadn't even gone to
bed, made him surge with joy. He'd twice gone down to her room
in the middle of the night, but she wasn't there and that made him
panic all over again, convinced that Ken had been wrong, that he'd
never seen her at all—or he'd seen her earlier, much earlier, and just
hadn't realized it because of the condition he was in, that they were
all in. He kept seeing the drowned monkey, the way it had given up
its being to bob there in a spreading stain of its own fluids, and as he
lay in his bed drifting in and out of consciousness, it kept sprouting
Lori's limbs and wearing her face and spinning round and round on
him in mockery.

The table was crowded. Alice was sitting on one side of her, two
people he didn't recognize on the other. There was a low murmur of
conversation, everything muted now, and he stood there a moment

feeling foolish, wondering how much she knew of what had happened the night before. Had he really been ready to call the police? Or was that just another hallucination? And what about her? Whether she'd meant to or not she'd lured him into the water and they both could have drowned, in which case this wouldn't have been a relaxed communal breakfast but a wake. So he didn't go directly up to her, but got himself a cup of coffee and stood by the door chatting with Rick Roberts and Royce Eggers and waited until she'd finished, until she put her spoon down and lifted her cup to her lips and let her eyes rove round the room. He gave her a little two-fingered wave and she waved back and in the next moment he was tapping Alice on the shoulder and then drawing up a chair to squeeze in between her and Lori. Alice turned her face to him, smiling. "Quite a party, huh?"

"Yeah," he said, conscious of Lori's eyes on him.

Alice was having waffles, the breakfast du jour (Diana Westfall and Susannah were out in the kitchen, mass-producing them) and she took a moment to broadcast syrup over her plate with a flamboyant swirl of one elbow. "Too bad about Flo's monkey, though. It's a shame, isn't it?"

He answered in the affirmative, though it was for form's sake only: he wasn't sorry to see it go, far from it. "Did you hear about it?" he asked, turning to Lori, who just shook her head.

"We think he must've got into the punch," Alice said, pausing to cut into a waffle, raise a glistening morsel of it to her lips, then put it down again. "I mean, all he had to do was snatch up somebody's cup, right? And I must have seen him ransacking the table a thousand times—"

"Something happened to the monkey?" Lori ran a hand through her hair and let it fall across her face so that each strand of it stood out electrified under the glow of the ceiling fixtures. He saw that there were flecks of weed in it, pond weed, dried now and so pale as to be almost translucent. A voice across the room said, "Badminton— anybody up for some badminton?"

"It drowned," he said. "We—Ken and I—went down to the lake, looking for you, actually"—he stared into her eyes but her eyes didn't register a thing—"and there it was, right there by the dock, floating facedown."

"I thought monkeys could swim."

"Not this one. Or maybe he was so far gone—"

"What," Lori said, "monkey suicide?"

"Stranger things," he said. "You were pretty far gone yourself."

"Flo's all broken up about it," Alice put in. "She loved that monkey."

"Badminton, are you nuts?" another voice rang out, and they all looked up briefly to see a balding man with a beard and pot belly who might have been Ginsberg, but wasn't, striding across the room. "I haven't even had my coffee yet."

To Lori, he said, "You remember any of that?"

"I went swimming."

"I thought you were going to wind up the same way as the monkey—I thought you *were* the monkey, at least at first—"

"Hah!" she said, and her face lit up for the first time. "Me a monkey? Monkeys climb trees, don't they? And then they screw up there, way high up in the highest branches?" Her eyes fell shut, almost involuntarily, as if she weren't even there, and then they snapped open again. "You want to climb a tree, Fitz? Is that what you want?" She pushed back her chair and rose, pausing a moment to glance round the table. "*Urk, urk, urk,* I'm a monkey," she said, humping her back and scratching under her arms. "Monkey see," she said, looking at him now, only him, "monkey do."

That afternoon, after most of the guests had left or were in the process of leaving, he was out on the veranda with a set of mismatched tools, trying to repair a porch swing that had collapsed under the collective weight of half a dozen enthusiasts who'd apparently been trying to get it airborne the night before. It was a relatively simple task, which involved replacing a bent eyebolt and two slats of the seat, and he was thankful for it, thankful to be focusing for once on something other than himself. And Lori. Always Lori. In his clearer moments, which, regrettably, seemed to be increasingly rare, he'd tried to analyze it, this compulsion to be with her, to have her, to chase after her even if it meant alienating his wife and son and making a fool of himself in front of everybody else. And for what? She was nothing special, as Joanie had kept telling him, no different from a million other half-educated teenage girls out there in the world—but she wasn't out there in the world, she was here, with him, and he'd gone to a place with her that week in the meditation house he couldn't begin to describe if he wrote ten theses. And there was a subject: *LSD-25 and Sexual Obsession.* How would they like that at Harvard?

He was down on his knees, probing beneath the broken seat with a screwdriver, when he felt a tremor run the length of the veranda and looked up to see Ken Sensabaugh standing over him with a cold beer in each hand. "I thought you could use this," Ken said, handing him a beer and easing down beside him.

"Yeah, thanks."

"Hell of a party, huh?"

"I don't know, I guess so. Tell you the truth, I could use a little less party and a little more purpose—whatever happened to that? Remember the way it was in Mexico? Or Newton? Remember Newton?"

No one wanted to admit there was anything wrong—they'd come too far for that—but there was a dawning sense that they were losing sight of what really mattered. More and more, they seemed to be going outward rather than inward, the parties become a raison d'être in themselves, as if they'd created all this for the benefit of celebrities, fashion models and Village types, as if they weren't a community of brothers and sisters anymore but a kind of performing troupe—and the weekend seminars, which had started up again, were a case in point. And worse, if this was an experiment, if it had anything to do with the discipline of psychology, then they had to admit that increased dosages, both in terms of frequency and potency, were proving problematic. Tim's son—Jackie—seemed barely able to speak anymore and he'd stopped going to school altogether back in May, Paulette was exhibiting signs of clinical depression and if she was taking incrementally larger doses of the drug it wasn't for enlightenment but escape, no different from what people were doing with Dilaudid and heroin on the street corners in Harlem. Joanie was on hiatus. And Lori had gone so deep inside herself nobody could fathom what she was thinking—or even, half the time, what she was saying.

"I don't know," Ken said, "I guess it's a work in progress."

Behind him, down the length of the veranda, two of Maynard's bandmates were pushing through the front door with their instrument cases and overnight bags, already on to their next gig, and if they were concerned with the finer points of the experiment under way here, they didn't show it. In fact, one of them—the tenor sax man, flattop, sideburns—set down his bags and lit up a joint, took a drag and passed it to his companion, who in turn set his own bags down to take it in two fingers and put it to his lips. "Shit, they got a lot of trees out here," the first one said. "I hear you," the other said, squinting against the light before reaching into his breast pocket and digging out his sunglasses. Fitz watched them till they picked up their bags, descended the steps and started up the drive to the car waiting there for them.

"Agreed," he said, setting aside the screwdriver in favor of an adjustable wrench, which seemed more adequate to the task, "but I wish it would *progress*."

"If you're talking about your thesis, don't go there, Jesus, not today—"

"My *fecis*, you mean."

"Right," Ken said, laughing. "Mine's made of shit too."

"But what I mean is it's coming up on a year now, ten months anyway, and I'm no closer to any sort of revelation—or breakthrough, maybe breakthrough's a better word—than I was on the beach in Zihuatanejo. And some of us—I mean, *Paulette*—are starting to scare me."

"You were pretty scary yourself last night."

"Point taken, but then that's what I'm saying: Where is this going? Is there any end in sight? Can we even call ourselves scientists anymore—or what are we, mystics? Partygoers? Bacchanalians?"

Ken raised the can to his lips and Fitz saw that he looked enervated, old, as if he'd aged a decade in a single night, the golden boy no longer—and not an adept either, just a weary explorer who'd all but given up on his degree to follow Tim, to be here, doing this. Like him. Just like him. "Come on, Fitz," he said, "I've got a headache—or no, you're giving me a headache. We're here, in the moment, okay? Isn't that enough?"

"Truthfully, no. Maybe Dick's on the path to enlightenment, maybe Tim is, but me? I'm just"—and here he had to pause a moment to let his emotions catch up—"lost. More and more, that's what I'm feeling, lost."

Tommy Eggers slammed out the door then, heading somewhere fast with a transistor radio in one hand and a can of soda in the other, and they both paused to watch him hurtle off the porch and jog on down the drive past the sauntering sax player and his companion. Almost in sync, they both took a long swallow of beer, everything raw and exposed on the cusp of that admission.

"Speaking of lost, Lori's still up in that tree. I don't know what she's on this morning, maybe nothing, and maybe it's only the aftereffects of last night, but as Charlie would say, 'She is *out* there.'"

As soon as she'd started in on the monkey routine at breakfast, she saw how much it embarrassed him in front of the others and just kept it up and kept it up, scratching under her arms and shuffling through the dining room and out the front door, chittering *urk, urk, urk* just to irritate him, until suddenly she broke away, bolted for the nearest of the maples lining the drive and hoisted herself up into its branches. And what did he do? He followed her like a supplicant and stood there beneath the tree, shading his eyes to peer up at her and trying to be a good sport, all in fun, and so what if Flora Lu was in mourning? It was only a monkey, after all—the laboratories of America were full of them.

He watched her settle back against the trunk, her legs straddling a branch twenty feet up, the soles of her feet like big pale moths batting at the leaves, her face high-flown and remote. The robe had fallen open and he saw that she was wearing panties and camisole only, no bra, and that stirred him despite himself. "Very funny," he said, bracing himself against the trunk. "Now come on down before you break your neck. Let's go do something—like a ride, you want to take a ride? We could go out in the country—"

"We are out in the country."

"You know what I mean. We've got the whole day ahead of us. Let's get away from all this"—he gestured to the house, the circus tent, the strangers wandering across the grounds like the remnants of lost tribes—"and go someplace, just the two of us."

"No, you come up here. Be a monkey with me."

"I don't want to play games. I'm tired of games. Last night, you . . . I was afraid you were going to hurt yourself, okay? If you want to know, my nerves are shot. So come down out of there. *Now.*"

In response, she rattled the branches and thrashed her feet as if she were about to lose her balance.

"Come down," he repeated.

"No, you come up."

He felt a flash of anger. "Go to hell," he said, and shoved himself away from the tree, which just stood there, immovable, locked into a being and purpose that antedated all this, the movement, the hunger, the eating, sleeping, shitting. "I'm going back in the house."

"Don't you want to fuck me?" she called, and when he didn't answer, she let out a long hoarse screech in perfect imitation of Flora Lu's dead monkey.

Now, draining the last of his beer and rising to his feet in the same motion, he said, "I'm worried about her."

And Ken, whose attitude all along had been why bother with a neurotic schoolgirl when you had Fanchon and Joanie and Susannah, not to mention all those women in bikinis out there sunning themselves by the pool, laid a hand on his arm. "You and everybody else," he said.

He was out in the yard one morning two or three weeks later, cutting back the high weeds at the edge of the lawn, glad to be doing his part—pitching in—especially since his contributions to the communal pot had been all but nonexistent in recent weeks, when he was distracted by what seemed to be the sound of a loudspeaker riding in over the treetops. He heard it—static, noise—and then he didn't. His first thought was that some local politician must be rolling up and down the streets of the village in a convertible broadcasting the usual promises and lies, but then the political season didn't arrive till fall, did it? Was there a mayoral race going on? He didn't even know who the mayor was, not that it mattered, as long as he kept clear of the Alte Haus and reined in his police force. But there it was: a loudspeaker, intermittent noise on an otherwise somnolent day, and it was nothing more to him than a curiosity, a minor irritation, like the deer flies settling on the back of his neck or the wasps and poison ivy lurking in the undergrowth. He wiped the blade of his sickle and went back to work.

There'd been a session the night before, conducted under the stars by Tim and Dick, and though it was almost noon practically no one was stirring besides himself. Somebody was stretched out on a chaise longue just off the front steps—was that Paulette?—and he'd seen a couple of the kids heading down the drive for town half an hour earlier, but that was about it, and if the sickle needed sharpening every once in a while and cabbage moths drifted through a shaft of sun like blotches on a movie print, it was all right, just another summer's day. He'd done only half a dose himself the previous night, along with Lori, because they both agreed—or at least he'd made the case and she went along—that things had gotten out of hand at the Fourth of July party, and not just because of the dosage, but the scene itself. They needed to get back to the basics. To the meditative. The inner, not the outer.

But here came that noise again, a crackling, a screech, a snatch of music, and he straightened up and looked off down the drive, but there was nothing there. Lori was asleep still, upstairs in his bed— their bed—and that was all right too. They'd come to an understanding in the aftermath of the party and scaled back not only the sacrament but the other amusements floating around the group— marijuana, hashish, amphetamine—and in the interval they'd spent most of their days and nights together, though she had a tendency to vanish without a word for hours or even days at a time, and where she went he didn't know and kept himself from asking. All he knew was that when she was around he felt he was soaring, with or without the sacrament, and he'd even begun to see a way around his academic dilemma—or at least a way to sidestep it. He was going to write about this, about Millbrook. About an ongoing experiment like no other in the history of the world, and there were no lab rats involved, no *monkeys,* because they were the subjects themselves. The idea excited him—liberated him—and when he told Lori about it she clapped her hands and laughed. "Will I be in it?"

"Of course, but all the names'll have to be changed—"

"What's mine going to be?"

"Yours? I don't know—how about just L, period?"

They were sitting on the edge of the bed in his room, and she gestured at his desk and the chaos of papers scattered across it, charts, diagrams, the abortive text and the thick sheaves of his notes, his endless notes. "What about all this? Your fecis?"

He shrugged. "I don't know."

"Let's burn it."

As soon as she said it, it sounded like the best idea he'd ever heard, and he pushed himself up, went into the bathroom and returned with the cheap tin wastebasket that was half full of wadded-up Kleenex and set it on the windowsill. The window was already open. All he needed was a match—and brandy, two glasses of the cut-rate Korbel brandy he kept in his desk drawer, for a toast—and if the smoke was a problem and he damned near set the side of the house on fire, it was worth it, definitely worth it.

But now the noise was inescapable, coming closer, booming, rattling, and he looked up to see a vehicle winding its way up the drive, a bus with some sort of cage or platform set atop it and people there, waving their arms and shouting. One of them began throwing things over the side—fuming cylinders that obliterated the air and bounced and rolled and drew a boiling green vapor out of the earth till it looked as if hydrothermal vents were opening up all over the yard. He just stood there, dumbfounded, while the noise came at him, clarifying until he realized it was music, or meant to be music, electric guitar, the screech of a flute, a bottom-heavy thump of bass and a superamplified voice crying, *Earthlings, we've arrived!* over and over. And here was the bus itself, bursting out of the trees in a skin of Day-Glo paint and shrieking past him and on up the drive to the house.

He snatched a glance over his shoulder to see Paulette lurch up from the chaise and bolt for the front door and in the next moment he was running himself, not for the house but for the woods, because whatever this was, he wanted no part of it. He ran till his lungs felt sodden and then pulled up abruptly, cursing himself. Why should he run? He lived here, didn't he? This was his property—or Tommy and Billy's anyway. But what *was* this? Who *were* these people? The music held steady and now there was a new sound intermixed with it: the horn. Incredibly, the driver was leaning on the horn as if he were stuck in a traffic jam, as if this were the FDR Drive at rush hour. That was it, he couldn't help himself, and in the next moment, outraged and baffled at the same time, he was circling back round to come up behind them, careful to keep his distance till he could begin to sort things out.

He saw that there was a whole tribe of them, men and women both, shaggy-haired, loose-limbed, in striped shirts, serapes, big-brimmed straw hats and cowboy boots, filing off the bus to sprawl on the lawn and pass joints and cigarettes from hand to hand, while a contingent mounted the steps of the veranda and one of them—short, muscular, cowboy hat—banged on the front door as if he belonged there, as if he'd been invited. That was when the door swung open and Dick's face appeared, flanked by Alice's and Fanchon's. Mouths moved, heads nodded, and then Dick and the women stood back and ushered them in, the whole mob—there must have been twenty of them, the ones on the lawn pushing themselves up to climb the front steps and disappear into the recesses of the house. The bus driver abruptly released the horn and a moment later he too headed up the steps and into the house—but the music, if you could call it that, never faltered. It just kept grinding on, a stew of feedback, static and distorted shrieks.

It was bewildering—and wrong, that too. The noise, let alone the spangled bus and the cowboy garb and all the rest, had to be a magnet for the police. They'd just plowed their way through the village, hadn't they? Shouting and waving and blaring their loudspeakers— and what if they'd tossed smoke grenades in the streets too? He snatched a glance over his shoulder, expecting to see the town's two police cruisers charging up the drive, sirens wailing, but there was nothing there but the glowing white stones and the trees that overhung them. Finally—he didn't want a confrontation; let Dick handle it, that was what he was thinking—he slunk around the side of the house and came in through the kitchen door, leaving it open behind him in case he had to make a quick exit.

There was a smell of cooking, a pot of something on the stove, fresh-baked bread set out to cool. And Susannah, her hair tied up in a kerchief, sitting at the table with a knife and the cutting board, dicing carrots. "What's going on?" he demanded. "Who are these people?"

"I don't know—the Pranksters."

"Pranksters?"

"You know," she said, "the writer? Kesey?"

"*He's* here? What's *he* doing here?" Even as he posed the question he knew the answer—these people, these clowns in motley, thought they had something in common with Millbrook, thought they'd be welcome, but that wasn't the case at all, not even close. Didn't they belong in California? Wasn't that where they'd come from? Well, let them go back there—and the sooner the better. He went to the swinging door and peered into the big room beyond and there they were, milling around, smirking, picking things up and setting them down again as if they were in a thrift store. He saw now that some of them were wearing face paint though it was three months to Halloween yet and that one—a man—had hair to his shoulders and a crow's feather cocked behind his ear. Another, incredibly, had a movie camera balanced on one shoulder, recording every slouch and gesture.

"So is Tim home?" the one in the cowboy hat asked. "I mean, can we see him? You know, get together?"

"Wild times," somebody said. "Let's do it."

There was a burst of ragged laughter. They all seemed to be leaning on one another.

Tim, as everybody in the house knew, was riding out the second day of a projected three-day trip by way of purifying himself and he'd given strict instructions that he wasn't to be disturbed. Which made it difficult for Dick, who gave an equivocal answer and wondered if he could show them around the estate, the meditation house, the lake—did anybody want to see the lake?

None of them seemed to care much one way or the other about the estate or the lake or anything else—they'd come for the party, only that—but then one of the women asked, "You got a bathroom in this place?" and everybody was laughing again. And not just laughing, but hooting, replete with catcalls and back-slapping and wiseacre jokes, and of course they were all stoned, all of them, because that was their business in life. At that moment, with Dick trying to make peace and distract them and get them back out in the yard, a tall broad-shouldered girl at the rear of the group swung round and spotted Fitz there at the door. "Hi," she murmured, smiling wide and raising the index and middle fingers of her right hand in a V-for-victory sign, her hair in pigtails and her eyes drinking up the light. She was dressed like the rest of them, more or less, in a pair of cutoffs, a buckskin vest and Indian moccasins decorated with colored beads, and that really didn't do much for him. It was childish, that was all. Like their bus and their rock and roll and their blissed-out smiles. They were like a negative image of the inner circle—or no, a cartoon version. He stared right through her and then, without a word, pulled the door shut, stalked through the kitchen and out the back door.

Sometime later, after somebody had mercifully shut off the music and the whole mob of them had sauntered off in the direction of the lake with Dick, Alice and Fanchon leading the way, he slipped back in the house and went up the stairs and down the hall to his room, wondering if Lori was up and if so whether she knew about the cyclone that had touched down in their midst. She wasn't there. She wasn't in the bathroom or Corey's room either. The bed still bore the impress of her and it was still warm, or maybe that was his imagination. He stepped out in the hall, called her name. Nobody seemed to be around. He thought then of the pool—she'd taken to swimming almost every day now, the activity imprinted on her after the night she'd almost drowned them both—and he went out to take a look, but she wasn't there either. Three of the Pranksters were in the pool though, two men and a woman, naked and floating on the kids' rubber rafts, their faces upturned to the sky. The woman—she was the same one he'd seen in the hall—held up a hand to shade her eyes and called out, "Hi, come join us!"

The sun was a terrible thing. He reached in his pocket for his sunglasses—his shades—and realized that in the confusion he must have left them in the kitchen. Everything was ablaze, the whole world, even the water, and where was Lori? "No thanks," he said, dismissing them with a gesture, and then, so as not to seem totally rude—like a shit, that is—he added, "Maybe later," though it was hard to overcome his resentment. Didn't these people realize what they were doing? The truce with the Millbrook Police Department wasn't going to last forever and though he wasn't the paranoid type he had noticed more airplanes buzzing the property lately, or at least since Ken and Charlie had drawn his attention to them. And that kid, Toby, he was a plant, a spy, Charlie was sure of it, though Lori denied it vehemently—and hadn't he read of cases where the police busted somebody on a possession charge and threatened him with the worst if he didn't go undercover and report back to them? Wear a wire? Tap the phones? The sacrament was legal still, but that wasn't going to last, and then what were they going to do? So no, he didn't like this, didn't like it at all.

"Who are you?" the woman called while the two men, one with a beard, the other without, floated around her.

He stood there, squinting into the sunlight, feeling foolish, as if he were the stranger here, and that rankled him even further. "'I'm nobody,'" he said, thinking of Lori, and the uncanny thing was, the woman threw it right back at him: "'Then there's a pair of us—don't tell!'" She laughed then, a harsh gargle of a laugh that ricocheted off the water and chased him all the way across the lawn, past the meditation house and down the path to the lake.

Lori was there, on the dock, the fated dock, surrounded by a dozen newcomers and a smattering of the inner circle too—Charlie, Alice, Dick, Fanchon—though most of the household was still keeping its distance. People were sprawled out in the sun, some of them wearing clothes, others not. Three of them were in the rowboat, horsing around, though it was still tethered to the dock, and everybody, including Lori, seemed to have wet hair. There was beer—six-packs that had magically appeared—and a brass hash pipe was circulating from hand to hand. Everything was convivial. A party. Another party.

Lori—she was in her bathing suit, hunched over her knees, her back pressed to one of the pilings—waved him over. She had a beer in one hand, a joint in the other. "You know everybody, Fitz? No? Okay, well this is"—and she gestured to the man beside her, who was dripping and naked and grinning like a thespian—"Paul, right? You're Paul?"

He was. And he reached up to take Fitz's hand, peering over his sunglasses as if to get a better look at him. "So I'm shaking the hand of a psychologist, right?"

Fitz nodded.

"So it's true—you're all psychologists, then? Jesus. I mean, you've got to see it to believe it, right?"

"I'm not a psychologist," Lori said.

Alice, who'd had her back to them, chatting with two of the other strangers, turned round now and said, "I'm not a psychologist either." She was barefoot, in a pair of wet shorts and a wet blouse. Her hair hung limp in her face.

The guy looked up at her, grinning wider. "Whew," he said, making a gesture as if he were wiping sweat from his brow, "that's a relief. For a minute there I thought I was back in the bin again—" He took hold of the post and pulled himself up, his equipment dangling in a way that managed to be purely natural and offensive at the same time. "Relax, it's a joke, man," he said. "Us? There's not a psychologist among us—or a shrink either. You know why? We're as normal as normal can be." And here he called out to one of the men in the boat—"Lee? Lee, you hear that?"

"No, what?" the one in the boat said.

"I said we're as normal as normal can be," and he tailed it with a laugh and Lee laughed too.

In that moment, while the conversation jumped off in a whole new direction, the three in the boat all adding asides to show how witty and relaxed they were, how with it, how cool, Fitz leaned down to Lori and whispered, "I'm thinking of going into Poughkeepsie if you want to come along. To the record shop there? Remember, I promised you?"

The look she gave him—and she wasn't wearing her sunglasses so he got the full benefit of her big unadorned eyes—seemed to close everything down. "You mean now?"

"Yeah," he said, the sun punishing his eyes, "now."

She made no move to get up, but just stared at him. He heard Dick laugh and glanced up to see him standing in a group at the end of the dock, in congress with the one in the cowboy hat, who, he realized, must be Kesey, the novelist, the celebrity, and all he could think was where's Maynard when we need him, match celebrity to celebrity, check and mate. He turned back to Lori. "Well?" he said, and she was already shaking her head.

"No," she said, "uh-uh. I don't think so."

In the morning, the bus was gone. He woke alone, in a prison of latticework shadows, the sheets, which could have been cleaner, smelling of mold and sloughed skin and of Lori, who could have been cleaner herself. She went around barefoot all the time, her feet calloused, toenails chipped, patches of grayish dirt caught in the hollows of her ankles, and each morning she slipped into the same shorts and top she'd tossed casually on the floor as she climbed into bed and never gave it a second thought. When they made love he liked to kiss her there, on the roughened skin of her feet and toes and work his way up first one leg, then the other, till all he could smell was her, the way she was in her essence, but they hadn't made love the night before. In fact, unless he was missing something, she hadn't come to bed at all, and that bothered him more than he would have cared to admit.

He found a few people sitting around the kitchen, looking fragile. Ken was there, hunched over his elbows at the table and staring into a cup of coffee, Fanchon on one side of him, Charlie on the other. Paulette was standing at the sink, mechanically working her way through the teetering piles of dirty dishes and crusted utensils that were the daily detritus of communal life, but then Paulette liked doing dishes because doing dishes was therapeutic—or at least that was what they all told themselves. He'd heard the hoots and jagged laughter of the carousal the night before, the sacrament circulating, the two tribes feeling each other out, but he'd stayed away from all that, from the commingling, the joints, the martinis, from dinner even (he'd taken himself down to the diner for meat loaf, mashed potatoes and wax beans, then to the local bar, where he'd lapped up generic brandy and watched a fuzzy baseball game on the television in the corner till things had had a chance to die down back at the Alte Haus and he could lurch up the stairs in peace and pitch blindly into bed). He had no use for these people. They weren't advancing the research. The fact was they were delegitimizing it with every sunburst of paint they sloshed over the battered fenders of their bus, every shriek of their amped-up music and every frame of film they took.

"So they're gone, huh?" he said, going to the cabinet to pour himself out a bowl of cereal, the Cheerios, Froot Loops and Lucky Charms they kept on hand for the benefit of the kids, basic nutrition, and who could argue with that?

Charlie nodded.

"Thank God, huh?"

"They weren't so bad," Charlie said. "They just think differently, that's all."

"Right, like let's put on clown suits and dance around for the TV cameras."

Nobody rose to the bait, though clearly they were all disgusted, he could see that. Or maybe he was kidding himself, maybe this was what it all came down to in the end: clown suits.

"They've got their own Ken, just like us—Ken Babbs," Charlie said.

"And he is the major domo," Fanchon said, "the right-hand man, just like our Ken, and isn't that funny?"

"Synchronicity," Ken said.

Charlie drained his cup—milk, he was drinking milk, and it left a faint white trace on his upper lip till he wiped it away with the back of his hand. "He's a good guy, he is, and smart as a whip—you would have liked him, Fitz . . . if you weren't hiding your head in the sand. Where were you? Don't tell me you were down at that bar again—"

He didn't answer. The cereal—Cheerios, little puffed loops of flour, sugar, starch and tripotassium phosphate—rattled into the bowl he'd set on the counter and now he was busy dribbling milk from the carton into it. The morning was almost gone. "Anybody seen Lori?" he asked.

6.

Nobody had seen Lori because Lori wasn't there. She wasn't in her room. She wasn't in the kitchen or the library or the pool and she wasn't in the rowboat or up in the tree or anyplace else he looked. The kids hadn't seen her—and he questioned them all (except for Nancy, whom he couldn't seem to find), trying to be casual about it, but that was a sham because he really had no interest in any of them since Corey had left and they knew it as well as he did. He kept telling himself there was nothing to worry about—Lori had gone missing more times than he could count, and she always came back—and yet there was something about that morning, about *the absence of the bus,* that turned everything upside down. But no, no, no, she wouldn't have gone with those people, no way in the world— she was part of this, this was her home, her community, and she was as integral to it as Fanchon was, as Tim, as anybody. Besides which, her backpack was still in her closet, all her clothes stuffed deep inside it and her shoes tucked under the bed, including the outsized pair of white tennis sneakers she liked to flap around in when she bothered with shoes at all. Her books were on her shelves still, her drawings on the walls. He told himself she'd probably just gone into town.

The missing link in all this was Nancy—if anybody knew where she was, it would be Nancy. But nobody seemed to know where Nancy was either, and yet that was all right, that calmed him—you didn't have to be Philip Marlowe to deduce that they'd gone off on an adventure together, a hike, clothes shopping, sharing a burger and milkshake at the diner or driving into Poughkeepsie. To the record store. For the Beatles, and who else now? The Beach Boys. The Animals—just try turning on the radio and escaping *them*. Eventually, he went up to his room, sat at his desk and tried to work, or at least read, but he couldn't seem to focus on anything except the bloated green bottle fly trapped against the windowpane and buzzing angrily, futilely, frustrated by the wall of glass interposed between it and a hospitable place to deposit its eggs, and what was this world coming to when you couldn't fulfill your destiny? Where was the next generation of maggots going to come from? Was nothing right? Nothing possible?

For a while he *was* the fly, and then he was inside the fly, an egg waiting to take nurture in a pile of dung, and Lori wasn't there and the afternoon was as bright as the open door of a furnace and he understood that if work, the notion of it, the need of it, had ever meant anything to him, it meant nothing now. The bed was right there, not ten feet from him. It only seemed natural to stretch himself out on it, close his eyes and listen to the decelerating buzz of the fly till it fell away to nothing. When he woke it was late afternoon. He didn't think of Lori, or not right away—he thought of brandy and soda in a tall glass and he went down to the kitchen (*Hey, what's up; Not much; You?*), poured himself a drink and took it out on the veranda. There was no one there, nothing moving, not even the dogs, the day stuck like flypaper to everything visible and the sun stalled in the trees.

He was just settling into the porch swing when he noticed a figure seated in a folding chair halfway across the sea of grass that swallowed up the drive and ran off into the forest in all directions. It was a girl, her back to him, and she had an easel propped up in front of her. For a moment, he thought it was Lori—the pinched shoulders, narrow waist, the flag of black hair—and he was already congratulating himself when he saw that he was mistaken. It wasn't Lori, it was Nancy. Which was fine. Nancy, out there on the lawn, painting. He took his time—he didn't want to push it, didn't want to jinx himself—but eventually, when the drink was just a rattle of ice cubes and a brownish tinge at the bottom of the glass, he got up from the swing and went down the steps and across the lawn to her.

She was using watercolors, dipping her brush in a paint-stained fruit jar and then touching it to the palette in her left hand, the painting a duplicate of what he was seeing over her shoulder, the lawn, the fountain, the drive, trees like grounded missiles and six different shades of green, and though he was no judge of art he couldn't help thinking she really wasn't half-bad. Which made him feel a sort of paternalistic pride, even if it was secondhand. She was his son's first real girlfriend, puppy love and maybe something more, though Joanie had put an end to that. He had nothing against her. She was a kid, that was all, and what the kids did among themselves was no business of his.

She must have felt his presence because she turned around just as he reached her, her eyes startled for the briefest fraction of an instant before she smiled and murmured, "Oh, hi, Fitz." And then, as if she needed to apologize, added, "I'm just painting."

"Looks great," he said. "Really."

She took the compliment in stride, cranking her smile up a degree. "Mr. Tortora, my art teacher at school? He said to keep it up over the summer because that's what a real artist does, practice, practice, practice. You really like it?"

"Sure," he said, "yeah, but listen, I was just wondering if you'd seen Lori around anywhere?"

"Lori?" she repeated, as if she'd never heard the name before. She leaned forward to dab at her painting, the green blotch there in the canopy of one of her reimagined trees, then straightened up and gave him a glance over her shoulder. "No, I don't think so. She wasn't at breakfast this morning, was she?"

He shrugged, as if it was no big deal. "Just wondering, that's all." He stood there a minute more, for form's sake, said, "Nice work," and strolled back across the lawn, retrieved his glass from where he'd set it down beside the porch swing and went on into the house to pour himself another drink.

Three days later, when she still hadn't turned up, it occurred to him to drive over to the college and see if she'd somehow gone back to her dorm room—if she even had a dorm room anymore. If she did, that would explain where she kept disappearing to, that would explain a lot, and as he slid behind the wheel of the first car he came to in the driveway—Ken's VW Bug, keys in the ignition, fuel gauge stuck on RESERVE—he pictured her living a double existence, the *enfant primitif* devoting herself to barefootedness and mind expansion at the Alte Haus, but privately pursuing her degree all the same. In a skirt and blouse and what, penny loafers? Sure, why not? If anybody could pull it off she could. But then it was August now and school wouldn't have been in session, would it? Unless they offered summer courses. *Did* they offer summer courses? He didn't have a clue. He'd been in Millbrook nearly a year now and he'd never set foot on campus, not once.

It wasn't much more than a mile from the gates of the Hitchcock estate, an easy walk, but he was driving because he was feeling a sense of urgency, an urgency he'd tried to contain over the course of the past three nights with prophylactic doses of alcohol and marijuana, but with little success. He needed her. He was blinded by her. And if he was drunk on cheap brandy at two in the afternoon, it wasn't his fault.

There were cars in the lot out back of the big gabled mansion that dominated the campus, more cars than he would have imagined, and that encouraged him—somebody was here, at least. It took him a while to park, the dimensions of things gone flaccid on him and the earth and its burden of lawns and trees and buildings moving even faster than the car, but finally he maneuvered the Bug into a shrinking space between two massive Pontiac sedans—or no, one was a Dodge—and got things squared away to his satisfaction before making his way across the lawn and up the steps of the main building. There wasn't a student in sight—nobody in sight, actually, not even a gardener or custodian. Bennett College, Closed for the Summer, like all colleges everywhere, and what was he thinking?

He was just about to try the door when a woman emerged, blinking against the light. Startled, he took a step back and made a clumsy swipe at the door, meaning to hold it open for her, but missing it altogether. "Oh," he gasped, "I'm sorry, I just—"

She was in her thirties, dressed in the black skirt and white blouse he'd pictured on Lori, she wore her hair in a flip and was squinting at him out of a pair of cat-eye glasses, and what was she, a secretary? Instructor? Professor? She said, "Yes? May I help you?"

"I was just wondering," he said, and the words seemed to bloat in his mouth, "if you were open. Or in session, I mean. For the summer? Do you have summer sessions? At all?"

They were standing there in the sun on the steps of a building twice the size of the Alte Haus and every bit as elaborate—gables, turrets, fish-scale shingles, bracketed overhangs, spindlework run riot—on a day that capitalized on silence. She gave him a long look. "The fall term starts the day after Labor Day."

"Because I was looking for one of your students—Lori Cunningham? And I thought she might be in the dorm. You do keep the dorm open for out-of-state students, foreign students, and, and—such? Yes? Right? Isn't that the way it works?" He smiled, but she didn't smile back.

"Any inquiries about our students," she said, enunciating carefully, "should be directed to the dean of women."

"Look, I'm not some deviant, if that's what you're thinking," he said, holding her eyes even as the building began to ripple and her face flew off and came roaring back again like a volleyball spiked over the net. "I'm a psychologist. And I just—who is the dean of women? Can I speak with her?"

"She's in Vermont. On vacation. She won't be back till school starts."

"Oh, come on, somebody must be in charge—I just need a way to contact her, this girl. I could leave a note—could I leave a note? There must be a mailbox, right? Doesn't everybody rate a mailbox? Even lowly undergrads?"

This was humor, or an attempt at it, but she wasn't smiling. And why was that? Because she was a hard cold icy bitch, that was why, and didn't he know the type?

"I'm sorry," she said, "but you'll have to come back next month."

Next month? Was she crazy?

"This is urgent, don't you get that? Can you even begin to imagine what I'm going through here? I don't want next month, I want *now*!"

"I'm sorry," she said, turning away from him to pick her way down the steps in her clacking flats so that all he was left with was a burning silhouette, and the thing was, she wasn't even attractive, wasn't graceful or helpful or sympathetic, wasn't Lori, not even close.

He tried the door—the door she'd just come out of—but the door was locked.

W as it a coincidence that Officer Salter was waiting for him when he left the campus and made a wide awkward turn onto

Franklin? He'd meant to turn right, to go back to the house and weigh his options, but at the last minute he decided to go in the opposite direction, thinking he'd drive up to Annandale, where Bard was, and see if he could find Toby, though Bard wouldn't have been in session either and if he'd ever known Toby's surname it eluded him now. He could picture him, though—the weasel face, the stringy hair, the way he laughed at the world and sneered and postured and put his hands on Lori as if she belonged to him—and that was enough. All he had to do was spot him crossing the quad—was there a quad?—or in one of the student bars or wherever, a burger joint, and see if he could get some *information* out of him, and what if Lori was with him? What then?

He never got a chance to find out because the police cruiser was right there, right on his bumper, and though everything was a bit hazy he knew enough to pull over and submit himself to whatever came next. There were the usual demands—"License and registration"—with which he was able to comply without too much difficulty, though the registration was in Fanchon's name and his license was still a Massachusetts issue because he hadn't yet been able to find the time to go down to the Department of Motor Vehicles and change it over, but now there was a further entanglement that went beyond the usual harassment and ticket writing and involved a question Officer Salter was putting to him at two-thirty-five on a coruscating high-summer afternoon that was redolent with the smell of hot tar and alive with the love song of the cicadas in the trees across the road: "Have you been drinking?"

He said the first thing that came into his head, which, in retrospect he thought was fairly witty, given the circumstances: "I'm a Mormon. It's against my religion."

"I'm going to have to ask you to step out of the car," Officer Salter said, and things moved quickly after that—the charade of the drunk test, the application of the handcuffs, the ride to the police station, the humiliation of the booking and the way everybody there stared at him as if he were a leper and finally the phone call to the Alte Haus. His hands shook as he dialed the number and listened to the clicks over the line, the phone pinned under his chin, the haze of alcohol receding like an ebb tide and trying to suck his legs out from under him so that he had to fight to remain upright. The phone rang in a vacuum. It seemed to ring forever before somebody finally picked it up with a soft expectant "Hello?"

"Who is this?"

"Tommy."

"It's Fitz. I need help. Is Ken there? Or Charlie or anybody?"

A silence. "I don't know."

"Well go look, would you? Tell them"—and here he felt something go soft inside him, as if he were about to start blubbering like an infant—"it's, it's . . . I'm in jail, okay?"

"What do you mean, *in jail?*"

"Please," he said, "please. Just get somebody."

He was all but sober by the time Ken arrived to bail him out after a period during which he'd fallen into a deep crushing sleep in a cell occupied by a shoeless white-haired man in a pair of overalls who kept repeating, *I did it, I did it, I confess,* and if Ken was rigid with anger that was only to be expected—it was his car the police had impounded. Beyond that, on the tight-lipped drive back up Franklin in Charlie's turquoise Chevrolet, Ken told him Tim was furious over the whole thing. "You of all people should know better. We don't need this kind of negative attention, we really don't—especially now, after Kesey and those jokers blew through town. And I'll tell you another thing—you're responsible for the towing charges and everything else, fines, whatever, you hear me?"

He murmured apologies all the way up the drive to the main house but Ken wouldn't listen, wouldn't stop. "And this Lori business, it's sick, Fitz. Wake up. You should hear what people are saying behind your back, Fanchon even, Alice, Charlie, everybody. Get a grip, man. Really."

The house loomed up to greet them, the fairy-tale house, the gingerbread castle, the home he'd come so far to find. He listened to the squeal of the brakes, the mechanical click of the handle as Ken swung open the door. "Can I just say one thing?"

"What?" Ken said, giving him a hard look.

"Fuck you. And fuck Fanchon too."

They might have come to blows—they should have; get it all out in the open for once, Joanie, Fanchon, Zihuatanejo and the lifeguard tower—but they didn't. Ken just squared his shoulders and went up the stairs and into the house while he sat there in the car to try to calm himself. He couldn't face anybody just then because Ken was right. He knew it, knew he was risking everything, but that didn't change a thing. After a while—and here came two of the dogs charging out the door to tumble across the grass in an explosion of pure animal joy, which in that moment was as depressing as anything he could imagine—he got out of the car, walked all the way around to the back of the house and slipped up the stairs to his room, just for a little privacy. A minute, a minute to himself, that was all.

He hadn't been there five minutes when there was a knock at the door. "Go away," he called, but Fanchon's voice came back at him, muted by the slab of the door, but sharp-edged and insistent all the same. "It is the telephone. For you."

He said nothing.

"Fitz?"

"Tell them I'm dead. Tell them the funeral's on Wednesday."

She knocked again, more emphatically this time, and he got up from the bed with a curse, not even bothering to hide the bottle of brandy he'd wrapped his hand around at some point and couldn't seem to let go of now. He crossed the room to the door and jerked it open, trying all the while to fight down something in his chest that felt perilously close to panic.

Fanchon took a step back, as if he'd startled her—he *had* startled her, but before he could sort out his feelings on that score (what was he doing? what was wrong with him?), she locked her eyes on his, announced, "It is Joanie," turned and walked away.

He went down to the kitchen, where the yellow wall phone with the extra-long cord was, and found it lying facedown on the counter. Alice was there, along with Paulette and Diana, the three of them sitting around the kitchen table with tall glasses of iced tea, playing cards. Alice's hair was bushed out, a mass of sun-bleached streaks and split ends that were testimony to a summer on the lake, a summer that seemed to have gone on from the beginning of time and was destined to go on till time ended and the universe became formless all over again. Her hair. Alice's hair. All of a sudden it was exploding in his face—*Pow!*—a supernova immolating itself right there in the kitchen. All three of them looked up at him, but he didn't have anything to give them, not gossip, explanation or apology, not even a greeting. Joanie was on the phone. *Joanie.* It didn't seem possible.

He picked up the receiver and eased himself through the door and out into the hallway, the cord trailing behind him. "Hello?" he said. "Joanie?"

"Hi," she said, and her voice didn't sound like hers at all so that when she asked, "How're you doing?" he thought it was some sort of trick, some stranger playing a gag on him—one of the kids, even, from the upstairs extension.

"Fine," he said, and everything seemed to fall back in place. Joanie. It was Joanie on the other end of the line.

"Fine? It's been weeks—weeks now, Fitz—and all you can say is *fine*?"

"Well, it's, I don't know—what do you want me to say?"

"I want you to say you miss me, miss your son. Couldn't you even call? Or what, write a letter? You don't have time for a letter?"

"I did call."

"Once."

"Okay, I told you, right, that we're not allowed to use the phone for long-distance? Because of the financial situation here?"

Her voice came right back at him and there was no feeling in it, no feeling at all. "You couldn't go to a pay phone? What happened, did somebody come in the dead of night and steal all the pay phones in town? What about the one on the wall in the back hallway of the bar—what about that one?"

This wasn't the conversation he wanted to have. Actually, he didn't want to have any conversation at all right now because everything kept shifting on him, the whole room, the whole house, all these *objects* that couldn't manage to keep still. He wasn't having a flash-back, he wasn't tripping, and if he was drunk he hadn't been drunk long enough or in a determined-enough way to give himself the D.T.'s—so what was this? Life? Life without the sacrament, without Joanie, without Corey.

She said something he didn't catch and then she said, "You there?"

He listened to the breath of the phone. After a minute—a pause—he said, "So what do you want?"

"What do I *want*? Are you kidding me? Are you drunk? Are you tripping? Don't tell me you're tripping, don't tell me that."

"I'm not tripping."

He heard her take in a deep breath, as if she were armoring herself, putting up the defenses so she could troop out into the field and give battle. "You told me you'd be here two weeks after the Fourth. That was over a month ago."

"Yeah," he said. "Yeah, I know."

"And you ask me what I want? I want you home, with me and Corey, your son—remember him?"

"I am home."

"Don't give me that shit. Tell me, how's your little slut? Has she fried her brains yet?"

He didn't respond to this. The phone receiver—what was it, plastic?—felt as ungainly as a redwood tree, two thousand years old and hairy with bark, pressed flat to the side of his head.

"What about Ken?" he said. "Don't you want to hear about Ken?"

"I've got news for you," she said, her tone shifting till it was brisk and mechanical, just the facts, "—I'm not going back there. Ever. It's wrong, Fitz, it's a disaster. Look what's it done to us. To me, Fitz, to *me*."

"Don't say that," he said.

"I swear to you, I'm not going back."

"Come on, don't say that."

He was going to say *I love you,* but it wouldn't have meant anything, not right then, because he was irritated and confused and so far between the salient points in his life he couldn't begin to imagine how he was ever going to navigate his way back. *Corey!* he thought then, *Joanie!* And even before she hung up and the line went dead he was thinking how very, very much he was going to miss them both.

Later—no, he wasn't hungry and no, he wasn't about to sit down to dinner and have to face everybody in the house, Tim especially— he took the back staircase down to Lori's room and checked for what must have been the twentieth time to be sure her backpack was still in the closet. It was. He flipped open the nylon flap and inspected the contents, but as far as he could see nothing had been removed—or added—which told him something he didn't really want to know. For a long while he sat there on her bed while the sun backed away from him inch by inch across the carpet till it hung suspended in the window and finally dropped out of sight. He was putting off what he most needed to do, which was go to Tim and explain himself, apologize, and at the same time see about the one thing that could begin to make this right, this whole day, this scene, as Charlie would put it, this terrible winnowing *scene*. Tim was the gander and he was the gosling. And though he'd been drinking brandy steadily off and on throughout the day, he couldn't feel it on any level beyond the physical, and what was the use of that? The sacrament, that was what he needed, revelation, the shining path. If ever he was ready, it was now.

There was music coming from the main room, a murmur of voices, the usual current of people plugged in and operating on the same wavelength. He avoided them and tiptoed up the stairs, hoping he'd find Tim alone in his room, which wasn't all that unlikely. Tim was up there most evenings now, at least while he was home and not out on the lecture circuit spreading the word and making the cash registers ring—it was as if he was withdrawing himself strategically, preparing them all for the break that was coming at the end of the year when he would fly off to India with his Nordic princess and leave them behind. Fitz listened at the door a moment, unsure of himself—he didn't want to intrude or interrupt anything, especially after what Ken had said about Tim being furious with him, though he couldn't really imagine Tim being furious with anybody for long.

At first he heard nothing, and then a sound came to him that froze him inside, a voice, a girl's voice, nasal and echoing, and wasn't that Lori? Wasn't that Lori's voice? Before he could think he gave the door a sharp declamatory thump with the heel of his fist and shoved his way in, ready for anything—only to find . . . Tim, dressed all in white in his long trailing *sherwani* and flowing trousers, sitting at his desk, alone. "Oh," he murmured, "I'm sorry, I didn't mean—can I come in?"

Tim had been writing in his notebook and he looked up now, the pen arrested over the page, and gave him a puzzled look that morphed almost immediately into his trademark grin. "Fitz," he called, "where's the fire?"

The room was warm. It had been a hot day, muggy, and the evening hadn't cooled things off at all. There was the sound of insects shrieking in the darkness beyond the windows and the periodic buzz of moths at the window screens. Fitz stood there, just inside the door, trying to smile back. "I just wanted to apologize," he said.

Tim frowned. "Yes, well, I understand, Fitz, I do. We all go through these things, but the point is we have to be on our very best behavior in a little burg like this, you know? We're members of the community now, but never forget it's a community of hicks and yahoos, conservatives, Catholics, and we don't need to be giving them any extra ammunition when we're in their crosshairs to begin with." He paused, set down his pen, interlocked the fingers of both hands and stretched his arms out before him. There was a bottle of scotch on the desk, a glass half full beside it. Moths flapped. The screens rattled. "Apology accepted," he said.

"Don't go," Fitz said suddenly, and he didn't know why he'd said it except that everything seemed to be closing in on him.

"Go? Go where?"

"India. Tibet." A pleading tone had come into his voice, a tone he didn't like, gosling and gander, but he couldn't help himself. "We're only getting started here, this experiment, I mean. We're, we're— we have *breakthroughs* coming."

Tim held up a palm to forestall him. "It's okay, Fitz, don't worry. You'll be in good hands with Dick. And Michael—Michael's going to stay on. And I'll be back before you know it, I promise." He swiveled around and gestured to the easy chair beside the bed. "Look, have a seat, why don't you. You want a drink?"

"Yes," he said, easing himself down. "Or no"—and he was the one grinning now—"drink is what got me in trouble. With our friend Officer Salter. What I was thinking is maybe a little taste of the heavenly blue? Will you do it with me?"

Tim gave him a long look. He controlled the sacrament, though he was more than liberal about it—if people wanted to trip, that was their right, the right to internal freedom—but he was the impresario, the ringleader, the dealer, and he held that power over everybody in the house. All you had to do was ask, but still, it was all in the asking, wasn't it? "It's kind of late," he said finally. "I *was* planning on finishing this," he said, gesturing to the notebook. He glanced across the room, as if there were an audience waiting in the wings. He gave it a beat, then one more. "But all things in time, right?"

"I don't know," Fitz said, "I just—I think I'm getting close. The last time, or no, two times ago, I saw the white light, the First Light, I mean—just at the end. It was like all the color went out of the world and there were no dimensions to anything, just light."

Tim was nodding. Sipping his drink and nodding. "I hear you. People who've died and been brought back to life report seeing that same light—in every case, absolutely. Though of course you've got your neuroscientists and their lab rats telling you it's no different than a light bulb flaring at the moment the power goes out."

"But they're wrong, aren't they?"

Tim shrugged. "I don't know, Fitz."

"I want to see the Second Light, I want to see God—or whatever passes for God when your mind peels back all the layers and there's nothing between you and the universe. You've been there, I know you have—"

Tim had the pill bottle out now, right there in his hand, the Delysid, LSD-25, with its preposterous warning label—POISON—when in fact the substance inside it was the only known antidote for the poison of the world, of consciousness, of non-God and non-knowledge and the pitiable grasp of humankind on the drawstrings of nature and the dead black reaches of space that swallowed everything like an insatiable mouth.

"Tell me you have. Tell me you've been there. Tell me you've seen *God.*"

Tim uncapped the bottle, shook six pills out into the palm of his hand, three each, a supernal dose, a dose worthy of all the gods there ever were. He winked. Grinned. Leaned forward over the cradle of his knees and stretched out his hand.

"Fuck God," he said, "let's get high."